Monticello
Ann O'Connell Rust

The Floridians Series Volume IV

Published by
Amaro Books
5673 Pine Avenue
Orange Park, Florida 32073

Copyright © 1991 Ann O'Connell Rust

All rights reserved. No part of this book may be reproduced in any form or by any electronic or mechanical means including information storage and retrieval systems without permission in writing from the publisher, except by a reviewer who may quote brief passages in a review.

First printing 1991

ISBN No. 0-9620556-5-4 (Volume 4) Softcover

ISBN No. 0-9620556-6-2 Hardcover

ISBN No. 0-9620556-4-6 (7 Volume Set)

Library of Congress Catalog Card No. 91-72853

Printed in U.S.A.

Cover Artist: Linda Taheri

Books by Ann O'Connell Rust

Punta Rassa

Palatka

Kissimmee

Monticello

ACKNOWLEDGMENTS

The author wishes to thank Allen F. Rust, Editor/Copy Editor, and Jim Brown and staff of Empulse, Gt. Barrington, Mass. And a special thanks to the kind people in Monticello and Apalachicola for their generous assistance.

AUTHOR'S NOTE

The setting of this story is Florida, 1889-1899. The history is as accurate as is needed for the story line, and all the characters are fictional.

Dedicated to: Raymond L. Hawk (Uncle Ray, born in Aucilla) who gave me the love of the telling of the tales. Gladys Folsom Harrington (born in Monticello) wife, mother, teacher, historian and lover of all that is Florida.

CONTENTS

BOOK ONE: *BULLSEYE*

CHAPTER I	THOMAS MEADE GARVIN	1
CHAPTER II	OLE PINEY CREEK	26
CHAPTER III	STETSON UNIVERSITY	37

BOOK II: *MY SWEET SORROW*

CHAPTER I	THE ARRIVAL	63
CHAPTER II	KISSIMMEE CITY	83
CHAPTER III	SWEET REVENGE	91
CHAPTER IV	FOILED AGAIN	115

BOOK III: *CHANGES ARE MANY*

CHAPTER I	THE WEDDING	133
CHAPTER II	MISS KATE	153
CHAPTER III	LONESOME PEN	165

BOOK IV: *THE FAR SIDE OF FOREVER*

CHAPTER I	ATHEA MANOR PLANTATION	181
CHAPTER II	THE PASSING TIME	191
CHAPTER III	CARRABELLE	206

BOOK ONE:

BULLSEYE

CHAPTER I THOMAS MEADE GARVIN

Callie heard the dogs barking long before she saw Slick ride up. When he rounded the barn and dismounted, Thom came out of the barn to meet him. As they talked, Callie finished cleaning the kitchen and laughed when she thought of the first time she had baked biscuits, and Slick actually spewed them out exclaiming, "What you trying to do, Callie Meade, kill yore Pa's top hand?" Well, her biscuits had improved in the ten years since she and Thom had been married, but even she admitted that they still couldn't compare to her ma's or Mattie's.

She called to them, "Why don't ya'll come on up to the house for a cup of coffee? Slick, is Mama Kate having a fit about that going away party she's giving for Jay? Did she ask you to have me come over? Hey, Slick? Thom, where did Meade and Willy run off to? Those two are going to be the death of me, yet." She laughed when she said it knowing full well that they knew how happy she was that Meade now had a puppy and could talk and say his name and...

Thomas Meade Garvin, a little over six years old, the son that Callie and Thom had waited almost four years for, had never uttered a word until six months ago. He was handsome, strong, lovable and the apple of his grandparents' (Kate and Parker) eye, not to mention his Uncle Jay's, Callie's younger brother. He did well in school, writing his ABC'S, doing his numbers and drawing and coloring as well as his fellow students - but talk, he could not.

This affliction had been especially hard on Thom, who had wanted a son more than almost anything in the world. Callie took his affliction in her stride and just loved Meade all the more, saying, "He's ours, and if this is the way he's to be, then we can't do anything about it." She and her pa had decided to take him to a specialist in Tampa when he was four years old, mainly to please Thom, but he could find nothing physically wrong with him. He had given them the name of a famous doctor in New York, but Callie decided to work with Meade herself and ignore the doctor's advice. Thom just drew farther and farther away from them, spending more time raising his bird dogs and an awful lot of time, when not on the cow hunts and cattle drives, drinking his shine and sleeping more often than not in the barn with the dogs.

Seemed to Callie that he couldn't stand to be around Meade. It just hurt him too much to see his only child like that, she reasoned.

All the people in the small town of Arcadia knew of his and Callie's troubles and understood his disappointment so they did what had to be done by catering to Meade more to make up for Thom's inability to show his son his love. The people in Arcadia were like that.

When Clay Willett's mother Cora passed away and Clay came home to Arcadia from his job on the Tampa *Tribune* in Tampa to handle the funeral, the entire town turned out to say their good-byes, Callie, Thom and Meade included. Cora had been a quiet pillar in the community, teaching piano and helping out at the school. It had been difficult raising a son alone. Her husband was taken when Clay was only two, and the town rallied around her just as they had Meade. The Jeeterses, who had no children of their own, took her and Clay in, and he seemed to belong to everyone.

It was at Miss Cora's funeral that Meade said his first words. Thom was offering his condolences to Clay at the church door, and Meade reached up to his pa and said big as you please, "Go home, Daddy?" When Callie turned around to see if her ears were deceiving her, he repeated it. Thom gathered him up, hugging him in his protective arms, and he and Callie ran to the buggy, fast as they could, and sped home. They needed to be alone with their happiness. Meade talked from that day on, and Thom actually let him have a puppy, one of his pure bred bird dogs that he thought so much of, and Meade named him Willy. They were inseparable, and the young family's lives changed from that minute on.

"It's like a cloud has been lifted, Ma," Callie told Kate. "We were all too hard on Thom. He was hurting so much, and even I couldn't see it. Why is that, do you suppose?" Kate wanted to say, but decided not to, that he could have tried as hard as you, my girl. I'm afraid your Thom was just being selfish, but she continued to rock and mumbled, "I'm not sure, honey." She got up and went to Callie, who had seen too much pain for one so young, bent down and kissed the top of her chestnut curls.

Kate thought, yes, my sweet, you had the compassion your husband couldn't muster. The entire town felt your pain but your husband couldn't; he just took to his shine. I don't feel sorry for Thom one little bit. You I feel sorry for 'cause your love for him is indeed blind.

She and Parker were so happy that some of Callie's problems had been resolved. When Callie and Thom told them that they wanted to go to Bullseye, Thom's parents' ranch outside of Crescent City in northeast Florida, for a visit and to attend his sister's wedding, they offered to look after their place on Ole Piney Creek and said that Slick could take care of Thom's dogs for the three weeks that they'd be away.

"He's so almighty particular about Dixie and those puppies of hers that you'd think they were his blood kin," Slick told Parker when he asked him to care for them. "I ain't so sure I can please Thom."

"Now, Slick, don't carry on so. It's just for three weeks. I ain't sentencing you to life, you know. Besides, there's not much doing right now, and it'll give you something to do besides lose your pay to Jam." Parker laughed at Slick's amazed expression. He'd known about their gambling ever since they'd been with him, over twenty some years, but hadn't let on. He just couldn't imagine anyone being so stupid that he'd gamble away his pay almost every blessed month. But Slick was the best hand with beeves he'd ever seen. Slick didn't protest any more. He just straddled Jackaw and rode over to Callie's and Thom's wearing a sick grin and shaking his head at how smart his boss was. "Knowed 'bout my gamblin' all these years an' nary a word did he say. He does beat all!"

Until twelve short years ago Callie had even refused to wear a dress or attend a town social, she had been such a tomboy. Then she fell in love with Thom, and her whole life changed. Thom had ridden for his pa since he was thirteen and had never missed the annual spring drive to Punta Rassa. That's where he and Callie met. Parker had raised her like a boy and had allowed her to accompany him on the spring drives just as he would have a son. Since his only son Jay got asthma every time he was around a horse, it was up to Callie to carry on at Tall Ten, and Parker began grooming her for that position soon as he found out about Jay's malady. Thom's father Pierce owned the Bullseye and was one of the largest ranchers in the state. After Callie and Thom married Thom moved down state to help Parker, and Parker built them a house over on Ole Piney Creek about a mile from the main house.

But Kate was right about Thom. Things just seemed to have come his way. He was handsome, had a ready smile and did all kinds of fancy tricks on his gelding. He had also won every contest he'd ever entered at the state fairs, and half the eligible girls in the state had been after him. It seemed like anything Thom wanted he got. He had also been popular with the other cowmen, had been a hard worker and very respected, and when he and Callie fell in love, every cowman in the state was excited for them. Theirs was a storybook marriage until Meade's arrival. After that the men had managed to tolerate Thom for Callie's and Parker's sake and had wondered why Callie didn't boot him a good one. The old Callie would have. But she had felt so guilty about giving him a son who was dumb that she had become almost docile, not one speck like the fired-up Callie they had known and loved.

"Parker, you wipe those boots real good 'cause Mattie just mopped the floor," Kate shouted through the screened kitchen door. "Here, Honey, take this old rag and give them a good one."

"Heck, Kate, I'll just go around to the porch. What are you women doing, anyway? A person would think that Jay was going all the way to China instead of just up to DeLand, I declare they would." He wasn't smiling. Parker Meade was an easy going man, who loved his family, did for them and always would, but he sure liked things as they used to be and without all this fuss. They were all excited about Jay's appointment as an art professor at the new John B. Stetson University up in DeLand, and Kate was giving a going away party and inviting his closest friends. It was her idea, not Jay's, but he seemed pleased that she'd want to and didn't protest too much. The town had already had a big shindig for him at the Young Hotel, but Kate wanted to put the icing on the cake, so to speak. She sure did like to fuss.

She came out to the front porch. Parker was still grumbling, so she sat down on the steps beside him. She was still a pretty woman in her middle fifties with a spark in her dark brown eyes. Her hand soon found his shoulder, and she patted it to calm him. "It turned out to be a beautiful day after all, didn't it, Honey? Why this morning I was sure we'd have a down pour. You remember how grey it was. Think we'll get that rain after all?"

Parker knew she was trying to smooth his feathers, so he went along with her weather report. "Don't think we'll get a drop, so you don't hafta worry about it spoiling your party, Missy." He pecked her on the cheek and added, "I just sent Slick over to Callie's to talk to Thom about his dogs. Sure hope he doesn't get riled up if Thom starts ordering him around. You know what a short fuse they both have."

"Well, mister, you're right - he'd better not. I don't know why Thom has to have his way all the time. He's spoiled, that's what he is. If he gets Callie all upset just before their trip and Jay's going away party, I just think I might give that young man a piece of my mind, that's what!"

"Now, Kate, I didn't mean anything by it. You just tend to your party and I'll tend to Thom. He's always had things come easy to him...."

"I know just what you're going to say, Parker - except Meade. And look how he handled that, would you just! Poor little tyke couldn't help the way he was, and a body'd think that it was the end of the world, just because..."

"Don't get going on that again, Honey. It doesn't solve a thing. That's all past now, and the three of 'em seem just as happy as can be..."

" 'cause he got his way, that's why. If she'd fallen in love with Clay Willett, he'd have been sensitive enough to know how to handle the situation, but Thom...well..."

Kate and Parker had discussed all this before, and both were getting a little tired of rehashing it. But Kate was right. Had Callie fallen in love with Clay, the town's only celebrity, except for Jay, things would have indeed been different. He was two years older than she and had been writing articles for the area papers since he was but a youngster of thirteen. He had become a top features writer for the *Tribune* by the time he was twenty and traveled all over the state. Clay had been sweet on Callie for as long as anyone in Arcadia could remember but knew that he couldn't offer Callie any kind of a decent life like Thom could. He left for Tampa just before her wedding. He came back home often, always making a big to-do over Meade to show Callie that he cared. The town was so proud of him and of Callie's brother Jay, who was well known throughout the South for his wildlife paintings, even being compared to Audubon. When Jay had been offered a position at Stetson University, they really had something to celebrate. The fact that one little town could have produced two such talented people was a wonder to them all, and they allowed their pride to show.

Kate joined Mattie in the warm kitchen and asked, "Did Callie bring down those guavas for the pies yesterday? I don't remember seeing them."

"Yassum, she sho nuff did. Dey's in a bucket on de back stoop, Miss Kate." Mattie chuckled at her and continued, "You be as nervous as when Miss Callie got married, I do declare you be."

"Between you and Parker declaring to the entire world about my nerves, Mattie, you are indeed going to make me nervous. Well, for your information, I don't feel nervous. And another thing, why should I be? Callie and Thom are getting a much needed vacation and are almost as frisky as two pups, and Jay is getting an opportunity that I never even dreamed of. So why should I be nervous, for heaven's sake?"

Mattie could tell that Kate was getting riled and began humming and speeded up washing the rest of the dishes. She went to the back stoop for the bucket of guavas and began washing them. "Miss, Kate, do you want me to peel dese and scoop out de seeds fer de pies?"

"Grief, Mattie! Now, why do you think I had Callie bring them down?"

She could see that her sharp tongue had hurt Mattie and immediately went to her and put her arms around the bent shoulders declaring, "I'm sorry, my dear friend. That was uncalled for. I guess you and Parker are right. I am a wreck. But I don't understand why, I really don't."

"Maybe it's 'cause Mister Jay done be goin' away..." Kate got tears in her eyes and turned from Mattie stating, "You are a very observant lady, Mattie. I told Beulah just the other day that you knew more about my family than I do, I declare you do. But it is indeed time he began a life of his own. Heavens, he's almost twenty seven years old."

"Miss Georgianna sho gonna miss him, ain't she? I'd a thought dos two done be married by now."

"You've got me there, Mattie. I don't know what's holding up their decision a bit more than you do. Parker seems to think that Jay's afraid he can't support her on what he makes from selling his paintings, but Louise said that she and John had offered to help out. But you know Jay - he's got that Meade pride and wouldn't hear of it."

"Well, maybe now dat he got him a good job all dat will change..."

"Not on what Stetson pays! I couldn't believe what they offered him. I really couldn't, and here it's supposed to be the top university in the entire state."

Kate began helping Mattie finish up the guavas and continued, "How do they expect to get qualified teachers if they aren't willing to pay a living wage? Now, in Jay's case, he can sell his paintings and prints to help out, but what about those other teachers? Did I tell you that Berta's and Layke's daughter, SuSu, is going to attend the Normal School at Stetson to study to be a teacher?"

Mattie looked perplexed. Kate continued. "You know, Mattie, SuSu is Berta's daughter by her first husband Reuben McRae...you remember Reuben, who owned South Spring up in Old Town on the Suwannee? He always had three helpings of your chicken and dumplings when he was here during the drive. Remember? He was built square and always happy...oh, you remember, Mattie. He died suddenly...real young." Mattie grinned when she remembered. Oh, how he had raved about her cooking.

Kate continued. "Then she married Layke Williams, who later became a state senator and...it is confusing, dear. Anyway, Thom's mother wrote Callie that she'd heard from Berta in Tallahassee, and Berta told her that SuSu will start school in September, too. She's already had two years of schooling, but Berta said that for some reason she wanted to transfer to Stetson. I told Jay to be sure to look her up, and I thought Georgianna was going to have a conniption fit."

Kate chuckled. "Mary said that she doesn't look a bit like Berta - must have taken after the McRae side of the family. She has auburn hair and huge brown eyes, and Mary said that she'd always been sickly looking until they moved up to Tallahassee. Seems to have really come out in the last few years and become something of a beauty. When I mentioned that to Jay and Georgianna, they both shot darts at me. I told Georgianna that if she was going to get jealous every time someone mentions another girl, maybe she'd better think about going to Stetson, too. And, you know what, she up and said that she had indeed been thinking of it. Jay was as surprised as I was. His mouth hung open and..."

"Miss Kate, Ah'm thinking dat you done stirred up a hornets' nest."

"What are you two carrying on about?" Parker said, pulling up a chair and sitting down at the kitchen table.

"You want a cup of coffee, Honey?" She reached toward the back burner for the blue enamel pot and poured the steaming, dark coffee into the tin cup. "Oh, I was telling Mattie about how jealous Georgianna got when I mentioned SuSu McRae."

"Having herself a good old time, wasn't she, Mattie?"

"Yassuh, Mister Parker, she sho 'nuff was. But maybe now Miss Georgianna put de vise on Mister Jay and we's have us another wedding 'round Tall Ten."

"Pierce said that SuSu was a beauty, all right. Said that when she visited Bullseye with Berta and they all went up to New York on the steamer, he was afraid that Thom's brother Thurmond was going to cancel his wedding plans, he was so smitten by her. Now wouldn't that be something if Jay and Reuben's daughter got together?" Parker added.

"Now, look who's stirring up trouble, would you, Mattie? Parker Meade, you better be careful or Georgianna will be shooting darts at you, too."

****

"Thom, watch out! You almost stepped on Meade!" Callie yelled, then started laughing at his expression. "Meade, you shouldn't have put your bedroll so close to your pa's side of the bed." She hugged him to her, tousled his brown curly hair and reached over to kiss her drowsy husband.

"Your ma's been calling the two of you for almost an hour. Now, hurry up so I can make the bed and get downstairs to help her with all the wedding fixings. Now, Thomas Garvin. This very minute."

"You're mighty frisky this morning, Honey," Thom said, pulling her down on the rumpled bed covers. "You're remembering your own wedding day, huh?"

"Thom Garvin, behave yourself," she whispered. "Can't you see that Meade's taking all this in?"

"And why shouldn't he? Any red blooded six year old should be able to see his folks love each other. Come here, woman..."

Callie squealed delightedly and soon they were all three rough housing on Mary Garvin's guest room bed, the star quilt and feather pillows flying every which-a-way.

"Grief! Thom get up from here. Your brothers have been up since daybreak and already eaten and got a ball game going in the side yard. Thurm sent me up to find out if you two had died."

"Already got a game going, have they? Well, Meade and I'll just hafta show them a thing or two, huh, son?"

"You betcha, Daddy. We sure will."

"Go down for breakfast first. Risa's got enough sausage and biscuits cooked for a pack of hungry wolves. Now, Meade, don't you gobble down your breakfast if you're gonna run and play. No, son, not that shirt. Put on the tan one, and we'll save the blue one for the train ride home."

Meade didn't argue with his mama but hurriedly looked at his daddy to see how close to being dressed he was. Callie smiled. He tried to do everything just like Thom and just as fast. She bit her lower lip and turned her head, not wanting them to see her emotion. Her entire life had turned around. All those prayers she'd said had been answered, and she'd never been this happy - not ever.

She found herself humming as she rolled up Meade's bedroll and then straightened the bed covers. She noticed that Mary had had Harriet put on the company sheets and pillowcases that she'd monogrammed. The warm lavender scent enveloped her and she sat down on the side of the bed. She stared out the window at the Garvin boys on the shaded side yard, where they had drawn out a baseball diamond far enough from the house so that Mary wouldn't have to worry about a stray ball breaking a window.

Their morning chores had been completed long ago, and Thurm, next to Thom in age, was pitching to the youngest boy, Holden, while Lanier, number three son, was fielding for him. They had scheduled a game after supper last night with Thurmond's wife Lottie's brothers and some of the young men from Crescent City, the closest town of any size to Bullseye. Pierce's cowhands filled out the team that he sponsored and had named the Garvin Bulls. Crescent City could sport two teams, and on a Saturday afternoon almost the entire town would show up at the town park to watch.

The night before while Thom and Callie lay awake talking, Thom said that he wanted to get Meade started playing ball when they returned to Arcadia, and even said that he wanted to join one the town's teams when they got back. Callie was so excited. He had not participated in any of the town's activities since he'd moved down to Tall Ten. Now, maybe he'll feel like he belongs, she thought.

Baseball had taken every town and city in the country by storm. The citizens of Crescent City were especially relieved because the year earlier, '88, had been so difficult due to the yellow fever epidemic that had hit Jacksonville to the north and was felt up and down the northeast coast. Many of the families that had been spared had owned their land since the territorial days and had given up and left, moving north or west. The smiles had waited for a long time before returning to that area, and they needed a healthful distraction such as baseball.

Thurm was the Bull's catcher, and Lanier was getting quite a reputation as an area pitcher. Since Thom had never really played much ball and was just getting the hang of it, they put him in the outfield, but being a natural athlete, it didn't take him long to catch on. Callie could see Meade sitting beside his grandfather underneath the red maple on the soft grass, yelling and clapping and encouraging his daddy's every effort. He could barely see because his grandfather had let him wear one of the Bulls' caps, and Callie got a catch in her throat as she looked at him pushing the cap back every few minutes so he could see his daddy.

Wait'll I tell Ma and Pa. They'll be so excited about Thom wanting to teach him. Won't they be surprised! I'd better get downstairs and help Mama Garvin. She'll think I've died up here.

Mary Garvin and Lucinda, her oldest daughter, and Lottie, and the bride to be, Sarah, were in the parlor preparing the bags of rice for after the reception. Mary had been so afraid that Sarah'd be an old maid. Of all her children Sarah had the sweetest disposition and was the most talented, at least in music. She was an accomplished pianist, played for the church choir, a very pleasant looking girl of medium build and quick to laugh. Everyone thought highly of Sarah. Her brothers and sister, except Holden and Bit, were married and had their own homes, so Sarah assisted Mary in the running of Bullseye. She'd just settled in like an old maid aunt. Thurm and his Lottie already had three children, Lucinda and her husband Freddie had two, and Lanier and his wife Jeanine were expecting their second child any day.

When Campbell Lewis moved to Crescent City from Jacksonville after his wife and two of his three children were taken during the epidemic, he opened the drugstore on First Street. He and Sarah took to each other right away. She'd always loved children, and his three-year-old, Elizabeth, was as crazy about Sarah as was her father. Everyone commented on how much she and Elizabeth looked alike. Both had dark, honey-colored hair and green eyes, and like her daddy and Sarah, a smile for everyone.

It amazed Mary the way Campbell embraced life after such a tragedy, and her Thom couldn't even accept his son's affliction. Now why couldn't Thom have had the strength he needed? She and Pierce had discussed it numerous times. They were very disappointed in how he had handled his situation, but their hands had been tied. Beulah, Mary's sister who lived in Arcadia, could not stand their not knowing of his reaction to Meade, so when they visited in Arcadia two years before she finally told Mary just what she thought of him. They had naturally known how upset he had been when he found out about

Meade, but neither Callie nor her folks had ever said a word to them - not once.

Mary watched Callie. It's hard to believe what a tomboy she was when she and Thom first fell in love. Look at her sitting there working on those rice bags right along with the other girls. Why, seems like only yesterday when we were at the state fair in Gainesville that she threw Thom headlong into the dirt when he had unthinkingly made the remark about her just now becoming a girl. He was spitting and spewing and with that surprised look on his face. Mary had told him to go after Callie, because she'd high-tailed it away from them and was determined to leave the fair and head back to Tall Ten, she was so embarrassed. Mary chuckled...

"Ma, what're you laughing about?" Lucinda asked. They all turned their attention toward her, and she started to respond, "Oh, nothing," but decided to confess.

"I was remembering the first time that I met Callie, and..."

"Go on with it, Ma," Lucinda insisted.

"Oh, all right. It was at the state fair in Gainesville - remember, Callie, when Thom introduced you to me and he made the uncalled-for remark about... let's see if I can remember....oh yes. He said, `Ma, don't let Callie's airs bother you 'cause she just became a girl,' or something like that..."

"What'd he say a thing like that for?" questioned Lottie.

"Guess you'd have to have been there to appreciate it, Lottie, but when he said it Callie got so upset with him that she tumbled him headlong in the dirt and marched off straight as you please..."

"I remember," Callie said with a grin. "He couldn't get over the airs I was putting on trying to impress his ma, and you know Thom. He likes everything just so."

"Callie, what would you do if Thom embarrassed you now?" Lottie interjected. Her sisters-in-law glanced at each other and wondered what she was driving at. Lottie did love to stir up trouble and seemed to enjoy telling everyone in town about it, too.

Callie thought for a minute and, remembering all the times in the last ten years that he had embarrassed her, decided to say as little as possible. "Guess I'd just hug him a big one and probably say, `Shame on you, Thomas Garvin.'"

Mary had to turn her head. She's had to grow up fast and think before she acts. I liked the old Callie better. These last six years have taken their toll, and guilt has become her companion. And that son of mine couldn't or wouldn't share it. Thank you, Lord, for giving him another chance. I just hope you give him a long life so's he can make up for his behavior.

Not being able to drop it, Lottie asked, "Sarah, what would you do if Campbell embarrassed you in front of other people?"

"For heavens sake, Lottie, can't you let it go?" Lucinda asked getting madder by the minute.

"I don't mind answering, Lucinda. Let's see. Well, I'd probably just change the subject then..."

"Well, I'd give Freddie a piece of my mind, I would...No, Jimmy, put that down! Ma, grab it!" Lucinda's two year old had reached the top of the parlor table and latched on to one of Mary's treasures. "I wonder if I'll let him see three, I really do!" commented Lucinda.

Mary did not like the direction the conversation was headed and especially didn't like Lottie's enjoyment of it, and said, "Lottie, is that Marcel I hear? Here, dear, I'll take these and finish them for you. Best check on him...he's big enough to crawl out of the crib, you know." She winked conspiratorially at Lucinda, who rolled her eyes at Sarah.

Lottie hesitated and said, "Miss Mary, I don't hear him."

"Well, unless my ears are deceiving me, I certainly did, dear."

Callie was so intent on getting the narrow yellow ribbon through the eyelet to secure the net sacks of rice that she didn't realize what was going on.

The shouting had become louder from the side yard, and Mary knew that Callie had much rather be outside watching the ball game than in the parlor sewing. When she went to the window, she pushed back the pale lace curtains so she could see better and decided that she'd suggest it.

"Here, Callie, I'll take your's, too, so you can join your men at the game. Now don't protest, dear. There are only a few more to do. Did you see Thom trying to teach Meade how to bat? It won't be long before those two are the stars of the Arcadia Rockets, huh?"

Callie jumped up and kissed Mary's cheek. "You said it, Mama Garvin. Not long at all." Her long legs raced out of the parlor just like the seventeen-year-old girl Mary remembered.

Mary thought, I hope she gets her old fire back. I love that child as much as my own, I declare I do.

****

Sarah was a lovely bride. She had decided to make her own gown, and Mary had helped with the delicate beading she'd sewn around the batteau neckline and the deeply scalloped full skirt and bell shaped sleeves. It was a lovely shade of pale green silk brocade that brought out the green in her eyes and complemented her golden hair.

Since Campbell had been married before, they decided to have just a small family wedding in the parlor at Bullseye. That suited Mary and Pierce, because their other children had had very large weddings with the entire state of Florida invited, it seemed to Pierce. He was not much for crowds, and Mary was wearying of them too.

Pierce and Mary stood together in the foyer. "Mary, the flowers are fine. What're you fooling with them for?"

"Just gives my hands something to do, Honey. What on earth is keeping Rev. Collins? You'd think he could be on time for a wedding, now wouldn't you? I'm just glad that it's only the family he's keeping waiting. Is that him riding up now?"

Pierce walked out the front door in a hurry and looked at his pocket watch as he did. "Right on the button, he is. One minute to spare." He turned back to her and said, "You can tell Lucinda to start the music, Honey."

"Well, before I do, I'm going to tell Lottie to get herself upstairs to tend to Marcel. I never heard such a racket." Pierce came back in with the preacher, and Mary turned to him and whispered in his ear, "Can you imagine what Thurmond was thinking of, bringing his entire family here? Nora Kay could have kept them, but no, they had to bring every last one of them. Listen to Marcel yell, would you just!"

Pierce shook his head in disgust, and while Mary was escorting Lottie, red with embarrassment, upstairs, he went over to Thurmond, who soon dragged the other rambunctious children upstairs behind their mama. Every head in the room was turned toward them, and every face said, "About time!"

"It's their own fault if they miss the ceremony, Honey. Don't look so forlorn. Everything will be all right." Pierce kissed her cheek and took her arm, nodded to Lanier, who was to escort Campbell in to stand beside the Rev. Collins in front of the fireplace that Mary had filled with every color of azalea in the yard, filling them out with the few remaining camellias.

Sarah came down the wide stairs holding her voluminous skirt up and smiling at the two of them. Mary handed her the family Bible that her grandmother had brought over from Scotland. It was so worn, she had covered it with yellow roses and maiden hair fern. Pierce nodded to Jeanine to begin her singing, and Mary, holding on to Sarah's arm, whispered that she looked so pretty. And she did - she just glowed.

The Rev. Collins gave his hurumph, clearing his throat, and Lucinda began playing the prelude. When Jeanine, who was very obviously large with child, began singing, Bit whispered to Holden, "She's gonna drop that baby right on Ma's parlor floor when she hits that high note. You just watch her." Holden, who had no sense of humor whatsoever, pursed his full lips, that always looked like he'd rubbed them with wild raspberries, and shook his head as he disgustedly glared at his sister. But when Jeanine hit the high note her distended belly shuddered, and Bit shot a side look at Holden. Sure enough, he was staring at the bottom of Jeanine's brown taffeta gown expecting to see something fall.

Bit almost had to leave the room, she was trying so hard to stifle her laughter. Wouldn't you think that he'd catch on once in a while? But not Holden. He never changes, and when she looked away from him, she glanced at Lanier. He was looking so lovingly at Jeanine and was so proud of her singing that Bit felt ashamed - but not for long. She somehow always managed to flip her mind to whatever pleased her.

****

"There is simply nothing for you to get so riled up about, Slick. Grief! Now, how many times have you heard a cat in the middle of the night, and close by, too? Huh?"

"That's so, Parker, but I'd swear on Miss Kate's Bible that that cat was after one of Dixie's pups. I mean it. It's not just a feeling you get often."

Parker thought on it, tamped the tobacco in his pipe, got up off the front steps and asked, "What kinda reaction did Dixie have...I mean did she act real nervous-like?"

"That's what I been trying to tell you. She was whimpering and walking all around that barn nervous as could be, and that pup of Meade's done almost jumped in my bedroll. You know how lovin' that one is. I'm not a'kidding ya."

"Well, do you want Jam to stay the night with you, and one of you can take watch while the other sleeps? Is that what you want to do?"

Slick threw up his hands and said, "I ain't sure what to do. I just know that if anything happens to those doggoned dogs of his, Thom'll have my head, and Callie and Meade to boot. Sure, go on and ask Jam - wouldn't hurt none." And with that he headed back for Ole Piney Creek.

Even before he got back to the barn, Slick could hear Dixie howling. Putting the spurs to Jackaw he swung around a tall stand of pines and called to her as he got off his horse. "Gawd almighty! That cat's after her in broad daylight. Would you look at this door - would you just! Six feet up the damned door he's clawed!" He had made sure that the barn door was secured top to bottom, because a puppy could squeeze out of the tiniest of openings, and that Willy of Meade's was a smart one. He didn't really believe that a cat would go after them in daylight, but he'd learned early in life to not second guess a wild animal. Squatting down, he continued to examine the splintered door, and when he looked down at the ground, he let out a yelp and looked around suspiciously.

He'd never seen the likes of it - paw prints the size of saucers. "That does it!" After calming Dixie and Willy, he got back on Jackaw and headed for Tall Ten and the bunkhouse. When I tell Parker and Jam about this, they'll have the whole town out here tracking him. Never saw one that big not even in the Cypress. "Uuumph! Lord help!"

****

Callie and Thom had decided to stay at Bullseye another day so Thom could play in his first baseball game. The Bulls were playing the top team in the region, the Bunnell Patriots, their rivals. It was a sunny February day with hardly a cloud in the sky, and as predicted the entire town had turned out. "I don't know how they stand to wear those hot uniforms, Mama Garvin, but doesn't he look handsome in it?"

"Thom wasn't caught short on looks, Callie," she decided to continue, "but he was caught short on thinking about others. Now don't," she said restraining Callie. "I need to say this. Maybe the middle of a ball game isn't the place, but you'll be leaving early in the morning, and this might be my last chance."

She could see that Callie didn't want to hear what she was about to say, but it needed saying none the less. "When Beulah told Pierce and me about how Thom was behaving to his own son, well, we couldn't believe it, Callie." She patted her hand when she said it, then continued. "We prayed over it and we talked about it but didn't feel like we could write him - you know - to give him advice. But now that things have done a turnabout, I want you to know how sorry we both are that we didn't help you out more.

"I want you to promise me that if he ever gets out of line - now Callie I mean it - if he ever starts drinking too much and doesn't treat you right, we want to know. Pierce and I both will take the very next train to Arcadia and straighten him out. I mean it! He might be thirty-one years old, but he's still our son, and I'll - I mean we'll not allow him to hurt you and Meade again."

"Now I've had my say and you can get back to the ball game, if you'll promise me. Please promise me, Callie. This is very important to me and Pierce. I just don't know what came over that boy that he'd act like..."

"Now, Mama Garvin, don't you start crying right in the middle of his very first game...now don't ya. I'm gonna promise only because I know it'll not happen again. You see, I've made up my mind that everything's gonna be fine. Thom's been tested, and I'll admit that he didn't do too good...I mean well...but then he's never had things not go right, you know. This is, I guess, the very first time, and he didn't know just how to act."

She thought a while, and before Mary could interject, she continued. "But I think he's learned...and if he hasn't, then it's up to me to teach him - that's what!" and she said it with such fervor that Mary knew that she and Pierce didn't have to worry about them any more. I believe that the old Callie has come home. I'm so relieved.

****

"Maybe you'd better not say anything to Miss Kate about that cat, Parker!"

"Are you out of your mind, Slick? If I told her that there was the biggest cat I've ever heard of stalking Dixie and her pups, and especially Meade's Willy, she'd drive us all crazy with her carrying on. Course I'm not gonna tell her!"

Jam spoke up, "I sent Bart in to town and told him to get the Hawley brothers and their dogs and to tell them not to come by way of the main house. He said he'd tell them, but you know their smarts is confined to cat hunting and not on how Miss Kate would take to them telling her about that cat. Hell, they just might ride right up to the main house and knock on your door and ask Miss Kate where we all are 'cause they've been told that we got us a big cat what needs killing."

Jam laughed while he said it, but Parker wouldn't put it past them. Those Hawley brothers were sure dumb 'bout most everything but tracking. Jeeters said that they couldn't read or write and showed up after the War like a lotta folks did and put up their shack 'bout two miles from town.

Parker said, "I never saw two men live like those two do, have you? Nothing but an old shack with a dirt floor, and have you ever in your life seen as many skins as they have hanging from the rafters?...Grief! Some of 'em aren't even cured and stink to high heaven."

Slick spoke up, "Hell, their dogs live better'n they do. But you gotta admit that they can out-track any body or thing the Devil done made. Never saw the like of 'em! It's like they become just like 'em and know their whereabouts and such."

"It's a good thing that they don't wanta be social. Whew! Just being within three feet of 'em is enough. But maybe all that's changing," Jam said. "What with that little girl taking up with 'em. Just as cute as a speckled pup she is. You ever seen her, Slick?"

"Seen her? Course I seen her. Now, which one of 'em's pokin' her, I don't know. Hell, maybe both Wilbur and Harry. Bet she ain't more'n fifteen years old, but Malady done told me Saturday night that she got 'em to take a bath and wear clean clothes - at least into town." He howled when he said it. "You don't ever get down wind of the Hawley brothers, even if'n you a animal. Nosiree."

Parker spoke up. "Ione Jeeters told me that the girl goes by Josey Peabody and comes from down near Naples. Said her folks were drowned in a storm while they were fishing, and since she didn't have any kin that she knew of, she just started walking. Ended up over near Johnson Slough near about starved to death, and the Hawleys found her and took her in. You know Ione. If there's anyone in all of Arcadia who can find out about a person, it's Ione Jeeters. Said that she was a sweet little thing and can read and write and sure knows her figuring."

"Malady said that Ione asked Josey to work in the store, but she said that she couldn't until she had paid back Wilbur and Harry for taking her in." Slick shook his head wondering at the intelligence of the girl. "I can't imagine anyone who would rather live with the Hawleys instead of the back room at Jeeters', can you?"

Parker spoke up. "Takes all kinds, it does."

****

"Meade, quit your wiggling! Your daddy's gonna hafta sit on you to keep you still."

"I bet Willy's forgotten me, Mama. I bet he won't even come when I call him and can't even fetch and..."

"Don't you worry about Willy. It'll be just like you've never been away in no time." Thom smiled down at him, patted his hand that was clenching and unclenching nervously.

Callie was looking out the train window at the countryside just speed by. "I know riding the train is a lot faster, Honey, but next time we go to Bullseye let's go by horseback. I'd like Meade to really see the land before it changes more. Almost everywhere you look anymore there's a house or some other building."

"That's mostly alongside the railroad. Heck, you go a little ways from the tracks and it's still as wild as ever. We've still got lots of good old Florida left."

"I'd like to ride a horse all the way to Mama Mary's, Daddy. If I could take Willy, I'd go tomorrow."

"Oh, you would, would you?" Callie grabbed him and pulled him to her. "And you'd just ride off and leave me and your daddy at home, would you?"

"Mama, I'd let you go with me...and Daddy, too, if he was a mind to. I bet Willy's near 'bout grown! I bet he's as big as Dixie!"

Callie smiled at the older couple sitting across the aisle from them, and they smiled back. She took Meade's hand in hers and patted his sturdy back. "We've been gone only three weeks, Son. He can't have grown much, Honey."

They had left Crescent City a day earlier because the ball game had been rained out. One minute there was not a cloud in the sky; then in no time the heavens opened up, and they all got drenched. Thom decided not to bother wiring his Aunt Beulah in Arcadia that they'd be in a day early and to take a chance on borrowing her buckboard for the ride out to their house.

Callie didn't mind getting home early. She was almost as excited about getting home as was Meade, and so what if it would be after dark. They'd ride over first thing the next morning to see her folks, and besides Slick would be there taking care of Dixie and the pups. She put her head back and closed her eyes, and the train's rocking back and forth soon had her nodding off to sleep.

****

Harry squatted beside the large tracks in front of the barn door. Being a man of few words, he grunted and shook his head in amazement. His brother Wilbur was leaning against the door picking his stained teeth with a straw, and when Harry grunted he interpreted.

"Big one. Big as we've seen," and said not another word. Parker looked from one to the other, then at Slick and Jam, who stood beside him. He decided to ask one more time. "Well, you boys going after him or not? I sure want him killed before Callie and Thom get back tomorrow."

Harry was drawing something in the sand and Wilbur seemed to understand what it meant, but neither responded to Parker's inquiry. Wilbur slowly turned, walked over to his horse and untied the only hound that they had brought, and which was not making any more noise than his masters. Wilbur led him over to the tracks, and he methodically sniffed all around and suddenly let out a howl that made Parker, Jam and Slick all jump like they were shot. They started laughing to cover their nervousness, and it was then that Parker decided that, even though the Hawley brothers and their dog were for sure different acting, just maybe they'd be able to do the job. Callie and Thom wouldn't be in until the noon train, and it'd give them all night on its trail. That should do it.

Slick and Jam were so amused at Parker's reaction to the Hawleys that they decided they'd best leave the scene and go on up to the house to sit on the porch steps so they could get a real good view of the show that the Hawleys were acting out for their boss. Parker almost never got ruffled, and they were enjoying his discomfort.

Slick slapped his skinny thigh near about laughing his head off. "Now if those two were drinking men, I could understand their slow acting, but I swear I never saw anything any funnier than Parker trying to get them to commit to taking on that cat, and them just as stubborn as any mule I ever seen have decided that they'll give him their answer in their own time. Look at him, would you just, getting redder in the face by the minute. Look at him."

"And next he'll commence with the pacing. Yep! There he goes. You reckon I'd better put in my two cents and save him?"

"Hell, Jam, let him stew a little longer. This is gettin' to be a battle of the wills...yep, he's got his hat off and is wiping his brow and.."

"Nope, I best go to him now. Cain't afford to have our boss have a stroke, now can we?"

Jam walked slowly down the sand path toward the barn and called, "You boys want me and Slick to go after it? Hell, wouldn't be much to it. We just thought you boys would like a crack at it first."

Wilbur screwed up his face, that Jam noticed was about three shades lighter than usual. Guess Miss Josey got him to wash with soap. He also noticed that his shirt and pants had been mended, and you could even tell what color they were. Wilbur ignored Jam just like he did Parker and said, "Let's go," and Harry followed him. They got on their horses. Their hound was baying his head almost off, and Wilbur turned around and said, "Be back tomorrow."

Parker looked at Jam and Slick. "Does that mean that they are or they aren't going after it?"

Slick was almost bent double, he was so amused at him. "Your guess is as good as mine. Those two ain't ever been accused of doing anything in a hurry, but I'd say that they meant they'd be back tomorrow with the cat slung over their horse. Their dog's already got the scent. Would you listen to him howl?"

"Well, you two had better stay here just in case that isn't what they meant. Never in my life have I seen such peculiar acting men. Sure can't let anything happen to Thom's dogs. Look at that Willy would you. Now that is a smart dog Meade picked out. He's almost got a hole dug deep enough for him to wiggle out of the barn. Jam, best fill it in and pack it hard. Thom's got some logs cut over on the wood pile. Best shore it up good and tight. Yep, that's one smart pup."

Slick thought, but was smart enough not to say, won't be too smart if it gets eat up by that big cat. Parker didn't like anything contrary said about Meade or his pup.

God! One more night of sleeping in that hot barn. Don't know if my poor old back can take much more of it. Guess it wouldn't be so bad if I wasn't havin' to listen for that blasted cat to start clawing at that door. Whew!

****

"Best we tell Miss Josey ta not wait dinner."

Harry didn't answer right away, then said slowly, "Hound's got the scent. Best not wait."

"She gonna worry."

"Gotta go now. He'll lose the scent"

"Want me ta go tell her, then catch up?"

"Hell, Wilbur!"

That's all Harry said as he reluctantly followed Wilbur back to their cabin two miles down the creek. Sure enough, Josey was at the door looking just as pretty and shiny and smelling like a whole forest of sweet smelling sand pines.

"I was getting worried about you two. I surely was. Here, Wilbur, let me take that. I told you that I can fetch water just as good as you can. I already got the greens and pone done, and Mr. Jeeters sold me this nice piece of side meat. Gonna be needin' more of that wild honey, Harry. Just about out."

She glanced at their hands and sure enough they had taken time to go to the creek to wash up before coming up to the cabin. They're coming along just fine, she thought.

"Could use a rabbit or squirrel for tomorrow's dinner. If you get one I'll do up that hoecake you like so much to go with the gravy, and wouldn't some swamp cabbage be good to go with it?"

Wilbur was the more talkative of the two. "Miss Josey, we goin' after that big cat at Ole Piney Creek. Ain't gonna be home 'fore tomorrow..."

"But, Wilbur, I already got it planned!"

He could see how disappointed she was. Her large, brown eyes were downcast, and her pouting mouth almost in her collar. He glanced at Harry, and his set jaw told him that they'd not be eating Miss Josey's stew but would be out all night tracking that cat. He surely hated to upset Miss Josey, he sure did, but what could he do? Harry wasn't one to change his mind once it'd been made up.

"Done promised 'em the cat, Miss Josey." He sure loved saying her name and looking at her long, dark brown hair. It was almost as pretty as a black bear cub's, it was, and just as shiny. She'd made her dress that was the color of maple leaves in November, that orange-red color, all warm looking. He continued looking at her, enjoying every minute of it.

Now what would it hurt if they didn't go after that cat for another night? Heck, he could get two fat squirrels in no time at all and cut her a cabbage palm so's to get the heart to cook. Heck, what would it hurt?

He decided to work on that stubborn jaw of Harry's, that he noticed had relaxed a little as he sat sipping the dark, sweet coffee Miss Josey had poured for him. She'd tried to fix up their place. Even bought the red checkered oilcloth for the table and hung curtains from the leftover fabric from her dress on the window. What'd it hurt to please her a little, he reasoned.

Since her arrival Harry and he had been sleeping in the shed beside the shack. They didn't get too wet when it rained but had promised her that they'd replace the palmetto thatch with a metal roof just as soon as they sold enough otter pelts. Wilbur had made her a bed, and crude as it was, it was pretty comfortable. He'd made sure that the ropes were strung real close together and had helped her stuff the ticking with corn husks. He had wished that he could have found enough feathers or some cotton but she said that it was real soft and that she just loved it. That pleased him. There wasn't much he wouldn't do for Miss Josey.

Josey knew that beggars couldn't be choosers, like her ma always said. She didn't miss her or her pa like she used to. It'd been awful at first. When Mr. Strobel came to the house early that morning even before daybreak and told her that their boat had been found washed up on the shore, broken into a million pieces, and that they had no doubt drowned, she gladly went with him over to his and Miss Rosemary's house and stayed for - she couldn't remember how many days. Seemed like everything in her mind just ran together.

She didn't even remember leaving. She just remembered that she had to get away. She went next door to their small house and reached up in the open cupboard above the cook stove and got the jar of money down. Her ma always said that it was for a rainy day, and she guessed that she had meant it for now. She went to her room off the kitchen and reached underneath the narrow cot for her Sunday shoes. Josey wasn't about to leave without her Sunday shoes. She wrapped them in an old newspaper that her pa used to wrap the fish for Mr. Perkins's fish house, and that's all she took.

She didn't even say good-bye to the Strobels, whom she'd known all her life, but went behind their house through the mangroves to the road, not much more than a path, toward Ft. Myers, where she bought a knife and other supplies. She walked and walked, seeking shelter under trees, and hot as it was had to cover herself with the light blanket to hide from the swarming insects. Rubbing her exposed skin with the skin of the wild oranges that grew along the way eased the itching, but she was near dead when the Hawleys found her.

When she lay awake at night listening to the hoot owls call to each other, she'd try to remember what it had been like before her folks drowned, but try as she, might she couldn't recall much. It was as if she'd shut the door on the past. At first it bothered her, because she didn't want to forget her ma and pa, but after a while she'd lie awake and just enjoy planning for her future.

She'd told Mrs. Jeeters that she felt she had to repay Wilbur and Harry for their many kindnesses, and she meant it. She did indeed plan to go to work for the Jeeters but not until after she straightened the boys out. They sure needed a lot more of her hard work, but when they learned to make themselves presentable and got the roof on and the floor in, as they had promised her, and when they did better on their eating, then she'd talk about taking that job - but not until.

Wilbur took his time as he finished up the pone, dipping it in the greens' pot liquor, letting it crumble in his mouth as he savored every mouthful. He and Harry hadn't ever eaten this good, he thought. He knew that Harry was outside the door pacing up and down just like a tied up dog in heat, but he couldn't seem to take his eyes off of Josey, who was humming contentedly while she did up the dishes. She sure did like things clean.

Hell, he thought, it ain't gonna cause the whole world to come to an end if'n we get that cat tomorrow night! He decided to stretch his five-and-a-half-foot frame up tall and approach Harry. Soon as he got to him he repeated aloud, "It ain't gonna cause the whole world to come to an end if'n we get that cat tomorrow night, Harry."

Harry glared at him and said, "I could'a told ya that's what you'd say." He turned abruptly and yelled over his shoulder, "I'll kill the damned squirrels!" He could see Miss Josey through the window, her head cocked to one side, smiling gratefully at him.

"It don't matter anyways," he mumbled as he headed for the woods. "That cat ain't goin' anywheres, not wid dose puppies around."

CHAPTER II OLE PINEY CREEK

Beulah heard the front door close. "Good grief! Who could be wanting a room at this time of night?" She put down her mending and called to her husband, who was outside the kitchen door. "George, aren't you through with those saddles yet?" She waited. Nothing. "There's someone at the front door." Still no response. "Well, I guess I'll have to answer it myself," she said disgustedly.

"For heaven's sake, Thom, why didn't you let a body know that y'all'd be coming in on the night train?" Beulah Young was Thom's aunt on his mother's side, and she and her husband George ran the Young Hotel in Arcadia. "Bet you haven't even had supper. Now would you look at how sleepy Meade is! Callie, did the poor little tyke get any supper? Here, come to your Aunt Beulah. George!" she yelled loud enough to awaken the dead, and that included Meade. "Has my boy had any supper? Poor little thing. I do declare, you two should have let a person know that you were coming in tonight. Did you even let Kate know?" She looked suspiciously at Callie.

"Beulah, we ate the sandwiches that Mama Garvin packed for us." She was about to say that they weren't hungry when Beulah said derisively, "Sandwiches! Huumph!"

Callie ignored Beulah. She'd practically been raised by her mother's best friend, and continued, "We'd planned to come on the noontime train tomorrow, but Thom was anxious to get to Ole Piney and Dixie, and Meade was just as anxious to get home to Willy."

"You are not going all the way out there without something to eat, young lady. Why don't you spend the night? Now, I don't mind you taking the rig, now you know that, but those dogs can certainly wait 'til the morning to see you. Thom, what's the hurry?"

George, who had come in while they were talking, spoke up, "Beulah, leave these kids alone and let them do as they please, for heaven's sake. If they want to take the rig, I'll get 'em a couple o' lanterns. It's pitch black out there. Now quit being so dadburned bossy." He said it with a smile 'cause he loved all two hundred pounds of her and knew she was a take-charge person.

Thom spoke up. "Aunt Beulah, you know there's not much I'd rather do than eat at your table especially 'cause I can smell peach pie just as sure as I'm standing here. Or is it cobbler?"

Callie knew that they'd be spending time in the Young kitchen, 'cause he dearly loved anything made out of a peach, especially with a glass of rich, creamy milk, and that's exactly what they were doing two hours later, still telling Beulah and George about the wedding and their trip with Meade, fast asleep on the parlor sofa, and Thom on his second piece of Beulah's deep dish peach pie.

They decided that they'd do as George had suggested and take his rig on back to Ole Piney that night. They'd be home a little after midnight. It was pitch black but with the lanterns it would be fine.

"Callie, you be sure to tell Kate that I need her here early Sunday to help with the chicken salad for Reverend Stewart and his new bride. I'm gonna miss his Eloise, I sure am, but you know how hard it is on a man to do without a wife for very long. She sure up and died sudden-like, didn't she? But Roberta Hundley wrote that this new wife is real nice, even if she is real young. And, Callie, do tell Kate to be sure to have Mattie make at least six dozen of her thimble biscuits for the salad, and...George, is there anything I've forgotten?

"Beulah, do you ever forget anything? I mean, the whole town of Arcadia knows that you run it. Hell, Thom, we oughta elect her mayor."

She grabbed his ear playfully and replied, "Well, Mister, you could've said that I didn't forget anything a few years back, but I'm not so sure any more."

They waved good-bye, and Meade sleepily said, "Bye-bye Aunt Beulah and Uncle George and..."

"Shush, Honey. Go on back to sleep." Callie turned back to wave. "You'll be seeing Willy before you know it. Shush!" Thom patted his head, that was in Callie's lap, and Meade snuggled deeper into her skirt.

"We'll be home soon, son. Real soon."

Jam said to himself, "Hell, I ain't sittin' out here a minute longer. Why should I? Those Hawley brothers are trackin' him. Why shouldn't I be gettin' my shut-eye same as Slick?"

He opened the barn door just wide enough to slip in and felt around until he got to the mound of hay in the corner. Slick was snoring away, and even his horse's whinnying didn't disturb him. Bet if he heard that cat he'd be wide awake. He thought a minute, so would I.

He remembered when that cowman over near Bartow, old man Simpson, was mauled so bad about three or four years back. That cat had jumped him when he went out to check his stock. Never was right after that. Lordy, I never seen such a scar as that. He never did get that cat. Someone said it must have killed near about a dozen calves before Roscoe Jones killed it near the same place as it messed up Simpson. Said it had a territory 'bout fifty mile wide.

Jam soon eased into his bedroll and was snoring right along with Slick. They neither one heard Callie and Thom ride up. Dixie didn't even awaken.

"Thom, here, take Meade while I get his things. I'll get ours in the morning," she said tiredly. "Don't see Slick's horse. Guess maybe he's not here? That's strange, 'cause Pa said he'd have him stay the whole time we were away. Oh, well."

Thom shushed Meade. "Go on back to sleep, son. It'll be light 'fore you know it." He watched Callie in the lantern light. She's gotten prettier, I declare she has. Face has filled out a little.

He was remembering their soft talk as they rode the dirt road home. He was glad he'd finally got the courage to tell her. Oh, how he'd wanted to all those years but just couldn't find the words. Clay Willett wouldn't have had that problem, he knew, but somehow words weren't easily come by for Thom. She didn't want him to say it, but he just had to. When he told her that he knew how hurt she was because he couldn't show Meade how much he loved him, she immediately interrupted, "That's all past, Honey. Don't Thom. Don't you fret yourself anymore about it. I understood then, and I understand now..."

"But Callie, I've got to put it in words. I've just gotta, and now seems to be the right time. You know how happy I was to have a son, but seemed like you just got farther away - you know - having to care for him and everything. Now, don't, Honey. I've gotta finish this. I guess maybe I was a wee bit jealous 'cause I had you to myself for all those years, you know. But when he couldn't even talk, well, something in me just sorta snapped. I just couldn't take hold..."

"Thom, that's enough. I don't wanta hear another word."

"Well, you're gonna hear these words, Callie. I'm sorry, I..." He couldn't go on. When Callie pulled his face down to hers, she felt the warm tears, but for once he didn't pull away.

"I love you, Thom."

"And I love you, Callie Anders Meade."

"Think I'll go out to the barn and check on Dixie..."

"Oh, Honey, she can wait 'til morn...", but he'd already got to the porch. Callie smiled, he's just like a mama, gotta check on his young. She went to their bedroom and lit the lamp that Beulah and George had given them for their wedding. Its soft glow shown on her rich brown hair as she loosened it. She was looking in the dresser mirror and humming happily as she brushed it. Think I'll put on my prettiest nightie for Thom. It'll feel good to be in our own bed, and tired as we are, I need to thank him the best way I know how for telling me how he feels.

She slipped into the soft batiste gown. I wonder if I should tell him about not feeling too well in the morning - no, I'll wait 'til I'm dead sure. Don't want to get his hopes up. I truly think that the Lord waited for Meade to get his voice before He sent us another.

She heard the shrill scream - seemed like it was right outside the bedroom window. "What on earth was that? Sounded like a cat!" she said out loud. When she looked out the window she saw Thom's lantern on the ground, but it was so dark that she couldn't make out what was happening. Then she heard voices and the scream again.

"That's from the barn! What on earth's going on? I know it's a cat!"

She ran to the door not bothering to pull on her robe and called as she ran, "Thom...Thom!"

"It's Callie, Jam. Don't let her come out here. Go stop her. She cain't see this. My God..."

"Miss Callie you stay there. Don't come out here!"

"Go to her, Jam! God, don't let her out here! She cain't see Thom like this!"

"What happened?" Parker asked Jam. "You say Thom? How on earth did it happen?" He was half asleep, rubbing his eyes and trying to comprehend when Kate came up behind him.

"What's going on, Honey? What's the matter?"

She heard him say, "I don't believe it! I just don't believe it!" Then he turned to her and opened the screen door. "Kate, get dressed. We've gotta go to Callie. Thom's been...he caught his breath as he held her out before him, "Thom's been killed, Honey. That damned cat got him! Now don't! Kate, don't. We've gotta be strong for Callie and Meade. Jam said she's carrying on something awful, and Slick is havin' an awful time keeping her from seeing him like that. I don't believe this! I just don't! Those Hawley brothers were supposed to get that cat!"

"But, Parker, they're not supposed to be here 'til tomorrow. Are you sure?"

"I know, Honey, guess they were anxious to get home." When they got to Callie she was still in her nightie and sitting on the porch steps with Slick right beside her. Kate was so wobbly that she had to be helped down from the buckboard, but when Callie called to her, Kate began to run. Parker was holding Callie and sobbing right along with her, something Slick thought he'd never see, and he was telling her that everything would be fine...just fine.

"It'll be all right, Honey. It'll be all right. Your ma and I'll take care of everything...now don't you fret."

"Callie, honey," Kate said softly, "Come on in now, and we'll just sit a spell and talk, and by morn it'll seem like a bad dream. Honey, come on in, please."

She checked on Meade, and he was sound asleep. She gently closed the door, and Kate was right beside her. "He's had too much to bear, Mama - too much. Now he has no daddy - oh, Mama - I don't think I can stand it. I just don't think I can..."

"Shush, Honey. The Lord doesn't give anybody more than they can bear, now you know that. Look at how he gave Meade his voice before he took Thom, so Thom could have some peace and joy, and now he's with the Father and will never know anything but happiness and..."

"Mama, do you really believe that? I mean, really?" she asked through streaming tears, trying desperately to stop them with the handkerchief Kate had handed her.

"Honey, if I didn't believe that, then I couldn't believe anything that was beautiful - like a newborn baby or an all-color sunset over the Peace River or the soft, comforting sound of a hoot owl in the pitch-black night as it guards its young. I couldn't believe anything, Honey, if I couldn't believe in the hereafter. The Good Book teaches it, and I believe it."

Kate was sitting on the side of Callie's and Thom's bed stroking her daughter's distraught face. She continued because she could feel Callie relax. "I know I'm going to see my ma and pa, sure as shootin', when I'm taken, and I'll get to see my beautiful first born, Henry Parker, so tiny and helpless. Oh, yes, my sweet girl, I surely do believe that when your time and Meade's time come, that Thom will open his strong arms to you and you'll be reunited and together again. I surely do."

"Then I guess I can make do with the time I've got left, Mama. Just as long as I know I'll see Thom again," and with that said, she put her head in Kate's lap, and Kate began singing to her just like she had when she was just a little girl, and Callie was soon fast asleep. Kate looked down at her, pulled the quilt up around her shoulders and tiptoed out to the porch.

The men had the lanterns lit, and she could hear their muffled voices coming from inside the barn. "I hope they don't go after that cat tonight. I surely do."

Parker came outside the barn and he and Jam were arguing. "He's tasted blood, Parker, and there's no stopping him now. Hell, he's probably still around here!"

"Well, if he is then we'd better get the lanterns outside and build a big fire. This family can't stand anymore, Jam."

"God! I never saw the likes of it. Thom couldn't have known what hit him! The cat must've been up in that oak and jumped smack dab on top of him, knocking the breath out before going for the...the throat. At least that's what me and Slick figured. Didn't know a thing. Never saw so much blood in my life. Hell, we didn't even hear Thom yell or nothin'. God! Poor Thom!"

Slick came out to join them and they all three stayed clear of the spreading oak above the barn. In no time they had a huge fire going with every lantern they could find surrounding the front of the barn. Parker joined Kate on the porch.

"How's Callie, Honey?"

"I got her calmed and she's resting. She's exhausted, and Meade hasn't even turned over, he's so tired. You going to wait 'til morn to get word to town?"

"We feel we'd better stay put. That cat's tasted blood and might just try to come back." He patted her hands, then took one in his. "God, Kate! It's a big one. Scratched so high on the barn door that it must be as long as a man."

"What'd cause a cat to go after a man, Honey? I don't understand it...I truly don't."

"Well, it's wild and can't think or figure like a human. I think those puppies of Dixie's drew it. But then we've always had puppies at Tall Ten, and I haven't seen a cat around home in years. Now, when we first homesteaded it, Logan and I must've killed near about a dozen of them before we cleared around our place. That's before we were wed, of course."

Kate interjected. "Maybe it's because it's in the thick woods here. You know Callie. She loves being in the woods, so the cat felt they were taking his place, so to speak."

"But, Honey, they've been here over ten years. I've heard some strange tales about cats though. You just can't figure them."

"Well, I don't like the idea of Meade and Callie being around here all alone. I surely don't. They're not safe way out here, not safe at all. I want you to promise me that you'll talk some sense into her, Parker. Promise me that..."

They heard the front door squeak from behind them, and they both jumped. "Promise what, Ma? You've gotta tell me. Promise what?"

"All right, Callie. I asked your pa to promise me that he'll insist that you and Meade come on home and not stay way out here in these wild woods..." She couldn't go on. She started crying then, and Callie went to her.

"It's my turn now, Mama. You need comforting, too. Go ahead and cry - it's my turn now."

Parker, not being able to see them like that, mumbled that he was going on to the barn and said that they were not to leave the porch. He brushed away the tears before he got in the light of the fire, but Jam and Slick could see how upset he was.

"Parker, I'll leave at first light for town. Tell me what you want me to do..."

"Before you do anything in town I want you to high-tail it to the Hawleys' shack and find out where in hell those two were when that cat jumped Thom - that's what!"

He couldn't continue and went on into the barn, sat on the mound of hay and began petting Meade's Willy, who had left the warmth of his mother and crawled up on his lap.

Slick could hear him whispering to Willy real gentle like. "Let him be, Jam. He needs his time alone just like Callie and Miss Kate do.

****

"Callie, it doesn't seem quite right for Meade to be taking that dog into the church. Not right at all!"

"Well, Mama, if the preacher doesn't think it's wrong, then it's not wrong. Besides, Meade needs to be loving something now. He needs to, Mama!"

"Leave it alone, Kate. No harm will be done," but Parker saw that determined set to her lips. Can't believe we've got a battle of the wills today of all days, he thought wearily. He decided to put an end to it.

"I want you two to listen. Now, I mean it! Callie's right, Kate. Just because Layke and Berta and half the state of Florida will be here for the funeral doesn't mean a thing!" He let it sink in and nodded toward Meade and Willy in the back of the buckboard. "Meade's having Willy inside the church isn't against any church rule I've ever heard of, and Callie is right about that, Honey." He took her hand, but she quickly took it back and pursed her lips even more.

But before he could continue, they were at the church, and there must've been fifty people out front and goodness knows how many on the inside - it was packed. About two dozen cowmen were hanging around the front door, and Kate shot a look at Parker that would have scalded a skunk. He could read her - she didn't even have to say it out loud. "If those young men think that they can get all likkered up and spoil Thom's funeral like they did his wedding, then mister, they'd better think again."

The funeral had been delayed for an extra day so the Garvins could get down from Bullseye, and the Senator and Berta, who had been in Kissimmee visiting friends, had wired that they would be attending. Kate was all a-dither. To think that a senator was actually attending Thom's funeral, and then Callie and now Parker said that it was all right for Meade to drag that dog into the church with him...well! But Kate was pleased about one thing. Thom would be buried in Arcadia at the Garvin's request, because they knew that it would mean a lot to Callie and Meade. Callie was so happy when they had suggested it, because Bullseye was so far away, and the idea of Thom being all the way up there would have been just too much for her to bear.

"Beulah said that Callie has taken hold and is doing fine, Honey," Mary Garvin said to Pierce as they left the hotel. The cowmen who were hanging around the porches took off their hats and nodded as the Garvins walked on the wooden sidewalk toward the church.

"Seems like only yesterday that we were walking down this same sidewalk for Thom's and Callie's wedding. Can you believe that it was over ten years ago..?" she began, but when she saw Pierce's set jaw she knew she'd not be getting a response. He'd not be saying much until they returned to Bullseye. He hadn't said more than a few sentences since they received the telegram about Thom. Mary sighed. He'll save his grieving time for when it's all over, and then he'll talk a streak about when Thom was just a youngster and when he broke his first horse and...

I've done my crying, now why am I getting started again? I'll think of pleasant things, I declare I will. Berta - I'll think of Berta and Layke. Gracious, I haven't seen her to talk to for ...it must be almost two years. Has it been that long? I can't believe it.

"Would you look at this crowd, Pierce?" Mary turned to Lucinda, who was behind her with her husband and their children, and repeated, "Have you ever seen such a crowd? My, how pleased Thom would be at all his friends coming from all over to pay their respects."

No one responded until Thurmond spoke up. "He'd be real pleased, Ma. Real pleased. Now, Lottie, don't get started with tears again. Honey..."

Mary turned around then. "Lottie, I know you're upset, but, dear, please keep it quiet." She started crying all the harder, and Mary took Thurmond aside and said, "If she can't control herself out here, how do you expect her to inside, son?"

"I know, Ma, but you know Lottie."

Yes, she thought, I know Lottie. At least she's a distraction.

"Would you just look at all the people who turned out, Pierce?" Why am I chattering so? I just wish someone in this family would say something so I could be quiet. Not even Bit's talking, and I usually can't shut her up. If I can only hold up my spirits until I return to Bullseye, then...

The Meades, Callie and Meade, were at the front of the church when the Garvins arrived. Mary rushed to the buggy.

"Kate...Parker...I..." When she saw Callie helping Meade down from the buckboard - and he was holding Willy so tightly that his head was around Meade's chin and his tail almost on the ground - Mary got such a catch in her throat she forgot all about being upset. If that isn't a picture! Dear Lord, you've given me back my Thom...you surely have.

"It's another sun-filled day, Pierce," Mary said as they entered the small church. People all up and down the pews nodded to them, but Pierce looked dead ahead. When Callie and Meade, who had put Willy down, followed Kate and Parker and Jay into the pew just ahead of the Garvins, Mary could hear the chatter, though muffled. Let them talk. That little Thom needs that hound, he does. Let them talk.

Preacher Stewart came out in his black funeral suit, and Marcella began to play the piano. He raised his hands to the congregation, and they all rose. But when she started singing the first stanza of *The Old Rugged Cross* in that high soprano that quivered so that it hurt your ears, Willy decided to join in with his howling, and the laughter that followed was so loud that the preacher had to raise his hands to the heavens again to quiet them. Marcella was flustered and flushed, and Bit finally let go and laughed so loudly that her father requested she leave the church.

Thurmond reached over to Pierce and said, "Now you know, Pa, that Thom is surely enjoying this." Pierce at first twitched his mouth, and Mary was sure was going to cuff Thurm a good one, but he, too, started to grin and shake his head up and down just like almost everyone in the entire congregation.

Meade turned to Callie and said, "I bet Daddy's happy that Willie can sing so good, don't you think, Mama?"

"I'm sure he is, but son, I want you to go with Uncle Jay out to the buggy and tie Willy to the wheel until after Daddy's funeral. Would you be a big boy and do it for me?" Jay took hold of Meade's small hand, and as they walked out of the church Preacher Stewart began.

"Praise the Lord! It's a glorious day when a son and the Father are united in His kingdom above. It's a time of rejoicing, not a time for sadness..." and Callie heard not another word he said. She was thinking only of Thom and could see him just as plain as anything with his handsome face looking down at Meade and Willy and laughing right along with them.

****

"Gus, I think I'm going to stay in Arcadia for a while," Clay Willett said as he helped Gus Jeeters, the only father he had ever known, unpack the new shipment of canned goods that had come in on the train. He could see Gus's concern. His raised, shaggy brows gave him away. "Not just because of Callie - now I want you to know that - but because Jay and I have decided to go ahead with the book we've been talking about."

"I thought Jay was going to DeLand to teach."

"He is, but before he leaves we want to rough draft the book and discuss the illustrations."

Yes, Gus thought, any excuse so's you can be near Callie and

Meade. Wouldn't you think a smart person like Clay would get the message that he's not gonna get to first base with her. Callie couldn't love him before Thom, and she sure as shootin' ain't gonna love him now. I'm not believing that book business, and neither will anyone else in Arcadia. He's just gotta be near her in case she looks his way. Poor Clay. He'll never learn, not ever.

Clay was reading Gus's mind and decided to continue. "If Jay can work on the illustrations before he goes to Stetson, then I can finish the manuscript and do the layouts..." and on he droned.

Gus and Ione had discouraged Clay from leaving the Tampa *Tribune*, where he was a features writer. He had won all sorts of awards and was quite a celebrity, and they were so proud of him. Just didn't make any sense at all to them that he'd throw away such a promising career just so he could be near Callie. No sense at all.

When Clay had told them that he already had an interested publisher in New York City, he thought that would impress them, but it didn't. Somehow, writing children's books just wasn't nearly as impressive as having his by-line on an article in the Tribune.

"I'll continue to write specials for the paper, Gus. It's not like I'll be giving up my association with them. This is something I've always wanted to do. There are so few good children's books published ..."

But Gus and Ione weren't buying a thing he said. "This is just another way for him to get close to Callie, being around Jay out at Tall Ten with Thom not a month in the grave. That's what the whole town will say, Gus," Ione had said when he tried to explain it to her. "I don't know about Clay's smarts. I declare I don't."

CHAPTER III STETSON UNIVERSITY

"You're not having the Queen of England for dinner, Katie," Parker teased her. "Grief! It's just Berta and Layke. You wouldn't be in such a dither if her husband weren't a senator, now would you?"

"Stop your teasing, mister. You know that I like to have things nice no matter who they are, and when's the last time we had someone important to dinner - now when?"

"Last night, Ma," Jay spoke up kissing her cheek. When she shot the questioning look at him he laughed and said, "Georgianna, Ma. She's important."

"Oh, for heavens sake. You two get out of my kitchen this very minute, and Jay, you mind your manners. I don't want you gobbling your food like a hungry cow hand, and go change your shirt. I bet it's two years old, and look, it's frayed around the cuffs."

"Better do what your Ma says, son. Miss Kate's in a dither all right. I'm just glad she didn't ask me to kill the fatted calf and..."

"James Parker Meade! Now that's enough. Fatted calf indeed! Fresh ham and Mattie's fried chicken are good enough for anyone, and that includes a state senator. Now, I mean it - git! Git!"

Mattie was enjoying their exchange and wondered, but did not ask, if Callie and Meade would be joining them for dinner. She knew that they had stayed in town after the funeral to spend some time with the Garvins, but no one had mentioned whether they were coming back to Tall Ten for dinner.

Kate had invited Clay, at Berta's and Layke's request, because they had become so fond of him when he had visited them in Tallahassee while writing the award-winning article on the making of a senator, using them as models. Had they known how the tongues would wag when the townspeople found out that he was having dinner at Tall Ten the very day after Thom's funeral, they wouldn't have asked Kate to include him.

Meade jumped off the hotel front porch and began running toward Callie. She and Rube, Beulah's hired man, were already in the Youngs' buckboard, and although she was not anxious to get back to her own home, she was anxious to get back to Tall Ten and the comfort of Kate and Parker. I'll ask Ma if we can stay there for a few days. I know I should go on home, but I can't. I just can't, at least not yet. She tousled Meade's curly hair and, as she looked at him, realized that he was already getting over his pa's death. *I wish grown-ups could forget as quickly as children. Why, he's already talking about asking Pa to help him with his hitting and catching.* She shook her head in wonder and through her tears smiled. *His recovery will make it easier for me. Maybe I'll be able to go on home after all.*

Mattie was on the back stoop when Callie and Meade rode up. *Look at her. She's got so stooped,* Callie thought. *She's not really up to fixing such a big dinner. I'll help her. I need to keep busy. Ma should have got Ettamae to come out to help her. I wonder if Ma wrote Pet about how Mattie's failing. Oh Lordy, we'll miss her so when she goes. She's as much a family member as I am.*

Mattie looked up when she heard the noise of the buggy. She thought that it was Senator and Miss Berta arriving early and was relieved that it wasn't. *Poor little thing looks so forlorn, and would ya look at Meade and Willy, would ya just. Just lak nothin' happen a'tall.*

She put her head inside the back door and called, "Miss Kate, Miss Callie done got home. You wants that Ah should send her up to ya?" but got no answer.

"Don' nobody hear nothin' in dis house," she grumbled while wiping her flour-covered hands on her apron. "Still gotta roll out de biscuits and do at least two more pans of chickens, and nobody 'round to hep."

"Miss Kate," she called again. Still no answer. She saw Callie kiss Meade, and he headed for Jay's workroom, and she couldn't believe it when she saw another buggy coming up the path. "Don' nobody in dis whole house plan on heppin' me wid dis highfalutin' dinner! Nobody!" she grumbled as she bent to lift the heavy pail of water.

Callie rushed to her. "Here, Mattie, let me get that. You've got no business trying to lift anything that heavy," but when Callie bent over she felt so faint that it was Mattie who was helping her.

"Miss Callie, you ain't got no business a'tall heppin' me. Now look what ya done. Almost got sick right here on de stoop. I'se gonna call yer ma. You sit right down here an' don' ya move. Miss Kate...Miss Kate." Callie was about to protest but knew it would do no good.

Now I'm sure. Oh, dear Lord, thank You. Now I've got another piece of Thom. She sat down and put her head down on her knees.

"Mama, don't you feel good?" Meade yelled as he ran to her with Willy nipping at his heels.

"Oh, Honey, I feel wonderful, really I do. It's just that I felt a little faint, that's all. I should have had more breakfast. Think I'm a little hungry and will have to eat an extra piece of Mattie's chicken."

"I will too, Mama. I'm gonna eat a whole chicken so I can grow big and can take care of you." Callie was laughing at him when Kate got to her.

"What's this all about? Grief! Mattie had me scared almost to death. Aren't you feeling well, Honey?"

"I feel great. I just got dizzy when I bent over. Think I'm just hungry. Mama, don't look so worried. I'm fine, honest I am."

"Why don't you just go on up to your old room and rest a spell, Honey? I'll help Mattie finish up." Callie didn't protest, and the worried exchange between Kate and Mattie went unnoticed.

"What's all this grumbling about, Mattie?"

"Oh, nuttin', Miss Kate, jes dat Miss Callie got back, and den Mr. Clay come up, and dey all at Master Jay's workroom, an Ah'm jes behind in de cookin', an..."

"I'm here now, dear. I'll let Callie rest for a while, and then she'll help with the table, and with the three of us we'll have it ready in no time. Besides, Clay and Jay have a lot of talking to do about the book they're planning." She began humming, and when Miss Kate hummed Mattie relaxed and knew all was well. That was her signal that her house and mind were in order and that she could take on anything that befell her. Mattie joined in. Callie could hear them harmonizing way up in her room as she stroked her stomach and smiled contentedly up at her Thom.

Kate rapped on Jay's workroom door. Parker had built him the two-room cabin before he was a teenager. He was allergic to horses and would never be able to assist him on the ranch, and Parker knew that he needed something of his own. Jay's teachers all said that he had a great talent, that he was a natural artist, and Parker could see that they were right. But it had been hard for him at first to accept that it would be Callie who would carry on Tall Ten, not his son.

He and Kate had discussed it many years ago. He wouldn't have, but Kate had insisted. "Why was it all right for Callie to dress, act and ride like a boy, but it wasn't all right for Jay to draw and paint?" she had asked. It was a puzzle to him, but somehow still not right. But when any of his hands said or intimated that Jay was a sissy, Parker had begun setting them straight. Pretty soon they accepted the fact that Jay was not able to be around horses and had begun visiting his workroom, and when Parker added the second room on to the original room to house all the animals that Jay had stuffed through the years, it had become a favorite hangout for the hands.

Clay was excited. He'd not been alone with Callie since before she and Thom were married. Oh, he'd seen her at church and at the store and even at the hotel without Thom during the period when Thom was having his problems, but not to talk to like they had from the time they'd been in grade school. He had analyzed his feelings hundreds of times. What was there about Callie that he loved so? He'd known other girls when he lived in Tampa - some intimately. His friends on the paper had introduced him to some very nice, intelligent, well educated young ladies, but none appealed to him. He'd even made the effort to keep company with two of them, but after a while he'd ask for an assignment that would take him from the area, and when he returned, he'd not contact them, hoping that their ardor would have cooled.

He could see Callie as she walked up the path toward the workroom. Meade got excited when he saw her approach and ran to the door.

"Meade, close the door tightly," Clay cautioned him.

Callie spoke up, "You know the moths will eat Uncle Jay's animals, Meade. Look at that bear cub. It's gonna loose all its hair if you let them in here."

"Don't worry about them, Callie," Jay said, "I put in enough borax to take care of any insect."

Clay embraced Callie easily and kissed her brow, while Meade hugged him around his knees. "Uncle Clay, did you see Willy's new trick? Did you?"

"Meade, let Clay be for a little while. I never saw such as you." But she smiled when she said it, and Clay patted his head and said, "It's all right, Callie. He knows that I want to hear all about Willy's trick, don't you, son?

"You bet, Uncle Clay. Mama, Clay and me..."

"That's Clay and I, son. Not Clay and me. Heaven's, I sound just like Ma."

"Mama, that's Blackie," Meade said as he held on to her hand. "Why do ya suppose it's called a black bear when it's brown?"

"That's the same question I asked Daddy Parker when I was just about your age, and he said that it was the group that was called black bears and didn't have anything to do with the color. So, all right, Blackie it is, and it's a good name for it."

Jay had allowed Meade into his workroom from when he was just a little tyke and had introduced him to his specimens while encouraging him to talk. He had named all of them, saying their names over and over, hoping that Meade would respond, and now Meade could call them by name. He was so proud of his achievement that he never missed an opportunity to let them know of it.

"Did I ever tell you about the time your great grandma and grandpa Meade had a run-in with a black bear? Well, Grandpa Parker was in the outhouse one morning real early at first light, and when he came out, what was standing there but a big old black bear."

"What'd he do, Mama?"

"Well, hold on and I'll get to it. He said he couldn't think of a thing to do, so he said, 'Howdy, nice morning isn't it'?' and walked slowly to the house and got his gun." She started laughing.

"Go on, Mama. Didn't anything else happen?"

"It most certainly did. He had forgotten that Grandma was in there, too - the outhouse was a two-holer, you see - and when she came out that bear was still there, and when she saw Grandpa standing there pointing the gun at the bear, she also said, 'Howdy, nice morning isn't it,' and Grandpa got so tickled that he put down the gun and laughed so loud that he scared the bear away. When Grandma got to Grandpa, she was so put out with him that she picked up the bresh broom and chased him all around the yard yelling her head off at him."

"Why didn't he shoot it?"

"Meade, the bear wasn't hurting them, so why should he shoot it? I bet I heard that story a million times while I was growing up."

"Meade and I have to name all the animals that Jay and I are going to feature in our book, don't we Meade?" Clay said.

"We sure do, and Mama they're going to write all about Willy, aren't you Clay?"

"That's Uncle Clay, young man. Don't you get too frisky just because you've been asked to help."

Clay could tell that she was just going through the motions, saying the right things but without having to think about anything. He held her arm possessively and took her into the room where Jay had the stuffed animals.

"Now, some of the animals already have names, like the bear cub we'll call Blackie, and the dog we'll name Wee Willy, The otter is Otis and the gator is Big Al. What did we decide to call the eagle, Meade? I can't remember." He winked at Callie when he said it.

"Oh, you remember, Uncle Clay. We named it Big Chief, and the great horned owl is Mister Wise, and we named the cat Arthur for King Arthur..."

Meade saw Callie begin to bite her lower lip and thought that she might begin to cry again, so quickly said, "Mama, this cat's not the one who hurt Daddy..."

"I know, son, don't you worry about Arthur. The cat who hurt your daddy is at the Hawleys' cabin, someone said." She looked at Jay, who had joined them, questioning him.

"Sis, they asked me if I wanted to stuff him, but I declined." He hung his head and continued. "I never in all my life saw such a specimen. It was beautiful." When he realized what he had said, he went to Callie and took her in his arms. "I'm so sorry. I shouldn't have said that."

"It's all right, Jay. I think that you should stuff it. Really I do. There's a place for all God's creatures on this earth, and they have a job to do just like humans. Meade, I want you to believe that, son. That cat was wild and naturally behaved as such, and had your daddy known that it was around, he would have been on the lookout..."

She got her breath and composed herself. "Don't worry about Arthur. I'm sure Uncle Clay will write a very good book about all your friends, and you've got to remember what I said...about all God's creatures having a place and..."

She couldn't go on. Turning as she left the doorway, she called over her shoulder, "I've got to help Mama Kate. Don't you get dirty, Meade. We'll be eating soon."

Clay watched her walk up the sand path to the main house. She hiked up her dark brown skirt above the ruffle of the starched petticoat. The noonday sun caught the red lights in her hair, that was pulled back with a large, brown, grosgrain bow.

I love her so much. I wish I could hold her and comfort her, but I'll have to wait 'til she heals more.

Jay watched from his perch on the stool beside his work table. The bright light shown through the clear glass panes onto his latest painting. He's hurting so much. I wish I could help him. He turned back to the sketch of the birds that he and Clay had decided to feature in the first volume of their Florida wildlife book. They had planned to go into the animals' habitat and do an almost textbook format, but then Clay hit on the idea of incorporating the animals in a fictional story about a small boy whose parents died, leaving him in the wilderness of old Florida to fend for himself.

Clay had completed the outline over a year before and had interested one of the top New York publishers in it. Jay's portfolio of sketches had been sent to them, and the letter that followed was very flattering. Jay knew that Clay's interest in the project was partially because of Callie and Meade, and now that Callie was a widow, his fervor for the book's completion was certainly intensified.

I hope it works out for him and Callie. Those two were always meant for each other. I just wish that I were as sure about Georgianna and me. I don't know why I have such doubts.

"Meade," Clay asked, "what do you think we should name the boy in the book? How do you like Jim or..."

"You should name him for my daddy. Thom's a good name, isn't it, Uncle Jay?"

Clay looked at Jay, and they both smiled and nodded. "I think that Thom's the perfect name. Now, if the editor approves it, then Thom it'll be."

"My daddy will like that. And don't forget, his dog's gotta be named Willy. Don't forget." He opened and closed the door quickly, as he'd been taught, and dashed outside running to the main house, following his mama as the men watched.

"We'll tentatively call it *"Thom's Wilderness Adventure"* just until we've had a chance to work on it. I'm getting excited, you know," Clay said. "Nothing's been done like it before. When J.M. wrote that he wanted it to be more of an adventure story than a textbook, I wasn't sure I liked that approach, but the more I work with it the more I like the idea. What do you think, Jay?"

"Well, it'll certainly give you more of an opportunity to stretch your creative talent, and I particularly like the idea of the wildlife having a distinctive personality all its own. For instance, last night as I was thinking about the cat that got Thom, I felt that we could use the incident in the book. Perhaps feature a friendly animal that could defend the little boy from being harmed by the cat or a gator or - well - you get the picture."

"The reader would learn while enjoying the excitement of the story. That's exactly what I had in mind," Clay interjected excitedly. He sat down, crossed his long legs, and using his hands expressively continued, "I think that Meade would be a perfect model for "Thom", don't you? He needs to be younger, of course, by at least two years. For instance, when the story opens, he should be about four or maybe even three, don't you think? You know, old enough to care for himself a little."

He stopped and listened and said, "Is that Callie calling us?" They listened and heard her call again. "We can continue this after dinner. But, I think we're on the right track," Clay said, his arm draped loosely around Jay's shoulder as they left the workroom.

"There're Berta and the Senator. That's why she was calling. It'll be good to see them again. They're an interesting couple and good source material for the lad's parents, by the way. Both very attractive, stable and intelligent with a fine sense of humor. Yes, I think they'll fit perfectly."

Jay smiled up at him. "I'm glad we're going to work on this together, Clay. I really am. But you know you'll have to spend a lot of time up in DeLand for it to work out."

"Yes, I know. But once I get the story outline and you get a feeling for the various animals' personalities, it shouldn't take us long to get approval from J.M., and I can return to Arcadia." He looked at Jay when he said it. "I need to be near her, Jay. Maybe she doesn't need me, but I like to think she does, nonetheless."

"I understand. Oh, she needs you all right. She needs your sensitivity. Now, I know Thom loved her. I never doubted that, and these last few months, well, I never saw them so happy. I'm glad she had that. I think that she'll forget the bad times and hang onto the good."

"Berta, Senator, so good to see you again," Clay said enthusiastically. "You've met Jay, haven't you?"

Berta spoke up, "We've not seen him for quite a while. Jay, it's good to see you again." She extended her hand, "And, before I forget, I want to congratulate you on your appointment to Stetson. Did Kate tell you that our daughter SuSu is attending? As a matter of fact that's where we were when we got word of poor Thom. We were visiting Senator Wells and family outside of DeLand."

She turned to Kate and said, "Kate, please let's sit on the porch. You know how informal Layke and I are, and besides, he can smoke his pipe out here. I don't like to have the parlor smelling of smoke, do you?"

They left arm in arm. Jay turned to Clay, "I think you're right. She'd be the perfect model, motherly looking but beautiful. I've never seen such blue eyes."

"What're you two whispering about?" Layke asked as he turned from Parker. "Admiring my lady-love, are you?"

Clay laughingly told him about their project, and Layke, who was as handsome as the day he and Berta first met, with a little grey at the temples and more weathered looking, got very excited.

"Use us for models? Wait 'til I tell Berta. Well, you've certainly chosen the female right, but I'm not sure about me. What do you think, Parker? I might be too handsome to be believable, huh?"

Layke always knows the right things to say, Parker thought as they walked up to the house. Guess that's why he's such a good politician, the best this state's ever had. I think the years he spent roaming from ranch to ranch gave him the feeling for our needs, and Berta has certainly helped. Those two seem as much in love as when I first saw them. You can just feel it, and Clay certainly captured it in his articles. I don't believe that there was any truth in what Mary Garvin told Kate about their having trouble a few years back. Now, I know Layke had the reputation of being a ladies' man before he and Berta were married. Heck, women came out of the woodwork after him. You would've thought that taking a ball in his thigh that left him slightly crippled would've turned them away, but it just seemed to draw them to him thick as flies. And maybe Berta did feel out of place in Tallahassee at first, but from the looks of it they've ironed it all out. I'm glad...

"Miss Kate, dinner's ready," Mattie called from the parlor door. Callie had joined her in the kitchen to help serve and was carrying on a conversation and humming just like her mama, and Mattie couldn't get over how she was acting just like she wasn't just widowed. Listen to her humming jes lak Miss Kate when her house be in order. Uumph! De young sho heal inna hurry. Dey sho do.

"Parker, would you bless the dinner, please."

"I'd be pleased to, Kate. It's always a pleasure to sit down to one of Mattie's meals." He winked at Mattie, who quickly lowered her head and covered her mouth trying to hide her toothless smile.

"Dear Lord, we thank you for this gathering of our family and our friends and would be pleased if you would bless this food for our health and our souls' spiritual food from your bountiful harvest. Amen."

Kate was so pleased that he didn't say, "Thank you, Lord, for dinner - let's eat," as he usually did. Her Parker could do a real good blessing and prayer when he put his mind to it. He saw how pleased she was, and that inspired him to enter into a lively conversation with Layke, Berta and Clay. Kate realized that it was as much to keep Callie's mind off of Thom as it was to be a good host. Her Parker was a lot like Clay and Layke. He was very aware of the folks around him, and he was happiest when they were happy.

I just wish that Thom had had more of Parker's compassion in him. Callie's life would have been so much easier, she thought as she studied her. But would you look at her? She's animated and talkative and just as much at ease as she used to be before Meade was born and when things were good. Maybe she'll have the good sense to learn to love Clay as much as he loves her - just maybe. Dear Lord, that is my wish.

The conversation turned to Jay's appointment to Stetson, and Berta proceeded to tell him about SuSu's reaction to the town of DeLand. "You know she's enrolled in the Normal School, don't you? She's always wanted to be a teacher; that is, after she got over the notion to join the circus and be the star of the show as the queen of the tightrope act." They all laughed. "I just know she'll love it, and goodness knows with Florida's rapid growth we need more and more qualified teachers."

"My mama's never wanted to be anything but a cowman, have you Mama?" Meade broke in.

While they laughed, Callie cautioned her son not to interrupt but said, "You're right, Meade, that's all I've ever wanted to be except a wife and mother, of course."

Clay saw the direction the conversation was going and so quickly asked, "Berta, did you have difficulty securing lodging for SuSu? I'll be spending a great deal of time in DeLand while Jay and I work on the book, and since I've not been there before - I guess it's one of the few Florida towns I've not visited - I was wondering about lodging."

Kate and Parker both relaxed when they saw Callie's expression change. She always listened to Clay - she always had. That was one of his charms, and, as usual, she was mesmerized, hanging on to his every word. And Berta, who was an excellent conversationalist, answered, "You'll have no problem at all, Clay. Why, DeLand is a delightful town. It's beautifully laid out with lovely boarding houses and hotels. Actually, I like it much better than Tallahassee in many respects, and with Stetson University, well, you'll not lack for cultural pursuits. We found lovely accommodations for SuSu at the College Arms. Just until she makes the adjustment, you understand. Avis Evans, who works there, is the widowed sister of Luta Brewster of Old Town and will certainly take special care of her, see that she eats right, and if she's not feeling well..."

"For Pete's sake, Berta!" Layke interrupted. "You know that SuSu is our first child to leave the nest," he said throwing his arms in the air. "The boys stayed on at South Spring to run the ranch, and I think Jonah will soon join Miss Trudy at the Stucky Hotel in Old Town. He's just not the cowman that Young Reuben is, and I think he's sweet on Myra Judson from Gainesville and is wanting to sink some roots. You probably haven't met Trudy Stucky, but she's the matriarch of Old Town and also its midwife. She brought the twins into this world and all Berta's children, and I'm afraid she's failing fast..."

"Don't say that, Layke!" Berta looked around at the up-turned faces. "She's not just a dear friend, but almost a mother to most of us in Old Town. It'll be difficult to think of home without Trudy there."

"I know the feeling, Berta," Kate said. "Parker and I feel the same about our dear friends in Tater Hill - I mean Arcadia, don't we, dear?"

"With all the excitement created by Disston and Flagler it's easy to forget our pioneers, isn't it?" Layke said. "Without the Trudy Stuckys and her like, our lives in this wilderness would be sorely lacking. I remember the very first night I rode into Old Town. Was almost dark, and my cowdog Tag and I pulled up rein in front of Stucky's Boarding House - I can remember it so clearly. Trudy came out onto the open porch that was lined with rocking chairs and introduced herself and said, 'There's some taters and pone and slab on the stove if'n you're hungry.' I fell madly in love with that woman on the spot," he laughed. "All hundred and fifty pounds of her, and her not five feet tall. We've been best friends ever since. Oh, the tales I've heard on the steps of Stucky's. Now, I'd embraced the cowman's life for the ten years before but hadn't really allowed myself to truly learn the fiber of the people who settled this state. Sitting on that porch in Old Town taught me more about our needs than all the rhetoric in Tallahassee, I can assure you."

Berta reached underneath the table and took his free hand, squeezing it. "Bet you can't tell how proud of my husband I am?"

Meade interjected, "I'm proud of my mama, too."

"We're all proud of your mama, Meade," Clay chimed in. "Berta, did you have a chance to tell Kate about staying at Henry Flagler's hotel in St. Augustine?"

"Why, Clay, I was going to save that for dessert." Berta said. "But since you've brought it up..."

"First, I'll take Meade outside so his mama can enjoy hearing it," Clay said. "Come on Meade. We'll find something interesting to do."

Layke turned toward Parker and said, "I've heard the story a hundred times. Why don't we men adjourn to the porch for a smoke?"

"Well, thank you very much, Layke. Here I get to tell about the most exciting thing that has ever happened to me, and you just up and leave. That's a fine howdy-do!" Berta reached up on her tiptoes and kissed his cheek. "Go on, Honey. I know you'll just be bored sitting through it again. Oh, my, Kate. I wish you could have been there. You just can't imagine!"

"Why don't we shoosh the men out to Jay's workroom, and we'll sit on the porch, Berta? Mattie, could we have our coffee there?"

Berta turned toward Mattie as she rose. "Mattie, I don't know when I've enjoyed a meal more. I've always said that no one could out-do Sadie's biscuits - she was our cook in Macon, Georgia, where I grew up. But, you know, I think I've met her match."

"Thank you Miss Berta. Dey turned out right nice." Callie held onto her ma's arm. "Ma, why don't you and Berta go on to the porch and I'll help Mattie clean up. Now, go on, I insist." Kate reached up and kissed her cheek.

"Thank you, Honey. We do have a lot of catching up to do."

"Now that the men aren't here I'll have the chance to tell you. Oh, I've been dying to." Berta took Kate's arm and pulled her to the two rockers. "Layke said that the legislature has decided on the state bird and flower and, I believe, even the state tree, and that he recommended that they commission Jay to paint them. Isn't that exciting? Now don't say anything. That's probably why he wanted to talk to him in his studio. We are all so proud of him. I think his work is much better than Audubon's, and so does everyone I've spoken to."

Kate was beside herself. "Wait 'til Parker hears this. I mean the honor of being considered even if he's not chosen." She sat down hard on the rocker and had difficulty composing herself.

"This town has truly been blessed - two celebrities." Berta continued. "I'm just as sure as I can be that their book will be a success. Oh, I forgot to mention to you. You remember the deMoya family?

You know the one who came to Old Town with their traveling medicine show and... oh my, that was before Layke and I were even married. Well, Etienne, the oldest of the three children is so beautifully educated. When his family left the bayou country of Louisiana and took to the road before the War, his uncle hired a tutor to travel with them so the children could get an education - they couldn't even speak English well. Apparently he was a remarkable educator, and the children were taught the classics, etc. Well, to make a long story short, Etienne, who is so polished and really should not be a cowman, agreed to teach at our little school in Old Town. The children are learning music - he is a very accomplished musician and sings beautifully - and French and, oh, you know. I truly believe that's what inspired SuSu. She was helping me run the house in Tallahassee and entertains beautifully, but she's twenty-one now and hasn't found her special young man."

Kate made all the right responses as she listened to Berta. "Mary Garvin said that she is a beautiful girl and that Thurmond was so taken by her when you last visited that they thought that he might try to worm out of his engagement. She really doesn't care for the girl he married."

"SuSu liked him too, but we were with them for such a short while. Mary and I've become quite close, you know. It's hard living so far apart, but we try to write often. When Reuben was alive and the children small, I never had a chance to meet you or the other cowmen's wives. I was so busy running the household, the same as you, I'm sure. But now that Layke feels that he needs to be out in his district and is called on to speak at the various functions - and I do have wonderful help in Tallahassee - I've enjoyed traveling with him. But those twins are a handful at ten years old, especially Raine. Oh, did I tell you that Wes has been accepted at The Citadel in South Carolina, where Layke and his father and brothers attended? Layke is so pleased that he wants an army career. He's been such a wonderful father to him, Kate, actually to all of them."

Kate thought, yes, once he got used to his job as senator. But I remember Mary saying how lonely Berta had been, and that he not only neglected her but the children as well, he was so dedicated to his role. Guess that's all over now, though. She seems so contented.

"Berta, whatever happened to that Graves girl? You know, the one who ran away with the Skinner gang and went to live at South Spring with you and Layke after they were hanged? I believe that Mary said she'd taken up with a riverboat gambler and had a baby by him and was running a dress shop with his sister up in Palatka, the last she'd heard."

"You're right, but Kate," she bit her lower lip and looked away as she spoke, "the most tragic thing happened. Did she tell you that I knew the gambler, Conner O'Farrell, when I was just a girl in Macon? His mother was widowed, and they moved to Macon from Ireland during the famine, and she opened a millinery shop. My mother bought all our hats from her. Well, his sister worked with her and learned the trade, and when she and Conner were... oh, I'd say about thirteen or fourteen, they all moved to New Orleans, and apparently the daughter, Maeve, became quite a well known milliner and dress maker in the city. I don't know the particulars, but Conner must have made a great deal of money after the War, because he set her up in a beautiful shop in Palatka right on the St. Johns River. Do you remember the terrible fire in '84?"

"I remember reading about it..."

"You know it destroyed almost all of the downtown business section. Well, Maeve was killed in it. Mary saw it in the paper and sent me the clipping."

"Meade - excuse me Berta - Meade, don't you dare get in that mud puddle. Now listen to Mama Kate. I'm sorry, Berta."

"It's all right. I believe that Wes splashed in every puddle he ever saw. Boys will be boys. Well, as I was saying, because I knew the family, though not well, and Juanita had taken up with Conner, Mary kept me posted on their relationship. I don't know if he ever married her, but Layke and I saw them in Kissimmee when we went for the ceremony when the first train arrived there. Apparently Conner had left the riverboat and had a very impressive position with Hamilton Disston overseeing his ship building and land sales and I don't know what all," she said enthusiastically.

She continued. "Juanita had changed so much, from just a country girl to... I guess you could say a ravishing beauty. She spoke well and was very mannered and behaved like a lady. She had apprenticed with Maeve in her shop and learned the business, and I was told later she had joined Conner in Kissimmee, and he had set her up in a dress shop."

"Oh, Callie, be a dear and bring us some lemonade, and Honey, please join us. We're having a real good woman's talk, aren't we, Berta?"

Berta turned to Kate after Callie went inside. "She's doing remarkably well, Kate. I feel for her so. When Reuben died so suddenly, though it wasn't horrible like poor Thom, it took me forever to get over it. At least she's financially secure, and I had such a struggle to keep South Spring going..."

"She's holding up fine. I truly believe she's still in shock though. To get back to Juanita, what happened to her? Is she still in Kissimmee?"

"Apparently not, because when Layke and I were there I actually got up enough nerve to go to her shop, but it was closed. The man who ran the candy store across the street said that she and her little girl - I believe he called her Delia Rose - moved up to Monticello and that she was supposed to have opened a shop there."

"Did the gambler...uh, Conner, not go with her?"

Berta seemed to be having difficulty controlling herself, so Kate started to change the subject, but she finally answered. "The man said that after Conner's sister was killed in the fire, he started drinking heavily and... I'm sorry, Kate, but knowing him as a very witty and such a bright and handsome man...it's difficult to think of him like that, you know - so depressed - and the man said that he'd lost his job with Disston and seldom came out of his house. So sad, isn't it? Such a dashing young man with such a promising future, and to let tragedy destroy him...well, I..."

"Berta, that's all right, dear. You're just too tender hearted." To herself she thought, she's certainly taking this particularly hard. I wonder if there isn't more to this than she's letting on. Mary intimated but never came out and said that she felt that Berta had an unusual interest in Juanita and him. I believe she's right.

"Here, Honey, I'll help you with that," Kate said to Callie, who had brought the pitcher of lemonade and enough glasses for the men as well.

"I'll go to the workroom with these, Mama. They might want some."

"If I know Parker they're probably all tippling some of his peach brandy, young lady. This lemonade will be too tame for them." She glanced at Berta and wondered why she had such a faraway expression. Normally she'd have responded.

"Well, here I was going to tell you about our stay in St. Augustine, and we've talked about almost everything under the sun but the trip. You know that the Ponce de Leon Hotel opened in January, and Flagler didn't even have a grand opening. Layke and I couldn't believe it, nor could the other senators and their wives. We'd all counted on being invited. I was so disappointed that Layke gave me an early anniversary present, and he and I took the train down. Well, Kate, I have never in my entire life seen anything as magnificent as the Ponce. The press didn't do it justice in their account. Some said it was superior to the Palmer House in Chicago, the Palace in San Francisco and even the Fifth Avenue in New York City. Can you believe that? And there are only about 4,000 inhabitants in that little town. He's done us proud, he has. We were surprised at the turn out, for there was no formal ceremony, but within thirty minutes there were a thousand people, they say, crowding the spacious rotunda and corridors and spilling out onto the Tropical Court, where the band played sweet music. Oh, it was grand! And the dinner menu...it compared with any fine hotel in New York or Europe, everyone said." Berta laughed. "When Layke inquired about the cost of the room, I thought he was going to faint, so I suggested that we stay at the other hotel he built, the Alcazar. That was certainly more suitable for our pocketbook. It's right across from the Ponce, separated by beautifully landscaped gardens, and occupies an entire city block. Oh, it's not as large as the Ponce, mind you, but we actually liked it better. It's a reproduction of a famous palace in Seville, Spain. The roof's of terra cotta tile, Moorish style, with towers and a huge swimming pool inside. I wish I'd brought the brochure telling all about it. But I'll try to describe it anyway." They continued to rock, and Berta talked with Kate hanging on to every word.

"The pool is the largest one I've ever seen with a skylight overhead, so there's a sunny atmosphere even in the dead of winter. There are dressing facilities on each end, and the ladies' side is closed off so we can swim in privacy. I really liked that feature. Layke said that the men's side was unique. The water goes into the rounded portions of the dressing rooms, and on their side it's possible to actually dive underwater and swim right out into the main pool, where there's a gallery overlooking it. There were two orchestras playing, one at each end of the gallery, and in the casino they actually have steam baths. Layke even had a massage. I could go on and on about the gowns the ladies wore, Kate, but I'd never stop if I got started. Oh, yes, we read that Flagler spent a thousand dollars to furnish each of the 540 rooms in the Ponce, and they all have electric lights. Imagine!"

Kate excused herself. "Now, don't you rise, Berta. I'll just be a minute, dear. You sit right here and enjoy that cool breeze. Goodness knows we don't often get 'em."

I do so wish I could have seen Conner, Berta thought. I feel Layke knows that I went to the shop and wonders what I found. Why couldn't I tell him about Conner? It's not as if I've been unfaithful, for I haven't. I don't think that fantasizing is a sin. I certainly hope not. But I'm so concerned about him. Maybe I should write to tell him how sorry I was to hear of Maeve's death - but that was five long years ago and I couldn't bring myself to write even then. I wonder what happened to his black friend. Did he desert him, too? He's had so much tragedy for a sensitive man. Why do I care so? Will I always care? I think I'll just make that trip to Monticello to see if Juanita is really there. That's what I'll do. Martha Taylor has been after me almost forever to pay them a visit. It wouldn't take long on the train.

***

Jay's new suit felt scratchy, and although it was cooler in DeLand than in Arcadia, he was still miserable. His mother had insisted that he buy it. "You want to make your best impression when you first meet your associates, now don't you?" There had been no use to argue with Miss Kate, so he helped her order the suit from the catalog at Jeeters'.

His mind was a-jumble. Here I am twenty-seven years old and practically scared out of my wits. I've never taught a class in my life. I know I'll be just the assistant at first, but heck, I'd better know something. Shoot! They know I've never taught art, well, except to Meade, and they wouldn't know about that, so why'd they ask me in the first place?

Jay continued to fidget and roll his new tan, felt bowler around and around in his sweaty hands. I'd better go on over to the College Arms to get a room, at least for the first week. I think that's where the McRae girl's staying - what's her name - oh, SuSu. I'm sure that's where they said she's rooming. Maybe I'll look her up. At least then I'll know one person when I start. Shoot, my hands are so sweaty I'd probably make her throw up when I shake her hand.

He rounded the corner and walked beneath the linden trees on the shady side. I've just gotta control myself. This is ridiculous! Maybe I shouldn't have been so firm with Georgianna. She really did want to come up here, but heck, I've gotta do this on my own. Now I wish I'd followed Pa's advice and gone to New York City and done some travelling. Maybe I'd feel less like a clod if I'd been anywhere besides Tampa. Grief! That's the farthest I've ever been from Arcadia except to the state fair in Gainesville. Grief! That SuSu'll think I'm some kinda freak, never having been anywhere or done anything but draw and paint and stuff dead animals.

"Oh, I'm sorry, did I hurt you?" he asked, holding the door to the College Arms ajar and staring down into two enormous, chocolate brown eyes and the most ingratiating smile he'd ever seen.

"No, of course you didn't. I'm not as fragile as I appear and should have been watching where I was going. May I help you find someone?" she asked in a low, warm, soft voice.

"I was just going to register - to the desk, you know. I'm hoping to stay here for a while before I start teaching. I'm an art teacher, you know."

It was very obvious that he was nervous. "Then your name must be Jay Meade. I just registered for your class, Jay. I'm SuSu McRae, and my parents are friends of your parents."

"I was going to call on you. Did you say that you were going to be my student? I can't believe it! Did they tell you that I've never taught before? No, of course they didn't. I imagine if they had that you wouldn't want to be in my class."

"Not so, sir. My parents think that you're the greatest artist this state has produced and...listen. Instead of standing out here in the hot sun why don't you register, and then I'll show you around the campus. It's just beautiful. I'm sorry. That's presumptuous of me. I'm sure you have plans for your afternoon..."

"Oh, no, I've no plans at all, and I'd love for you to show me around." He thought, Oh, if I could only tell you how I'd love for you to show me around. Is this why I couldn't make a commitment to Georgianna? Be still my heart! Be still! I bet she can see it thumping clean through this tacky suit, or at least hear it.

Why is he looking at me like that? How brave I've become since my arrival. It's hard to believe that I've been here almost a week and already know the town backwards and forwards and have made friends and...why is he looking at me like that? He is so good-looking! Why didn't mother tell me? Did she say that he was spoken for? Well, Mister Jay Meade, she's going to have to fight like the very deuce for you, sir. I can't believe how sensitive he is. I was sure that he'd be a real clod from Arcadia. What a beautiful smile he has!

Jay's mind was racing. I can't seem to move. If I take even one step, I think I'll fall over these too-big feet. Grief! To just open the door and almost fall over her! She's the most beautiful girl I've ever seen. Doesn't look a bit like her mother, and I don't remember Reuben that well, but seems to me that he was not very tall and built square and, she's so dainty. Biggest eyes I've ever seen. I'd love to paint her sitting in a canoe on a turquoise lake with dark brown cattails, the color of her eyes. Is she laughing at me?

"Professor, didn't you say that you needed to register?"

"Oh, I'm sorry." He calmed down and continued. "I've a lot on my mind."

"Would you like for me to wait for you? I could wait beneath that tree over there. Why don't I do that?" I've got so brazen! I can't believe I said that.

"Oh, please do, SuSu." She started to say, I'm called Sue here, but didn't. She loved his soft drawl.

"I'll be under the tree, Jay. Don't hurry." She turned from him and he quickly looked away.

Now maybe I can walk without falling all over myself. She's going to wait for me. Whew!

They left the College Arms and walked west on New York Avenue, turned north on Woodland Blvd. and walked past the churches toward the main buildings. She could tell that he was as impressed as she had been but was also intimidated. She decided to put him at ease.

"And this is Chaudoin Hall, where I'll be moving within the month, but Mother wanted me to stay at the College Arms, where Avis Evans could keep her eye on me." She laughed and looked up at him. There he goes again looking at me like I'm peach pie. Oh, I'm loving it!

They walked on. "And here, Professor Meade, is Science Hall, where you'll teach and, I hope, I'll learn. I'm truly looking forward to it. Perhaps you don't know that adjoining the Heath Museum is a room containing a collection of well over seventy Florida birds, another gift from Mr. Stetson." His expression was so open and excited! She laughed. "I knew that would impress you, Jay. You see, Layke has filled our dinner hour with tales about what an interesting and uniquely talented young man you are. Heavens, I've grown up on tales about Jay Meade."

He actually blushed. "Are you poking fun at me SuSu McRae? For if you are, I have some tales to tell also." He let that sink in and took her arm firmly as they crossed Michigan St. and continued. "It seems that there once was a slight waif of a girl by the peculiar name of SuSu. She had enormous brown eyes and through her perseverance and daring decided to become the tightrope star of the circus. She dreamed of wearing a skimpy gold and green, shiny costume..."

"They didn't tell you that! Surely they didn't! All right, Jay Meade...Truce?" She put out her small hand to shake his, and he grabbed her before she stepped right in front of an oncoming buggy. The driver barraged their ears with, "Crazy kids! Don't watch where they're going...crazy kids!"

They stared at each other, neither moving. Finally, Jay said, "I'll walk you back to the hotel. I'd best make my appearance at the office or they'll think I'm not showing."

They hardly spoke all the way back, but their minds didn't stop for a minute. *I wonder if he likes tennis, or maybe he prefers baseball?*

Is she truly real? I do so hope she is...I do so hope...

****

"Mr. Meade, sir, you have visitors," Alma said while knocking on his door. Jay had moved into Stetson Hall two weeks earlier and was still not used to it. *It can't be SuSu because she has an early class and won't finish until four o'clock, and then she has a lab after that.* He was not quite awake but answered Alma and asked her to tell them that he'd be in the lobby soon. He rubbed his eyes and splashed them with cool water from the blue china wash bowl. Taking the soft towel he wiped his face, tanned from the afternoons on the shell tennis court, and couldn't help but smile when he remembered last evening.

He and SuSu had both had late classes, but she had challenged him in a game of tennis. Since they both were novices it had truly been a comedy of errors. He couldn't believe how graceful she was. She seemed to glide across the court, and the rather large group of onlookers had gathered and seemed to enjoy watching them.

It was obvious to SuSu that every girl in Jay's classes had fallen madly in love with him. The head of the department, Professor Chalmers, was old, at least sixty or so, fat and bald. He did have a nice manner and was an excellent teacher, but when Jay taught, all the young ladies hung onto his every word, and they all seemed to require special assistance.

Who on earth could be wanting me this early? he questioned while hurriedly getting dressed. On his arrival he had gone to the Kilcker Brothers Men's store and bought a new suit. At least this one didn't scratch. It was a dark tan and seemed to blend with his dark hair and eyes, and he loved it. It was so soft, and SuSu had admired it.

There had not been a single day for the past month that they had not been together. She had art classes three days a week, but they'd managed to get together for meals at La Villa or an ice cream or a tennis match or lawn bowling, that was very popular on campus. He preferred croquet, and so did SuSu, but their favorite pastime was just walking around campus and sharing. Once in a while they'd go to the chapel in Elizabeth Hall for a concert. He'd hardly had time to think of Georgianna, and when he did, he'd quickly change his direction. SuSu seemed ever present.

Last night the moon was full, and after he'd accompanied her back to Chaudoin Hall he'd retired to his room with plans to work on his next day's lesson plan, but his mind wouldn't settle. Lying on his narrow bed with his arms behind his still damp hair he stared out the single window in his narrow room. There was a slight breeze, and the heavy curtains moved lazily as he looked through the tall tree tops that blended into the blue-black night. When the moon came up over the trees, it seemed to edge them in silver, and the ever changing clouds were moving so swiftly across the sky that Jay's throat tightened as he watched.

If I painted this the way it really looks people would say that it looked fake. Gosh, I've never seen such a night. I wonder if Susu is watching it and if she's thinking of me, he thought dreamily.

He got up and with his head in his hands thought, I've got myself in one helluva mess! I truly think the world of Georgianna, but when I think of SuSu I know beyond a doubt that I can't live the rest of my life without her. I want to protect her, but I know she's probably stronger than I. I want to kiss her so that it's all I think of. I know that I make a fool of myself when she's in class. Grief! Even Professor Chalmers has noticed. He's finding my fascination very amusing, the old goat! When he walked me to the dorm yesterday he reminded me that, "You're the teacher, Meade, not that the McRae girl isn't extremely attractive. But, Meade, you do owe some attention to the other students." He did chuckle when he said it, thank goodness.

"But what am I going to tell Georgianna? Heavens!" he said aloud. I've written her only twice since I arrived. I know she must know something's up. Maybe I should write Ma or Callie and ask for advice. No, Callie's got enough worry on her mind. But what am I to do?

There was knocking on the door again. "Mr. Meade, sir, dos ladies sho is gettin' impatient 'bout you not bein' der. Dey sho is..."

"Alma, tell her, or them, that I'll be right down," he said excitedly. SuSu must have brought a friend. He was having a deuce of a time getting his cowlick to cooperate, and even the hair wax couldn't control it. "Oh, to heck with it!" Boyishly he bounced down the stairs to the lobby. Sitting on the long, grey settee were Georgianna and her mother. Jay's eyes almost bugged out of his head, and his heart most certainly skipped a beat. All he could think was, I'm in for it. Look at old lady Latham trying her darndest to look pleasant. Oh God, SuSu, I wish you were here - no - I'm glad you're not. Oh, I don't know what I'm glad about!

"Georgianna, Mrs. Latham, why on earth didn't you wire that you were coming? I can't believe that you're here!"

"Why, Jay," Mrs. Latham said, "I didn't know that professors could be so, well, uh ..."

"Mama, don't! You know that Jay always gets tongue-tied when he's excited. It's so good to see you, sweetheart. I've missed you so." She reached up on her tiptoes and kissed his cheek sweetly.

Oh, Lordy! he thought. Oh, Lordy! I'm in for it!

"I saw her Sue! She kissed him standing right in the middle of the lobby. I couldn't believe it!" Doni Browning, one of SuSu's new friends, exclaimed. SuSu knew beyond a doubt that Jay's girl and her mother had come from Arcadia to protect their claim on him.

"I believe you, Doni. I hadn't mentioned it to you before, but Jay has been keeping company with a girl from his hometown for a long time. He told me, not exactly in detail, but he didn't say that they were engaged or anything like that..."

"The way she was hanging onto him would indicate that they indeed are, Sue. Oh my! You should've seen her!" Doni was a very excitable girl, very theatrical. She was plump and on the plain side but very bright and from the small settlement of Middleburg, southwest of Jacksonville, where her family was in the turpentine business. She, too, was planning on a teaching career, and she and SuSu had the same classes. She was the only one SuSu had confided in regarding her affection for Jay, and it appeared to SuSu that Doni was more concerned about Jay and whats-her-name than she was.

"Don't you think that we should go over to rescue him?"

"Of course not! Jay's a grown man and I know he'll be able to handle the situation."

Actually, she was not as confident as her words conveyed, and not knowing what else to do she suggested that they go straight to their science class.

"Well, I, for one, think you're making a big mistake. If I were as crazy about him as you say you are..."

"Doni, be still! Now just what do you think they are going to do? You know he has class in half an hour. Do you think she's going to accompany him there? Now really, dear, I think you're over-reacting."

But accompany Jay to class Mrs. Latham and Georgianna did. Mrs. Latham insisted, and when Louise Latham insisted, Georgianna did her bidding. Jay said that he thought that it would be all right for them to visit, at least for a short while, just so he could show them his classroom and studio, but that they would have to find something to do for the rest of the morning until lunch time while he had classes. He suggested that they meet him at the St. Elmo for lunch, but he would not be able to spend much time with them afterwards because he had afternoon classes.

He was in a dither, Mrs. Latham could tell. "I wonder why he's so nervous, Georgianna?" she asked as they walked slowly on their way back to the Melrose Hall boarding house.

"He's just excited about our surprise visit, Mama. You know how excited he can get," she said sweetly.

My daughter is a nincompoop! She really is. Can't she see that he's got a lot on his mind he's not telling her? I can't believe what a dumb child she is. Heavens, she's no child - she's almost twenty-one. If I hadn't insisted she'd never have come up here. He's probably got him another girl. I'm sure of it. Why, he couldn't even look me in the eye. If he thinks for one minute that he's going to squirm out of this marriage, he'd better have another thought. When Louise made up her mind about something, she was a bulldog of determination and never stopped until she got her way.

Nincompoop! That's what Georgianna is!

"Doni, I'll see you in a little while," SuSu whispered as they walked down the corridor of Science Hall.

"Good girl, Sue. Don't let her get away with it."

SuSu didn't hesitate and walked right into Jay's classroom. When he saw her, he knew that she knew. *Gosh, how'd she find out? I know she knows Georgianna's here. Look at the set of her shoulders! Grief!*

SuSu smiled sweetly to reassure him. *He knows that I know. Is that the girl and her mother actually sitting in the back? I just bet that it is. She's a rather pretty little thing. Poor Jay. That mother of hers is not going to give up - but neither am I - neither am I.*

SuSu walked right up to the front of the classroom and handed Jay the note. He averted his eyes and almost died on the spot. *When he reads that, he'll know how to handle the girl and even her mother...that is, if he truly loves me. Oh, I do so hope he does, 'cause I love him something fierce!*

Doni was anxiously waiting outside the classroom door when SuSu came out smiling broadly. "What happened, Sue? Now don't you say *nothin'* cause..."

"Oh, something's going to happen all right, when he reads that note."

And happen it did. Jay couldn't wait to read it. The light lavender scent from the pale pink paper quickly found his nostrils. He turned his back to the class. Louise Latham looked at Georgianna suspiciously. Georgianna looked at Jay. He opened the note. She saw his hand go quickly to his open mouth restraining the outburst as he slowly read SuSu's almost childish scrawl. *She can't have you, Jay Meade. You're mine. I love you. SuSu*

BOOK II:

MY SWEET SORROW

CHAPTER I THE ARRIVAL

The Year 1889 Monticello, Florida

Juanita stroked Delia's sleeping face. Six years old is too young to know loneliness, she thought as she looked down at her daughter. Her black hair was confined to two large braids cascading over Juanita's grey twill skirt. She has Conner's hair and his pale eyes to drive me to distraction and beyond. Why couldn't she have had my blond hair and blue eyes? But, no, she'll always be my reminder of her da - Oh, dear Lord! Why did I have to meet him? Why couldn't I have been content to have the love of a fine man like Etienne...so intelligent. She smiled to herself, manageable is a better word. Why, he'd do her bidding whenever she crooked her little finger. But Conner - Conner O'Farrell - she couldn't tame that one.

The noise and swaying of the train with its hard wooden seats reminded her of the mail stage she'd taken from Ft. Myers all the way back to Palatka so many years ago - ten to be exact. She had hoped to see Conner again. She'd never felt that way about a man before, not even when R.J. Skinner, the notorious bank robber, had made her his woman, and she not much more than sixteen. At least R.J. hadn't smelled like those cow-eyed lads she'd grown up with in LaBelle. He'd been the answer to her prayers - her way out of the Glades - her way to the exciting world beyond...or had it been?

Juanita's young life had been filled with the characters she'd read about in the books she'd borrowed from her friend Lonnie. She'd lie awake in the small, dark room on her ma's and pa's farm, that hugged the Caloosahatchee River, and dream of the world beyond LaBelle. Her folks had been content with raising their dumb old chickens, tending their stock, making quilts, canning everything in the whole entire world and attending the tiny church whenever a circuit preacher arrived in the hamlet.

But not Juanita. She knew that there was an exciting life just waiting for her, and by golly she was gonna have it. She was going to travel the river for as far as it would take her, maybe even all the way to the big gulf, the Gulf of Mexico. She couldn't even imagine what it would look like - smell like. She'd sneak to the river whenever her ma wasn't looking, and lying underneath the spreading oaks, their arms reaching out, touching the trees on the other side of the high bluffs, she'd dream of those faraway places she'd only read about. The Spanish moss flowed from the trees' rough branches, mingling with the moon vines that covered them, hovering over her as she dreamily plotted her course.

She knew her destiny, and it certainly wasn't to stay in that nothing LaBelle and be buried in that little old nothing graveyard, where the weeds meandered all over the graves just like it was their place of rest too. Upstart weeds! She wanted a giant marble headstone, as big as they could make it, and with her name etched in fancy letters and maybe even an angel or a cherub on the top. Oh, my! Something different. Yes, something different. Juanita wanted a life that was different, unlike her sister Bonnie's. Never anything in the whole, entire world like her sister Bonnie's. There she was, stuck in LaBelle with babies tugging at her sagging breasts and getting old before her time. Not Juanita!

Delia's life will be different, she thought as she wiggled slightly, lifting Delia and straightening her skirt. I sure don't want to arrive in Monticello all rumpled. I must set an example so Rose and I can be admired by the town's ladies, so they'll shop at Cherie's House Of Fashion. That's a good name. She rested her head on the back of the straight seat. Cherie's House Of Fashion - yes, it's just right, just sophisticated enough.

Juanita had been billed as Cherie when she was the tightrope star of the deMoyas' traveling medicine show. Etienne thought it sounded more romantic than Juanita, and she agreed. Conner had always called her Cherie. It all seemed so long ago - the medicine show - her life with Conner on the steamship *Savannah* as they sailed the St. Johns, and their life in Palatka. She tried to position herself more comfortably but didn't want to disturb Delia. Finally resting her head against the train's small window she concentrated on those by-gone days, the days before Conner.

She remembered the breath-holding excitement when she walked the tightrope - high - alone - feeling the audience's anxiety, their admiration, as she effortlessly glided across in her beautiful silver and aqua costume. She could hear their shouts and applause. But suddenly Conner's sad face appeared, blocking out everything, releasing the pain, the pain that she'd had to live with since the fire in Palatka that killed his beloved sister Maeve.

He had not been able to accept the fact that Delia had been spared from the fire in '84 that leveled Palatka's downtown section, including

Maeve's shop, Monique's. And Harrison, Conner's black friend whom he'd known since they lived in New Orleans, had not been able to explain it to Juanita. The once witty, handsome man she'd loved more than life itself disappeared, caught in the Devil's snare as he blotted out all memory of that fateful night with his drinking, drinking, drinking. Not even Harrison, his best friend - actually his only friend - had been able to penetrate that black wall of self-pity. She and Delia had been ignored, forgotten, as Conner wallowed in remorse.

Harrison had tried to justify Conner's actions, but he, too, had finally given up. He left Conner in his darkened room, the room that was filled with the pieces of Maeve's charred letters from Monsignor Vincent Haut of New Orleans, her dear Vincent, her friend, whom she had loved. But she had not been aware of her own true feelings. Conner had been trying to paste the bits and pieces of the letters together for almost five years. Harrison had dared not describe the room to Juanita, because she would not understand. How could she understand Conner's obsession when Harrison could not himself?

Enlightenment had not come to Harrison, no matter how much he prayed. How could a man ignore and reject his own daughter, even if she was illegitimate, he questioned over and over again. Conner had loved her so and had been the typical doting father until the fire. Harrison was finally convinced that his, Juanita's and Delia's presence was not helping Conner to heal. Voltaire was right, he realized. *"Sorrow is a disease in which every patient must heal himself."* Yes, Voltaire was right.

So they left Conner in Kissimmee. Juanita, Delia and Harrison along with Juanita's friend Rose and her son Seth embraced a new life in Monticello, the town that Harrison had lived near when he had been owned by Samuel Baker, proprietor of the plantation Fairlea. He had been sold to the Simpsons of Louisiana when just a youngster, and that's where he and Conner met.

He had left Conner a note telling him of their whereabouts. But he'll not follow. He's content to be miserable. I just hope he gets enough to eat and will bathe and will at least try to resume work. I'm sure Mr. Disston will take him back, and on he worried as they approached Monticello. The train jostled him. The fat lady sitting next to him bombarded his poor ears with her mountain of troubles. He could see the lights of Monticello in the distance as the train slowed. On the woman droned. Won't she ever shut up? he thought, rising, excusing himself as he reached into the compartment above their seats for his small trap.

There's Juanita! Thank God! But I'd better not be too bold, or some southern gentleman will have my manhood severed and fed to his hogs. The War'll never be done with - not in Monticello. I'm black and they're not about to let me forget it. I'd better be careful.

Juanita was holding Delia's hand tightly. Seth, who was as tall as she and just ten years old, left his mother and grabbed on to Juanita's other hand. All three were gaping. "I've never seen the likes of it, have you Rose? I bet there are a million lights!"

Rose couldn't respond, she was so excited. Electric lights had only been read about, never seen. The largest town she'd ever been in was Kissimmee, and it was not much more than a hamlet. Seth and Delia released themselves from Juanita's protective hands and began twirling around and around, first in shadow, then in light, laughing so loudly that the departing passengers stood aside and smiled at them. When they saw Harrison they ran toward him shouting his name.

"Don't you two misbehave," Juanita called after them. "Have you ever seen them so excited?" she asked, taking Rose's arm. Two fatherless children, she thought. I doubt that Seth even knows who his father was. Rose certainly won't tell him, and I could never go against her wishes. I wonder if Joe Bob's looking down at him saying 'what a handsome son I have.' He's more than likely looking up at him from the Devil's fiery furnace, she thought, smiling devilishly. I bet if Rose'd run away with him, like I did with R.J., that he'd have married her. Then, poor little Seth would've had a daddy. Guess it's best that she didn't. Best that Seth thinks that she's his aunt, that his own mama died when he was born and that his Aunt Rose took him in. Frankly, I'm glad that Delia knows her da - that she knows that she has one. I just hope that she can remember how much he loved her before - before that dagblasted fire. That's what I hope.

But Juanita's thoughts were soon interrupted. Harrison, along with the rambunctious children and the trunks and traps piled high on the wooden wagon, approached them. "Miss Cherie," he said in his practiced darky speech, "de Madden House done sen' a buggy fo' to fetch ya."

"Harrison," she whispered, "I don't want you to feel like you hafta speak like that. Now, I mean it. There is no reason whatsoever to put on that talk. Why, you speak better than any of us here."

"Miss Cherie," he hastened to interrupt, "Ah knows dese folks, an' if'n dey hears me speak proper-like we all be in fer a heap o' trouble."

She could see by his stern expression that her protesting would do no good, so she shrugged her slight shoulders, sighed, and tried to grab Delia, who had decided to use the mound of trunks as a mountain, climbing to the top before Juanita could stop her.

"Delia Rose, you be careful! For heaven's sake, Seth, grab her. She's for sure gonna fall and break all her bones! You'll be the death of me yet, Delia Rose O'Farrell! Do you hear?"

Juanita used the name O'Farrell, although she and Conner were unmarried, and had so informed him loudly while desperately trying to penetrate his conscience. "I bet you've spread your seed up and down the whole Mississippi River and the St. John to boot. I'll just bet you have, Conner O'Farrell, Your Majesty, sir!" But Conner would just sit there grinning that familiar grin. Why do I love him so? she'd ask herself silently, never aloud, and before she'd allow the tears to fall, she'd give him another lash. "If you think Delia Rose is gonna be nameless like all those other bastards you've spawned, you, sir, think again. Delia's got a name. It might not be sanctioned by your fancy priests or even a preacher, but there is no denying who her da is, Mr. O'Farrell."

He'd sit, the grin slowly fading as he slipped into a drunken stupor. "I give up, Conner, I really do." She'd pull off his boots, get him in bed, cover him with the quilt and sadly leave, allowing the welled-up tears to slide down her flushed cheeks. Invariably, Harrison would be there - he was always there.

"Cherie, would you like a nice cup of tea? Here, let me fix some. I pulled some beautiful lemons from Mr. Ammon's tree." Trying to sooth her grief he'd chatter about the goings on in Kissimmee and often would refer to the Monticello paper, "*The Constitution*", that he had subscribed to months before. At first Juanita thought it was because it was his hometown paper, but after a while she realized that he was preparing her for the inevitable parting, leaving Conner, and he wanted her to have a familiar place to go to. Oh, how he glowingly praised Monticello, commenting about what a progressive town it was, ripe for the pickings, perfect for a dress shop.

It would be the first time that Harrison and Conner would be separated. He had even cooked Conner's mess during the War when they rode with Capt. Dickison, the Confederate Swamp Fox. But unknown to Juanita, Harrison had not been able to leave Kissimmee without his ace in the hole. He'd taken the liberty of writing Maeve's and Conner's friend Monsignor Haut from St. Ignatius Church in New Orleans. He'd received an answer to his first letter but none to his last. He'd described Conner's condition in hopes that the priest would write Conner, but to his knowledge he had not, and not much went undetected by Harrison.

Apparently Fr. Haut had been ill, because he mentioned that he was taking a trip to Florida to spend some time in Jacksonville with his friend Fr. William Kenny, pastor of the Immaculate Conception Church, and that if he was well enough, he'd contact Harrison to arrange a visit with Conner. Months had gone by with no word. That's when Harrison began working on Juanita, glorying in the tales of Monticello. He said that it was near enough to Tallahassee that she'd probably get business from the senators' and representatives' wives and that there was an overnight train directly to Savannah, where she could select her fabrics and notions in person. Oh, what an exciting picture he painted! But he knew that he could only plant the seeds, because Juanita was clever and would certainly be on to his plan.

Needing more self assurance before making such a move, Juanita sought out Rose, who was an excellent seamstress and had made her living taking in sewing after her parents had died of the fever in Alva. It was strange that Juanita even remembered her, for she'd seen her only once, the year she ran away with R.J. But if there was anyone in the whole world who loved to plan, it was Juanita, and Rose fit perfectly into her plan. R.J. used to say that the South would have won the War if Juanita had been a general.

But she was also practical. She could envision the fancy sign above her beautiful shop, but she could also see the mountain of work. The seamstresses she'd hired for her shop in Kissimmee wouldn't be willing to relocate, she was sure. That's when she thought of Rose Shorter. She'd learned years ago that she had moved from Alva to Basinger on the Kissimmee River just south of the town of Kissimmee and was working as a cleaning lady at one of the boarding houses. But would she still be there? There was only one way of finding out, so Juanita and Delia took the boat to Basinger. She had had no trouble finding Rose and Seth, and there was certainly no mistaking who Seth's father was. He was the spittin' image of Joe Bob, R.J.'s younger brother. Rose had never married, and when Juanita told her of her plan, Rose decided that it was time to make a new start for her and Seth away from Basinger.

But there was work to be done. Rose was a mess. Her hands had been roughened from the years of hard work, and her skin completely neglected. Juanita insisted that Rose and Seth move to Kissimmee so she could work on her. She smeared her hands liberally with scented creams and even had her wear gloves as she slept. She gave her facials of stiffly beaten egg whites to minimize her enlarged pores. She taught her how to use face rouge sparingly so it looked natural. Thank goodness her hair was naturally curly. Juanita styled it in the latest fashion, and she and Harrison worked on Rose's speech nightly.

Harrison's patience with Rose was amazing to Juanita. Why, he could be a professor in a leading university if he weren't colored, she thought. But then he'd have to leave us, and we're his family. Once she asked Conner if Harrison had ever had a woman. He became enraged. Why, she could never figure out. Maybe because Harrison was like a white man in a black skin, and there wouldn't be a suitable woman around. She had noticed that he got all soft-like when Mrs. Montgomery's maid Tisha came into the shop. She was a mulatto and as pretty as any woman Juanita had ever seen, but she didn't have much education. Harrison wouldn't have had much to talk about with her. She laughed when she thought that he'd have to teach Tisha like he, Maeve and Conner taught her. But Harrison did seem to make sure that he was around whenever Tisha came to pick up Mrs. Montgomery's packages. Juanita wondered if he was seeing Tisha on the side, but when she mentioned it to Conner, again he became livid. Conner had apparently placed Harrison on a pedestal, and there was no room for any high-yeller gal in his life, Juanita deduced.

The Madden House wasn't far from the depot. They passed by row after row of brick buildings that lined Dogwood Street, and her and Rose's excitement was as great as the children's. Juanita had read in the paper that most of the wooden buildings had been burned throughout the past years and replaced by brick ones. When they passed by the St. Elmo Hotel, that was still under construction, she had to contain her outburst. She had confided to Harrison that she wanted her shop near enough to it so that the visiting winter guests could become her customers. She'd also told him about the money she'd been saving for over ten years. R.J. had given her his share of the gold doubloons he'd stolen from the cowmen in Punta Rassa the night before he and Joe Bob were hanged in Old Town. Juanita hadn't said where she got the money, just that she'd been saving up for her big adventure. That plus the money she'd made when she was with the medicine show and with Maeve in her dress shop would give her more than enough to get started and maybe to even buy a place not far from town, where they could all live, she reasoned.

She'd been worried that she would have to invest all her savings in her shop in Kissimmee when Conner lost his job with Disston Enterprises, but by then she had developed quite a sizable clientele - actually she had had more orders than she could handle.

When Harrison helped her down from the buggy, he was smiling. This is a good move, he thought. I just hope Conner will miss us enough to get himself straightened out. He hadn't told Juanita that he'd left Conner some money along with the note.

The Madden House was warm and comfortable looking, of red brick, and located on a lot south of the courthouse. It sported twenty rooms. Rose looked ill at ease, but when Juanita took her arm and smiled reassuringly at her she relaxed. "Oh, Rose, I'm so excited! This is going to be just as we planned!" Rose still had her mouth wide open, looking at the imposing wooden courthouse, all lit up, massive oaks surrounding it. About then the courthouse bell rang nine o'clock, and while Juanita and her entourage stared at it, she felt someone staring at her. Her big blue eyes soon rested on a man standing under the street light on the opposite side of the dirt street. Had she been more observant, she would also have seen him at the depot on Railroad St. and would have noticed that he had followed her buggy down Dogwood at a comfortable distance.

He was not an unobtrusive man, for he stood well over six feet and was built square, carrying over two hundred pounds. His sandy hair was straight, his complexion ruddy and his eyes small and grey. His full mustache covered thin, pale lips, and pinned to his left shirt pocket was a badge that read Marshal. He was Boyle Coleman, town marshal of Monticello.

As in most small towns there were few secrets, and in Monticello everyone knew everyone else's business. So when Juanita wrote to the court house for information concerning available buildings for her dress shop, the word traveled fast. Earlene Drysdale, who worked at the courthouse and was a cousin of Millie and Buford Bailey, proprietors of Madden House, ran across the street and gave the word to Millie, who in turn wrote Juanita about her and Buford's empty building on Jefferson St. and also about their lovely hotel. The fact that someone desired to open a couturier shop in downtown Monticello was enough fodder to keep tongues wagging for months. It was true that there was almost every kind of store in town, but a fancy shop such as they envisioned had never even been thought of. Juanita was a celebrity long before her train arrived.

In her letter to Millie Bailey she had told her that traveling with her would be her small daughter, her business associate and her young nephew and a colored man who had been with her husband's family since before the War and who would need accommodations. Her husband, Conner O'Farrell, would join them later when his work with the honorable Hamilton Disston came to an end. Millie answered Juanita's inquiry immediately. She stated that there was an available building that would be perfect for her needs with living quarters upstairs and a storage shed in the back for her colored man. When Juanita read that, she got furious. Harrison is not just a colored man! He's Harrison, for heaven's sake! Her response was very direct. She informed Mrs. Bailey that she would like to engage two rooms for the night and an appropriate room for the colored man, Talmai Harrison, formerly of Fairlea Plantation. She had hoped that would have some bearing on the type of lodging Millie gave Harrison, for Fairlea had at one time been the pride of Jefferson County and was located southeast between Aucilla and Monticello. She also informed her that she and her partner, Rose Shorter, would like to see in person the building she had described before making any kind of decision. Millie purposely did not tell Juanita that she and Buford were the proprietors of the building in question. Actually there were several empty buildings in the downtown area.

Boyle Coleman leaned against the building across from the hotel, his hands fidgeting deep in his pockets as he observed that Millie was right, that Juanita's husband was not with her. He allowed a slow smile as he wondered how much time he'd have to work on her before the husband arrived. Did he send that nigger to watch over her? he wondered. I just bet he did. But I've dealt with his kind before. She's a pretty little thing. Not much bigger than my ten year old, but she sure isn't built like her. Whew! Would you look at those tits just sticking out there for the whole of Monticello to see. He used the back of his square, freckled hand to wipe the saliva. He was actually smiling broadly. Guess I'd better welcome the little lady to town. Somehow wouldn't be neighborly of me to not.

Harrison was standing beside the trunks while Juanita and Rose registered at the oak desk. The room was attractive enough with dark red brocade on the matching mahogany love seats and heavy forest green and red draperies over ecru lace panels at the long windows. Juanita could tell that one of Mrs. Bailey's passions was crocheting, for there were doilies and scarves on every available table as well as the love seats.

Delia, at her mother's request, was being looked after by Seth. He held her hand tightly, but her legs weren't restricted and were swinging as high as her long, navy blue skirt would allow as she attempted to kick the rose figures in the patterned rug. "Stop that, Delia! Your ma said for you to sit still and behave. You better stop, you hear?" But Delia paid no attention to Seth's protestations and continued swinging her legs high and staring at the man who stood framed in the doorway. He took up the entire space.

Harrison glanced his way but didn't allow his expression to change. Trouble just arrived, he thought. Conner had often said, "Beware of the man with darting eyes and nervous fingers." Harrison wanted to scratch the back of his neck, a familiar gesture when he was worried. Juanita turned from the desk and saw him as he gave in to the urge. What now? she thought. She was feeling tired after the long journey. She felt someone staring at her, and when she glanced at Delia and followed her gaze toward the doorway, she soon found him.

Quickly she turned back toward Mrs. Bailey. Her throat became dry, and she cleared it before answering her inquiry. "Yes, Mrs. Bailey, Miss Shorter and I plan to stay until we find suitable lodging. Do you have weekly rates?" she asked. Juanita knew the value of a dollar and always sought a bargain. The rates were acceptable and Juanita responded, "That will be fine, Mrs. Bailey. Harrison, will you see to our baggage? Seth," she called, avoiding looking toward the doorway, "Help Harrison, dear."

The man slowly approached and Millie said, "Good evening, Boyle. What can I do for you? Buford's in the back if you need him." She figured that he was making a social call even as late as it was 'cause he didn't seem to be in a hurry. "How's Ardeth feeling? She get over that cold?"

"She's fine, Millie. Just fine." His voice was low and hesitant. When he didn't move toward their living quarters in the back, Millie felt obliged to introduce Juanita and Rose.

"Boyle, this is Mrs. O'Farrell and Miss Shorter."

Juanita nodded slightly, saying, "Mrs. Conner O'Farrell. Perhaps you've heard of my husband? He's in charge of the Hamilton Disston Enterprises in Kissimmee."

"Boyle is the town marshal," Millie continued before he could respond to Juanita's question. He tipped his hat, then removed it while bowing slightly. Rose acknowledged him with a soft "Good evening."

"We've really had a busy year around here," Millie said. She hurriedly added, "Not that Monticello is a bad place to settle in, Mrs. O'Farrell. Just seems like we had a lotta riffraff come through town lately, but Boyle and his deputies saw to it that they left in a hurry," she said laughingly.

Harrison could hear the muffled exchange between them as he and Seth carried the trunks upstairs, and when she laughed he wondered just what it was that the marshal and his deputies had done to hurry their departure. Juanita's not liking that one. She's on guard, and from the looks of him I'd better be too, he thought.

Boyle Coleman was a small town boy, who had done well at everything that he'd attempted. His father had been the principal at the Jefferson Academy ever since he had arrived in Monticello to assume that position in the late 40's. Born in England and graduated with honors from Brown University in Rhode Island, John Coleman was a much sought after bachelor on his arrival. He married Mary Kendrick, a local girl from a fine family, and had four children by her. After her death he married Lucy Scott Rhodes, a local beauty, and Boyle was their only child who lived. He was his father's pride and joy and a town favorite. When he was accepted at Brown University, the entire town came out to send him off. He was just a big, strapping boy of sixteen when he went away, and he, too, was graduated with honors and anxious to return home to Monticello. But instead of returning home to a good life he came back to war.

He and his father differed on the South's position, and when Boyle joined the Jefferson Beauregards, Company E, 3rd Florida, his father was conspicuously absent at the train depot, where the entire town turned out to send Boyle and the other young men off. He fought in practically every major battle for four years and at the War's end had attained the rank of Major. Until his father's illness their relationship was strained, but before John Coleman died, he and Boyle had again become close.

But the War changed Boyle. He was no longer the happy lad who had enlisted, and when he married Ardeth Little, the town's tongues really wagged. She was a mousy little thing with no more personality than a bed bug, they said. Her father and mother ran Little's Livery stable on the corner of Washington and Olive Streets, and it was rumored that Ardeth had given her favors to every boy who'd worked there. When she gave birth to Boyle Lester Coleman six months after their wedding, it appeared that Buddy, as he was called, had arrived with the assistance of Little's shotgun. For six years afterwards Ardeth had a baby almost every year, and she and Boyle had become pillars of the community.

When Boyle ran for town marshal to fill the position of Rooster Burns, who had accidentally stopped a bullet from Trib Henry's gun down by Lickskillet Creek, he was unopposed. The town knew that they had elected an intelligent, brave man who was concerned about the community. He was one of the Monticello Jefferson's baseball coaches, an active member of the Methodist Church and seemed attentive to Ardeth, who had assumed a position of respect since their marriage and his election. What they didn't know was that when Ardeth failed to respond to her husband's "needs" that he made sure that they were satisfied elsewhere, usually in the jail cage behind barred doors with any wench he locked up. No one would have believed the women had they spoken up - they knew it and so did Boyle. It was easy to put on a front for all of Monticello to see - they saw just what they wanted to.

Boyle was so bored with the dull ladies of the night that when he heard of Juanita's expected move to Monticello without her husband, his lust was heightened. He fantasized, he plotted, he planned. When she finally arrived and he saw her at the depot in the lamplight, all blond and tiny, and, he thought, helpless without her husband as Millie Bailey had said, he had no doubt that she'd anxiously receive his advances. Oh she'd fight a little - he hoped that she would - but he was positive that she'd give in to his desires.

God, he was tired of Ardeth! At first she had been an active partner, but now he couldn't even get a hump out of her - she just lay there. Oh, how she used to groan and moan and carry on. Hell, she hadn't let out a peep in over two years. And when his deputies Tully and Smith weren't around, he'd get his dose.

Only once did he almost get caught. That Deese woman's old man Tyson had beat her to a pulp, and Boyle had brought her to jail for protection when Tyson ran off. Never knew when he'd get likkered up and return, Boyle had told her. God, she was good! Never had such a poke - certainly not from Ardeth. So, he saw to it that she needed protecting often. One night when he left home to go to the jail to check on that "poor woman", as he explained to Ardeth, he and she were going at it, and had the front door not had a creak in it, Smith would've caught them.

"That you, Tully? " Boyle called while trying desperately to pull his pants up and button them.

"It's me, Smith. What're you doing here at this time o' night, Marshal? Saw the light on and thought maybe something was up."

"Oh," Boyle answered, finally getting his pants buttoned, "Ardeth baked an extra pear pie and thought poor Mrs. Deese would enjoy a piece." He came out of the cell. Smith noticed that his boots were unlaced but didn't say anything or really think much about it. The marshal wasn't known as a fancy Dan, and if he wanted to walk down to the jail from his house only six blocks away with his boots unlaced, well, let him. He worked hard and could use some comfort, Smith thought.

"I'd have brought you a piece, too, if I'd known you were going to be here, Smith. It was as good a LeConte pear pie as I ever ate. You know Ardeth, always thinking of the less fortunate."

That was the last time Boyle saved the Deese woman from her abusive husband. Boyle Coleman was a careful man. At least up until now, for he was determined to have that fancy, little, sweet-smelling Juanita, who was not even broke in good. Determination was one of his strong qualities.

Millie had had Buford clear out the back storage room and put in a cot for Harrison. The light shining through the small, paned window above him played on the crates stacked alongside the opposite wall. *Madden House LeConte Pears, Sweetest in the South, Monticello, Florida* was stamped on the sides of the crates. Buford and Millie not only owned the hotel, but they had bought ten acres of land just outside town and planted LeConte pears, the reputed answer to the orange in the northern part of the state.

Harrison couldn't relax enough to allow sleep to visit. Over and over he allowed his mind to wander. He remembered the first time he'd seen Conner and then Juanita and when Delia was born and on and on his thoughts hopscotched, never settling. Maybe I've put too much faith in the Whites' ways. I probably should have given into my desires and bedded Tisha, but I know I'd not have been content. But maybe it is as Thomas Paine said, *"It is necessary to the happiness of man that he be mentally faithful to himself."* Yes, perhaps I should have listened to the wisdom of Mr. Paine. This could be the beginning for me as well as for Juanita and Rose. I know there are several Negro schools here - perhaps I can get a teaching position.

Juanita mentioned driving out to Fairlea. That's the very first thing I'm going to do tomorrow morning. I'll inquire about it. I wonder if Mister Marshall came back from the War alive and if he sold it or rented it ... He turned over and thought, this has got to be the lumpiest mattress I've slept on since Conner and I visited Avalon Manor. He chuckled and wondered what ever happened to the poor, ignorant boy whose mare they confiscated, the one Conner named Guinevere. If I ever have a horse I'm going to name her Guinevere. His breathing became steady and he didn't stir the entire night.

When first light came he awakened with a smile on his face. He had dreamed about his and Conner's narrow escape from the Delta Sun, when the irate Mr. Ed Longwood had caught Conner with his young, buxom wife Sophie, and Harrison and Conner had had to jump overboard into the sluggish Mississippi while Conner, trying desperately to pull up his trousers, dodged Ed Longwood's bullets. It must have been a humorous sight from the deck, because Harrison could still hear the uproarious laughter from the amused passengers.

I'll always have my memories, he thought, sighing, pulling on his work boots. Tisha wouldn't have been a part of them nor would she have cared probably. I can share with Juanita. She understands how I feel about Conner. That's important - more than finding myself a woman...or marrying... or...

"You awake, Harrison?" Again Buford knocked on the storage room door. Harrison had gone out behind the building and found some tall azaleas, where he had relieved himself. He hadn't dared to ask to use the bathroom off the lobby. Had Conner been there, he would have insisted that he share his room, stating that he was his manservant, and no one would have questioned him. But with just Juanita and Rose there was no way that he would be accepted, and he knew it. Buford heard him coming up the back steps and said, "Thought you'd gone back to Kissimmee," and laughed. He was a jolly man, who obviously loved good cooking. "Mrs. Bailey's got some grits and biscuits cooked up if you'd care to have some." Harrison assured him that would be fine and asked if there was some place where he could wash up. He was directed to the pump back of the tool shed.

"Seems like a real nice colored man, Millie. Real polite and clean. Miss Juanita said that he'd been brought up on Fairlea but that when the fever and blight hit back 'fore the War started, he got sold to a plantation up in Louisiana." Buford stirred his hot, black coffee.

"And she said that he served with the mister during the war, cooking his mess. Maybe he can work out in the pears 'til the mister arrives. Give him some spending money and help us out at the same time," Millie added, asking if he'd like a fill-up.

When Juanita and Rose came downstairs, they were soon joined by the other guests for breakfast. Millie set a good table, Juanita noticed. Linen napkins in silver napkin rings, ornate silver flatware and pretty, dark blue and gold edged china. Juanita took the lead and began to converse with Mr. and Mrs. Hunter Nasworthy from Thomasville, Georgia. They were looking for property near Monticello, because Mr. Nasworthy had a saw mill near the Thomasville Railroad between Monticello and Thomasville, and the schools were much better in Monticello, Mrs. Nasworthy said. They had always sent their children to private schools, but after the Jefferson Academy had earned such high honors, they decided to move closer to Monticello so their children could attend.

Juanita turned on her charm when she heard that. She could see potential customers in Mrs. Nasworthy and her four school-aged children. Rose relaxed and even entered into the conversation, stating that Seth, her niece's son who lived with her since his ma's death, was looking forward to attending the famous academy. Seth and Delia fidgetted and could hardly wait to escape the room. He had spied a rope swing in the backyard and a weeping willow that was beckoning him.

Why is Aunt Rose carrying on about the dumb old school, anyway? She knew how he hated it. When I grow up I'm gonna go back to Basinger and become a boat captain. That's what! Don't need to go to any high falutin' school to be a captain. Nosiree! And Delia, heck she don't take to school a bit better'n I do. She could learn to cook real good and be the boat's cook. She'd like that. She sure loves to eat. Would ya look at her shovel it in, he thought while rolling his eyes at Delia, who was being glared at by Juanita.

"Delia Rose, now don't you gobble down your breakfast, young lady. My, my, my. You'll have an upset tummy, dear. Why, you'd think that your da and I hadn't taught you a speck of manners." Delia had seen the rope swing, too, and was hoping that she and Seth could escape their folks eyes long enough for a turn on it. Why'd she hafta get all dressed up anyway? Heck, all they were gonna do was look at some old buildings.

"Mama, maybe Seth and I can have Harrison look after us. Why can't he, Mama? Why?"

"Now, Delia Rose, you know why." She smiled at the family at the table next to hers. "Children are always in a hurry, aren't they?" she murmured sweetly. Three more prospective customers, she thought. She had told the Nasworthys of her shop and stated that she and Rose would have an extensive line of children's fashions. There would be no more need for folks to travel all the way to Jacksonville or Savannah, and she hoped to find just the perfect shop very soon, for she was so anxious to take the train to Savannah to purchase her supplies.

"I was privileged to assist my dear sister-in-law in her exclusive shop, Monique's, in Palatka, but she was taken from us in that terrible fire in '84, you know. May the saints preserve us!" she exclaimed dramatically.

"Oh, are you Catholic, Mrs. O'Farrell?" Mrs. Nasworthy asked, knowing that there was no Catholic Church in Monticello, the closest one being in Tallahassee.

"Oh, no I'm not, but Mr. O'Farrell is. I was raised in the Baptist Church and Rose is Methodist." She and Rose had decided before their arrival to become active in the two largest churches in town for business purposes. Juanita hadn't attended church since she left LaBelle except for the few times when she accompanied Maeve to Mass, hoping that if she became Catholic, Conner would marry her. Not that he ever went to Mass. Maeve could usually persuade him to accompany her during Lent when he was on shore, but that was it.

Millie was clearing their table and overheard the conversation. She got real excited about Rose's being Methodist and proceeded to tell her all about the women's groups and how the town marshal's wife, Ardeth Coleman, was president of their sunday school and would no doubt be making a call on her the first chance she got.

When she said that, Juanita thought, so the marshal's wife is active in her church, is she? Maybe she's not paying enough attention to her own hen house. I don't like that man. There's something false about him. Harrison noticed it, too. It's hard to believe Mrs. Bailey didn't notice it. Gosh, he was almost drooling. But I guess we see just what we want to.

Harrison handed Millie's cook Virgie his empty plate. She smiled her most ingratiating smile up at him and proceeded to tell him her life's story. What on earth makes every woman I meet think that I need to listen to their drivel? I don't give a fig if her old man ran off with the baker's housemaid and I sure as hell don't care that she was just a girl from a no-good family and that she's had two babies for him - at least he thinks they're his...

"Miss Virgie," he interrupted after he'd finished his coffee, "I hates to interrupt ya, but Miss Juanita done ast me ta fin' out 'bout my old home, Fairlea. She wants dat Ah pay it a visit 'cause she know how much Ah been missin' it."

Virgie patted him on his shoulder. "Harrison, forgive me fer burdenin' ya wid mah problems. Ah should be 'shamed o' maself. Ah certainly should. Why, Mister Marshall and Miss Sutton's daughter Ruthann an' her husban' Morris done move ta Fairlea an' fix it up real nice. Mah cousin Shirlee work fer dem an say it lak a palace. Got acres an' acres o' tobaccy an' cotton. He put in five acre pears an' another section in watermelons..."

"So Mr. Marshall couldn't part wid it. Ah'm glad. Ah knows dat his mama an' papa, Marse Samuel an' Miss Edwina, are smilin' in heaven fer sure," Harrison added.

"Virgie, do ya tink Ah be outta line ta pay it a visit? Miss Juanita would sure lak ta see it. She heard me an Mr. O'Farrell talk 'bout it all dese years."

"Why, nosiree. Miss Ruthann be proud ta haf a visit wid sech a fine lady lak Missus O'Farrell, Ah'm shore. When ya gits dere be sure ta speak ta Shirlee an' tell her ya is a friend o' mine. She'll take ya 'round de whole entire place. Miss Ruthann married Mr. Morris Ledeau. Don' matter dat he be old 'nuff ta be her own papa. He kind an' got more money den he know what to spen' it on. Owns mos' de Aucilla Valley, he do, an' mos' de railroad ya see here 'bouts."

Millie rushed into the kitchen, put down the tray of dishes and asked Virgie if Henry was laid up again. "Noam, he be fine." She thought better about what she said and added, "But ya knows, Miss Millie, dat back could be actin' up on him again. Ya knows how it jes up an' grab him somthin' awful. Ah ask Josephus if'n he can stop doin' de yard chores an go see ta him."

All she got from Millie Bailey was a suspicious "huruump!" Unsaid was what they were both thinking. Back, my eye! More like stump whisky.

As soon as Millie went back to the dining room to finish clearing up, Virgie said to Harrison, "Ah bes git Josephus ovah ta Henry's. He gonna mess up de onlies' job he evah been able ta keep. He gitten ta be down raght shifless, he is." She sighed deeply, and Harrison used her distraction to escape.

Juanita and Rose were distraught, Harrison could see. When Juanita pursed her lips, that was a sure sign that her mind was on something unpleasant. "I don't want lines before my time," she would often say. Delia was sniffling while Seth practically dragged her. They were reluctantly following Juanita and Rose down Jefferson St. That's when Harrison saw the marshal. He was leaning against the door of the Puleston Mercantile building on the opposite side of the street, trying to appear nonchalant but not succeeding.

Conner often said, "The best way to destroy an enemy is to change him into a friend." But, you, my enemy, are likely to remain so. His thoughts were interrupted when Juanita saw him and shouted, "Harrison! There you are! I really don't think that there's a suitable shop in all of Monticello. Why, the building Mrs. Bailey showed us is just a big old square nothing - just a nothing, isn't it Rose?"

Rose didn't hesitate, "We could divide it, you know, Juanita. You know, make a work room in the..."

"Rose Shorter!" Juanita was by now even squinting - an absolute no-no. "You know good and well that'd just look like a great big old square room all chopped up. That's what!"

Rose didn't pursue the matter, but neither did she lower her head, Harrison noticed. I think maybe Miss Shorter has found some starch in her backbone, as my Ma Sarie used to say. That's good for Juanita and good for Rose.

"We've just gotta look somewhere else. I know there's gotta be another building more suitable. You know, in town or maybe on the very outskirts." She looked up and right into the admiring eyes of James S. Denham, the Mayor of Monticello, who had joined Boyle Coleman and who gallantly tipped his dark grey hat. Boyle gave the appropriate "Good Morning, Mrs. O'Farrell and Miss Shorter." and bowed slightly. Not waiting for them to respond he quickly asked, "Is there something disturbing you, Mrs. O'Farrell? You seem to be distraught." The way he emphasized the Mrs. made Juanita want to spit in his little eyes, but instead she responded wisely, "Marshal, actually there is something bothering Miss Shorter and me. We were told by Mrs. Bailey that there was a suitable building in town for our dress shop, but alas, we have not seen it."

Harrison stood a good six feet away from them. He wished that he could congratulate Juanita on her tactics. She's going to use him. I just hope she's not getting in over her head. He's not as easy to fool as some of the others she's worked. Not easy at all. I'd better think of something. But before he could come up with a diversion, Boyle spoke, "Well now, ladies, you indeed are in luck. I'd like you to meet our Mayor. May I present Mayor James Denham. I'm certain that he can assist you in every way and that includes any real estate venture, huh, James?"

"I'm glad to make your acquaintance, ladies, and to officially welcome you to Monticello. Millie told me of your expected arrival, and I and my missus are most pleased. I'm sure she'll be a most faithful patron, eh, Boyle?"

Juanita wore her most ingratiating smile but thought, I wish Conner were here. He'd punch that gun-toting marshal in the nose. I wish Harrison were White - he'd give him what for! But all she could do under the circumstances was continue to smile lady-like and pretend that the marshal was not practically licking his chops as he admired her openly - brazenly. Had the Mayor been taller he would have seen it, too.

Harrison decided to make his move and quickly caught up with them and said, "Scuse me Missus, but Ah needs ta speak ta ya. Sorry, sirs, to interrupt ya but de business be urgent." He tipped his hat as politely as he could, and Juanita and Rose said in unison, "G'day, gentlemen," and joined Harrison, Juanita gratefully, for she could read Harrison. Rose was anxiously waiting to find out what the urgent business was.

Delia began to jump up and down and shouted, "Is my da here, Harrison? Is he here?" Juanita got such a frog in her throat that before she could clear it, Harrison had picked Delia up and taken Juanita's arm and escorted them across the street away from Boyle Coleman's curious eyes.

"No, Miss Delia, he ain't. But don' ya fret, 'cause he be here by and by." What he didn't say was "and before that marshal tries something he shouldn't with your mama." Juanita saw his concern and squeezed his arm hard. She glanced at Boyle. His mouth was open as he intensely studied them. She didn't like what she saw, and when Harrison's hand found the back of his neck, she knew that he, too, was worried. *I don't know what I'd do without him. He's the best friend I've ever had, but Lord, why'd You hafta send me one who's colored? What protection can he give me? Oh, dear Lord, where's Conner?*

She suddenly felt weak all over, light-headed. When Harrison saw her start to faint, he quickly put Delia down, grabbed Juanita, holding her up underneath both arms. Rose turned and asked loudly, "Juanita, what's wrong? Are you sick?"

The next thing Juanita knew was that she was being lifted up and carried. She could feel the badge dig in to her side. He smelled of wintergreen. *Oh, God, not now! Why now? Conner...Conner O'Farrell, what've you done to me? If I'm with child I'll...I'll...* She lost consciousness.

CHAPTER II KISSIMMEE CITY

Fred Saunders and his wife Doris owned the confectionery on Orange Street across from Juanita's old shop, Cherie's, in Kissimmee City. The shop was now empty with no sign of it's ever having been occupied. Conner used the large showroom only to walk through as he sought the darkness and solitude of his own room, looking neither right nor left. Closing his door soundly behind him he removed his hat and reached for his bed, slowly lowering himself onto it. Turning on his side, his eyes open, he followed the pattern of the wallpaper in the dim light.

"I'll be back for you, Doris," Mrs. Craig called as she closed the door of the confectionery. The tinkling bell rang out loudly as she said it. She glanced at Cherie's and tried to see if Mr. O'Farrell was there. He was the town's curiosity. She and Doris and Mary Austin had just been discussing how strange he'd become and wondered if the woman who claimed to be his wife would ever return to Kissimmee. She'd best not, she declared to herself. This town doesn't need the likes of her. She should have taken that no-good Irish with her.

They'd quickly forgotten how proud they had been of the attractive shop when Juanita first opened it, and also how the tongues wagged when the town's wealthy ladies went in and out for their fittings. It wasn't until after one of the busybodies had found out that Juanita and Conner weren't married and after Conner had lost his high position with Hamilton Disston that they'd turned on them.

Conner couldn't sleep. He didn't even feel like having a drink - hadn't had one in months. He just went through the motions of living now. After Juanita and Harrison left Kissimmee, it'd taken him only a few days to admit to himself that he was actually alone. For the first time in his almost fifty years he was alone. Fred Saunders had promised Harrison that he'd look in on Conner from time to time. Harrison had paid him handsomely to do it, and Fred was an honorable man.

Fred had waited for a while after Juanita and Harrison left town to check on Conner. But when he missed seeing any sign of life over there, he decided that he'd better have a look-see. He hadn't told Doris about the money Harrison had paid him. Didn't know exactly why he hadn't. Fred told Doris, "Think I'll look in on Mr. O'Farrell. Don't like the idea of a neighbor dying right before our eyes. Now Doris don't make a fuss. Don't matter that you don't like him. You know it's the neighborly thing to do." And before she could stop him he was gone.

He could hear her protesting loudly. "Neighborly! Didn't see Mr. High and Mighty Irish being neighborly to us. Sticking his nose up just like a millionaire, he did, all the time he's been here. And him worshipping idols like they say them Catholics do." Actually she'd never seen Conner go to church because there wasn't a Catholic church anywhere around. But being suspicious of anything and everything that she didn't understand, she suspected the worse. Catholics easily fell into that category. "Idol-worshipping Irish, that's what he is!"

She had allowed herself to like Juanita, though reluctantly, and was particularly fond of little Delia. She had to admit that Juanita had always been pleasant to her, and she could tell that Fred had been taken with Delia, too. "Don't seem quite right, them not even married and having a baby, and me and Fred trying as hard as we can and can't have a one. Don't seem right!" she said over and over.

Fred knocked on the front door of Cherie's. There was no sound. He turned the knob - it was unlocked. He knew that the second room on the right was the one Conner'd taken after he had become ill when his sister had been burned to death in Palatka. If Doris had known that he had stuffed leftover fresh ham and biscuits under his jacket, she'd really have kicked up a fuss. Nag - nag - nag. Harrison had asked him to take food to Conner and to tell him that his missus had cooked some extra and thought that maybe he'd like some, or to tell him some tale like that.

Fred knocked softly on Conner's door at first, then called, "Mr. O'Farrell, sir, it's me, Fred Saunders. You know, from the store across the street. Got some nice fresh ham and biscuits that my missus cooked. Thought maybe you'd enjoy some." No response. "I'll just leave 'em outside your door. I'll be back directly with some hot coffee to help you down it. Plumb forgot the coffee." He placed his ear against the door, and still no stirring did he hear.

Fred pulled the front door to behind him, and when he looked across the street, he could see Doris peeking around the curtained window. When he came in she didn't look up nor ask how Conner was - just busied herself with the coconut pralines she was counting. But he knew she was curious. He was trying to figure out how he could return to Cherie's with the coffee.

"Doggone it!" he said aloud. "The man needs our help!" He said more gently, "Think I'll take him some hot coffee, Hon. Is there any left from this morning?"

She pursed her lips tight, shook her head and whirled around, and out of the room she went mumbling about how if he was a man he'd not be misled by that fancy Dan, and on and on she fussed. He followed her, turned her around roughly, she threw off his hand. "Now listen to me, Doris," he said firmly. "The man is sick. He's our neighbor, and the very least we can do is to be sure he gets help if'n he needs it. I thought that Reverend Stokes preached on that very thing Sunday, miss."

She was not going to allow his logic to interfere with her anger. "He didn't say one word about feeding a high and mighty idol-worshipping Irishman, Mr. Saunders. Not a word did he say about that, sir."

She turned from him swiftly, untied her apron and threw it on the kitchen floor, and bursting through the door she ran up the stairs. Neither one had heard the door bell jingle announcing Thelma Craig's entry. When Doris saw her, she didn't even stop - just kept running up the stairs to the sanctuary of their bedroom. Fred was right behind her. He stopped when he saw Thelma, and over his shoulder he called, "I'll be back in a minute, Thelma. Got something that needs tending to." Thelma saw the look in his eye, and when he unbuckled his belt and started to remove it, she was out of there in jig time. She didn't close her mouth until she got home, having puffed all the way down Orange Street.

She hadn't heard Doris's hollering, but the Riggses next door did; they'd heard it many times before. Jonathan said to his wife, Lora Sue, "Guess Doris done got out o' line again. You'd think that fool woman would learn now, wouldn't you?" Lora Sue meekly nodded and continued stirring the stew. I'll take some healing ointment over to her soon's I see Fred leave, she thought. I declare she must like him beating up on her. Seems like mos' every few months she asks for it.

Lora Sue would hear her neighbor hollering her head off and out would come the healing ointment. It was just lard mixed with wintergreen, but it did soothe a welt. She'd pay Doris a visit as soon as Fred left, as he always did, for Johnson's Saloon, where he'd stay for hours while Thelma and Lora Sue listened to Doris expound on what led to the beatings.

Doris was very dramatic and could really put on a show for them, as good as any they'd ever seen given by the traveling shows. They'd massage the ointment into her welts and commiserate with her while enjoying every minute of the drama. Doris especially enjoyed the sniffling and allowed it to last for as long as it took to tell her tale. Then it would miraculously cease as she declared that was the last time she'd allow Fred Saunders to mistreat her.

But this time Fred didn't head for the saloon. Instead he carried the big pot of coffee straight to Cherie's. Lora Sue was hesitant to go to Doris, what with Fred just across the street, so she took to the front porch with her jar of salve tucked inside her apron pocket and sat darning Jonathan's socks while watching and waiting. She hadn't been sitting long until Thelma joined her. She must have darned at least three socks before Fred came out of the front door of Cherie's. His head was lowered.

"It doesn't look good, Thelma. Looks like he's going on home, but for how long we won't know. Guess Doris will have to hang on to her story a little longer."

Finally Thelma, who was easily bored, went on back to her house. When there was still no commotion coming from next door, Lora Sue also retreated to her kitchen to clear up the dinner dishes. She didn't want Jonathan to get out of sorts. Not that he'd take his belt to her. He had no reason to. She always did his bidding - always.

Fred Saunders sat down hard on the kitchen chair. He lowered his head and his hands soon found it. He was actually crying. He'd never in his entire life seen anything like it - never. Doris was still upstairs. He hadn't been gone long enough for her to get over her mad - usually took her at least half a day.

She was really put out with Lora Sue and Thelma. Where were they when she needed them? Fine thing! Freddie beating up on her about that heathen Irishman and her best friends not even there to comfort her in her time of need. "I'll just stay up here 'til he calms down," she said to herself.

Fred rose, poured himself a cup of coffee and went out to the back stoop. He needed air, fresh air, after what he'd just been through. He'd never seen a handsomer man in his life than Conner O'Farrell. Always dressed up to beat the band. Spotless white suit and wearing a Panama and smoking those black cheroots. And that little girl of his, his spittin' image. What'd she think of her daddy now? What?

When Fred got back to Conner's room, he noticed that the biscuits and ham were gone. He decided to knock and tell Conner that he'd brought the coffee. He started to turn the knob but could see that the door wasn't shut. He could smell the acrid stench of urine even before he got inside. There was a little light coming underneath one of the shades that was raised about two inches. It was then he saw Conner all crumpled up on the bed in the corner next to the wall. He couldn't tell what was piled up beside the bed, but when he raised the shade saying, "Mr. O'Farrell, it's me Fred Saunders. I've got your coffee. Let me up this shade some more so you can see, sir," the roaches began scurrying all over the place. When he turned the impact of the room hit him. Pasted all over two of the walls were charred pieces of paper, handwritten letters. There was not a square foot of space that wasn't filthy and cluttered. Conner didn't stir but Fred knew that he was alive, or he wouldn't have been able to take the food inside. I've got to get him out of here, is all he could think.

It was obvious that Conner hadn't been strong enough to get to the bathroom at the back of the house. Fred had to be careful where he stepped. The stench was so bad that Fred tried holding his breath but felt that he had to tell Conner what he planned to do. "Mr. O'Farrell, I'm going to get you out of here. Now don't you go gettin' mad at me, sir. It's for your own good I'm doing it." When Fred lifted him he realized that every bone in his body was clawing to get out. "Gawd Almighty! Get off him! Now!" he brushed the roaches, swatting the ones he could and stomping the ones he could get to. "Gawd Almighty! Mr. O'Farrell! How come you let yourself get in this shape, sir? Oh, Lordie - Oh, Lordie!"

He pushed the door ajar and headed for the only other room in the back. It had been Harrison's. Conner's head dangled. He was ashen. Fred laid him down on Harrison's unmade bed and hurriedly went back for the coffee. He closed the door to keep the stench in and, he hoped, the cockroaches as well. He lifted Conner and held him gently like a small child. His long legs were doubled up underneath him. He spooned the coffee into his partly opened mouth. His eyes were open but didn't seem to be focused, and he sipped the coffee without protesting.

"Mr. O'Farrell, I'm going for Dr. Clayton. You need some help, sir, and I think it's more'n food or coffee." Still no protest.

Fred left for the doctor and made sure to go out the back door. He didn't want any more gossip about the poor man, and that Lora Sue would be sitting on her front porch just waiting to spread her lies up and down the whole town.

He decided that when he returned, he'd take the doc in the back, too. He didn't want him to see that room, and he'd stop on his way back by Elvira's to see if she and Roy could come over to help him clean out that place. He knew Miss Cherie hadn't left it like that, and sure as shootin' Harrison hadn't known 'bout it. Must've been holed up in there like that this whole time. Now why didn't I go over there the very day they left? I should've. Poor man! Poor, proud man!

Doctor Bishop Clayton was a dour man. He rarely smiled or said anything for that matter but was highly thought of by everyone in Kissimmee City. He was one of the first doctors to settle there after Hamilton Disston bought up all the land and began dredging the Kissimmee River. It was rumored that he'd been a leading physician and teacher up in the Richmond area, but he didn't talk enough for anyone to find out for sure. Somehow Fred didn't want to share Conner O'Farrell's plight with the doctor, but he did want his professional help. When Bishop Clayton first looked at Conner he was shocked. He turned toward Fred and asked, "Why'd you let this man get in this condition, sir? Heavens, he's almost starved to death!"

Before Fred could tell him that Conner was not his responsibility, he was receiving orders rapidly. "Strip him down! Get this filth off him. My God, man, be quick about it!"

Fred heard Roy and Elvira calling at the back door and he answered. "I'm here in the back. Hurry on in." Elvira was a robust colored woman from over Ocala way, and she and Roy Peterson had been one of the first colored families to settle in the Kissimmee valley. Roy had been the butler at the Tropical Hotel. They knew everyone, and everyone knew them. When something needed done most folks thought of the Petersons. They had eight children, six of them strapping boys, as nice and polite as any children anywhere. Didn't have a lazy one among them. When Fred stopped by their place on Drury St., he only had to ask for their help one time. They put down what they were doing - Roy had been mending a harness out by the barn, and El had been in the garden with three of their smaller children. She took off her apron, washed up at the pump and told the girl on the porch, who was about twelve, "Yore pa and me'll be back soon as we can. Don' let the younguns leave de place, heah?"

Unknown to Fred, Conner O'Farrell had befriended Roy on more than one occasion. Once when one of the dock hands had got out of line and begun shoving Roy around for no reason at all, Conner had straightened the man up physically and verbally. Roy hadn't forgotten it. He was also acquainted with Harrison. Harrison didn't have any black friends, and Conner had thought it wise for him to attempt to establish some sort of relationship in the black community, suggesting that he get to know the Petersons. So Harrison had made it a point to seek out Roy, even if only for short evenings on their front porch. After Maeve's death he had confided in Roy about his concern for Conner. His grief was so pronounced that Roy was surprised when Harrison decided to accompany Juanita to Monticello, but then he figured Harrison, being the smartest black man he'd ever met, knew what he was doing.

Fred didn't have to introduce the Petersons. Doctor Clayton took El's arm and left the room. "Mrs. Peterson, I want you to get Mr. O'Farrell bathed and into some clean clothes. Then I'll examine him thoroughly. Mr. Peterson, would you and Mr. Saunders come with me, please?" They followed him out to the front porch. "The man is close to death, I'm afraid. We need to get someone to stay with him around the clock, and I want him fed every hour. Mr. Saunders, I'd like for you to have your wife fix some tea with honey and add the juice of an orange. Mr. Peterson, do you think your wife would be able to assist her?"

Fred spoke up, "Dr. Clayton, I'll tend to Mr. O'Farrell. But I would appreciate it if El would get him some clean clothes, though. My pants would probably come only to his knees." He would have said it laughingly to anyone other than the doc. One didn't feel comfortable showing any humor around the doc.

"That would be fine. That would be fine."

No point in asking Doris to help, Fred thought. Actually, I'd rather she didn't. Me and El can take care of Mr. O'Farrell. Fred had never considered calling Conner by his first name.

When Fred returned to Cherie's, he went to the back room. El had already bathed and dressed Conner and made the bed and was waiting for him. "Roy'll be back quick as a wink wid mah boys, Mr. Fred. We get dat room cleaned up and aired out for Mr. O'Farrell in no time. Darlene'll bring some good pine soap scrub, an' we have dat room smellin' jes lak de woods after a rain storm." She gave a little laugh and hummed as she went about straightening the room.

Now why can't Doris be happy like that? He shook his light brown hair. Maybe it's because we don't have any younguns. I bet she'd be happy then. Not that she's unhappy all the time. But that woman can get her mind set just like she has about Mr. O'Farrell, and there's no changing it.

Fred and El took turns staying with Conner. Dr. Clayton visited daily. He'd started him on porridge with cream and honey the second day, and by the fourth day Fred had him up walking. Dr. Clayton insisted that he walk him every two hours. Back and forth the length of the house he'd walk. By the end of the first week he was actually joking with Fred. But Fred noticed that his eyes had lost their old glint. He was not the Conner O'Farrell who had moved to Kissimmee City almost nine years ago. Fred had been an admirer of this man, and if he could, if it were humanly possible, he'd help him regain his verve for life, no matter what Doris thought. He'd make Conner his cause. Fred Saunders had never had a cause before. It excited him.

When the letter came the end of that second week, Fred was excited for Conner. It appeared to be very important. But when he gave it to Conner and Conner read the return address, he didn't even bother to open it. He just stared like he didn't know where he was. Fred got concerned. He had come too far to allow an old letter to upset him. "Mr. O'Farrell, I'll fix you some tea, and you can read your letter out in the sunshine," he suggested. "You know that the doc wants you in the sunshine every day." But Conner got up and like a sleep walker went into his old room and curled up on the bed. Turning toward the wall, he stared at the flowers on the wallpaper.

Fred found the letter on the floor outside Conner's room unopened. Monsignor Vincent Haut, % Fr. William Kenny, Immaculate Conception Church, Jacksonville, Florida, it said. So the priest he's been talking about is in Florida. Do tell! Fred put the letter on the kitchen table and kept vigil at Conner's door. Should I open the letter? He decided that was just what he was going to do. "I'm not gonna let him do this to himself. Not Fred Saunders," he mumbled aloud.

CHAPTER III SWEET REVENGE

Ardeth Coleman never had much use for Millie Bailey, not that she'd ever let on to Boyle or anyone else in town for that matter. She tried to be pleasant to everyone in Monticello, especially since Boyle had been elected marshal. She had known for as long as she could remember what the townspeople thought of her. They'd never tried to hide their feelings. But when she caught Boyle Coleman for her husband, she was sure their gossip would stop. After all, he was the catch of Jefferson County, or so they thought. Heck, it didn't matter that she was pregnant. Half the girls in town were when they wed, she told herself, even if it wasn't true. She had said it so often that she'd even convinced herself. But now she was the Sunday school superintendent of the Methodist Church, just about the most important position in the entire town - at least to her.

She sat in front of her dressing table mirror braiding her long hair. It was her most redeeming feature, and even she knew it - light brown with golden highlights and so thick that the braids were almost teacup size. "If he thinks for just one little minute that he's going to shame me in front of this town, he'd better think again!" she declared aloud. "Picking that little high-falutin' woman up and carrying her all the way to Madden House for the entire town to see, and Millie spreading the news fast as she could. I'll fix him! I'll fix Mr. know-it-all Coleman!"

Ardeth had the habit of talking to herself and had to be very careful when she was upset. She got up and closed her bedroom door just in case one of the children was still awake and would hear her. She sat back down and watched her image in the mirror and continued her harangue. "He's so stupid that he even thinks that I don't know about all the others." She squinted her small brown eyes dramatically. "Doesn't he know that I gather up his dirty clothes? Now, how does he think I could miss seeing his gummy drawers after he's had a poke with some no good whore? How?"

She was really getting into it, her face not six inches from the mirror. "Bet Clara thinks that it's me he's poking." She smugly thought, she always has that funny smile on her black face when she delivers the laundry. Bet every one of her kin in the entire black community thinks he's a real man. "Hummph!"

She blew out the lamp, and as she pulled up the cotton sheet she smiled. "I'll just write cousin Freddie's wife Doris and ask her all about this Miss Cherie, I will. Sounds like a fancy whore's name to me. Bet that's what she was in Kissimmee City and is foolin' everyone here. Bet she doesn't even have a husband like she claims."

She slept soundly and didn't hear Boyle come inside. He glanced down at her and thought, God! I married myself one ugly woman. But things are looking up - looking up real good. He thought of how small Cherie felt in his protective arms. He sat down on the rocker beside the bed and pulled off his boots. I ought to be able to break her in about a month if I work real fast. He climbed into bed and turned on his side away from Ardeth. His mind was methodically plotting how he could rid himself of her. I'll think of something. Should be a snap since I'll be the one investigating my poor wife's demise. Suddenly, Harrison's black face appeared. He smiled as he thought, maybe I can kill two birds with one stone - a blackbird and an old crow. He wanted to laugh out loud but, instead, fell into a deep sleep almost immediately.

Harrison drove the buggy, and Juanita, Rose and the children were enjoying the country side as they rode slowly up the lane to Fairlea. They'd have had an earlier start had Juanita not been feeling poorly that morning, and Millie had insisted on fixing her some camomile tea with honey and taking it up to her room. Juanita wasn't letting on to her about her suspicions. None of her prying-eyes business, she had decided. "Oh, Mrs. Bailey, you shouldn't have. I'm feeling so much better. I was just so very tired after that long trip from Kissimmee and the excitement of finally arriving in Monticello. Why, I don't know what came over me, fainting like that."

Millie wanted to reply but decided not to. "This cup of tea'll fix you right up Mrs. O'Farrell. Harrison said that you all will be riding all the way to Fairlea today. You sure you're up to it?"

"Oh, I feel fine now. Just needed a good long rest, that's all. Why Rose and I were worn to a frazzle even before we left Kissimmee. What with packing all the fabrics and notions not to mention my wedding gifts - you know - my china and silver and the likes."

"I know that must have been a real chore, and y'all will be glad to get settled in some nice house. You might want to stop by the Reases' property for a look-see on your way to Fairlea. It's a real nice house and plenty big enough for all of you, even when Mr. O'Farrell joins you. Even has a little playhouse for Delia, made just like the big house. Mr. Rease was always thinking up something new and different for little

Mary. Poor little thing didn't see her seventh birthday - the fever, you know. Was it as bad in Kissimmee as it was in Jacksonville and here?

Juanita shook her head no.

"We lost a lotta families here. Now Loretta and John Rease weren't taken along with little Mary. But would you believe both of 'em came down with typhoid not two months after the angels took Mary - not two months..."

"We'll be sure to stop by the Reases'. Does it have any property with it? My husband insists on some acreage, about ten or so acres. I believe he'd enjoy putting in some of those LeConte pears and maybe some watermelons.

Millie studied Juanita. Why am I so suspicious of this girl? There is something that just doesn't ring true, and the way Boyle scooped her up and looked at her like he could eat her with a spoon...something just doesn't ring true.

Millie answered, "Has about twenty-something acres, best I remember. John put in a couple acres of pears and even peaches. Did real well with them, too. But his main job was on the railroad up to Thomasville. Gone a lot of the time, and you know how hard it is getting good help. But Harrison will be a big help to you, I'm sure. Seems like a fine colored man, he does." She chuckled. "I believe that Virgie'd be sweet on him if she thought he'd give her the time of day. I take it that he's not got him a woman."

"No, Mrs. Bailey, he doesn't have a woman but knowing Harrison he'll want to get us all settled in before he'll even consider looking for one. He's so devoted to the mister and is such a responsible man..."she didn't get to finish. "Delia! For heaven's sake don't carry on so! What is it dear?"

"Mama - Mama - we're going on a ride all the way to Harrison's old house. You coming with us?"

"Don't jump up and down so. For heaven's sake, you'll throw up all your breakfast."

Millie couldn't help but laugh. "Children just can't seem to stay calm when there's a trip coming up. I remember Ray and Floyd would drive us near about crazy every time Buford and me'd even mention going to Aucilla to visit his ma and pa, and that not but ten or so miles away. They'd carry on for days. Over and over they'd ask, 'How much longer, Mama? How much longer?' They're living up in Thomasville now, and we just about never get to see them. We thought when the train started running that they'd get home often, but they have their own families and businesses to care for. Ray runs the mercantile store for Mr. James J. Parker and ....."

Juanita pretended to listen. She could tell that she missed her boys.

****

Doris Saunders was humming loudly as she went about her chores. As usual Fred was at the Irishman's. It didn't anger her as it had before - before she received the letter from Fred's cousin Ardeth. Fred didn't know about it. Didn't even know she'd received it. That delighted her, to be able to put something over on her husband. So that Miss Cherie was trying to pass herself off as a married lady, was she? She chuckled aloud. I'll just fix that one. Monticello will be buzzing about that whore when Ardeth reads my letter. If Freddie thinks he can ignore me and the store and play nursemaid to that Irishman while leaving me alone most of the day and night, he's got another think coming. I'll fix the whole lot of 'em. I just wish I could see that Cherie's face when she learns her secret's out. I just wish I could.

She poured the dark syrup candy on the buttered pan and set it beside the pralines and lemon drops. All of a sudden the smile turned to a grimace when she remembered little Delia's delight when she or Freddie gave her a piece of candy. Shaking her head to clear the image of the beautiful, happy child she said aloud, "Serves 'em all right, taking my Freddie away from me. Serves 'em right!"

****

The curtains Juanita and Rose were hanging on the front windows of their new shop were white polished cotton with turquoise and rose fleur-de-lis scattered throughout. Rose had added deep ruffles of the rose and turquoise on the bottom and covered the channel back chairs in the waiting room with the same fabric. Big paper roses were placed in tall china vases beside the French doors that led to the back room. Juanita had found the vases and fabric on her first buying trip in Savannah. It was so much easier shopping there. Why, she was in the warehouse shopping after just an overnight on the train.

They'd been in Monticello for almost a month. By now she knew she was indeed pregnant and still wondered why...why now of all times. She had been very upset at first, but Rose, dear warm Rose, had been so excited and happy for her that Juanita soon relaxed and accepted the inevitable. Her main concern was whether she should write to Conner to tell him. She decided not to. What good would it do, she reasoned. He'd not even care. After much deliberation, she decided to tell Harrison, and he, like Rose, was delighted.

"I don't understand you two. I really don't. Why, you'd think that I was the Queen of Sheba the way you're carrying on." Then she'd get that faraway look, and they knew she was thinking of Conner - the old Conner. She remembered his wide, crooked grin when she told him about Delia. He had changed so much - couldn't do enough for her and waited on her hand and foot. She'd never seen such a change come over a person. And Maeve, who Juanita thought would be upset when she found out, especially since she and Conner weren't married, got to her writing desk soon as she could to write Vincent the news. She was almost as solicitous toward her as Conner.

Those Irish are a peculiar lot, she thought. They surely do have a thing about children and family. She'd never seen a closer relationship between two people than Conner's and Maeve's. At first she had resented it, but as she got to know Maeve better and was told about their life in Ireland during the famine, the miserable trip on the overcrowded bark to America and how they were shunned when they got to Macon, except by the other Irish Catholics, she began to understand, at least a little. Juanita understood survival. But she'd never understand Conner's deep depression and hell-bent decision to destroy himself when Maeve died in the fire...never!

Juanita knew how anxious Harrison was to pay a return visit to Fairlea, so she suggested that they go straight there and then stop by the Rease property on their way back to town. They had been so busy for the past month getting the shop remodeled that they truly hadn't found the time to look at it again before making a decision about buying it.

Seth and Delia had been enrolled in school, and Millie had given Juanita good room rates, because they had not been able to find a house to rent. Millie had noticed that there had been no letters or telegrams from Juanita's husband and wondered what the matter was. She finally got up enough nerve to ask, and Juanita replied, "Oh, Mr. O'Farrell is not a writing man, Mrs. Bailey. I write him often though. He's always concerned about Delia's and my welfare. When his work is completed in Kissimmee, he'll let us know. It shouldn't be much longer. I would like to find a place for us before he joins us. He's also not one for a mess, likes everything around him orderly, you know. That's why I'm anxious to take another look at the Rease property. Harrison'll take us by there on our way back to town this afternoon."

But Millie continued with her concern, especially since Boyle Coleman had started hanging around the hotel so much. Even Buford had commented on it. "Seems to me that Boyle isn't as interested in our checker games as he is in that pretty little O'Farrell lady. Don't suppose that he and Ardeth are having trouble, do ya, Hon?"

It wasn't like Buford to pick up on anything like that.

She put her crocheting down in her lap and responded, "Well, mister, he'll have himself one mighty hard time getting around Mr. O'Farrell's man Harrison. He watches her and Delia like a hawk, he does. But you know, I was wondering the very same thing about him and Ardeth. She's gotten so uppity since she became president of the Sunday school that you'd think she was the one with the college education and not the Smiths' dirt-poor youngun."

Buford squinted at her. "You never did like Ardeth, did you Millie? I mean, I don't think I ever heard you say a kind word about..."

"And just what kind word could I say? I'd be willing to bet that she even gave her favors to Raymond and Floyd - I'd be willing to..."

"Now, you don't have one shred of evidence on that..."

"And how'd you be knowing that, Mr. Bailey? How?"

"I'm their daddy, and I do believe I'd a found out about it if there was any truth to it."

"Well, you can take up for her if you want to, but it'd serve her right if Boyle got the wandering eye. He's a wonderful man, and she's just not good enough for him and you know it!"

Boyle had begun working late almost every night at the jail since Juanita's arrival. In the past he'd helped Professor Hamilton with the boys' cornet band at the school and coached the baseball team, but he'd begged off lately, saying how busy he was with all that paperwork at the jail. His every waking minute was zeroed in on but one thing - how he could get to Juanita. He knew he'd have to get rid of Harrison, so he plotted and planned. If he could just arrange it so it looked like Harrison was somehow responsible for Ardeth's early demise, then that would be the ideal solution. He told Ardeth that his paper work had tripled since Simpkins had become sheriff. She could tell by his clothing that he'd not been visiting any of his whores, not even that

Cherie who was passing herself off as a married woman, and she had the letter - the letter to prove it. When the time was right she'd make sure that the entire town knew about that lying little blond whore - maybe on the very day of the opening of her fancy shop. And on Ardeth plotted.

****

Fred Saunders was in a quandary. When the letter arrived from the priest and Conner regressed to going back to his old room, curling up on his bed, facing the wall and ceasing to talk, Fred knew that he had to do something desperate. But what? Finally, he gave in to his desires. Taking a sharp knife he lifted the wax seal on Conner's letter. He read:

My dear Conner,
It is with deep regret that I read Harrison's letter of this summer past, telling me of your continued grief at the loss of our beautiful Maeve. But, my dear boy, she is as she was on this earth, surrounded by beauty and a host of angels to guide her and, I'm sure, completely happy while awaiting our arrival.

Fred put the letter on the table. No wonder Conner didn't want to read this. It's all about his sister. But he continued reading: *As you can see by the return address, I am no longer in New Orleans. My health has disintegrated in the past few years, and the bishop approved my move to St. Augustine, where as you know it's much warmer. At present I'm staying with my good friend, Fr. William Kenny, but will soon join Bishop John Moore's staff in St. Augustine. I'll be assisting at St. Monica's, our dear Maeve's church, in Palatka a few days a week or as my health allows.*

I do hope that this letter finds you much improved and that you've accepted the Almighty's will. He knows what is best for us, my son. I'll stay in touch, and if you're up to traveling, please come see me in St. Augustine or Palatka. It would give us both added strength to be together.

Don't you see the pattern, Conner? This is as Maeve would have wanted it, for us to be near each other.

May our Almighty Father bless you. I remain your devoted friend,
Vincent

Fred re-sealed the letter, got up from the kitchen chair, scraping it on the wooden floor, walked straight to Conner's room and did not bother to knock. "Mr. O'Farrell, I want you to join me on the porch for your morning sunbath," he said forcefully.

Conner did not stir. "Here, sir, I'll help you up, and if you don't mind I'll read you your letter."

Still no response. Fred continued. "There might be something important in it."

At last Conner spoke. "None of the goddamned priest's business! Why can't he leave her alone?"

"Mr. O'Farrell, don't fight me now. Doc said every day - every day you're to get some sun."

"Get your hands off me, Saunders. That goddamned doctor doesn't know what he's talking about!"

Fred was smiling. He's coming around now. Getting his old spunk back. He didn't drag Conner exactly, but he did strongly assist him. Conner squinted in the bright sunlight, plopped himself on the rocker and lowered his head. Fred sat in front of him, opened the letter and watched Conner's reaction as he read. He interrupted him only once. "Harrison's always been a traitor. Thinks he's got to be bossing me every step of the way..."

"Mr. O'Farrell, as soon as the doc says you're strong enough, I'd be happy to go with you to St. Augustine or Palatka. I've got cousins there who I haven't seen in a long time. About time I took a few days off. Doris can mind the store."

Conner didn't protest. Fred pulled his chair alongside Conner's and began rocking and whistling *When Johnnie Comes Marching Home.* Out of the corner of his eye he noticed Conner's foot keeping time. He smiled. He looked across the street toward the store and could see Doris peeking around the curtains. What's she up to, he wondered. Hasn't given me a speck of grief in over a week. She's up to something. Not like her to be happy. Hell, she's even been humming and singing lately. Not like her at all.

****

The big day arrived. The new sign had finally arrived on the train from Thomasville. Juanita and Rose had been so upset that it had been delayed. They'd expected it for over a week. After school every afternoon they'd sent Seth and Delia to the depot to check on it. It was perfect! When Seth slipped the pasteboard from around it, Juanita was afraid he'd let the knife slip and damage it. Harrison helped him remove the last piece, and they all exclaimed, "It's beautiful!" *Cherie's House Of Fashion. Juanita J. O'Farrell, proprietor - Rose Shorter, assistant - discriminating fashions for women and children - Jefferson Street, Monticello, Florida.*

Little did they know what this day would shatter their happiness. It came early in the morning even before they opened their doors for business. Invitations had been sent to all the prominent people in Thomasville, Tallahassee and the surrounding towns of Lloyd, Capps, Aucilla, Waukeenah and Lamont. The *Constitution* carried a long article about Juanita and her apprenticeship with Maeve and her shop in Kissimmee. Excitement was high at the Madden House. Every room was filled, and Millie and Buford had planned an afternoon reception in honor of the opening. The Monticello Cornet Band was to play, and Mayor Denham was scheduled to cut the ribbon. The red, white and blue bunting rippled in the soft morning breeze on each side of the newly hung sign.

Boyle Coleman was decked out in his finest suit, rich brown gabardine. It was seven o'clock. Ardeth called after him, "The children and I'll be down for the ceremony about nine, Boyle." He, unsuspecting, left. He still hadn't come up with a plan regarding Harrison and Ardeth, but Juanita had seemed to warm up to him, so perhaps the urgency wasn't as necessary as he had thought. Buford and Millie had both exclaimed at the lack of correspondence from Mr. O'Farrell in Kissimmee, so perhaps things weren't as Miss Cherie would lead you to believe.

Smith came running hard toward Boyle, yelling his name. "Good Lord, Smith, what's happened?"

"Just came over the telegraph, Marshal. Trib Henry escaped the work camp and was holed up at Miccosukee Sinks but got away." He continued breathlessly. "Frank Bond caught him running away from his store, where he'd set it afire, but since Frank ran off without his gun and Trib somehow got hold of a Winchester rifle, he couldn't stop him. You know, over in Lloyd, Marshal. Frank's got Gorman, Lee and Bryan after him. You want that Tulley and me should ride over to bring him in? They say he's riding over this way, right towards Monticello!"

Boyle didn't take much time to respond. "Well, if he's coming this way, then he's headed for Barlows' place. He sure has a hankering for that black woman." Boyle saw Harrison walking toward Cherie's. "I'll join you soon as I deputize some more men, Smith. If there is a lower down skunk than Trib Henry, I've not met him. God! Even shot Rooster Burns cold dead!"

Smith turned toward the jail, and Boyle hurriedly followed Harrison down Jefferson Street. Here's my answer. I'll use him as bait. "Harrison," he called. "Wait up."

Harrison slowed down. I don't like the sound of this man. He's been just too friendly lately. I've been waiting for over a month for him to make his move and this might be it. Even Juanita's let down her guard, but maybe it's her condition that's caused her to mellow. He's methodical and cunning. I wish he were stupid.

"Yessuh, Mister Marshal. What could Ah be heppin' ya wid?"

Boyle wanted to respond with just what he thought. Son-of-a-bitch - putting on that darky talk. Doesn't even suspect that I've been overhearing him, listening right outside the shop window. Speaks like a goddamn Harvard professor. Goddamn surly nigger! "Harrison, Smith just brought word that Trib Henry escaped the work camp and was holed up at Miccosukee Sinks near Lloyd but got away, but not before burning down a building. Smith and Tulley are riding out to head 'em off but I need some more men. Consider yourself deputized, and I'll get Buford and Alfred Knopp - he's always in his store before light. Don't want anything to spoil Mrs. O'Farrell's shindig, now do we?"

"Nawsuh, we sho don', suh."

"Buford's got an extra horse and I'll get some rifles from the jail."

Harrison was suspicious. Got no reason in this world to deputize me what with all these white men around."

"I'se not too good wid a gun, Mistuh Marshal. Mostly cooked Mistuh Conner's mess durin' de Wah."

"No matter. Trib just needs to see lots of men surrounding him. Probably give up peaceful then."

Who the hell does he think he's talking to. I can read, and that Trib Henry's robbed and killed more than even R.J. Skinner's gang. Just because he and his gang's been captured every time they've escaped doesn't mean that he hasn't still got friends all around these parts supplying him with horses and guns. He's got another reason for wanting me with him, and I don't like it one little bit. "Ah bes' go tell Miss Cherie wheah Ah be a-going..."

"Oh, I'll tell her, Harrison. Want to get Buford and that extra horse anyway. I'll meet you at the jail," and he moved swiftly, not like a big man at all. Harrison suspiciously watched, then turned, crossed the street and slowly walked toward the jail. Where are you when I need you Conner O'Farrell? Probably got yourself back together and in the midst of a hot game on the St. Johns. I certainly hope so, my friend. He got all mellow.

Ardeth placed the letter in her best navy blue handbag. She pulled on her gloves, adjusted her straw hat, smoothed out her navy blue skirt and confidently went out the screened porch on to Walnut Street. She had sent the children on ahead. Franklin played lead cornet in the band, and Marylee and Josephine were marching with the church's youth group. Marylee had been chosen to carry their Sunday school banner and was fidgeting so nervously that Ardeth asked her to go to Mrs. Baker's house, where all the ladies of the Sunday school were gathered, and to tell them to await her mother.

Ardeth had planned everything to the last detail. She'd pretend that she had been so upset on discovering Cherie was an unwed mother, deceiving them all with her lies, that she had prayed and prayed for guidance, and at last had been given her answer. She'd had a visitation, an apparition, you might say, in the middle of the night. Oh my, it had been so scary! It had instructed her in her duty to her fellow church women and all the good women of Monticello. The imposter must be exposed, it said, and sent from their good Christian community in disgrace and instructed never to return.

She quickened her pace. At Lucile Baker's she rapped on the door. There was no response. "Lucile, it's me, Ardeth." She heard nothing, not even the usual chatter. She opened the porch door and tried the front door. It was locked. "Lucile, where on earth are you? It's Ardeth." Still no answer. "Where are the children?" she asked out loud as she peered down Jefferson St. Where are the Jefferson Rifles? I know they're going to perform. They've been strutting ever since they bested the Jacksonville Gun Club. She also became aware that there were no buggies on the street and no one meandering around. Something's up! I'll go to Ovieda's, she'll know what's going on. She checked her lapel watch - 8:30 - Jefferson Street should be teeming with people and buggies. Maybe I should go by the jail. No, I don't want to see Boyle. Can't stand to even look at him anymore.

"Seth, it's going on eight o'clock. You and Delia go on over to Mrs. Parkhill's." Juanita was putting the finishing touches on her hair. "Now mind your manners, you hear? And Seth, do see that she doesn't get dirty playing croquet, would you? Rose and I'll be over to get you this evening after the party. Delia Rose O'Farrell! Did you hear what I said?" Juanita, exasperated, turned toward Rose, "Rose, would you be a dear and go with them? Why am I so antsy? Grief! I hope I don't throw up!" Rose's concern was ever present, just like an old setting hen, Juanita had thought more than once.

"Mrs. Parkhill's colored boy Jacob will watch over them, Juanita. Now you know how dependable he's been. Too bad his ma has such a bad reputation, but Ovieda Parkhill is as good a Christian woman as I've ever known." Rose called over her shoulder as she left, "I'll be back directly. Do you want me to do anything while I'm out? Did you remember to order the tea sandwiches from Mr. Budd's?"

"Why, Rose Shorter, I believe you're anxious about our opening. I'm not! Truly, I'm not! It's like play acting. It's just like the performance by the Monticello Amateur Club at Carroll Hall the other night. Just play acting." Juanita got up from the dressing table and embraced Rose. "And just think, Rose, when Mr. Perkins completes the opera house, then we'll really see some wonderful performances here. Imagine!"

Juanita sadly remembered how excited she'd been when she opened her tightrope act over ten years ago. She wondered if anything would ever again be as thrilling. Having Delia and worrying about Conner have really taken their toll, she realized. She wished she could be carefree again like she was with R.J. and even Etienne. She wished she could find time to read again. Oh, how she missed it. Heavens, she hadn't read a thing since Poe's *Annabelle Lee*, that Rose had given her. She sat down and with her head in her hands wondered why things couldn't stay the same and why she didn't like the new Juanita, so proper and business-like. I don't like me at all. This should be a happy day, she thought, but it's not. She went down the stairs slowly, and Millie came rushing toward her.

"Mrs. O'Farrell, did you hear? Did you hear that Trib Henry escaped the work camp and burned down a store in Lloyd and is headed this way? Boyle came and got Buford and your man Harrison, and they're after him," and with that she sat down hard.

"When did you hear all this? Does Rose know? And why, pray tell, did he take Harrison? Why Harrison?"

"I'm sure I don't know, but take him he did. Even borrowed one of Buford's horses for him to ride. They think that Trib's headed for that colored woman's place. You know, the one he'd taken up with, that Barlow woman, you know, Jacob's ma. Poor thing, he's such a nice colored boy and to have a no-account ma like that..."

"Good Lord! That boy's taking care of Delia and Seth over at Parkhills'!" Juanita was out that door and dashing down the deserted street before Millie could stop her. "If he touches just one hair on Delia's head I'll...I'll.."

****

After the train pulled up at the Palatka station, Fred Saunders and Conner O'Farrell were almost the last to get off. Conner had not been back to Palatka since Maeve's funeral Mass and the subsequent burial at the Westview cemetery, because there was no Catholic cemetery near by. He would not even say her name, and finally those around him stopped saying her name in his presence. He and Fred walked the four blocks to St. Monica's, a small frame church in the heart of town. Fred had telegraphed Fr. Haut of their impending visit and the day and time of their arrival, but he was not at the depot. Perhaps the fact that he was not well had prevented his meeting them, he thought. As he and a reluctant Conner climbed the steps of St. Monica's, the door suddenly opened, and a frail, stooped man wearing a big smile extended his arms to envelope Conner, who, like a small child, nuzzled the priest's shoulder. Fred noticed that Fr. Haut had been a very handsome man, and underneath his white, curly hair were fine features and intelligent eyes shining through eyeglasses. Although he was now stooped, Fred was aware that he had once been a tall man. Fred stood aside and looked away. They did not speak.

Fr. Haut finally broke the silence. "We've grown old, my boy."

"Aye, and that we have, Vincent."

Fred took the opportunity to excuse himself, stating that he wanted to return to the depot to see to their bags and would get them settled in at the Putnam House. He couldn't believe it when Conner had said that it was only $3.00 a day. Doris would have had a fit if she knew how much he was spending on this trip. Grief! Three dollars would feed them like kings for an entire week.

He took the mule-drawn railway to Putnam House, passing the orange trees that lined the street. Palatka was certainly different from Kissimmee. While the desk clerk was registering them, Fred picked up the *Palatka Times* and whistled out loud when he read about the new waterworks and the fire hydrants. He read that Putnam County now had over 11,000 people. The clerk noticed his reaction and asked if this was his first visit to Palatka. Fred said that it was and that it was indeed the largest town he'd ever been in. "We now have over 450 residents in the Palatka Heights area alone, and the new fire hydrants..."

"I'm glad to see that. My friend's sister was killed in that big fire in '84."

When the clerk asked the name of the deceased and Fred told him, he exclaimed, "Why, I knew Miss O'Farrell ever since she moved here from New Orleans." He sort of laughed and continued, "My mother always wanted me to ask her out, but I had the feeling that she was somehow taken, spoken for, you understand."

"I wouldn't be knowing about that. My friend never speaks about her. It still hurts him to think of it, you know."

Fred was met by laughter upon his return to the rectory. Fr. Haut and Conner were on the veranda soaking up the late morning sun, sipping tea and visiting. They were actually talking about Maeve. He was amazed at how relaxed Conner appeared. He was smiling and remembering. "Vincent, do you remember the expression on Maeve's face when I opened my valise and presented her with the money I'd earned at Ridgeland Manor, enough to start her own shop? Remember?" He rushed on excitedly. "And Mum! She sat down so hard that her chair skittered out from under her, and when she looked up from the floor we were all open-mouthed, laughing. She, being Mum, red-faced with embarrassment, exclaimed in her most ferocious voice, `Now why're ya howling like a bunch of banshees, I'd like to be knowing?' And remember how Maeve counted and recounted the money..."

Vincent Haut indeed remembered. He remembered everything about his Maeve. Those memories and his love of the Father were his life's blood. When he saw how Fred was looking at Conner, he realized that the lad had more than one friend. He could now add Mr. Saunders. Vincent sighed and relaxed in the wicker chair, his white head leaned back against the soft cushion and he finally felt at peace. Now maybe I can join my Maeve. Her boyo is on the mend, and perhaps he'll go to the girl Juanita and his lassie. I'll speak to Mr Saunders about the possibility before they return to Kissimmee.

Vincent joined Conner and Fred for dinner at two o'clock at the Putnam House dining hall. When Fred saw the menu he was hesitant. He'd never seen anything like it, not in all his forty three-years. He would have felt out of place had Conner not been there. Conner's white linen suit was much too large, since he'd lost so much weight, but he still turned heads when they entered the spacious room. His black hair was now grey at the temples, but that only added to his demeanor. There must have been over a hundred people dining. Fred's only good suit was not well tailored, he knew, but Doris had kept it covered in the trunk, and he wore it only on Sundays and at funerals and the like.

When the waiter approached their table, Vincent and Fred were making light conversation. Fred was hoping that Conner would order first, and Conner, sensing Fred's apprehension, did just that. "Doubt that you'll want the broiled quail on toast, Fred. Get enough of that in Kissimmee, don't you?"

When Conner called him Fred instead of Saunders, Fred felt warm all over. He laughed a little, "That's for sure a fact,..uh...Conner."

Conner looked up from the menu, his brow was raised, he smiled warmly and continued, "Think I'll have the breast of veal with tomato sauce. I'll start with consomme Julienne." He clicked his fingers. A waiter in an impeccable, starched uniform was there immediately. "What is the Macaroni Milanaise? I'm sure it's Italian."

"Yessuh, it got tomatoes 'n bell peppers 'n onions 'n lots o' spices."

"Gentlemen," Conner continued, "Are you ready to order? Vincent, you begin."

"Think I'd like the baked pompano with port wine sauce - yes, and I'll start with the consomme, too, and boiled sweet potatoes and new green peas. I'll wait until later to order dessert."

"Would you lak ta order da wine, suh?" the waiter addressed Conner.

"I'll wait until Mr. Saunders decides on his entree. Fred, have you decided? The spring lamb with mint sauce looks good."

"Yes, that does look good." He'd never tasted lamb in his life but had grown up with mint in his tea, and his ma used to put a sprig in her ambrosia - said it gave it a sit-up taste. "Yes, I'll have the lamb and mashed potatoes and peas..."

Conner intervened. "You might enjoy the Cabinet Pudding with brandy sauce, Fred. Very tasty, I'm told. If it's good enough for the White House, it should be good enough for us Floridians, huh?"

"That it should," Fred responded and felt a warm glow as he relaxed.

"Now for the wine. Would you like Mumm's extra dry or the Haute Sauterne Rising, gentlemen?" Conner inquired.

Vincent said that they'd bow to his expert taste. He selected the sauterne. "Then we'll have our cognac and cigars on the verandah afterwards."

Fred kept thinking, a good thing Doris can't see me. She'd have some kinda fit. He'd never had such a day. The wine released his inhibitions, and he joined in the light conversation. Vincent could see that he was a sensitive man, a smart man, with not much education, but considering that he'd grown up in the wilderness, he held his own with the two of them.

They retired to the veranda, where Conner and Fred began discussing Kissimmee's growing problems: the fact that they still didn't have electric lights, that the city council seemed more interested in having an opera house than in lighting the streets, that they now had over a thousand residents, that John Watson was doing a fine job of representing them in the legislature, the first Episcopal Church was being built on the corner of Mitchell and Sproule Streets, and they finally had a newspaper, *The Kissimmee Leader.* Conner explained to Vincent that his old boss Disston had signed another contract with the state and had started canal operations in the lake chain east of Lake Tohopekaliga. He had built a brick sugar mill and warehouse south of East Lake Tohopekaliga on the new canal's bank. He also built a spur connecting the narrow gauge *Kissimmee to Narcoosee Railroad* to the mill but still sent the raw sugar to Savannah for refining.

"He's done a lot for our area. He now employs between three and four hundred workers on his plantation, many of them Italians who come from Tampa by train. They finally got around to naming the lake area - it's now called Sunny Side - and he named the plantation St. Cloud for the city in Minnesota. It's a lovely name, isn't it?"

Fred interjected, "And we finally got us a public school. Took us long enough. A small, four-room frame building over on Church St., and Mr. Towne is the principal. That Miss Alice Brown from up in Pennsylvania teaches the primary grades, and is she a looker!"

Conner raised his brow, "Why, Fred, didn't take you for a wandering man." He laughed at Fred's expression, and Fred could tell he was having sport with him. Fred continued, "Got us another hotel, too, the Osceola Hotel, and lots of new people moved down from Georgia and Kentucky."

Fred seemed to have had his say, he sat back, relaxed and listened to Conner and Vincent. Conner was animated and, oh, so eloquent. The ladies and gentlemen on the veranda were eavesdropping, engrossed in his tales of his life on the Mississippi and the St. John. He won't be in Kissimmee much longer, Fred thought, as he watched him. I can tell by that far away look in his eyes. He's hankering for Miss Cherie and little Delia. The priest knows it, too.

A gentleman who was having a brandy with a group of businessmen next to Fred arose, tipped his hat to Fred and asked, "Would you like to see today's paper? It seems that wily Trib Henry has escaped another work camp up in Monticello." He shook his head in disbelief. When he said Monticello, Conner and Vincent both stopped talking. Fred thanked the man for the paper, and when he saw the headlines, quit reading and handed the paper to Conner, who was obviously anxious.

"TERRIBLE TRIB HAS TRIPPED THEM AGAIN" Just over the wire came this disconcerting news: The slippery gang leader, Trib Henry, has again escaped a work camp outside Lloyd, Florida, about ten miles southwest of Monticello. To show his total disdain for the law he purposefully burned down Frank Bond's new store, and before Bond could stop him he escaped into the area of Miccosukee Sinks while brandishing a Winchester. The authorities in Monticello were alerted and with ten deputized men surrounded the house of Pearl Barlow, the Negress Henry had taken up with on previous occasions. Marshal Boyle Coleman of Monticello reported heavy gunfire from her premises and sent in a deputized colored man named Harrison to check on it. The man has not been seen since, and it is presumed that he was either captured or is an accomplice of Trib Henry. It is a well known fact that Henry's gang members are scattered in that section of the state and the colored man, Harrison, is new to the area. Marshal Coleman said that he'd been under suspicion for some time concerning other matters but that he thought...

Conner dropped the paper on the table. He was ashen.

"Conner!" Fred and Vincent exclaimed at the same time.

****

Harrison could see Pearl Barlow's small house through the overgrown weeds. The dog fennel was window high. There was no obvious activity. Now why'd Coleman bring me along? he questioned over and over. He's a slick one. God! I wish Conner were here. Buford's horse,

Colonel, chestnut and sleek, felt good under him. He had to admit that the weight of the Winchester did, too. They'd pulled up beneath a large sweetgum about a quarter of a mile from the old Stedham place, where Pearl lived. The main house had burned down years ago and no one had claimed it. She and her boy Jacob just moved into the little house that was once servants quarters and made themselves at home. She had at one time done housework for some of the town's ladies, but when Trib took up with her (her brother Dyke had ridden with Trib for going on ten years) she said that she didn't need to work for any white women.

The Parkhills had hired Jacob when he wasn't much more than a boy, seven or eight. He was bright and handsome and well liked by the townspeople. Their only fault with him was his complete devotion to his no-good mama. He walked the five miles to and from town every morning and night, never staying over even though Ovieda and Ed Parkhill had fixed up a room off the tool shed for him. He still shunned it with, "I best be gettin' on home to my mama."

Seth was so upset with Delia that he couldn't control himself. "Now you know what your Ma is goin' to say, Delia Rose. You rightly know what!" But Delia continued to twirl 'round and 'round on the corn sack swing. It wasn't until Jacob came down the back steps, and hearing and seeing all the commotion that he decided that he'd better intervene.

"Miss Delia, yore ma ast me ta mind you and mistah Seth and ta see dat ya don' get yore clothes dirty, now din she?" Laughing loudly, Delia continued whirling around, not paying a bit of attention to the two of them. Jacob, stern-faced and wearing his most authoritative expression, fists planted firmly on each side of his too short trousers, decided that he wasn't going to accept any more of Miss Delia O'Farrell's shenanigans. After all, he, Jacob Barlow, was in charge. He was only two years older than Seth and since Seth's arrival in Monticello two months earlier, they had become friends. The Parkhills' house was two blocks from Cherie's, and after his chores were all done he, Seth and Harrison quite often played hit and run baseball in the Parkhills' field out back. It got so that there'd been a game going most afternoons for the last few weeks. He was the only colored boy, but that didn't matter to Seth or the others.

Jacob had begun arriving home later and later, and his ma didn't take to that. After he went by Mr. Slocum's for the day's groceries, then down by Cricket Creek to get her shine from Pope, it'd be mostly dark when he got home. Seemed to him his ma wasn't feeling any too good of late. She'd just about bite his head off when he got home. At least he didn't have to put up with that Trib Henry. He was glad and hoped they'd be able to keep him on the work gang this time. Didn't like that one at all. He'd hit him only a few times, but seemed that when he was around all Jacob was allowed to do was go to Cricket Creek for shine, then back to the creek to fish. They told him not to show his ugly face 'til after dark, and that he'd better bring home some good vittles. So when Trib was around, Pope's wife Twila always had a Dutch oven of rabbit or squirrel stew or something for him to take back home. Jacob never figured out how they knew when Trib was at his ma's, 'cause it was supposed to be a secret. But that Twila sure did make a good stew and always tucked in a few biscuits for the cane syrup Miss Parkhill gave him.

Delia sat on the Parkhills' back steps, chin cupped in her small hands and pouted. Thinks he can boss me around. Both of 'em think they can boss me around. Boss! Boss! All day long. I'll be glad when all the goings on are over at the shop, I will. She was startled by the sound of horses. Hopping up and running around to the front of the house she saw a bunch of riders and Seth and Jacob holding on to Buford's horse. Amidst all the commotion she heard Trib Henry's name and something about burning down a store, and try as she did, she couldn't understand what it was all about.

Mr. Parkhill came running down the front steps with Mrs. Parkhill right on his heels telling him to be careful. It was then that Delia saw Harrison riding down York St. carrying a rifle in his hand with the marshal right beside him. She was so excited! She tugged on Seth's shirt sleeve and he jumped almost a mile. "What the...!"

"Delia Rose, you come back here, young lady," Mrs. Parkhill called, and before Delia could turn around, she was beside her pulling hard on her arm exclaiming, "You want to get yourself trampled? For heaven's sake, child, they're riding off to capture Trib Henry!" Under her breath she said, "Poor Jacob, poor thing," and pulled Delia up the steps and into the house.

Delia had no idea what capturing Trib Henry had to do with Jacob and really didn't care. She was still mad at him for bossing her around. All she could think was, guess now we can't play croquet. Never get to do a blasted thing I wanta. Not ever! Then Mrs. Parkhill told her to sit and to stay put until she told her to move. She ran all over the house pulling the curtains closed and locking the doors and yelling at

Mooney to get the other rifles out of the closet, and, oh my, she was excited. Delia heard pounding on the front door, but she had been told to stay put and didn't attempt to answer it. Mrs. Parkhill was so put out with her that she lambasted her again. "But you told me to stay put, so that's just what I'm doing," she cried.

"Who's there?" Mrs. Parkhill asked just above a whisper.

"It's me, Seth, and Jacob. We want in."

Mrs. Parkhill pulled the curtains back just a little to make sure. You'd think that she could tell it's Seth by his voice, Delia thought. Boy, she's sure scared of something. Things might not be too dull after all, if I don't hafta sit all the blasted day long on this old chair.

"So there you are. We been looking all over creation for you. Why'd you just run off, Delia Rose? Why?"

"Run off! I didn't run off. Mrs. Parkhill dragged me in here and made me sit down and told me not to move. I never had so many bosses...!" and she pursed her lips and began swinging her long legs, almost tipping over the chair.

"You could'a told a body where you were going, ya know!" and with that said he sat down on the stairs. Jacob followed Mrs. Parkhill into the kitchen, and Mooney and the two of them entered into a deep conversation. Delia heard words like *posse* and *hanging* and did Mooney say *yore ma* - whose ma? She strained but couldn't hear, and when Jacob came into the parlor, he sure looked worried.

"What's the matter, Jacob? What's all the fuss about?" she inquired.

"It's not for yore young ears, Delia Rose. Not for you to hear." He went over to Seth and whispered something to him, and, boy, did that make her mad. They treat me like a big dumb old baby. Just like one. When Seth followed Jacob outside, he looked just as worried as Jacob and called over his shoulder, "You lock the door behind us, Delia. Now mind you, do what I tell you."

"Lock the door behind us - boss - boss - boss!" she called after him. She opened the door a crack and saw them as they hugged the side of the dirt road looking right then quickly left. She slipped out the door and followed them.

Boyle Coleman was huddled with the posse; only Harrison was off to the side. "Any you men know anything about Miss Cherie's colored man? I mean how long's he been with her?"

Buford spoke up. "He told Millie that he cooked her husband's mess in the War and said for a fact that old Samuel owned him over at Fairlea 'fore the blight and fever hit and then sold him along with his ma to a man in Louisiana."

"But do you know if any of it is true, Buford?" Boyle asked.

Ed Parkhill spoke up, "Seems to me that it could all be made up. I mean, have you seen any husband? Millie said she hasn't even had a letter from him. Could it be that they showed up in Monticello to help Trib escape the work camp? Now, you know Dyke Barlow's been riding with him for a good ten years, and he's black as the ace of spades. Maybe him and this man who calls himself Harrison are in cahoots." He let that sink in.

Boyle was warming to the task at hand. "Yes, that's the very reason I insisted on him riding with us. But I don't for a minute believe that Miss Cherie knows if what he's saying is a lie, a fine upstanding woman like she is." He let that sink in then continued. "I'm going to send Harrison in there, and if Trib's already there and doesn't fire on Harrison, then you'll know for sure that they're in cahoots. And Trib's probably laughing his head off at us right now, thinking that we're too dumb to figure it out."

"Yeah," they all said in unison.

Seth and Jacob had completed their mission of alerting all the people in close-in Monticello about Trib's escape. No one thought that he'd be stupid enough to come into town, but then he did burn down Frank Bond's building in broad daylight, so no telling what that crazy man would do. Some of the Monticello Gun Club members who had planned to perform down Jefferson St. that day had stayed and were dispersed throughout the town keeping vigilance. Seth could see how anxious Jacob was and said, "I'm gonna warn mah Ma, Seth. Now Ah knows what folks thinks 'bout her, but she still mah Ma."

"I'm going with you!"

"No, you ain't. No tellin' what he'd do ta ya if'n he's dere lak dey says."

"But Jacob, maybe if we're together, we can get your ma out of the house so she won't get hurt..."

"Now, Ah'm not a goin' ta let ya get yaself kilt on mah account."

Seth could see that he was weakening. "Well, you're my friend and I know you'd do the same for me."

Jacob lowered his head and pretended to not hear him, but Seth followed close behind, and Jacob didn't tell him to leave. They didn't see Delia following, because she stayed in the shadows of the buildings. They hadn't given her a second thought since telling Juanita, who met them while they were on their rounds, that she was locked inside the Parkhills' house and wouldn't leave until Juanita sent for her.

When Jacob got to Cricket Creek, he decided that he'd stop to get his ma some shine - that always pleased her. But there was no one there, not Pope nor Twila nor even the dogs. He'd never been there when there was no one guarding the still. "This is sure 'nuff funny, Seth. There mus' be a mighty lot o trouble brewin' if'n Pope an' Twila ain't heah. Mighty lot!"

Delia was getting tired. She'd never in her life walked four long miles, and her new slippers were hurting her. Every bee in the whole world was buzzing around her head, and she was sweating and would have been crying but didn't want Seth to hear her. If she could just have figured out how to get home she'd have turned back. Looking around she saw nothing but a bunch of woods and couldn't even distinguish the path she'd just left.

When Seth and Jacob left the shack's porch and were no longer in sight, Delia wearily climbed up the worn steps, and, not having the strength to follow, decided to see if there was anyone home. Maybe they'd take her back to Monticello and her mama, she reasoned. She knocked on the door and no one answered. She lifted the iron latch and peeked inside. She was just so tired that when she saw the bed in the corner she crawled up on it and was sound asleep in no time.

****

"Now, Twila, I done told ya we ain't gonna get involved wid Trib this time. He ain't ever brought us nothin' but heartache, no matter that he's yore cousin."

Twila Thomas, never one for many words, gave her "Huruumph" sound, but Pope went on. He was used to her guttural sounds, and they no longer carried much weight. "I never minded ya keepin' him in shine, and I never minded ya givin' that woman and her boy shine and food. Now, did I ever say anythin' to ya about it?"

Finally, words visited Twila. "What could ya say? Neighbor helps neighbor, and 'sides he paid ya good fer it. Onliest money ya ever had Brother Pope!"

Pope Thomas knew he had now passed the high water mark and that there'd be hell to pay. When Twila called him Brother Pope, it was a sure sign. But she was right about one thing. The only time money was his was when Trib was in the area and in need of shine. Pope had been a circuit preacher for a few years but mostly got paid in food and lodging, and that's when he met Twila. Her ma and pa had him stay at their cabin over in Capps about five miles from his and Twila's spread on Cricket Creek when he was just a young man making his church rounds. They'd homesteaded their place back in the late seventies. Trib never went to Pearl's without stopping by their place to get his shine. Pope didn't much like the man, and it wasn't because he took up with a colored woman. It was just that he was downright mean. If he had let the truth in, he would have admitted to being afraid of him. He knew Twila was, at least she was a little bit scared. But she sure liked getting real money and would put up with Trib's meanness.

When Trib rode up this time, his poor horse lathered and near about ridden to death, she let her fear show. "What ya mean ya burned down Frank Bond's store? Good grief, Trib!"

He laughed hysterically, wiped the shine drooling from his dirty chin, and with beady eyes gave a full account of the incident. "God almighty, ya should a seen him runnin' out in his old yeller underdrawers, yellin' his head off. God, ya should a seen him!"

Twila whirled around and looked at Pope, her face full of fright. He'd never seen her like that. Finally, she asked, "What'd Frank ever do to ya, Trib? I mean, did he turn ya in or somethin'?"

"Hell, no. Never seen the bastard in ma life. Fancy store, brand new, with his name in big letters all across the front. Stupid bastard!" His eyes were getting wilder and wilder. Pope couldn't for the life of him think of what to say, but he needn't have concerned himself for Twila took care of it.

"Trib, ya rightly know that the law'll ride over to Pearl's fast as they can, now you know that."

"Hell, yeh. I'm countin' on 'em doin' jes that - right in my trap."

Twila and Pope looked at each other. "What trap?" she asked.

"Hell, you don't think that I'm gonna be there without some guns, do ya? Dyke and Strawman are on their way there right now, and with you two that'll give me six guns." He howled with laughter.

Pope found his tongue. "What ya mean with us two, Trib?"

"Jes what I done said, Brother Pope. Jes what I said. Ya don't think I've been keeping you in this shine business without ya havin' to pay back, now do ya?"

CHAPTER IV FOILED AGAIN

"Mistuh Marshal, suh, Ah don' think it's a good idea fer me to jes ride up to dat house. Dey don' know me an'll shoot me fer sure, suh."

"Now, Harrison, do you think that I'd send you in there if Trib Henry is there? Why, there is no way that he could have arrived from Miccosukee Sinks in that amount of time. He doesn't even have a horse, and it'll take him 'til late this afternoon to get here, that is, if he decides to pay Pearl a visit at all. He's certainly not stupid enough to come straight here knowing full well that we'll be checking her out," and on he droned.

Harrison rolled his eyes to the heavens. He knows darned good and well he's in there and that they'll blow my head off. God! Where are you, Conner O'Farrell? Where are you when you're needed?

Aloud, he said, "Well, Ah'll go warn dat woman dat he's a comin', suh, but Ah'm gonna hug close ta de high weeds so's not ta be too good a target."

Boyle shook his head that he understood and rejoined his men.

"When he gets about half way there, I want you to move in slowly, Buford, and circle around back to the west side, and, Ed, you take Harry and go around on the opposite side. Don't want them sneaking out the back door, now do we?"

He was getting excited. His shirt was soaked along his broad back and armpits. Well, I'll be rid of at least one of my obstacles. I'll have to think of something else for Ardeth though. Funny how things just played right into my hands. Would never have figured it to happen so easily. He smiled.

Harrison hadn't gone fifty feet when he ducked into the high brush. If he thinks I'm stupid enough to walk right up the lane, he's not as crafty as I thought. He went in about twenty five feet and headed straight for Monticello. From where Boyle and the rest were positioned they couldn't see him. It had never occurred to Boyle that he'd disobey his orders. Colored men took orders.

"Buford, start to circle now and take Barnes with you, and, Ed, you'd better do the same." He took a long breath and continued. "Just as I thought, gentlemen, Harrison's one of them. If Trib is in there he'd have blown his head off by now, if he didn't know him."

To himself he thought, they've caught him for sure by now, and I'll get to shoot the black bastard myself. He was salivating as he wiped the sweat from his forehead.

The front door suddenly opened and a barrage of fire seemed to come from every direction. Boyle hit the ground hard as did the others. Harrison could hear it from where he was and couldn't help but grin. He heard a rider and hit the high brush. He looked up and saw Jessup Gregory hauling it to town to get the story in the Monticello *Constitution*. Harrison looked longingly at the horse's rear and wished he still had Buford's. It was going to be a long, hot walk back to town.

He didn't see Seth and Jacob at first nor hear them, he was breathing so hard, but they heard him and burrowed in among the palmettos and thick brush. Seth could see him approach but didn't recognize him at first. He saw Jacob pick up a long stick and get ready to use it. "Harrison!" he called in the nick of time.

"What the world you two doing here?" but he knew even as he said it. Everyone in town knew how Jacob felt about his ma.

"Jacob, you're not going to your ma's. Now, I mean it! The marshal has about ten men, and they all have guns. If Trib knows what's good for him he'll give himself up, and your ma'll be just fine."

But Jacob knew she'd be full of shine and probably not even know what was going on. "But Harrison, I gotta go. I jes hafta."

He had given in to his fear, and Seth and Harrison had a hard time restraining him. "What are you going to do for her, boy? Listen to all that gunfire. What are you going to do, use that great big stick on them, huh?"

Jacob was now crying uncontrollably, his chest heaving. Seth began patting his sweat stained back and telling him that he understood but that Harrison was right, that maybe they should just go on to Twila and Pope's house to wait for the shooting to stop. Then they could go to the house to see his ma. Jacob thought on it, got up and followed them - they could hear the constant gunfire all the way there. They were only about a quarter of a mile from Pope's and Twila's place.

Ardeth Coleman practically raced to Ovieda Parkhill's just a few blocks down the street. There was still no commotion, and for the life of her she couldn't understand it. Supposed to be a fancy parade and goodness knows what all. Where are all the band members and the Sunday school class? Loudly she knocked, then called, but no answer did she get. Ovieda and Mooney had taken shelter in the back shed, the one that she and Ed had fixed up for Jacob. They had plenty of guns and ammunition, and as she sat crouched inside the dark room she thanked her Ed for having taught her how to handle a rifle. There were times in one's life when you had to cast aside your ladylike ways and take care of matters. If she had been honest, she would have admitted that she loved the excitement of it and had much rather be doing this than giving the big fancy party she'd planned.

Ardeth, totally flabbergasted by the turn of events, decided to go on over to Madden House. She didn't want to, but if anyone in the entire town would know what was happening, she knew that Millie and Buford would. She just hoped that she wouldn't run into that Cherie woman. Probably already in her fancy shop, she thought. But I'll fix her, and I'll fix her this very day. Thinks she can pull the wool over my eyes and over every other decent woman's in Monticello.

Her steps were determined. She didn't see the Monticello Rifle Club members behind the pillars and uncompleted walls of the St. Elmo Hotel, but they saw her. Denny whispered, "Miss. Ardeth sure is in a hurry. Maybe she's got news. You want me to go find out?"

"Not gonna know if you don't," Jim replied.

Denny got up slowly, raised his head high and informed the other men behind him that he was going to halt Miss. Ardeth. He called to her and she stopped dead, turned around and panted, "Denny Mattox, what in the dear Lord's name's going on around here? Where is everybody?"

"I was hoping you had word from the marshal, Miss. Ardeth."

"Word! Word about what, pray tell?"

"Word about Trib Henry busting loose from the work gang and maybe heading this way. Didn't the marshal..."

She screwed up her pasty face and gritted her teeth like she could've bitten clean through a wagon tongue. Denny knew then the marshal had neglected to inform his own wife. Everyone in the blooming town knew but the town marshal's wife. That was a good one. He could hardly wait to get back to the other club members to tell that one.

Ardeth stomped her foot, got red in the face, and Denny was afraid she'd have a fit right in the middle of downtown Monticello. But she finally spewed out, "And just where are the marshal's children, Denny Mattox? Could you at least tell me that?"

"I saw Franklin and the band head for the courthouse, and the Sunday school girls marched over to the Methodist church, Miss. Ardeth. Marylee and Josephine were with them."

"Well, I never...I never..." and she mumbled all the way down Washington St. to the Madden House, the letter forgotten for the moment. Forgot to even warn his own wife. I'll be the laughing stock of all Jefferson County, I will. "I'll get you, Boyle Coleman! I'll get you!" she said out loud.

When Ardeth finally got to Madden House, huffing and puffing, she addressed Virgie, who had been in the front room with the front door barricaded. "Let me in, for heaven's sake. You'd think that everyone in this entire town had lost his mind - everyone! Millie, it's me Ardeth. Let me in!"

"Miss Ardeth, Ma'am," Virgie said. "Let me hep ya off wid dis..."

"I don't need any help because I'm not going to be staying. Where is Millie? I mean this is ridiculous! Just because Boyle and most of the men have lost their minds, there's no need for the rest of us to follow suit."

Millie rushed into the front room. "Just what are you yelling about, Ardeth? You know what's going on just as much as the rest of us. Why, it's your husband who dragged our men all over creation looking for that outlaw, now isn't it?"

Ardeth plopped herself down on the love seat. "What..I..mean, Millie," she emphasized, "is why has this town gone crazy, locking all the buildings and pointing guns at you as you walk down Jefferson St.? Have you all gone crazy?"

That did it. Millie had been waiting to tell Ardeth off for years, and now seemed the perfect time. Bending from her ample waist, she put her contorted face close to Ardeth's and answered, "Well, Mrs. Coleman, I'll tell you whose lost his mind and gone crazy. That husband of yours, that's who. Taking most every grown man on a wild goose chase, if you ask me, ruining Mrs. O'Farrell's opening, the parade, my party and Ovieda's big shindig. Why, it's the first big affair she's planned since Miss Carrie up and died. Near about two years of mourning, she's done. Now you rightly know that, Mrs. Coleman." Millie straightened up, standing erect, queen-like, and said, "Now, if you'd please leave Madden House, Mrs. Coleman, so I can tend to my guests who came all the way down from Thomasville and Tallahassee and are very upset by the state of things, I'd be mightily grateful. Good day to you," and she turned around and marched off to the rear of the hotel. She hadn't bothered to tell Ardeth that she'd wired the folks early that morning that perhaps they'd best not come on account of that doggoned Trib Henry. She was out ten rooms' rent, she was. Spoiled the whole day. Doggone Boyle Coleman anyway. Ruined the whole blasted day. She couldn't figure him. He didn't usually overreact like that. Usually was a common-sense man, and on she fussed.

Ardeth left Madden House and marched herself straight to the courthouse to get Franklin and then to the church for Marylee and Josephine and then the six blocks home. She was planning her next step all the way. *I've vowed to not let this day go by without putting that riffraff Cherie in her place, I have. And do it I will. Soon as I get these three fed and settled in, I'm just going to pay a visit back to the church and fill Clarice Baker's ears. There won't be a lady in all of Monticello who'll have a thing to do with that woman.* Her excitement had lost some of its fervor, though, and after their main meal she decided to take a little rest as she did every afternoon. It was almost two o'clock when she awakened.

"Franklin, now you look after your sisters, you hear? I'll not be long, just going to the church for a short while. Josephine, now stop that sniffling. For heaven's sake! Marylee, what's wrong with the two of you?"

"But Mama, they said that Trib Henry might be heading this way..."

"Who said that? Who?"

"Why, Smith told us. He came back for more bullets and..." Franklin was getting into the drama of it.

"Smith Livingston doesn't know beans, Franklin Lee, not beans!"

"Then why's everybody in the whole town barricaded in the courthouse, Mama? Why?"

"You mean to tell me that Clarice Baker and the other ladies from the church have moved over to the courthouse with everyone else in this town?"

"Mr. Hollister said that him and Mr. McNaught was going to escort them right after dinner. He was afraid for them to be in the church without protection."

Ardeth couldn't believe it. It was the second time this day that her plans had been stifled. "Lily livers all of 'em! Spineless, they are. You three go to your rooms, do you hear? To your rooms, and if you're scared of your own shadows then crawl under your beds. I never - well, I never," and she sat and rocked in her and Boyle's bedroom and conjured up all the ways she was going to have her say about Cherie and how she'd show the letter to the ladies - her ladies. But she needed to be alone with them so she could tell them properly.

****

It was Sunday morning when Conner O'Farrell arrived in Monticello. He had left Palatka on the afternoon train immediately after having read about Harrison in the special edition of the Palatka paper. Fred Saunders had insisted that he lend him the money for the trip, and for once Conner wasn't too proud to accept it. "I'm not concerned, Mr. O'Farrell," Fred said, reverting back to the formal tone he had always used around Conner. "I know that you'll pay me back soon's you're able."

But how was he going to explain the lack of money to Doris? he wondered. It was like a light went off in his head. He decided that he'd tell her that he'd been robbed while in Palatka. Robber lifted his money right out of his pocket while he was walking to see his cousin, Morris. Took the silver money clip and all. Boy, she'd be angry - she'd given him the money clip for their tenth wedding anniversary. Whew! She'd be mad. He was loving every minute of it. Besting Doris had become very important to Fred - that and taking care of Conner.

"Did you see him, Virgie? I can't believe my eyes, so distinguished looking, just like I pictured he'd look, " Millie commented nervously rubbing her pudgy hands together.

"Yassum, Ah seed him, all right. Fine thing ta come ta town de very day after de Devil done sen' his wrath on us."

"Well, I don't care what they're all saying. I really don't. I'm sure Trib's long gone by now, probably all the way to Georgia. Spoiling our big day like he did and causing us all to worry so. I think that Boyle Coleman is making a big to do over it. The way they're carrying on you'd think Mrs. O'Farrell's colored man was in cahoots with that ne'er-do-well. Nice colored man like that. Trib's on his way to Georgia, I'd say."

She left the kitchen, stopped by the back door and called to Henry and Josephus, who were sitting inside the shed with the door open, swatting flies and not doing a lick of work. "You two think 'cause this is the Sabbath, you can play the lazy men, huh? Just because Mr. Buford's riding all over the country chasing robbers is no reason for you to be idle. Henry, I want you to clean up that side lot. Now, do you hear? If Trib Henry's crazy enough to ride up to the courthouse for all of Monticello to shoot at, then you can take to the shed. Now, Henry!"

She turned and mumbled something about him being shiftless and Virgie snickered. Miss Millie can sho 'nuff get ta dat one - sho 'nuff. But she be right. Dat fool man ain't about ta be ridin' up Jefferson St. wid dos trigger-happy boys hidin' 'round every building hereabouts, and she be right 'bout Harrison, too. Don' care what dat newspaper be sayin' 'bout him.

Millie had known the very minute she saw him who he was. Didn't know how she knew, she'd later relate over and over again, but know she did. She'd almost been tongue-tied when he walked up to the polished mahogany desk she and Buford had made up in Thomasville. And when he inquired in that delightful brogue of his whether or not she had a Mrs. O'Farrell staying with her, she had trouble finding her voice. "Would you be Mr. O'Farrell, sir?" She could see the devilish glint in his pale eyes. He removed his panama and replied formally, "That I am, Miss....??"

"Oh, I'm Mrs. Millie Bailey, Mr. O'Farrell." He took her hand and raised it to his lips, and she thought she was going to die on the spot. But all changed when Juanita came down the stairs. She'd been at the door of her and Rose's room when she heard him. There was no mistaking Conner's voice. She bit her lower lip and thought, I wish Delia weren't at the Parkhills'. Oh, she'd be so excited. Am I excited? Should I let him see my excitement? What does he look like? Has he gained his weight back? Oh, dear Lord, just let him love me again. Grief! How will he react when he finds out about the baby? I'll not tell him - not now. Why's he here? You don't suppose that fool editor wired the other newspapers about Harrison, do you? That's it! That's why he's here. Not for me and not for his little girl. He's here for Harrison.

She straightened her barely-five-foot height up as tall as she could, and holding her head high, regally glided down the stairs. But when she saw him her heart ached. He's so thin - I don't think I can stand it. He's still handsome. Millie's face expressed her admiration. She thought, oh, if she could have seen him before he became ill...!

"Conner, you've arrived," she said with a slight smile. She held out her arms, and he bent to kiss her cheek.

"You look well, my dear, doesn't she, Mrs. Bailey?" but before Millie could respond, he was inquiring about Delia.

"She's at the Parkhills', just down the street, dear. With all the commotion about this terrible Trib Henry and..."

"And Harrison, Cherie. Where is Harrison?"

By the way he asked, both she and Millie knew that he'd read the newspaper's accusations.

She lowered her head and with a catch in her throat responded, "We haven't heard, Conner. No one has come back from the posse all night..."

"Mrs. O'Farrell, that's not quite true. While you were sleeping, Smith came riding in to get more ammunition from the jail. They have the gang holed up at that colored woman's place, and he said they think it's just a matter of time 'til they can go in and capture them. Boyle said they oughta be out of bullets 'fore long."

"And, Harrison, Mrs. Bailey? Was there any mention of him?"

She replied softly, "Mr. O'Farrell, I'm sorry, sir, but they all think that he's in with that outlaw, Trib..."

"Absurd!" he shouted. "It is positively absurd! Whose harebrained opinion is it, would you please answer me? Whose?"

Millie could see that he was getting out of control and answered, "That Boyle Coleman's, you know, the town marshal's. Maybe they didn't shoot at Harrison when he sent him in..."

"Sent him in, did you say? Sent the man in?" He was now wild-eyed.

Juanita interrupted, "Conner, they don't know Harrison like we do, dear." She added for the sake of Millie, "Now, we both know that he's a gentle man..." She couldn't finish. Conner was livid. She was afraid that she was going to be sick...

"Where, may I inquire, is there a mount in this God-forsaken town? Or do you rely on ox and cart?"

"Conner, there's no need for..."

"No need, Cherie? No need? Is not the best friend I've - no, we've - ever had being falsely accused of assisting a scoundrel? Is he not, Cherie?"

"Well, yes, he is..."

"Well, yes, she says." He threw his long arms up in disgust.

"I've had it, Mr. High and Mighty! I've had it up to here and beyond!" and with that exclamation she whirled around and dashed up the stairs. But, being Juanita, she left the door ajar just in case she felt like hearing his retort - and, hear it she did.

"Mrs. Bailey," he said grandly, then softened his voice and murmured, "Millie," Juanita crouched beside the door and opened it a crack wider. "Would it be a bother to you or one of your people to secure a suitable mount? I would make it well worth you while, my dear."

Juanita bit her lower lip and stroked her rounded belly. He's not looking the same, but he is indeed in rare form. Your da's here, boyo. He's with us now.

Conner had been given specific directions to Barlows' by the rifle team and Capt. Martin Dewitt, who volunteered to accompany him. Conner had been so concerned about Harrison that he had neglected to eat, and as they approached Pope and Twila's he called to Martin to hold up, that he needed to beg a drink of water. He saw the light bounce off the rifle barrel in the front window. He glanced at Martin, and his expression told him that he, too, had seen it. He decided to call out and identify himself, probably just some frightened backwoods man protecting himself, he thought.

"Hello there! My companion and I are friendly wayfarers in need of..."

He didn't finish. "Da! - Da!" Delia burst out the door with Harrison on her heels.

"What the devil!" is all Conner could think to say.

"I knew you'd come! I knew it!" Harrison stood to the side and observed Conner as he put the squirming Delia down.

"Harrison, what the devil is this child doing here? Her mother thinks she's safe in Monticello. Delia Rose, come out from behind Seth and explain your actions, young lady." She could tell that he wasn't real mad so slowly approached from behind Seth and began babbling about getting lost and never getting to do anything. Conner knelt down and took her in his long, thin arms. "You know that your mum and I wouldn't know what to do if anything happened to you, now you know that." But he was thinking how much like Cherie she was even though she was the spitting image of him.

Harrison could see that he'd filled out somewhat. Must've gained a good fifteen pounds. Needs another twenty or so, though. Still has those dark circles under his eyes. He took Conner's hand, and then they were in each other's arms. Conner pushed him back and said, "One would have the entire state of Florida believing that you, my man, are in partnership with a scoundrel."

Martin spoke up, "Mr. O'Farrell, you must know this man well, sir?"

"Know him? Know him? Why, Martin, I created him," and Harrison saw the familiar crooked grin and devilish glint in his eyes, he hadn't seen in over five years. *He's back. Now we can get on with our lives.*

Seth had been told to return to Monticello with Delia in tow and to go directly to Madden House to tell her ma and Rose what had happened. Jacob told them emphatically that he'd not return to Monticello with them and that he was going with Harrison. No one argued with him. Harrison informed them of what Boyle had done, sending him in as bait. Martin Dewitt couldn't believe that Boyle would have done such a despicable thing. "Boyle Coleman is highly thought of in Jefferson County. I can't believe that he would act in that manner."

"I'll not rest 'til I see the foolish expression on the marshal's face," Conner said. "Perhaps his wisdom took a holiday, sir. Or perhaps he's been in Monticello far too long. It happens you know. I've seen it many a time. The town might consider another candidate come election time, hmm?"

"I believe that you, sir, are right. Sheriff Simkins will not take this accusation lightly, I'm sure, and will certainly make the necessary changes."

"It would appear, Martin, that that statement could prove to be prophetic," Conner replied. *I'm believing that I just placed an entertaining idea in the Captain's head.* He glanced at Harrison and had to restrain his laughter. Harrison smiled and turned his head away from the captain. *I dare not let him see the sport he's having with him,* he thought. *He might be more astute than he appears.*

They could hear sporadic gunfire as they approached. Martin called to Smith, who was under a sweetgum tree busily reloading their rifles, sweat pouring down his stubbled chin. "'Bout time you brought us help. Trib must've had a goddamned arsenal stashed in there."

When he looked up and saw Harrison, he anxiously raised his gun. Martin yelled, "Not so fast. Put that damned thing down!"

"What's he doing here? He's supposed to be in the house..."

"Supposed to be?" Conner questioned while getting off his horse and staring down at a perplexed deputy. Again he said, "Supposed to be, you say, sir? This man whom your marshal purposely sent to be slaughtered, is a friend of mine and has been for longer than you've been allowed to breathe." Conner continued while Smith cowered before him. "This man went to Monticello to assist my wife and daughter until I could join them. Where, may I inquire, does this marshal of yours get his information regarding my friend? Would you be telling me that, sir?" He was surly and thoroughly angry.

Smith, not wanting to get involved, merely replied, "I'm just a deputy, mister. I don't know nothing."

"On that, I heartily agree. And now, would you please inform this marshal of yours that I'd like to have a word with him." Harrison stood beside the tree and had to turn away. He's in rare form. I believe it was an Irishman who said, *"No man can be free until he conquers himself."* Yes, it was a Mr. O'Shaughnessy. He said it well, Conner. Are you now free, my friend? I'll give the marshal three S's - Surprised, Suspicious and, I hope, in the near future, Suspended.

Boyle was indeed surprised and suspicious. He, too, knew who Conner was the minute he saw him, and seeing the disrespect in Martin Dewitt's eyes, he knew he was in for trouble.

****

Ardeth hurriedly fed her family and told them to get on their Sunday clothes. "But, Mama..." they said in unison.

"Do as you're told. Robbers or no robbers, you know Brother Taylor will be conducting services."

"Not unless he came back, he won't."

"What did you say, Franklin? You don't mean to tell me that Simon Taylor's gone and lost his mind, too?"

"That's just what he up and done, Mama. Him and Mr. Emory said that they were needed more at Barlows' than at the courthouse and that Miss Clarice and Miss Ellen could lead the singing and praying good as they could, and..."

"Oh, shut up, Franklin! Shut up, do you hear!" and Ardeth mumbled about being tricked again all the way back to her room. She slammed the door while her children, eyes large with fright, shook their heads.

"Poor mama," Marylee sniffled.

"Stop your sniffling, Marylee!" Franklin ordered. "And if you're afraid of your own shadow, go crawl under your bed!"

"You're mean as Mama, Franklin Lee," Marylee cried, then she and Josephine ran to their rooms and closed their doors securely.

Franklin positioned himself at the front window so he wouldn't miss any activity that might just march down the street. Needing some kind of protection, he got up, went to the fireplace and returned to his chair with the iron fireplace poker. Feeling much more secure he began his watch. He hadn't been there more than an hour before Conner and Martin Dewitt galloped past on their way out of town.

"Mama, Mama," he yelled.

Ardeth was out her door like a shot. "What's the matter?"

"I just saw Captain Dewitt and a stranger hightailing it out of town, and they were for sure in a hurry!"

"A stranger, did you say? Oh my, maybe they had to call in some of the men from over Aucilla way."

She looked hard at her youngest son, who she knew was inclined to exaggerate. "Franklin Lee Coleman, are you sure?"

"Yessum, I'm sure. I never saw him before."

"Well, it's not like Martin to leave his men unless something's up. He's gotten so high and mighty since they elected him captain." She thought some more and, not being able to control her curiosity any longer, said conspiratorially, "Now listen to me, Franklin. I'm going over to the St. Elmo site and ask some of his men what's happening." She thought and added, "Your Pa might be in some kind of trouble. Now you lock the doors and don't even let on to the girls that I'm gone. Do you hear?" Remembering her purse containing the damaging letter, she went to her room for it and her shawl, even though it was unseasonably warm, and out the front door she charged on her mission.

"Just who did you say that man is? Mr. O'Farrell, did you say? But she doesn't even have a husband, and I've got a letter in this purse to prove it!" She was red faced and spewing by now.

"Now Miss Ardeth, I don't know nothing about it. I'm just telling you who he said he was, and he told Capt. Dewitt that that colored man Harrison was his man and had been almost forever and didn't know any Trib Henry and that the marshal was a fool and... oh, I beg your pardon, Ma'am. I didn't mean to repeat that, but that's what he said."

She stormed through the opening for the front door and around the pillars of the hotel and as fast as her long brown skirt would allow raced toward Madden House brandishing the letter in the air and shouting for all of Monticello to hear about the harlot and liar and...

"Miss Ardeth's gone and lost her mind, Harvey. Gone and lost it. She must be plenty worried about the marshal. Do you think we oughta send for Doc Shetland?"

"Captain Dewitt gave us our orders, now didn't he?"

"Well, yes, but seems to me..."

"Seems to me that we best do his bidding, that is, if you like being in the gun club."

"You're right - orders are orders."

"Open up this door, Millie! Open up, I say. I got proof right here! Proof! " Ardeth pushed Virgie out of her way as she burst inside.

"You got proof of what, Ardeth? What's this all about?"

"Now, Millie Bailey, maybe you'll believe me!"

Juanita and Rose appeared at the top of the stairs. Juanita being concerned about Conner ran down shouting, "Mrs. Coleman, is anything wrong?"

"So there you are - you harlot!"

"Ardeth!" Millie shouted. "What on earth are you talking about?"

"Married she says she is? Proof, Millie, I've got proof! She's lying and has been ever since she arrived in Monticello!"

"That's quite enough, Ardeth! I said that's enough, do you hear? Mr. O'Farrell has this very minute left Madden House and would be here still with his wife if that fool husband of yours hadn't gone and falsely accused Harrison. I think you've up and lost your mind, I really do!"

"You'd believe these two before me, wouldn't you, Millie? You never did like me. Oh, don't deny it. I've always known it."

Millie took Juanita by the arm and apologized. "Mrs. O'Farrell, I'm so sorry about this disturbance. She's not herself - worried about her husband, you know."

Ardeth slammed the door and grumbled all the way down Washington St. ignoring the disbelieving faces peering out from behind the drawn curtains. On she shouted, "Whole town's against me...all of you...all of you... I see you peeking out those windows... I see you...you'd believe that whore over me, and here I am, the town marshal's wife, and you'd believe..."

****

"I do appreciate your thoughtfulness, Rose. Really I do," Juanita whispered as she helped her pack her and Seth's things. Millie had been more than accommodating, especially since she'd lost the rent on the ten rooms. Rose, Seth and Delia could take the large room in the front so Juanita and Conner could be alone.

"Are you gonna tell him? about the baby, I mean?"

"I haven't decided. I declare, I think the only reason he came at all was because of Harrison and..."

"Now, Juanita, you know better than that..."

"Know better! Indeed I do not. He was out of here in no time soon's Mrs. Bailey got him a horse. Why, I hardly had time to ask him anything. Not even about the shop and..."

"Juanita, Mrs. Bailey said the way he looked at you, so loving like, you know, that it was plain to see how much he missed you..."

"She said that? She really did? You wouldn't be telling a body that just to make her feel good, would you, Rose Shorter? Would you?"

"Of course not! You know me better than that. I declare, Juanita!" and Rose left the room seemingly in a huff. Well, she almost said it - at least something like it, but no need for Juanita to have to have the exact words, for heaven's sake. Rose couldn't even remember the exact words, but she knew that Mrs. Bailey said something about how much he must have missed his wife and little girl or something like that.

"Seth, you found her where? Where did you day? Dear Lord in the morning. Delia Rose O'Farrell, I've a mind to spank you right here in front of the whole town. I'm not believing what I just heard!" Juanita pushed the strands of her blond hair back from her brow with one hand and grabbed Delia with the other and dragged her up the stairs, Delia yelling the length of the stairway. "When are you going to learn to mind, Delia Rose? When? Now you sit there and don't you move 'til your da comes back, miss. He'll for sure have words for you!"

Juanita slammed the door hard, and Delia got up immediately. "Every time I turn around somebody's making me sit and telling me to not move! Every time!" she grumbled. She jumped up on the bed and, liking the way it felt, hopped off and did it again, keeping her ears open for any creaks on the stairs.

Seth and Delia hadn't been back in town but a few hours when Conner, Harrison with Jacob behind him on Buford's stallion and

Martin Dewitt came riding in with the news that Trib Henry and his gang had finally run out of ammunition and had been captured. They first thought that Pearl had been killed but soon found out that she had just passed out from too much shine. Strawman and Dyke had been slightly wounded, and Pope and Twila were shaken from the experience and would await trial with the rest of them. Sheriff Simkins was due back in town the next day and would see to it that they got a fair trial. The streets were filled with the people shouting about the capture. They were relieved to be out of their hot homes - all except Ardeth Coleman who had taken to her room, locked herself in, and even her children couldn't get her to come out.

****

The soft glow of the lamp light played on Juanita's loosened hair. What a festive evening they'd had. Millie and Buford had set a good table, and Conner was in rare form. Millie had wired Thomasville and Tallahassee, and some of the guests had been able to make the afternoon train. Mayor Denham declared Monday a holiday and all the schools would be closed. The Monticello Rifle Club and Cornet Band would perform as planned as would the various groups. Cherie's House Of Fashion would finally have its grand opening.

Why am I not excited about it? Juanita wondered. I thought I'd die with excitement before. But not now. All I can think about is Conner. You'd think the dagblasted bugs would chase him and Harrison inside. Why, he acts like he's holding court with all those men around him laughing and drinking. All except that Boyle Coleman. He's ashamed to show his face. I can't believe he'd pull such a stupid trick as he did on Harrison. In cahoots with Trib Henry! Really!

She heard the hall clock chime midnight. Still no Conner. Her mind was hopscotching all over creation. She couldn't relax. When she heard the door across the hall close, she knew that Mr. Frazier from up Thomasville way had finally decided to retire. She listened for the familiar footsteps and, finally they came. She turned the lamp down low, crawled into bed and turned on her side away from the door. She could make out his every movement.

He's taking off his coat, now he's draping it over the chair. Now he's sitting down and removing his boots, now his pants and shirt. As always he'll drape them over the back of the chair. Conner's always been neat, even when he's drunk. Be still my heart. Lordy, he'll hear it. Why don't

I have more control? Did I put on too much toilet water? I only splashed a little. I know how he hates it, says he likes to smell a real woman, whatever that means.

She felt him ease himself down on the bed. She could smell the brandy and cigar smoke. *Why do I love him so? He doesn't deserve it. If he doesn't touch me I think I'll die. God, he's not going to. Is he snoring? I don't think I can stand it if he's snoring. Probably poked every whore in Kissimmee and on the St. Johns. Doesn't need or want me. Only came here because of Harrison.*

By now Juanita had worked herself into quite a state and was trying to restrain her heaving and sniffling but not succeeding. She didn't even remember how she ended up in his arms, but in his arms she was, and he was saying, "Shhhh - shhhh, Cherie. You'll awaken all of Madden House."

Oh, dear Lord, I'd forgotten how much I... "Conner..."

"Shhhh, Cherie..."

Afterwards she lay awake, her body tingling all over. I'll not tell him about the baby, not for a while. If he knew, he might leave me. I don't know what I'd do. Oh, Conner, I love you so. Why can't you love me at least half as much?

BOOK III

CHANGES ARE MANY

CHAPTER I THE WEDDING

1891 Old Town

"Luta," Trudy called. She was upstairs resting. "Luta, for heaven's sake, where are you?"

Leander's daughter-in-law, Dollie, answered her. "Miss Trudy, Miss Luta done gone home fer de pot o' chicken. She be back directly."

Trudy lay back, closed her weary eyes and declared to herself, I'll not miss that wedding. I don't care if it takes all of Old Town to carry me to the church. Brought that child into this world and all her brothers plus the twins. Not gonna miss it.

Dollie opened the back screen door, threw out the dish water and looked at the darkened sky and said a little prayer. "Dear Lord, give Miss SuSu a sunny weddin' day, like You give me an' Jefferson." The clouds were forming above the hanging tree, the big oak behind Stucky's and McCoy's. R.J. and Joe Bob Skinner had been hanged there in '78, and then those rustlers who tried to kidnap little Wes not long after that.

Dollie went about her morning chores and thought, not gonna be no more hangin's on dat ole tree what wid all de lawmen 'round. Everybody gotta go ta Cross City to de courthouse for trial. Not much goin' on in Old Town dese days, jes de same old thing day in, day out. Gits up in de mornin', git de water from de pump, stoke up de stove, git de water goin' fer de grits and coffee, slice up de pork slab, git de biscuits roll out - same old thing. Least ways mah chillun go to school now dat Mistuh deMoya 'sist on it. Dat man gotta have de patience of Job. Anyone who can teach Little Leon to carry a tune gotta be de smartest teacher in de whole wide world. Why dat play dey put on for Christmas near 'bout the bestest thing Ah ever seed, de bestest thing dat ever happen in Old Town, 'ceptin' de hangin's, dat is.

Trudy called out again, "Dollie!" No answer. "Dollie!" Dollie closed the kitchen door slowly, mumbled that she was coming and shuffled to the bottom of the stairs. "Miss Trudy, Ah be here."

"'Bout time you answered. Where have you been, anyway? A body could up and die while you pussy-foot around in that kitchen doing nothing. You best not be breaking my Ma's good china, gal. You best not!"

"Bes' not dis, bes' not dat. Why, dose old dishes got more cracks and chips out of 'em den a snaggle-toothed bull gator, dey has. Jes 'cause dey come all de way from Alabammy, a body would think dat dey be gold..."

"What'd you say, gal? You best not give me any sass, or Jefferson and your ma'll have your kinky head lumped up good..."

"Old woman," she said aloud. Why, I remember when she be real nice ta me, but ever since she broke dat hip, she turn into some kinda mean. Poor, Miss Luta. Even her bes' friend cain't do right fer her.

"Gal, you come up here and get Beauty and take her for her walk. She's been suffering all morning long waiting for you. Where's Little Leon, anyway? Why does he think I pay him good money for..."

Dat ugly old dog's gonna be de death o me yet. Combs her hair jes lak she a real person, she does. Worse thing Mistuh Bud and Miss Luta evah done was give her dat ugly dog. Said it'd be company fer her 'cause she couldn't come down de stairs. Company, my foot! More lak trouble, Ah'd say, and Little Leon cain't hardly git his lessons studied an' chores done fer prissin' up and down de street wid dat dog, and her a lookin' out de window at dem sayin', "now ain't dat a beautiful dog. Dollie, ain't mah dog beautiful?" Well, it ain't beautiful, Miss Trudy. But Ah'll allow dat it's de cleanest dog in de whole United States o' 'merica. Poor Little Leon hafta bathe dat ugly dog mos' every day. Ah wonder it's got any hair left on it. Ah nevah in mah life heard of a dog havin' its own bed and her havin' Daddy Leander carvin' it pretty wid birds an' flowers on de head board jes lak it was fer people, an' her a-layin' up in dat big old bed from Alabammy makin' it fancy bed covers jes lak for a person. Well, de whole town knows she's gone an losted her mind, dat's what. Onliest one 'round who don' knows it is Miss Trudy herself.

Dollie rocked and rocked and glared at the Stucky china in the breakfront. "Doze dishes 'bout as ugly as dat old dog, dey is. Jes about."

She hopped up when she heard the bell ring at the front door and began dusting the breakfront.

"Dollie, who's there?" Trudy yelled. "Is it time, yet? Dollie!"

"It's me, Trudy. It's Luta."

"I know who it is, for heaven's sake. Don't you think I know that voice? Been having to listen to it for over thirty years, even before the War!"

"Dollie, how has she been?" Luta asked while putting the heavy iron pot of stewed chicken on the wood stove.

"Been? How's she been? Well, Miss Luta, Ah tell ya. She been at me again 'bout dat china and dat dog, dat's how she been."

"Now, Dollie," Luta responded shaking her head, "You know how upset she is that she can't give SuSu and Mr. Jay a big fancy party all by herself - you gotta know that. Why, Trudy's given every important party for over forty years, and it's very upsetting for her to have to just lay up in that bed and be helpless. Now you know that, Dollie."

"Miss Luta, Ah'm not a fussin' 'bout dat. Ah knows all dat but..."

"What're you two mumbling about down there? Luta, make that gal take Beauty out, she's about to bust a gut!"

"We're coming, Trudy. Be right there."

"Now, Dollie, you listen to me. Trudy Stucky's been the best friend this town's ever had, to your pa-in-law, to your husband and to your mama. You don't remember about when times were real bad 'round here and about when she opened up this very boarding house to colored and white alike when the big hurricane hit. Good thing, too, 'cause Leander's house blew down just like it was made out of straw, and Miss Trudy for sure saved their lives. I'll avow that she's got mighty cantankerous this last year, but you've gotta think of how frustrated she is. How'd you like to be stuck up there in that bed knowing you'd be there the rest of your life, huh? How'd you like that?"

Dollie lowered her head and said exactly what Luta wanted to hear. "Ah be mizzable."

"See - that's how Trudy is - miserable!"

But Dollie really wanted to say, "Ah'd lak havin' nothin' ta do all de day long but have folks, white and colored alak, treat me lak Ah's a queen an' bring me food and empty my slops and comb mah hair and me not havin' ta do anythin' in de blessed world but sleep and yell at evuhbody all day long. Now, Ah'd lak dat." But she was sure smart enough to not let on to Miss Luta that that was what she was thinking. One thing you could say 'bout white folks - long as ya said what dey wanted to hear you could do mos' anythin' ya wanted, long as ya did it quiet lak. Dollie had learned that when she was not but knee high and got along just fine most of the time.

****

There had been many changes in Old Town since Berta and her first husband arrived before the War. Jonah McRae, Berta's middle son from her marriage to Reuben, and his wife Myra, formerly of

Gainesville and from the prominent Judson family, had taken over the actual running of the Stucky Hotel. They had an understanding with Trudy that she'd remain in her own room upstairs. Myra understood her prominence in the small town and also Jonah's affection for Trudy. Berta and Layke had bought Jonah's share of South Spring so he could purchase the hotel, and he and Myra had rented the old Simpson place on the outskirts of town so they could have their privacy and Trudy could continue her proprietorship, at least in appearance.

Myra Judson McRae was a sweet girl, small but not fragile, and had a great enthusiasm for life. She loved everything around her, especially Jonah. They had elaborate plans for the hotel but would wait until Trudy passed on to implement them. With Trudy's assistance they had planned the wedding reception for SuSu and Jay Meade. The Meades were taking the train from Arcadia to Gainesville and would spend the night at Myra's parents' home before riding out to Old Town with Jonah and Myra for the wedding and other festivities.

Berta and Layke, her son Wes, who was home from The Citadel in South Carolina, and the twins, Raine and Tucker, arrived in Old Town by steamboat a week earlier. The Suwannee was high from the spring rains and already running over its banks. It was a worry for all around. Berta had promised her oldest son, Young Reuben, now called just Reuben, and his wife Leonora that they'd be at South Spring to assist with the entertaining, although SuSu and Jay had requested a small wedding with just the two families present along with their closest friends. But as in most cases, the list grew and grew, and Berta, being a seasoned hostess, knew that Leonora could use her help.

Their two young sons were a handful, Samuel, four and a half, and Oliver, barely two. Little Sammy was the spittin' image of Young Reuben at that age, and Berta doted on that child. She didn't get to be with him and Oliver often, now that she and Layke spent most of their time in Tallahassee, but when they were in South Spring, she was the typical proud grandmother. Actually Layke was as crazy about them as she was and, being a demonstrative man, showed it. It had rankled Trudy that Leonora felt that she had to go all the way back to Perry to deliver them. Why she'd delivered Reuben and every baby in and around Old Town, and why the Olivers felt that Leonora wouldn't get the proper treatment with a midwife she couldn't figure. But as they said, Doc Bodine had delivered Leonora and all the rest in her family, and she wanted to be near her mother.

There had also been many changes at South Spring through the years. Berta and Layke had added on to the main house to accommodate their growing family, and Reuben and Leonora lived there. Pierre deMoya and his wife Elysse had built a small house down the road about a quarter of a mile. Reuben had fixed up Big Dan's and Willa's small cabin, and the Starling family had moved in. Bernice was a good worker as was Moses, who also helped on the ranch. He rode with the other cowmen during the cow hunts, and their five children were company for Sammy and Oliver. Myrtice and Ezekiel's house had been torn down so Reuben and Moses could put in a larger vegetable garden and enlarge the chicken coop.

Etienne deMoya had moved into town so he could be closer to the school and had never married. Some said it was because he had never got over his feelings for Juanita Jane Graves and somehow couldn't forgive her for running off to live with that riverboat gambler, Conner O'Farrell. As far as anyone knew he had never married her, and although it was reported that she had changed her ways and had become quite a respected business woman in Palatka, Kissimmee and now Monticello, it still didn't seem to affect Etienne's feelings toward another woman. Mind you, they tried. Almost everyone of Emma and the Sweede's eligible daughters had made a play for him but didn't get to first base.

He was in his late thirties and apparently a confirmed bachelor. Even Leonora had invited her very pretty sister Charlotte down to South Spring for the summer once and entertained lavishly for her, inviting the young people from as far away as Fannin Springs and Newberry. Etienne attended the parties and entertained the guests with his singing and guitar playing but didn't give Miss Charlotte a tumble - nothing - so for the past few years folks just let him be.

There were so many school children around Old Town now that it took Emma Haglund and Etienne both to teach the lot of them. Those Beatty children from south of the Suwannee and the Haglund brood from up at North Prong seemed to drop a babe about every two years, and it had got so Miss Trudy had to call on Doc Dorsett and also had to train Karine Haglund, now Miller, to assist her. But since Trudy broke her hip, Karine had become the number one midwife in Old Town.

McCoy's Dry Goods was still the only store in town, but since Palmer and Davis had passed on, as had their wives, the Stuart Laughlins from Ocala had bought it. He and his wife Rabel ran it and lived in the back quarters, just like the McCoys and their families had. Stu was a cousin of the McCoys, and everyone in the entire county liked him and Rabel. Now, if those two weren't a pair, he diminutive, not much over five feet tall but well proportioned and strong as could be, and she a good foot taller and weighing in at a respectable two hundred pounds.

The funny thing about them was that they had six children, three boys and three girls, and so help if every one of the boys didn't take after Stu, and the girls were as big as Rabel. But once the phenomenon had been discussed at length on the Stucky porch for the first few months, folks forgot about it and just took to enjoying their good natured ways. When Rabel laughed the entire town shook, and Stu's hearty laugh was near about as respectable.

SuSu's and Jay's plans were as follows: After the wedding reception they'd drive the buggy to Gainesville to the Worthington Hotel, spend the night, then take the train to Arcadia, where they'd stay for the three months before SuSu had to assume her teaching position. She had been accepted in the Whitesville school in Middleburg, southwest of Orange Park, formerly called Laurel Grove, and not far from Jacksonville. Jay had resigned from his position at Stetson, and he and Clay Willett, Callie's new husband, had needed that time to put the finishing touches on their children's book, *Thom's Wilderness Adventures.* Since they had sold their book, he would now have enough money to take off a year or two to pursue his art.

He and SuSu had a master plan. They both wanted to settle on the Gulf in or near Appalachicola, Jay to study the wildlife on St. George Island and she to be nearer Tallahassee. Berta and Layke had spent a great deal of time with their children at Alligator Pt., a peninsula in the Gulf south of Tallahassee, as did the other senators and their families. SuSu had learned to love that area of Florida and had sent applications to Appalachicola and Carrabelle, but they had no openings. She was excited that there was an opening in Middleburg, because Berta had relatives in Jacksonville, and it would give her and Jay an opportunity to get acquainted with them.

Berta could not believe the turn of events. "I've done everything right and proper, dear Lord, now why are You sending these rain clouds to spoil SuSu's wedding day? Why?" Layke chuckled at her ineffective wrath. "Honey, you're supposed to shake your fists high and stomp your little feet if you want the Lord to pay attention."

"Mr. Smartie, what would you know about it anyway? Now, why would He do this to SuSu, answer me that. There was never a sweeter or better daughter in the world than she. Now, Raine - well, she's a different kettle of fish, Mr. Williams. I never saw two girls so different!"

"Might be that they have different fathers, missy!" and with that and a swat on her rounded behind he hugged her to him. They stood and looked out the kitchen window. "Does it seem like thirteen years, my sweet?"

"I can't even remember when you weren't with me, Honey." She sighed, then wiggled free and away from him. "Fine thing, trying to distract me when you know how much I have to do. Now get - go on - get out of my kitchen!"

"You didn't say that thirteen years ago, Miss Berta. Whew! You couldn't get enough of me then."

"Layke Williams, you shush. Someone might hear you - I never..." and she, too, chuckled and fussed and smiled. But he was certainly right, she couldn't then, and she couldn't now. Oh, it wasn't as it had been. They were middle aged now, and their love-making had lost some of its fire, but she still burned all over when he touched her and giggled like a silly school girl. Oh, it wasn't the same, but in many ways it was better, so much better.

"Mama, do you see that cloud? Mama!" SuSu shouted.

"I'm in here, Honey. Yes, I see it, but by the time we're due in town it'll all be over. Now don't you fret."

"Why do you say that? How do you know?"

"I know because as Layke would say, I've ordained it, or something like that. He knows full well that I'll simply not have this wedding rained on, and that's that."

"You're teasing me, aren't you?"

"Yes, I'm teasing you, but as Trudy would say, `the Lord will have his say and his way' and she's right, of course. But I'm almost sure it'll blow over. It's just an early summer squall, 'cause it's coming from the southeast."

"Oh, I hope you're right. There's going to be such a crowd that I know the little church won't hold them all. I just know it. I just wish

Aimee could have come. Micanopy isn't that far, but I understand, I really do. I'll be that concerned when I'm with child."

"Of course you will, SuSu. Aimee's always been a good friend, but you're probably right about the crowd. Leonora said that Rev. Smythe had a wagon load of chairs brought over from Newberry, and they plan to put them out in the front yard and to leave both church doors open so at least some of the folks can see, and I'm sure all will be able to hear."

"SuSu, please don't spoil your day with that frown. Now go on into the parlor and help Leonora and Elysse with the rice bags, and would you please check on Raine. I declare when we come to South Spring, she goes absolutely wild, just like a renegade Indian she is." And it was true. Berta had told Layke only the week before that he would have to speak to that child. Not much of a child any more, only twelve years old and starting to develop. She was as tall as Berta and still running around barefoot as a yard dog and ...

She thought of all the money they'd spent sending her to the best schools, and the minute she'd get home Berta would find her in Tucker's old pants, legs rolled up and a rope around her waist holding the too-big things up. She almost died on the spot when Mrs. Wainright and that gossipy Tilly Ryan came calling last year, and Raine came right into the parlor dressed like that. Berta excused herself, practically dragging Raine to the hallway, and let her know just how many weeks she was going to have to stay inside the house doing penance for embarrassing her that way.

Raine promised that she would never do it again and had kept her promise as far as Berta knew. But the big elm beckoning outside her bedroom window was just too tempting for her to ignore for long, and when Berta took her afternoon nap as she always did, out Raine would go in Tucker's pants, shinnying down the tree, then dashing out back of the house to the creek. There was always a lot of activity there, all boys, and that suited Raine just fine.

Why Tucker never told on her she didn't know, but he never did, and it wasn't that he particularly admired her for going against Berta's orders. He knew that she had to be busy doing something all the time, Raine being Raine. The worse punishment Berta could have inflicted on her was to make her stay still. She was not the reader he was, except maybe *Tom Sawyer* - oh, how she loved that book, and she did love to recite poems, not gushy old stuff, but very adventurous and dramatic poems like *"Paul Revere's Ride"*. Actually, this was the one poem she knew all the way through. She'd go into great theatrics when she got to the part about him climbing the tower of the Old North Church. And the dead people in the church yard... oh, how she'd carry on with not a peep out of her enthralled subjects. Why, there must've been twelve stanzas in that poem, and she knew every word. When she finished she'd look around at the admiring faces and glory in their ardor. She never bothered to learn another poem, because she didn't have to. Raine never did more than what was absolutely necessary.

She tolerated Tucker. They weren't especially close, but he did take up for her whenever necessary. He was certainly as intelligent as she, but she was quicker to learn everything and had been since birth. They were also unlike in appearance, he fair like Berta and she more like the Williams side with dark brown hair and hazel eyes. No one would have guessed that they were twins.

Tucker didn't seem to have any adventure in him - Raine was curious about everything. The only time her daddy had ever spanked her was when he caught her dissecting a frog, and it still alive. He felt sort of bad about it later while she was wailing. She informed him that she just wanted to know what made it able to jump and make that croaking sound, and she wouldn't have been able to find out if it'd been dead.

Later, he had told Berta, "Now, Honey, I know that if she were going to examine the frog that she shouldn't have done it while it was alive, but Berta, she's only five, and a child that age can't reason like you and I..."

"Layke," Berta said sternly, "I just pray that she wasn't enjoying that poor little thing's pain..."

"I'm sure she wasn't. She didn't think of its pain. She just wanted to see where the croak was coming from."

"Raine has you hoodwinked, Layke Williams!"

"No, honestly, I can understand why she..."

"Let's go to sleep, dear. We'll talk about it in the morning."

They didn't, but Berta kept a keener eye focused on Raine, that is, until she'd get too busy with the other senators' wives or when they were in South Spring. Oh, how Raine loved South Spring! She could hardly wait for the session to be over so they could all go for a long visit. Every waking moment she was busy with Bernice's and Moses's oldest boys, Henry and Jessup, who were nine and eleven, respectively, and sometimes Tucker. They were at the spring swimming or at the river fishing or building a raft or riding horseback or climbing a tree or hunting rabbit or squirrel or just meandering all over the place.

But Raine knew that there was one rule she had to abide by. When Berta had Bernice ring that dinner bell, she'd better be within earshot and at the house within a few minutes. As long as she did that she and her ma got along just fine, and Raine had the run of the place. She was politically aware at an early age. When her pa would inquire as to what she and Tucker had been doing, she knew just how to play him. She had to virtually sit on her enthusiasm and just give short sentences highlighting their activities. Tucker would follow her lead, never giving away anything he shouldn't, and Layke, being an astute student of people, allowed them their ruse.

Berta had long ago given up on teaching her how to do any kind of hand work or cooking. Raine had a hearty appetite; actually, she ate more than Tucker, and when Berta informed her that she'd have to learn how to cook and run a house one of these days, she replied, "I don't think so, Mama. I'll just pay someone else to do it." Berta replied, "Yes, Raine, that's probably just what you'll do all right," and shook her head in bewilderment.

When the time came for the wedding party's departure for Old Town, the skies had not given in to Berta's wishes. They were still just as threatening as they had been earlier that morning, but only a few sprinkles of rain had fallen. Berta and Layke were hurriedly trying to corral all the family, Berta telling which buggy each should ride in. Everyone was yelling and SuSu was getting more upset by the minute. Finally she shouted for all to hear, "Whose wedding is it, anyway? Whose?"

Raine jumped off the wagon and enthusiastically joined her older sister and yelled, "Yeh, whose?"

"Raine Trudy Williams, you get back in that wagon, you hear me, young lady?" Berta admonished her. Layke threw up his hands, "The Meades will think we're uncouth bumpkins with this kind of behavior. I want everyone of you to remember what this day means to SuSu and Jay, and I'm sure being McRaes and Williamses you'll hold your heads high with pride and behave accordingly."

They all, even the grown children, hung their heads. Finally Reuben added, "We're happy for you and Jay, SuSu, and we all want your day to be perfect. Now, as the senator said, let's behave with some kind of dignity." He hesitated, then gave into a devilish grin and said,

"For at least the ceremony, then afterwards we can kick up our heels at Stucky's and..."

"You wouldn't dare, Young Reuben! You wouldn't!" SuSu shouted. Wes playfully slapped him on the back. "Reuben, I think SuSu's taking your threat seriously. Better reassure her. She's as nervous as a cat."

"Well, well, Wes the peacemaker. At least you've learned that at school. I was just teasing her and she knew it. She's just going all girly on us."

Leonora grabbed on to Sammy and Oliver, who had decided to hop off the back of the wagon after she had told them to stay, threatening them with a spanking. They were surrounded by pots and bowls and trays of food that she, Elysse and Berta had been preparing all week, and Bernice had been engaged to keep the boys still, to no avail. The lightning began without warning, streaking across the dark sky. On its heels the thunder roared. While the men put the whips to the horses, the women and children gathered the tarps for a quick cover should the rains come before reaching town and shelter.

"Guess the Lord had his fingers in his ears, Miss Berta," Layke whispered so SuSu couldn't hear. She hit his thigh with an ineffective swat, then nestled into his shoulder. His arm encircled her. SuSu watched from the back seat. I hope Jay and I will have that much love in our marriage, but as she thought it she remembered there was a time when she was just finishing up her schooling in Tallahassee that she sensed a tension between her parents.

Layke was so busy that he often didn't come home for supper, and Berta was alone a great deal of the time. She and her mother were close but not close enough to discuss any problems that existed in Berta's marriage. She always made excuses for Layke and went about her day-to-days without complaining. But SuSu, being the oldest child present, was very worried. All seemed to change after they took a trip to Kissimmee in '83 for the big ceremony welcoming the first train into the wilderness town. They came back like two young lovebirds, and she noticed that Layke hadn't missed coming home for either dinner or supper since. Oh, he might have to go back to the capitol afterwards, but he had become a very attentive husband.

When SuSu started keeping company with Jay, she wished that Berta had confided in her. Finally, on her last trip home to Tallahassee, she had got up enough nerve to ask Berta what she felt made her marriage to Layke so vital. She had replied, "SuSu, honey, don't hold anything that's bothering you inside. It can fester and grow beyond your control. If you can't confide in Jay, not your innermost thoughts exactly, but the things that you feel the need to share, then perhaps Jay's not the right husband for you.

"I was such a child when I married your father, not quite seventeen, and had truly led a sheltered life. But Reuben was a wonderful man, gentle but strong, as much my friend as my husband. He was probably the finest man I have ever known. Now don't misunderstand what I'm saying, dear. Layke is a good man and the most exciting creature on earth - there's something magnetic about Layke - but I can't seem to... well, I guess you might say chat with him about everything like I could with Reuben. He has a volatile temper, as you know, about injustice and prejudice, and of course that's good since he's entered public life. I find it all very exciting, but I also find it difficult sometimes to express my feelings to him, especially if it has to do with me, not you children. We can discuss you all at length. But your father was a philosopher and...oh, I don't know."

"I think I understand, Mama. I guess Jay's more like Daddy. He's a gentle man, and we can talk about everything for hours. That's one of the things I love about him, I guess. He's a good listener, too, and when I'm with him time just flies by."

SuSu had determined that Berta had finally been able to tell Layke that she was lonely, and he had been so busy that he hadn't noticed it. That was why there had not been the happy singing and teasing in their home on Calhoun Street like there was in South Spring. Heavens, at South Spring Berta and Layke would sit on the front porch and talk and giggle, and she'd do her hand work, and he'd smoke his pipe and read to her. SuSu would sit just inside the parlor so she could listen to them. He read beautifully with great expression, his deep bass caressing the words. He and Berta were especially fond of James Whitcomb Riley's works. SuSu had given him a volume of his poetry for Christmas once. Layke said Mr. Riley captured the common man in his work and like Samuel Clemens could poke fun at everybody without their taking offense.

Even Raine would sit still for him to read *The Raggedy Man* and had named her only doll that still had arms and legs 'Lizbeth Ann like in the poem. Nobody could even touch 'Lizbeth Ann. She perched prominently on Raine's bed pillow, and she would lovingly take her off the bed at night and place her high on the highboy and would make her stay there until Saralee had made her bed in the morning, and then only Raine was allowed to place her back on the pillow.

The rains let loose when the caravan pulled up to Stucky's. There was already a large gathering filling the parlor and dining room. Trudy had made Leander and Jefferson bring her downstairs and was shouting orders to everyone. Several of the men, all in their Sunday best, got tarps that she had had Leander bring up on the porch earlier in case of rain, and they spread them on the ground in front of the front steps, and four of them held a large cowman's cook tarp up high so the entourage wouldn't get wet. Reuben and Wes brought Berta's wedding trunk inside and carried it upstairs to the changing room. Leonora was having a time trying to keep Sammy and Oliver from getting off the tarp that was now filling up with water. Finally, Elysse and Pierre were able to get down from their wagon to give her a hand.

Berta's umbrella was useless. The wind blew and the men had a terrible time holding the tarp. Trudy kept saying as how it might be a hurricane, and Bud answered patiently every time she declared it that there wouldn't be one at this time of the year. Dollie overheard the conversation and said to herself, now dis whole town gonna know dat ole lady done losted her mine - hurricane, mah eye!

Etienne deMoya was helping Pierre and Elysse carry the food into Trudy's already overflowing kitchen, and Trudy was yelling at Dollie and Luta and Emma to be sure to not crush the wedding cake and to make sure it got put in a safe place. All hell broke loose when up rode Jonah and Myra with Jay, Kate and Parker, and Myra's parents. Jay, who was not supposed to see the bride on their wedding day because it would bring bad luck, had everyone yelling at him over the claps of thunder that he'd better not come in. Jonah yelled back at them that they had to come in, because that big maple on the side of their house decided to pay them a visit and fell right into the front parlor, and Myra's pretties had been soaked. SuSu was so upset that she took to the changing room upstairs and was crying so loud that you could hear her above the thunder.

Raine told Tucker later that night on the way back to South Spring that that had to be the best wedding she'd ever been to. It didn't matter that it was the only one she'd ever been to, and that Layke had to stop Ringo every mile or so for her to hang her head over the side of the buggy to throw up. Each time she did Berta would repeat, "Poor thing, getting sick on her sister's wedding day, poor little Raine."

"Poor Little Raine, nothing. If she hadn't tried to eat every plate empty, she'd not be sick," Layke admonished. What they hadn't been told by Rabel Laughlin, who decided that they'd had more than enough problems for one day, was that Raine and Emma Haglund's grandson Bobby had been discovered underneath the lace covered long table, and by the time they had been found they had devoured two entire plates of Agnes Beatty's deviled eggs and goodness knows how many ham biscuits, and both were just about green when she got to them.

The rains never did let up, but Berta was finally able to calm SuSu enough to get her dressed. Preacher Smythe sloshed through the mud to Stucky's and, crowded as it was, managed to make room for the bride and groom in front of Trudy's mama's chiming clock. SuSu came down the stairs on Layke's arm, and the greetings were as enthusiastic as they had been thirteen years before when Berta and Layke were married in that same room in front of the very same clock. Some of the old timers were dead and gone now, but those who had been there remembered that bygone day and couldn't help but make comparisons between the two couples. SuSu wore Berta's mauve faille wedding dress. Berta had had to take in the waist, but aside from that it was perfect. Her rich auburn hair was worn high off her forehead, and the heavy curls cascaded down her back. On her arm she carried a cascade of gardenias and ivy that Myra had fashioned from the large bush in her side yard. Their fragrance couldn't hide the smell of the wet wool of the men's suits, but no one cared. They gazed at her enormous chocolate eyes and how lovingly she was looking at Jay in his new, dark grey suit and black satin waistcoat.

Jay almost cried when he saw her. They forgot about the wind-swept rain - they forgot about how hot it was with all those people crushed inside Trudy's parlor - they forgot about everything in the world around them but their love for each other. When the preacher finished the readings, he asked Layke to say a few words. Layke had planned just what he wanted to say but due to the storm knew that he'd have to shorten his speech so the men could get over to McCoy's and Bud's blacksmith shop, rain or no, for their spirits. So he approached SuSu and Jay and asked them to go up three or four steps so all could see Mr. and Mrs. James Parker Meade.

Reuben called out, "Make it short, Layke!"

"Yeah, don't give us one of your long-winded speeches, Senator," Frank yelled.

"All right, boys. But this needs to be said. I had planned to speak about what makes a good marriage and the pitfalls, etc., but when I saw SuSu looking at her young man with those tremendous eyes and her abundant love shining through, I decided that any words of wisdom I might find to say would be superfluous. Their obvious love and respect for each other will bring them enough happiness for two lifetimes."

Everyone applauded and yelled that he was right, and Trudy said to herself, Reuben would be so proud. I just hope he's looking on. Aloud she said, "Amen, now let's eat," and so they did.

Kate and Parker stayed on at Old Town for a visit and filled Berta and Layke in on Callie and Clay. They had been married the year before, just a small wedding for the family and a picnic in the church yard afterwards with their oldest and dearest friends attending. She and Clay had waited for a respectable time after Thom's death. When Callie found out that she was not pregnant with Thom's baby, it was so devastating to her that Kate and Parker were afraid she was going to have a breakdown. But Clay was there and helped her through it, as he had other times in her life.

They took the train to DeLand for their honeymoon. After a few days visiting SuSu and Jay they rented a cottage in New Smyrna Beach on the Atlantic and spent a week relaxing and roaming the beautiful white beaches before going to St. Augustine, where Clay had a writing assignment on Henry Flagler. They were his guests in the Ponce de Leon Hotel, and Callie said later that they had been treated like royalty. They had even been invited to tea by the new Mrs. Flagler, the former actress. And as the newspapers reported, Alice did have the reddest hair and greenest eyes you can imagine. It seemed like everyone there knew who Clay was and about the book that he and Jay had written.

Callie had been a nervous wreck about the invitation. She was sure she'd make a fool of herself and embarrass Clay, so for weeks before the honeymoon she and Kate had practice tea parties just so she could learn to balance those little cups and saucers and tea cakes without spilling everything all over the place. Clay said that it wasn't that important to him that she have the fanciest manners in the state, but Callie felt that it was time to take her place beside her husband, just as she had tried to for Thom, and if that entailed fancy manners, then by gum, she'd have them.

When Berta asked Kate if Callie had resumed her delightful carefree manner, Kate replied, "She's scared, Berta. She's afraid that this baby will have something wrong with it. Now, I know Clay has reassured her over and over again as only he could, but I can tell that she's truly concerned."

"But, I thought the doctors said that nothing physically had been wrong with Meade, didn't they?"

"Yes, nothing physically, but Callie has got it in her head that she was somehow responsible for him not being able to talk all those years. Don't ask me why." Kate added, "Parker is as worried as she is. He checks on her everyday - didn't even go on the cow hunt, and I almost had to hog-tie him to bring him here. The fact that he was willing to stay for a visit these past few days amazes me. Guess it's because of you and Layke."

****

The dog days of August had passed, but the flowers around Kate's front porch still required daily watering. Oh, how she missed Mattie. They'd buried her in the Meade family plot with the approval of her children six months earlier. Every one of her children had made it to the funeral and burial. It was the first time that Callie and Pet, Mattie's daughter and Callie's best friend when they were growing up, had seen each other since Pet had moved back to Bartow. She had married and now had four children. She looked the very same, had added a few pounds, and Callie would have known her anywhere. "It is the first time in years that Callie has been the old Callie," Kate remarked to Parker.

As sad as Mattie's passing was to all of them, they were glad that she had just slipped out of this world and joined the Lord quietly enough that even she didn't know it - sound asleep she had been. Kate found her the next morning when she hadn't appeared to fix breakfast. She had called and knocked on her door with no answer. She knew! She eased open the door, and sure enough, Mattie was lying there peacefully. She'd even picked some flowers the day before, selecting every variety in her garden, arranged them in a vase and had it sitting on the low maple dresser beside her bed. Kate said that she looked like she had placed them there on purpose, but then Mattie always had loved her flowers.

Kate refilled the watering can from the bucket and soaked the ferns along the house-wide front porch, all the while keeping her eyes toward the black clouds forming in the southwest. Parker had said earlier, before he left for town, that he hoped Clay would go ahead and move them into Arcadia so Callie would be closer to Dr. Spooner. Beulah had already set aside a room for them, but for some reason Callie was determined to stay at Ole Piney for as long as she could. Kate couldn't for the life of her figure that girl. As concerned as she seemed to be you'd think she'd be anxious to be near the Doc. Doc Spooner had said her due date was about September the tenth, not that any babe arrived when it was supposed to, and the tenth was tomorrow.

Where is Parker? He should have been home hours ago. If anything happens at Ole Piney, I'll just have to leave without him. Oh, I miss Mattie. I'm just glad she knew about the baby. She had been so worried about Callie. Kate sat on the rocker, got up, positioned the cushion again, and declared out loud, "I'm going to have to replace these covers. My, I hadn't realized how faded they are." She sat down again and thought, that's something I can do this winter. I need things to keep me busy. Even though Callie and Meade are close by, seems that I seldom see them. Now that Mattie's not here to keep Callie in biscuits and cakes, she's had to learn to cook, and Clay, well, that man is as good a cook near about as Mattie was. It's something to see the three of them in the kitchen, and I can't get over how Meade's grown - about half a foot lately.

On she rocked and on she looked at the sky getting blacker by the minute. Kate Meade was not used to being alone. She'd always had her children or Mattie or Parker or the cowmen around. Parker had been after her to get someone to take Mattie's place, but Kate hadn't found anyone in all of Arcadia to suit her. Beulah had told her of at least half a dozen women, but they were either too young or too old or just - well - just not Mattie. Beulah had also informed her that she was through - through with trying to help her - that she could just do her on cooking and washing and cleaning and every blasted thing that Mattie had done for her. And she had, except the washing. Parker had brought Darlene out from town to do that and the ironing, but she sure wasn't a Mattie. Couldn't even get the girl to talk, hardly at all.

Kate needed to keep busy, but Beulah was right. There's too much to do around this place for one person to try to do it. She thought about when Susu and Jay were home for those few months, how they were a big help, but now that they're up in Middleburg, she was right back to having it all to do herself.

All right, James Parker Meade! I just bet you're still at the feed store talking and laughing, and here I am all alone with a blow coming up that looks like a real dandy. I just wish Callie didn't live so far away. It'd take me forever to hitch up Boss Man and drive out there, and sure as shootin' that sky would open up and all the Devil's droppings would fall on me and ...

On Kate stewed and on she rocked. When she saw the rain approaching nearer and nearer, she hopped up, grabbed the watering can and ran inside, but not before her backside got pelted. Pushing her damp hair back from her face she closed the windows in the parlor, fighting the lace panels, then up the stairs to shut the southwest windows in Jay's old room - the pine floor was already wet - muttering to herself she grabbed the rags from the bottom of the dresser and began wiping the floor.

The sky suddenly lit up. "The Devil's loose!" her ma used to say when Kate was just a tyke, one of the few things she could remember, for she'd died when Kate was real young. She sat on Jay's bed and thought, Pa used to say "The Devil's beating his wife with a frying pan", when it would thunder.

Where are you, Parker? Why'd you leave me all alone with not even Mattie here? She eased herself down onto Jay's quilt-covered bed. She began to sob, not that she was actually afraid, for she wasn't. She was just lonely, for the first time in her fifty-eight years, and she wasn't feeling any too well either. Seemed light headed when she ran up the stairs, and seemed to be having trouble breathing. The storm raged on and Kate knew that she should go to their room and close the windows, but somehow her legs didn't seem to want to work.

Then the pain suddenly struck her chest like a fiery poker and ran down her left arm, and she knew that she was in for trouble. All she could think was, not now, dear Lord, please wait 'til after Callie's baby comes...oh, please for Callie's sake. I beg You not to take me...

"Meade, don't wander off too far this afternoon. We might need to get you in a hurry, you know," Callie cautioned.

"I won't. I'll just take Willy down to the creek for a swim. I can hear you from there."

Clay looked at him. I believe Callie's right, never saw a kid grow as fast as he has these past few months. He's looking more like Thom all the time, even walks like him. I'm glad actually. I want Callie to have good memories. I wonder if a mother's state of mind affects the unborn like they say, but I've not been able to find anything written that's truly conclusive. I hope not. Callie is so uneasy about this baby. Oh, she's happy all right but also apprehensive. It's no wonder...

Clay sat on the small front porch that faced the barn and watched Dixie, Thom's prize possession, and reportedly the best bird dog in the area. He was surprised that Callie hadn't wanted to get rid of her after Thom was killed, but she said no, that it wasn't Dixie's fault, and besides she was something else that Meade would have as a reminder of his daddy. And, of course, Callie was right.

Clay could see the dark clouds through the tall sand pines and river oaks. Going to have us a storm. Lots of wind in those clouds. I just wish Callie had agreed to go to town this morning. The baby's dropped, and I'm sure it's in the birth canal. When Clay had asked Callie if the baby had been as active as it had the day before, she had said that she guessed babies had to take a rest, too, and laughed, so he knew that it was just a matter of time.

It's my fault, he thought. I should have packed our things and headed for town. Hope this storm's over soon. As soon as it is, we're leaving. I'll not take no for an answer, Callie Anders Willett. I so hope it's a girl, Cora Anders Willett. Mama would be so pleased, and if it's a boy, James William for our dads. He laughed when he remembered Meade's response when they told him the proposed names, "Well, you can't call him Willy 'cause we already got us a Willy."

"We'll probably call him Jim or Jimmy. Which one do you like, Honey?"

Meade answered, "What's wrong with James? I got a friend called James, and he's real nice."

Clay continued his vigil. Wish I'd gone over to the big house for Kate. I'd feel a lot better if she were here. He saw the rain approaching and ran for the barn, rang the triangle and called Meade. Meade answered, and he and Willy got to the house just as it let loose.

"Whew!" Meade exclaimed. "Got us a gully washer, Mama. Whew! Me and Willy... I mean, Willy and I," he smiled, pleased that he'd remembered, "we got out of there in jig time. It's really coming down, ain't it, Clay?" Quickly he corrected himself. "I mean, isn't it?"

Clay tousled his brown, curly hair and began pulling off his soaked shirt. "Hand those to me, you two. Gracious me, you'll catch your death."

Clay's skin glistened. He was heavily muscled from lifting those heavy sacks at Jeeters' from the time he was old enough to help out in the store. Callie thought, I need Clay's calm. I need his strength. What she hadn't allowed herself to dwell on was how much she missed Thom. Oh, how she missed him! Clay was a wonderful man, her best friend, very affectionate, and she knew he could probably read her mind. She never allowed herself to think of Thom when Clay was around - only in the dead of night after Clay was sleeping beside her. Then she'd remember and glory in her memories. She felt that Clay knew, but she just couldn't let her love for Thom go quite yet.

Clay mentioned Thom often at first. She thought that it was for Meade, so he wouldn't forget his daddy. But she now knew that it was for her as well. She couldn't believe that he wasn't even jealous. Most men would be, but she guessed Clay knew that she needed her memories. She was afraid that she'd hurt him, and he was the last person on earth she'd want to hurt. But Callie couldn't understand why she couldn't love him like she did Thom. It bothered her something terrible, and she wondered if that was why she was so jumpy - nervous.

CHAPTER II MISS KATE

There was quite a gathering at the Arcadia train depot when the two o'clock arrived from Bartow. Beulah had George in tow so he could see Parker's new acquisition, Meade's filly. Gus Jeeters and the Davis brothers were there, too, and most of the old timers who had known Callie, Clay and Meade from birth. It was to be a surprise for Meade. Parker hadn't even told Kate about it. It was about time that Meade had a real horse, not that he was too big for his pony, and Kate would be especially pleased that he got it from Morgan and that Mattie's boys broke it.

Parker had been thinking about the horse ever since Callie and Clay had been married. He wanted Meade to have something of his own besides Willy, something to take care of. When Callie announced that she was with child, Parker sat right down and wrote his friend Morgan Murphy at his horse farm, Tralee, in Bartow, where Mattie, her husband and children had lived and worked before Mattie's husband was killed. All the horses on Tall Ten had been purchased from Tralee, and Parker had told Morgan that he wanted the best cow pony he had in his stable and knew he'd not let him down.

When the telegram arrived in Arcadia telling Parker when to expect the cow pony, Lucy took it over to the Young Hotel as Parker had requested and gave it to Beulah. Poor old George couldn't read the telegram because he'd become so shaky these past few years, so much so that Beulah wouldn't let him out of her sight. He'd just about withered away, and everyone was concerned about him. Beulah had sent Sap, Mattie's youngest boy, who had stayed on in Arcadia and worked for the railroad, out to Tall Ten with strict instructions to not let on to Kate about the cow pony. Sap took his little boy Toad along with him and told Kate that they wanted to visit his mama's grave and do a little fishing at the pond. She wasn't the least suspicious.

He was able to slip Parker the telegram, but he also gave him the latest cattle notice. Brand changing and cattle rustling had become so rampant that Parker had taken to branding his on their bellies and using ear croppings, hoping that it would help. This notice was from H.T. Lykes, warning people against "penning, milking, driving or shipping cattle that carried this brand." A couple of rustlers had been shot only a week before outside of Titusville, and the patrol hanged the other two - they had stolen over two hundred head. Parker, Jam and Slick made up a shotgun patrol and rode all over DeSoto county at least once a month and had done so for the past year. Parker decided not to show Kate the latest notice. She was nervous enough as it was awaiting Callie and Clay's baby. He did promise her that he'd not ride patrol around Callie's due date though.

The minute Parker saw the colt he knew Morgan had not let him down - she was a beauty. She was a rich chestnut with three white socks and a white star in the middle of her forehead. She pranced down that ramp with her head held high. "What a princess you are - what a princess!" Parker said stroking her. Gus Jeeters called out, "Parker, the saddle you ordered came in on the *Mamie Lou* two days ago and it's a beaut!"

"I'll be by to get it in a little while. Gotta beat that storm home. Here, Beulah, let me help you with George. Well, what do you think about the filly, George? She's a princess, isn't she?"

George looked off into space just like he hadn't heard him but then said, "Gonna blow, little lady. Gonna blow."

"I know, Honey, we'll get home right away." Beulah looked sadly up at Parker, tears welled up in her faded eyes. Sap and Toad and Little Lily, called Lillily by most, were on the platform when the train came in. When he saw how dark the sky had become, he approached Parker. "Mister Parker, you want me to take the filly out to you tomorrow morning so's you can ride back to Tall Ten? Gonna start blowing soon. Wouldn't be no trouble a-tall."

"That's a thought, Sap." Parker thought on it but, wanting to be the one to surprise Kate, decided, "I'll stay a minute at Jeeters' and head on back fast. If it comes up real bad, I'll just stop at Lonesome Pen. Know I can get that far if I hurry."

And that's what he did. Having to hand lead the filly slowed them down, and by the time he arrived at Lonesome Pen he was soaked clean through. Even his slicker didn't keep his seat dry. He looked at the rain-sleek filly and said, "Maybe we oughta call you Thunder or Lightning, Princess. But I'm sure Meade will come up with just the right name. He's good at that."

They waited out the storm for over an hour. "Kate's probably giving me a real tongue lashing, Princess. Good thing she's not scared of a storm." He sat with his back against the palmetto thatched side and thought, maybe she hitched up Boss Man and went on over to Callie's. I hope she didn't. I wanta get a look at her surprise. Boy, she's gonna have a fit!

"Meade, get another dry log off the porch. Make it pine, I wanta heat this room up in a hurry. Can't get over how much the temperature's dropped in such a short time. Hard to believe it's September. More like January. It's actully chilly."

"Callie," Clay called toward the kitchen. "Can you see if Dixie got inside the barn?"

"Don't see her, Honey, so guess she did."

"Here she is," Meade yelled. "She's on the porch. Can't she come inside, Mama? Can't she?"

"Go on, and let Willy in too. Won't hurt a thing. Never saw such a storm. Can't be anything big or we'd have heard something about it, wouldn't we, Clay?"

"You know that Parker would've sent Jam or Slick over to tell us, Honey..."

He didn't get to finish his sentence. The expression on Callie's face told him that her time had come. "Callie - Callie, maybe you'd better lie down, Honey."

"My water broke," is all she said as she stared at the puddle on the kitchen floor.

"I'll ride for Kate. Now come on and lie down. We won't have time to get to town."

"But it took forever for Meade. We'll have plenty of time."

"Now, Honey, you probably won't have such a long time this go. They say it's easier after the first one. I'll ride for Kate."

"But the pains have already started, Clay, already."

The fury of the early fall storm was almost hurricane force. He told Callie to get in bed and stay there and Meade would sit beside her and keep the fire going and that he'd be back within the hour with his granny.

"But what if the baby comes before you get back?"

"I doubt that we'll have to worry about that, son. Your Mama's labor just started. It'll be a while yet."

He fought his way to the barn for the buckboard. He was all thumbs. Even had trouble getting the mare hitched. It seemed to take forever. He was soaked even before he left Ole Piney lane. He kept thinking, I know Callie's brave and I know Meade will do just what I said, but I could be wrong about this babe.

"Giddy-up, Dolly!" I just hope Parker's home, too. I remember Kate said that he'd promised to not do patrol 'til after the birth. Lordy, I never saw so much rain. Can hardly see. He wiped his face constantly trying to see the road that was now just a sheet of water. It'll take at least an hour to get to the Big House in this flood, then another hour to get back. I hope this baby's not in a hurry.

"Giddy-up, Dolly!"

Clay drove Dolly right up to the front porch. Although the rain had lessened, he was surprised to see the windows open. He shook off his slicker and dropped it on the rocker. When he looked down he saw that the cushions were sopping wet. That wasn't like Kate to leave the cushions out when a storm was coming. Aloud, he said, "Something's up!"

"Kate," he called as he stuck his head inside. No answer. "Parker! Anyone home?" Still no answer, The kitchen window was open and the table was soaked. Dish cloths were blown onto the floor. "Kate, oh, Kate! It's Clay!"

He ran upstairs, and when he saw the mess in Kate's and Parker's room, he knew that if she were home she would have closed the windows. The door to Jay's room was usually kept closed except when it was beastly hot and additional air was needed. The door was ajar so he peeked in. He didn't see Kate at first, she was slumped on the floor between the bed and dresser.

When he rounded the bed he saw her. "My God, Kate! What's wrong?" Her eyes were open. "Dear Lord, she's dead!" He knelt down beside her, put his ear down to her heart, checked her pulse. It was barely beating.

What am I going to do? She's had a heart attack, I guess. Where's Parker? Did he go to town for the doctor? No, he wouldn't have left her alone. He'd have sent one of the cowmen to town for him. Should I move her? I can't leave her here on the floor. "Oh God! Poor Callie!"

He sat on the edge of Jay's bed and declared to himself that he had to get his thoughts together. I should put her on the bed, cover her, go to the bunkhouse and get someone to ride into town for doc. That's what I'll do. "I'll go get Jam or Slick!"

Burt, Jam and Slick were all in the bunkhouse. They'd hightailed it back when they saw the clouds come up, and after Clay got to them they didn't take long to get saddled up. The rain was down to an occasional sprinkle. Slick went back to the big house with Clay and said that he'd sit with Kate. Clay left him sitting beside Kate, talking to her and telling her to hang on that Jam and Burt were riding for the Doc and Parker. He patted her hand and talked.

"Make tracks, Dolly!" Clay shouted aloud. "Make tracks! Giddy-up, old girl. I want to be the one to greet my baby. Hold on Callie! Oh, Honey, please hold on!"

Parker knew something was up when Burt and Jam came toward him. He got excited when he asked, "Is it Callie's time, boys?"

They looked at each other.

"What's wrong, Jam? What's happened?"

"It's Kate, Parker..., well, it's Callie too - I mean..."

"Kate? What's wrong with Katie?"

"Clay thinks she's had a heart attack or something like that, and we're going for ..."

Parker didn't wait. He had Chief in a gallop with the filly galloping beside them even before Jam finished explaining.

"Please, God, not my Katie - not my Katie!"

"Mama, does it hurt real bad? Mama, why're you groaning? Mama, you want me to go to the big house for Granny Kate and Clay? Do ya, Mama?"

"Shhh, Meade. Shhh! It'll be all right, honest. Ohhhhh! Ohhhhh, dear Lord."

She didn't want him to know how scared she was, but the pain was excruciating. Her tight fists were white, and her nails dug into her palms. She could feel the baby's head. Oh, Clay where are you? She had heard herself call for Thom earlier, and poor little Meade asked her why she was calling for his daddy. She couldn't find the words to explain, she just shook her head and put the knotted sheet into her mouth to prevent the yelling. She didn't want to frighten Meade, but she couldn't seem to restrain the outbursts.

He'll not get back in time, I just know it. What's keeping them anyway? The storms over. What's keeping them..?

"Mama, he's here. Clay's here!" Meade yelled excitedly as he ran toward the porch. Willy and Dixie were barking and clawing at the door. Clay had thrown off his slicker and hat on the porch but didn't bother to remove his mud covered boots. He'd decided to not tell Callie about Kate. He'd lie if he had to. Kate would have expected it.

"Honey, how're you doing? Jam and Burt went for the doc."

"Where's Mama? Where is she? Ohhhh!"

"Here, young lady, until she can get here, let's see how far along you are."

"Don't you touch me, Clay Willett! Don't you...Ohhh!"

"Callie, listen to me. You know I've been reading up on childbirth. Now, I don't know as much as Kate, but I do know a few things, young lady. I'm going to examine you to see how far along you are..."

"You'll not!"

"Callie, why're you fighting me? Why?"

She began to cry then. He could tell that she was exhausted. After all, she'd been in labor over three hours.

"Meade, I want you to stay in the kitchen, son. Your Mama's time is here, and Mama Kate can't get here for a while. I'm going to close the door. Now, everything is going to be fine, but you're to stay in there, or would you rather go outside? The storm's over, and I'm sure Dolly could use some attention, since I didn't have time to wipe her down. Would you do that for me, son? I'd appreciate it."

"Sure, Clay. She's probably cold, huh?" Meade was glad to have something to do.

"Now, Callie, let's see what our precious baby is up to. Grief! Callie, you didn't say that it was just a matter of minutes. Why didn't you tell me?"

She turned her head toward the wall and seeing the lamp that Thom's Aunt Beulah and Uncle George had given them for her and Thom's wedding present, she began to sob - just couldn't seem to help herself.

Clay was almost as exhausted as she and certainly as worried. Reading about childbirth was one thing - experiencing it, another. He had made up his mind that Doc Spooner should tend to Kate first and had told Slick that he'd be able to take care of Callie and the baby, that it was more important for the doc to stay with Kate. But now that he was here he wasn't so sure.

What's wrong with Callie? Doesn't she want their child? He knew that she didn't feel for him as she had for Thom. It really had not bothered him that much, for he knew she loved him, and he knew she respected him. But this rebellious attitude was new. Maybe all women go through this during childbirth, he thought. Maybe they're angry at us men for causing them so much pain...maybe...

But he didn't get the chance to finish his thought. Callie sat up and yelled so loud that Meade burst in the door yelling, "Mama, what's wrong, Mama?"

"Meade, you go on out, you hear!" Clay thought better about it and decided, "Do you want to help your brother or sister come into our family, son? Do you?"

"Oh, yes." he said relieved. "Oh, yeah, Clay."

"All right. I want to explain a few things about giving birth..."

"Ohhh!" Callie called out again. Clay pulled up the sheet then told Meade that he was to stand over by the pile of clean rags and to hand him the old sheet pieces that Callie had washed and carefully packed for her trip into Arcadia for when she needed them.

"Sure I can do that. That's easy."

"Good! Callie give a good push, we're about there..."

"WE? Where do you men get this WE? Ohhhh!"

"That's right, Honey. We're almost there. Here we are. Oh, Callie, we have a daughter. Now, Meade, don't get upset. You've seen Dixie give birth and there's not much difference."

Even before Clay had a chance to tie off the cord, Meade was beside him. "She's funny looking, isn't she, Clay? I mean all red and...would you listen to her yell! Boy, she sure can yell, can't she, Clay? Mama, listen to Annie yell! Boy!"

"Kate! Katie!" Parker called as he rushed upstairs.

"Up here, Parker," Slick called from upstairs.

"Oh my God! Slick, is she..."

"She's doing all right, she's doing all right," he whispered, patting her hand.

Parker was on his knees beside the bed. "Hang in there, Katie, hang in there. Burt and Jam will be back with Doc any minute, Katie, any minute. Guess what, Katie. You'll never guess what this crazy old husband of yours has up and done, Katie. That's why I was so late coming home, Honey, that and the storm. I got Meade a colt. Got him from Morgan. That's where I was. I wanted to surprise you, Honey, you and Meade. Oh, Miss Kate, she's a beauty - she's..." At that point Slick left the room and Parker broke down.

"Oh, Katie, don't leave me, Honey - don't leave me. I'm sorry I wasn't here - I'm so sorry..."

****

"Jay, if you feel you need to go to Tall Ten, you must go. I know it'll mean a lot to Mama Kate and Dad. He said it would be a long recovery, and you could begin work on the sequel to your book. I'll get along just fine."

"Honey, I know I should go but, well, I don't want to leave you.."

"You'd get a chance to visit little Annie and maybe pick up some pointers."

"I haven't decided to tell the folks yet, SuSu. They've got so much on their minds. Clay said that Dad won't even leave Tall Ten, that he's gotten so thin that they're as worried about him as they are about Mama."

"I think you need to be there. After all, I'm only a few months and feel fine, and we have good and attentive neighbors and..."

"I don't think I could stand it if anything happened to you - I really don't"

"Oh, Jay, I love you so," and she was in his arms.

Sap was at the station waiting for Jay. They hadn't spent much time together since they were teenagers, but when they were together the time apart evaporated. "Miss Kate was some better the other day when Toad and me rode out. Mr. Parker said she had learned to say a few words and can walk holding onto the back of a light chair. It's slow but she's trying."

Toad had latched on to Jay's small trap and was trying his best to carry it. Jay decided to tell Sap about SuSu. "Haven't even told Mama or Dad, Sap. Not even Callie, but looks like SuSu is in the family way."

Sap hit him a good one. "Here, Toad, don't be dragging that." He took the small trap, and Jay slung the large trunk into the back of the buckboard. On almost every building in town there was a cattle notice posted. "Looks like the papers are right. Clay sent me an article from the *DeSoto County News*. I didn't know the rustling was as bad as this."

"Worse - worse. Some of the ranchers in these parts would as soon steal Mr. Parker's cattle as not. Got so all his men hafta carry a rifle and a pistol too. Real bad, Jay. Real bad. Found a whole herd they stole jes' 'fore they loaded 'em on a boat over in Tampa jes' las' week. Judge gave 'em a year and a day. Real bad. Mr. Parker's had to hire him two more men and said to me he's not too sure of 'em, that they might be in cahoots wid a gang."

Toad was in the back of the buckboard singing at the top of his lungs. When Jay turned and looked at him, Toad turned his head and shut up fast. "I like to hear you sing, Toad. Don't stop on account of me."

"That boy always singing or talking. Lily Mae said she was sorry she evah teach him ta sing." He laughed proudly when he said it, and Toad resumed, but kept it low so just he could enjoy it. They passed Lonesome Pen, the cow pen about half way between Tall Ten and town. Two cowmen were there, and Sap said, "Think those are the two your pa hired."

"They're not but boys. Don't look like the kind Pa would hire on."

"Mr. Parker not thinking too straight of late he's so worried 'bout Miss Kate. Jam and Slick told me that they done told those boys that if'n they cause your pa any trouble that they can expect to say howdy to their maker 'fore they hit twenty year."

"What'd they say?"

"Don' know. They didn't say nothin', I reckon." They chatted the entire three-mile trip, Sap telling him about the filly Parker had bought Meade and how much little Annie looked like Callie, spittin' image of her ma, and they seemed to be gettin' along just fine. He told him that a lot of ranchers had started planting citrus on account of the rustling and asked Jay if anyone had written him about how nice the new mule-drawn street car was. Why, they had it running all the way from the river far as Coon Prairie.

"Things sure have changed since we were boys, haven't they, Sap? Even before the railroad came things had changed. But we aren't as sophisticated as Bartow with its Summerlin Institute and the cornet band. Have you ever heard it? And a lot of the streets have even been paved. Makes it real nice. Some Englishmen started a Jockey Club, and they have racing tournaments over at Ft. Meade. I know it's still just a frontier town, but it's still progressive, and they're always having a dance at one of the opera houses.

"I'm hoping that since Arcadia was named the county seat and they built the new court house that we'll see this town truly grow. But not much chance unless they stop running the cattle down main street. Can you believe that they'd run them past the fancy DeSoto Abstract Co. and the First National Bank Building? Somehow, doesn't seem smart. It's outlawed in Bartow now. But, we've got such a bad reputation. When I tell anyone up in Middleburg or Orange Park that I'm from Arcadia they start laughing. Honestly, they do. All they seem to read is about rustling between the ranchers and gunfights and everything bad. When I try to tell them about the great picnics and dances and church activities, they don't even listen. We've got a lot to live down before new settlers want to come to DeSoto County, we really do.

"Now you take Middleburg, it's mostly just a lumber town - turpentine and the likes, but it's such an easy-living little town. The school where SuSu teaches, it's in an area they call Whitesville. Just has a general store, blacksmith and such, but there's always a dance or a picnic or something going on at the church. The one SuSu and I attend, the Methodist Church on Main Street, well, the people are so friendly. And, we can catch a steamer at the end of Wharf Street and go to Green Cove Springs or to Jacksonville. There really is a lot to do. I do love sitting on the shores of Black Creek and sketching. There's a different feel to the land there. You know, in some areas they say that the elevation is near 250 feet. Imagine!"

When Parker opened the front door, Jay had to quickly control his expression. He wasn't prepared, even though Clay had written him that Parker had got thin and that he and Callie were very worried about him. Jay hugged him, trying to keep the tears from forming, but Parker didn't have Jay's control and clung to him helplessly crying. Sap couldn't stand to see him like that, so he got busy taking Jay's trap and trunk out of the buckboard. Toad tried to help, but Sap fussed at him, "You git back up there. Don' you see Mistuh Parker an' Jay need alone time? Now, git!"

Toad hung his head low but rolled his big eyes up enough to witness the scene on the front porch. Toad didn't like to miss anything. Jay turned to Sap, "Come on in, Sap. I'm sure there'll be some lemonade or tea made, and just bet I can rustle up some cookies."

"Things aren't like they used to be around here, you know, son." Parker said. "Callie brought over some biscuits, and Darlene churned up butter, and we have some blackberry jam your ma made last year, but cookies we don't have."

"Beulah did send Irece Whaley over, you know, Wilvern's wife, but you know your ma didn't take to her too good. She'd rather have a good colored woman, I know, but Irece needed the work on account of her little boy being sickly. I guess she'll hafta do 'til we can find someone else. She's not much of a cook, either, but is strong as an ox and can lift your mama and do for her and clean. She's real good at that..." and on he rambled. Jay and Sap exchanged knowing looks.

"Dad, don't you worry about any cookies. I just hope Callie's biscuits have improved."

"Heck, Callie didn't make them, Clay did. He can almost out-do Mattie when it comes to biscuits." Parker heard the chair scraping the floor above them and knew that Kate had heard Jay. "Your ma's up. We best get up there fast, or she'll try to come down those stairs..."

He didn't finish what he was going to say, he was so anxious to ward off Katie's descent. "I'm coming, Katie. Don't you try those stairs!" Jay followed him slowly. He wasn't anxious to see his mother. He knew she'd have to have changed a lot, and it saddened him. But he wasn't prepared for the changes. Her left side was partially paralyzed, eye drooped and mouth turned downward. It was like she was two people. She realized his discomfort and tried hard as she could to smile and finally managed to say, "Jay."

"That's the first word she's said all morning. That's good Katie. That's real good, Honey. I believe you've been practicing the whole blessed morning. That's what I think."

She took the pad down from the top of her washstand and wrote, "Don't treat me like a baby, Parker. Welcome home, Jay." Jay removed the chair and put his arms under hers, lifting her up, and round and round they went. It was something he had done since he was big enough to lift her, and she had always enjoyed the sport of it. He couldn't believe how light she was.

"Mama, I've got wonderful news. Guess what? I'm gonna be a daddy."

He held her out from him, and she gave him a crooked smile and her eyes danced. Again she said, "Jay."

He thought as he watched the two of them, why can't things stay the same? I'm afraid my baby won't ever get to see his grandparents.

After he, Sap and Toad drank their tea, Jay went into his old room, closed the door and climbed wearily onto his bed. I don't understand the order of things, I guess. I wish SuSu were here. I miss her so. He turned over and faced the window. He stared at the water oaks and willows that grew thick around the pond. He was remembering when Thom had come galloping up over twelve long years ago, and Callie, who hadn't seen him in six months, had been trying so hard to be lady like. But when she saw her Thom she forgot all about being a lady, hiked up her dress and ran fast as her coltish legs could take her. She hopped up on Thom's horse and with her arms clinging to him he sped her toward the grassy slope and the privacy of the draping willows.

He remembered Mattie saying, "Miss Callie ain't evah gonna be no house woman what with cleaning and cooking and the likes," and Jay had thought but didn't say that he didn't like the new Callie one bit, that he liked his sister carefree and riding like the wind and....

Clay had written that little Annie had given the smile back to his Callie and that he was so relieved. He'd been very worried about her. Jay thought, I wonder if our baby will change things between me and SuSu. I've heard that it sometimes does. It surely did for Callie and Thom. Oh, I pray that things stay the same. I don't know if I can stand much more change, Lord, I surely don't. He thought of Kate and Parker and how frail they had become and Thom's being killed and finally gave into his grief. Sobbing uncontrollably, he buried his head in the feather pillow.

CHAPTER III LONESOME PEN

"Jim and Bobby, did you say? Hell, they ain't no Jim and Bobby!" Reason Harris spit out. "Jam, what's happened to Parker anyway? Now, I know Miss Kate's not doing good, but Parker Meade's always been as smart a rancher as this state's ever seen, and for him to hire on those hands without checking up on 'em don't make a lick of sense."

"It's like this, Reason, he's desperate, that's what he is, and with Callie having her baby and not able to help out and Clay not knowing much about Tall Ten... well, he's just given in to a terrible case of the worries, that's what!"

Slick hit his fist down hard on the pine table and exclaimed, "I done told Mister Parker that those two ain't what they say they are and who they say they are! I knowed it the minute he came riding up with them. Now what cowman comes into Arcadia telling everyone within earshot their life's story, about all those ranches they worked on? Hell, they ain't even seventeen year old, and if they'd worked on that many ranches they'd hada start 'fore they could walk. Mister Parker said they were just tall-telling, but I knowed they were flat out lying. That's what! Lying!"

Reason looked from one to the other, got red in the face and burst out with, "They're Sloan Pickett and Turner MacClellan sure as shootin'! Rode with the Brady gang up in 'Bama 'fore they even got to Florida. I'd stake Pintsize on it, and that's the best cow pony in this whole state!"

"Jay said that when he and Sap rode in they were at Lonesome Pen justa sittin' on their mounts doing nothin'. I'd be willing to bet they were meeting men from the Brady gang and telling 'em just where the beeves are. Hell, don't make one bit of difference if Parker branded their bellies and cropped their ears, those thieves they're selling 'em to don't give a cotton- pickin' damn if'n they're stole!" Jam added.

"You wants that I should go tell Parker?" Reason asked. Jam and Slick said in unison, "We sure do!"

Then Jam said, "Jay's over at Ole Piney visiting Callie, so maybe we'd best wait 'til he gets back. Maybe he can talk some sense into Parker."

Reason wasn't letting up on it. "I know for a fact that they're the two that shot Roy Prevatt over near Melbourne - blew him right out of his saddle. Only witness was his wife Maybelle, and she ain't been able to say a word since it happened, 'most a year ago. The sheriff got her to draw their picture and asked her what color hair they had and everything, but even though she couldn't talk and don't know how to write, she sure as hell could shake her head, and when he got to brown hair she shook that old gray head to beat the band. So he got a real good description and put those drawings up on 'most every pine tree in the whole county. I can't believe that some of those posters didn't find their way down here - $100.00 reward money on 'em. Roy's children are offering it. We thought that they'd be hidin' out over near Big Cypress Lake, you know, near Ft. Drum. But to think that Parker Meade done hired 'em on..."

Jam spoke up, "Maybe we'd best not wait on Jay coming back. Maybe we'd best all ride over to Ole Piney and tell Callie and Jay what you suspect, Reason."

"Suspect? Hell, I know, and if'n I could come up with one of them posters I'd have proof to show Parker - indeed, I would!"

"Seems too hot for January," Clay said, while handing Jay and Callie the tepid tea.

"Sometimes gets to well below freezing up in Middleburg," Jay said. "Can't imagine why most every farmer and rancher around there are putting in citrus. Some of them are giving up on beeves altogether and're raising hogs along with oranges. Said they're tired of all the problems with rustlers, and talk is that within the next few years the state'll require fences..."

"Not in our lifetime, it won't," Callie interrupted.

"I'm not so sure, Honey, they're talking about it in Tallahassee."

"Yes, Clay, they're talking about it. Talk! Talk! That's all it is!"

Jay frowned. Why is she so out of sorts with him? She hasn't said a kind word to him since I got here. She'd never have talked to Thom like that. He felt Clay bristle, something completely out of character. There's something wrong in this household, he thought.

Callie finished nursing Annie and put her in her cradle. Slick's right, Jay thought. She's the spittin' image of Callie. Callie returned to the front porch. She looks worn out, but that's not surprising. She's up before first light taking care of Annie, then cooking enough to take over to the big house, then back to Ole Piney to tend to her own family. But Clay is right beside her helping, and Meade's good about chores. I know she's worried about the folks, but I think it's more than that.

Meade came riding up on Princess Stella announcing, "Three horsemen riding up - might be rustlers, Ma!"

"Meade Garvin, if they were rustlers do you think they'd ride on the main road? Do you?"

"Well, no, Mama, but Granpa Parker said you can't be too careful these days." He slid off Stella, pulled her after him and informed her that he was going to hide her in the barn just in case they were bad men, that he sure didn't want the best filly in all of DeSoto county to get stolen.

"Parker should be given a throne in heaven for giving Stella to Meade. I never saw..."

Callie interrupted Clay, "Throne in heaven, my eye! Grief Clay! The horse is much too big for him - can't even get on her without help. Don't know what possessed him to do such a dumb thing!"

Jay noticed that Clay was biting the inside of his cheek. He's sure frustrated.

Finally Clay said, "What's wrong, Callie? Are you tired, or are you hot? You haven't had a kind word to say since Jay got here. I think that he deserves a little peace and quiet after such a long trip and..."

"Oh, you do? You really think that, Clay? Well, I deserve a little peace and quiet myself. Work from sunup to sundown and up most of the night with Annie. Don't I deserve some of that wonderful peace and quiet, mister?"

About then Jam, Slick and Reason galloped up. They could sense the tension in the air. Jam broke it by saying, "Need to talk to y'all." And even before he dismounted he was telling them about Reason's suspicions.

"I don't think we need any more bad news at Tall Ten, Reason, I really don't!" and with that Callie whirled around and walked back into the house.

"What's wrong with Callie? Boy, is she out of sorts," Slick said.

"She's run down, that's all. The baby saps her strength, and then she feels responsible for Kate and Parker. She's plenty worried about them," Clay answered.

"You need to get someone out here to help her, Clay. Heck, she's practically runnin' Tall Ten and... well, she needs someone to do the chores."

Clay could tell how worried Slick was. "I've already made up my mind to do just that, Slick. I'll talk to Sap about him and Lily Mae moving out and living in Mattie's quarters if Parker approves, but I can't get him to commit to anything. I know Kate likes Lily Mae, and it just seems to be the answer. Every time I bring it up Callie turns a deaf ear."

Jay spoke up, "If Sap says it's all right then go ahead. I'll talk to Dad. Callie doesn't need to worry about the big house plus the ranch. It's too much for one person to handle."

"Well, what're we gonna do about those boys?" Jam questioned.

"We don't know for sure that they're the same ones who shot Roy Prevatt, now do we?" Jay stated.

"No, but I think someone had better tell the marshal so he can wire Melbourne to find out. If they are the killers, then they're as mean as anyone I've ever heard of, and they for sure are on Tall Ten for a reason, and it sure as heck ain't the $15.00-a-month pay," Reason said emphatically. "Where'd Burt go? Ain't he ridin' shotgun patrol over near Lonesome Pen with them?"

"I didn't see him when Sap and I rode out," Jay said.

"Should've been with them - left with them. You don't suppose that they killed him and..."

Callie burst out the door. "I don't want y'all talking like that in front of Meade! You hear? Those two might be innocent of all you're talking about - might be just who they say they are..."

"If they are, Callie, then they don't have anything to worry about, do they? The marshal does need to be alerted so we can get to the truth."

"Well, Mr. Willett, I for one don't want any blood spilled on Tall Ten. You'd better be sure that they're the ones. It's my ranch, you know! Do you hear? "

"The whole county hears, you Callie!" Clay let that sink in, then turned around and told Meade that he was to stay with his mama and went to the corral to saddle Dancer. Jay drove the buckboard back to the big house to tell Parker what was going on, and Clay, Reason, Jam and Slick rode for town.

Callie and Meade stood on the porch watching them ride off. Callie was biting her lower lip and questioning why she had talked to Clay like that. *What in the world's wrong with me? I hate myself when I behave like this.* She was sniffling so loudly that Meade put his arms around her waist and buried his head in her apron. "You're gonna be fine, Mama. I'll take care of you. Don't you worry; I'm here. Those bad men aren't gonna get you and Annie. And they sure aren't gonna get Willy or Princess Stella. Nosiree!"

****

"You should've taken care of him, Turner. Could've made it look like he was trampled to death. Wouldn't take much to stampede these stupid beeves."

"Hell, he ain't ever gonna get loose from those ropes. By the time they find him he'll be dead as a doornail, and we'll be long gone. They ain't gonna know who done it and can't prove a thing, now can they? I said can they, Sloan?"

"Don't exactly know, but I'd feel better if you'd killed him."

"Yeah, like you done old man Prevatt and got the whole goddamned state after us!"

"They ain't caught us, have they? By the time Brady and Fisher get here and run that herd over Myakka way to Ft. Ogden, Swaim'll be on the Peace with the *Crying Loon* just a waiting for 'em, then it's out to Charlotte Harbor, then riding the Gulf all the way to Key West and our gold. This lousy $15.00 a month won't even keep us in shine."

"You best not be countin' it 'til Brady shows. He should've been here over a week ago. What the hell's keepin' him?"

He could see the riders in the distance, and they were hauling it. "Whoa! What the hell? What're they all riding out here for? Bet that old woman up and died! I'll just bet!"

Clay turned to the others and said, "I'll tend to them, men."

Jam thought, sure hope your imagination is working good. If these boys are the killers, they've gotta be desperate.

Sloan sat quietly, his hand resting on his thigh next to his revolver. Clay watched Sloan's fingers drumming slowly. Sloan was the first to speak.

"Something going on at Tall Ten, men? Me and Bobby waiting for Burt to come back from checking the herd."

Clay responded, "Miss Kate took a turn for the worse, and we're riding in to get the doc and bring out Mrs. Young and Irece to help out. Y'all give Burt a while, and when he catches up, be sure to tell him. And better come on into town, because I have to buy feed and supplies for you to take back to Tall Ten. The family won't be leaving Miss Kate, and Parker will need all the help he can get - all right?"

"Sure - happy to help out. We'll be in directly." Sloan's grin of satisfaction was not lost on Clay.

Stupid, smart-ass writer. God, some people are flat out dumb, Sloan thought. The fact that neither he nor Turner could read or write didn't faze him.

"Where's Burt?" Slick whispered. "Where the hell is Burt? I bet those bastards done killed him!"

"Now, Slick, we don't know that, and like Callie said, we don't want any blood spilled on Tall Ten."

"Well, if Parker was his old self, you'd be seeing a mighty lot of their blood. Callie's gone and got soft, that's what."

"Don't go on like that. She's right about us not being positive that they're the ones who killed Prevatt. You'll have to agree with that."

"Well, Clay, I got a gut feelin' that's jes' who they are all right, and Parker would be on them with his cow whip and everything else he could lay a hand to if he was his old self - that's what!"

Clay said to himself, I've got to think on this. He could be right.

****

The more Burt struggled the tighter the ropes became. "Sons o' bitches! Wish they'd gone ahead and killed me!" But, I gotta get word to Tall Ten. Goddamned ants crawling all over me gonna drive me plumb outta my mind. All I'd need is a rattler to decide to pay me a visit - probably crawl right up my britches leg.

Burt was wringing wet. "That does it! Goddamned blow flies! Get offa me, you goddamned flies! Get..go on get..Jesus! I hate you, you goddamned flies!" He began to sob.

As soon as the foursome was out of sight, Clay called a halt. "Jam, you think Burt's around here some place? Maybe they didn't kill him. Maybe they just tied him up and left him for the cats. If he's around here and he's alive, we need to get to him and..."

"You wants that I should circle back for a look-see?"

"Yes, that's exactly what I want you to do. It's obvious that they're waiting for someone. Jay said that they were there when he and Sap rode out this morning, and that's been over six hours. You might as well go with him," Clay said to Slick and Reason. "If they are really a part of the gang you'll be needed. I'll have the marshal wire Melbourne and wait for the response. In the meantime we'll get a posse together, and if need be, we'll join you."

"Good thinking, Clay! Damn!" They put their spurs to their mounts, and Jam turned around to Slick. "Hell, he's smarter than Thom ever thought to be. You see the way he play-acted for those two, and they believed every word he said. That Clay Willett has got some smarts. Too bad Callie don't know it."

"Quiet, Jam! Did you hear that moaning? Did you?"

They stopped dead still. Reason had gone on around to the west, the heavy brush was dry - hadn't had much rain since early December.

"Might be Reason." Jam replied.

"Don't think so less'n he's hurt. I'd swear I heard moaning. Listen up! There again. Now don't you go makin' noise. I need to hear," Slick cautioned.

"Now, how'd I make so much noise that you couldn't hear, huh? You come to be some kind of bossy of late. Near 'bout as bossy as Callie, and you ain't even had a baby!"

Slick ignored him. "I know for a fact that it's Burt." He got down and followed the noise. They must've done a good job of hiding him. Good thing these palmettos ain't the sawtooth or I'd be cut to pieces. He used his rifle barrel to push the clumps of palmettos aside - rattlers used them for cover. Maybe my mind's playing tricks on me and I didn't hear a thing. Maybe.

Slick stopped and Jam said, "You must've heard a ghost, Slick. There ain't nobody anywheres around here. Hell, I'm gonna go on into town."

"Well, I ain't gonna give up this easy. Burt sure wouldn't give up on me this quick. Go - go on!"

"If he thinks he's gonna make me feel bad about going, he can think again. Old fool! Hearing things again. Why, he's got so hard o' hearing, I hafta yell as it is," Jam mumbled as he rode off.

Jam saw Reason riding from around the hammock. He had his arm in the air, but not wanting Sloan or Turner to hear, said nothing. He rode toward him, and trying to get out of the palmettos and into the brush, he skirted the sand pines. "You see anything, Reason?"

"Not one thing. If he's around here they sure hid him good."

"Maybe they buried him."

Reason retorted, "Hell, those two ain't goin' to the trouble to bury anything less'n it's gold."

"Well, I'm going on into town. If the marshal gets up a posse, I'll ride with 'em. You comin'?"

"Don't think I'd better. If they're waiting for the Brady gang, think maybe one of us oughta be here so we can see what's going on."

Jam laughed, "That Slick swears he's hearing moaning. Old fool. He'll be here 'til dark. He sure hates to be wrong about anything. He's gotten like a cantankerous old woman."

Jam turned around in his saddle and said softly, "See ya," and using the hammock as a blind, galloped off.

Slick whispered, "Maybe I'd better get up on you, Toby, so's I can see a good far piece." He thought, I'd swear on a stack of Bibles that I heard moaning, but maybe Jam's right. Maybe I'm just hearing things.

He saw Reason approach but could tell by his attitude that he hadn't found Burt. "Wanted you to know that I'm goin' to ride to the back of that pine stand and wait, Slick. If that gang shows, they'll make enough noise for me to hear from there."

"Go on, Reason. I'll join you directly. Just wanta look a little longer."

Clay rode past the DeSoto Abstract Company building, waved to John and Clarence Polk, who were sitting on the steps of their mercantile store and rode on to the courthouse. Marshal Jennings was down Wachula way, Chubb said, so Clay went to the telegraph office. His mind wasn't on Sloan and Turner, and it wasn't on Parker and Kate - it was on Callie and her behavior since Annie was born. At first she'd become her old self, smiling, laughing easily, carefree. But the past few months she'd... well, she was impossible to please. She didn't seem to want him to touch her, recoiled whenever he as much as hugged her. Clay knew that he needed to talk to someone about it, but who? Kate couldn't respond, and Jay wouldn't understand. Maybe all women got like that after giving birth, he thought. I know she's run down and worried, but it's more than that. I can't write, can't seem to get my thoughts together. She's even fussy with Meade. I've never seen her like this.

"Good afternoon, Lucy."

"Afternoon, Clay. How're Callie and the baby doing?"

"To tell you the truth I'm worried about Callie. She's so tired, you know, taking care of the baby and Kate and Parker. It seems to have worn her out."

Lucy laughed. "I know all about that tired business, Clay, indeed I do. After Buster was born Homer threatened to send me back to Wachula. Now don't laugh, he truly did. You know what a mild mannered man Homer is most of the time, but he won't take sass from any woman, and guess I was so tired that I was some kinda fussy." She laughed as she said it.

"Guess I've been a bit edgy myself lately. It hurts to see Parker and Kate like this. But that's not what I came in for. Looks like we might just have us a problem at Tall Ten."

"My, my, what kind a problem?"

"You know those two young men Parker hired?"

"Sure do, still got fuzz on their faces. Everyone in town wondered why he'd hire 'em."

"Reason Harris just returned from working Thom's dad's ranch up in Crescent City and told Jam and Slick that those two are wanted for killing a man up in Melbourne about six months ago. Now, we don't know for sure that they're the ones, but Reason surely thinks so. I want to send a telegram to Sheriff Murrhee to get an accurate description, and if they fit it, then think we better get a posse and round up those two. When Marshal Jennings comes back from Wachula, he'll have a surprise waiting for him."

"My - my, won't he though!"

Slick sat on Toby, sweat dribbling down his chin. He had taken his hat off and was fanning himself with it. "Let's mosey on over to that shade oak, Toby. No need in us cooking ourselves in this hot sun. I can hear just as good from over there. Now, Toby, I know I heard moaning. Don't care what that smart-ass Jam says. He's been gettin' on my nerves of late. Can't say a blessed thing without him wanting to argue 'bout it. Hell! Might as well be married, if'n I hafta put up with that."

He stopped in the shade and told Toby that he'd ride him over to Lonesome Pond in a little while, that he just wanted to give Burt another chance to moan.

"Now you take Burt," he said to Toby. "He don't argue like Jam, real pleasant to be around and....Shhhh, Toby! Listen up! Did you hear that? By gum, there ain't no mistakin' that. That's sure 'nuff a genuine moan if I ever heard it. Yep, there it goes again."

He slid off Toby and began walking toward the sound.

"Gawd almighty, Burt! Look at ya - Gawd almighty!"

****

"Meade, lets you and me and Annie ride over to see Mama Kate - see how she's doing."

"You feeling better, Mama?"

"I wasn't sick, Honey. What're you talking about?"

"Oh, I thought that maybe you weren't feeling good because of the way you fussed at Clay. Don't you like Clay anymore, Mama?"

"Why on earth would you ask a body that? Course I like Clay. He's my husband."

"Well, that's how Leon Rivers talks to me, and he sure don't like me."

"How do you know he doesn't?"

"Cause he told me so, and that's just how he talks to me, just like you talk to Clay. Everyone in the whole school knows that Leon don't like me."

"Doesn't, Meade. Doesn't like you, not don't like. Sit down, son. I need to talk to you. Now, I know I've been out of sorts lately what with having to get up with Annie and tending to the folks, and I guess that I have been short with Clay, but it certainly doesn't mean that I don't like him. He's a wonderful man and..."

"I like Clay, Mama. I like Clay as much as I did Daddy - sometimes more. Is that wrong? I mean, that I like him more'n Daddy? Just sometimes though..."

"No, son. I like him more than I did your daddy sometimes, too. Really I do."

He seemed relieved. "I'll get Dolly hitched, Mama. You want that I should help you with Annie?"

Callie had to turn around, quickly - the tears had started, and she didn't want Meade to see them. She shook her head no and ran for the bedroom. Lord, what's wrong with me? Why can't I act right? Maybe I am just worn out like Jay said. Oh, Clay, when you come home I'm gonna talk real nice and be so loving and do what's right, and I do love you. Really I do.

****

"Clay, here it comes." Lucy wrote furiously and handed the message to Clay. When he'd read it he said, "We've got to get the posse, Lucy. Got a perfect description. You think Homer can leave the store? I'll go on over to the courthouse and tell Chubb what I heard. Maybe I'll go to the depot to get Sap. Oh, Lucy, send this message to Sheriff Murrhee. *MEN FIT DESCRIPTION. STOP. THINK THEY'RE WAITING FOR BRADY GANG. STOP. FORMING POSSE BECAUSE MARSHAL JENNINGS IN WACHULA. STOP. WILL KEEP YOU INFORMED. STOP. CLAY WILLETT.*

****

"Sorry I ain't got any water, Burt. Does this feel good? I mean those old rope burns sure can hurt a fellow." Burt couldn't respond. All he could do was moan. "Now hold on if'n you can, and I'll put you up on Toby and we'll go on over to Lonesome Pond, and that water'll help ease you. Wisht I had some salve for those rope burns, surely do, and something for the skeeter bites. Now you hold on. Here, put your arms 'round my neck, and I'll have you up on Toby in no time at all. Wish Reason wasn't so far away. I'd have him to help us."

When Slick realized that Burt couldn't hold on to Toby, he climbed up behind him and steadied him and slowly headed for the pond, talking all the while, telling him as how Reason recognized the boys as killers of Roy Prevatt over in Melbourne and how he couldn't understand why none of those wanted posters had got down to Arcadia, and on and on he rambled. Burt's head bobbed up and down bumping against his chest. He was covered with welts. The blow flies, mosquitoes and ants had left their marks.

Slick knelt beside the small pond and pushed aside the burr weeds and shooting stars and pulled up some cattails. Then he dug down deep til he got to the gray clay soil along the ponds edge. Burt was stretched out on the bank under the pond willows. Slick stripped his clothes off and smeared him with the warm clay. "Now, this won't do the job like Miss Kate's salve, Burt, but will ease you some. It'll help take the itching and sting away. Them Indians been using this stead of salve for a long time. Don't that help, Burt? Now, don't that ease it a little? Thought it would. Yep, those Indians been a lot smarter than the White man in a lotta ways, ummmm, a lotta ways."

Burt didn't respond, but Slick could see his heart beat. He almost jumped out of his britches when the red shouldered hawk screamed in the willows above him and anxiously looked up when the flock of white ibis flew over, their wings making a strong, thrashing sound. Nervously he made himself look at Burt. Gawd, Burt, I never in my life saw the likes of this. Damned blow flies 'most ate you up...Gawd Burt...

****

"Does that look like Brady? Hey, Turner, is it or ain't it?"

"Can't tell from this far. Could be. Must be at least six of 'em, but I..."

"Hold up, you two!" Reason yelled. He had seen the posse from the other side of the pine stand and recognized Chubb's stallion, so knew who it was. He had his rifle pointed at them and was grim faced.

"What the hell!" Turner yelled. "What ya pointing that gun at me for?"

"Well, I'll be telling you since you asked so nice like and since the posse is here..."

"Posse!" Sloan yelled.

Reason said in his most authoritative voice, "I'd not be gettin' too close to that revolver, Turner - or are you Sloan?"

"What you talking about, mister? I'm Bobby..."

He didn't finish. Clay rode up with Sap beside him. He had borrowed a rifle from deputy Chubb, and had it pointed right at the two of them.

"Boys, we just got a description from Melbourne that seems to fit the two of you. Chubb, you want to take Sap and disarm these two imposters."

"What's this all about?" Turner asked. No one had even noticed Slick with Burt sitting in front of him riding Toby from around the hammock until Slick called out. When he did, Turner and Sloan knew the jig was up.

"Don't you put your nigger hands on me!" Sloan yelled at Sap. Sap smiled at him, and made sure that he rubbed his hands up and down his arms as he took the revolver from him, and said, "Now look at how black this here white boy done got, deputy Chubb. Would ya just."

Chubb smiled at him and said, "Why, Sap, I do believe that black color might be permanent. You did say that once it touches you it won't come off, didn't you?"

"Yessuh, that's how I got mine. Some old nigger wipe his black hands all over me, and look what happened?"

Sloan and Turner had their heads down and didn't say a word, but the other men got a big laugh out of Sap's sport with the two killers.

Chubb, Homer and Tyler decided to stay behind just in case the Brady gang showed and suggested that Slick take Burt on into town with the other men. Jam was so concerned that he re-emphasized the need for him to see to Burt. "Yep, you best take him on in, Slick. He sure is in need of a doctor. Never saw such as that."

"Told you I heard moaning. I sure 'nuff know a moan when I hear one."

Jam just shook his head. He's going to be hard to live with from now on for sure. Bet I'll hafta listen to how he saved Burt's life and how I didn't believe that he heard anything. Hell, might as well be married having to listen to him carry on over and over again about hearing that moan... Gawd! Might as well be married!

BOOK IV:

THE FAR SIDE OF FOREVER

CHAPTER I ATHEA MANOR PLANTATION

Spring 1893

The watermelons and potatoes had been harvested, and later in the summer the cotton and corn would be ready. The LeConte pears were doing for middle Florida what the orange was doing for the peninsula. Harrison and Conner had put in ten acres of pears and tobacco each and an acre of paper-shell pecans and another in peaches. The rest of the forty acres they put mostly in watermelons. Conner had taken to the gentleman farmer role as easily as he had the gaming tables on the steamers, and many times Harrison had said to Juanita, "He's come home, Cherie - come home. I've never seen him so happy."

"Well, I'll admit he loves to run things. You'd think he was an authority on every subject regarding plantation life, now wouldn't you?" she responded warmly but with a touch of suspicion.

Juanita continued to drive the two miles into town most days joining Rose at the shop. Melvia Small had been hired to look after Young Nolan, who was now three and a real handful. Juanita had thought that Delia was willful, but Young Nolan, named for Conner's da, and called Young by the colored people on Athea Plantation, had the temperament of his own da, even though he did not resemble him. He was a beautiful child with a shock of curly auburn hair and big blue-grey eyes fringed with long black lashes. Melvia and the colored women on Athea spoiled him beyond all reason. Juanita finally just threw up her hands and prayed.

After Conner arrived in Monticello, he and Juanita began looking for a house. He never questioned where she got so much money, and she didn't volunteer the information. Besides, she thought, it's none of his blasted business - he's not my husband. The Rease Plantation, that Millie Bailey had suggested that she look at, had suited her and Conner. But he had insisted on changing the exterior as well as the name. His mum's family had come from the small town of Athea in Ireland. He was not fond of the colonial period of the Rease house. He preferred the style and openness of the French houses that he had admired in New Orlean's with their long balconies across the second floor bordered with intricate iron grill work. Juanita had never been to New Orleans but had seen pictures of houses of that type and found them intriguing. But, being Juanita, she also found the need to fight him. At first she reasoned that it was her money, or at least most of it, and she should certainly have some say so as to the name and decor. But Conner had received some money from the sale of his Kissimmee property from Fred Saunders, who had acted as his agent, and continued to correspond with him, so she gave in to his wishes, not really reluctantly, for she knew that his taste was impeccable.

She couldn't for the life of her understand why Conner had given Saunders the time of day. They were pleasant enough people and had always been kind to Delia, but for Conner to have befriended the storekeeper...well? Once, when her curiosity could no longer be stifled, she had opened a letter from Fred. She couldn't believe how formal he was. It was Mr. O'Farrell this and Mr. O'Farrell that. Grief! You'd have thought that Conner was some kind of king the way he was writing.

She understood that he had a way about him and people who had barely met him would seek his advice on almost any matter. Why, he was asked to accompany just the most influential man in all of Jefferson County on a trip to Virginia to help him select a hunting dog, and Conner had hardly been in Monticello more than a few weeks when he was asked. What could a gambler possibly know about a blooming hunting dog, she had asked Harrison. She couldn't believe his reply. "Cherie, Conner has that extra sense some people are blessed with. I've heard that the Irish have that instinct."

"Instinct? Harrison, you have to be daft! He's playing Mr. Turnbull just like he would one of those Mississippi gamblers, and you know it full well. If he spoils my chance to make something of myself here in Monticello, I'll...I'll...well, I don't know what, but I'll think of something." But he didn't spoil a single thing, and the very next month Mr. Sherrott asked him to accompany him to Kentucky to help him select a race horse, and Conner, big as you please, went with him. What really irked Juanita was that the blasted dog was the envy of the entire county and that the horse had won every race Mr. Sherrott had entered him in. And Conner, well, he just took it in his stride, just as if he were gifted with all those special powers. She couldn't believe him. She really couldn't. But she couldn't help but get a kick out of it. He had the whole town bamboozled. Juanita liked that.

And when they opened John Perkins' Opera House in '90, just who do you think he asked to be the main speaker? Conner O'Farrell, that's who. Juanita thought that she'd for sure die before, during and after that night. It indeed was the most exciting thing that had ever happened to her, even more than the night she debuted on the tightrope. She and Rose and their four seamstresses had worked so hard for over four months before it opened to have the elaborate gowns ready. People from Tallahassee, Jacksonville, Thomasville and Atlanta, not to mention the dignitaries from Washington, D.C., were to be there. And to think that Conner had been asked to introduce all those people, and she'd get to sit in the special box and, oh my, she was excited.

She fumed and ranted and raved over every detail of her gown and Rose's, and that Mr. know-it-all Conner was amused by it all. Finally, when she simply could not decide on the fabric and design, he sat down with her, took her hands in his and said, just like he was some grand French couturier, "Cherie, you are to design a creamy silk gown with blue silk trim - not a harsh blue but a soft periwinkle blue. I can see it," and he closed his dark fringed eyes. "It should have the Roman leaf design edging the full skirt and the off-the-shoulder bodice, and there should be blue rosettes at the sleeves to accentuate your still beautiful arms. Here Cherie, give me a pencil and I'll draw it." Juanita sat with her mouth open until she realized that he was serious. She got him the pad and pencil, and he, as if he had been drawing all his life, drew the gown. With a very studious expression he handed it to her and said, "You might add some black fringe at the sash, it is popular in New York City, but aside from that I believe it might be what you had in mind, but because of your heavy schedule the design escaped you. You are working much too hard, Cherie - getting those little fatigue lines around your eyes and mouth, my dear."

When she realized that she had pursed her lips, she relaxed and thought, what does he mean by my still beautiful arms? And what does he mean by those tiny lines at my...She rushed to the mirror and, sure enough, she could see them. Doggone you, Conner O'Farrell, I'm getting tired of having to put up with your...!

Rose and the other ladies were laughing at her, and Juanita, being without much sense of humor, whirled around and said over her shoulder to Rose, "Well, Rose, here is his majesty's design. What do you think?

The Monticello Opera House was on the second floor of John H. Perkins' business block. The bottom floor of the building housed his mercantile establishment, sewing machine depot and a seed store. It took up an entire block across from the court house, and it was beautiful, boasting perfect acoustics, a sweeping stage and a sizable orchestra pit. Flanking the thirty-foot proscenium were two off-stage boxes of Moorish design, and that's where Juanita and Conner would sit, right along with just the most influential people in the entire state. The main auditorium seated about four hundred, and the balcony another two hundred. It was reported that all of the seats had been sold for the opening night performance. When the chandeliers, gas lit, arrived in Monticello, the entire town turned out to approve them. And the beautifully hand-carved doors, framed in stained glass, and the grand staircase were talked about and praised for their beauty in every home and business establishment in the town. To think that little Monticello could have such a grand building was almost beyond belief.

The building was constructed in the Romanesque Revival Style, and how Conner knew that was beyond Juanita, but he did and talked about it by the hour, boring her almost out of her mind. But the men in town who gathered around to hear him expound at length at the St. Elmo Hotel seemed to hang on to his every word. She knew that she should be proud of him, and she was, but he mostly made her aware of her ignorance.

Oh, well, she would say, and go about her business of dressing the most influential women in that section of the state. If he'll just let me run my business without interfering, then all will be well. Her patrons would travel by train from Thomasville and Tallahassee. They'd arrive in Monticello, get registered at the St. Elmo Hotel more often than not, and go to Cherie's House Of Fashion for their appointment. Juanita never saw a patron from out of town without an appointment. By the next day she'd have several sketches for them to make a selection and fabrics to choose from. It amazed Juanita that they would come so far for their special gowns. It also delighted her.

When she inquired of the senator's wife from the Jacksonville district how she had heard of her creations, she replied, "Oh, Berta Williams, Senator Layke Williams' wife, recommended you. She said that your gowns were as lovely as any she had seen in New York."

My, my, so the distinguished senator's little South Spring wife approves of my work. Should I be flattered? I wonder why she has never visited Monticello. Oh, how I'd love to fit her. I heard that she's gotten a little stout...

****

The Conner O'Farrell family was well thought of in Monticello. Such a handsome family, everyone declared. The fact that their marriage had not been legally sanctioned was no one's business, and only they, Harrison and Rose were aware of it. Conner would accompany Juanita into town three or four times a week and would usually spend his days at the St. Elmo Hotel. The hotel was considered by the townspeople to be on a par with the prestigious hotels in the North. It had sixty rooms with a fireplace each, an orchestra furnished music morning and evening. There was a fine livery stable attached and well supplied with shooting wagons and camp outfits for hunting parties.

With such a grand hotel, six daily meals, a railroad connecting with northern and midwestern cities, and only five hours from Jacksonville, Monticello prepared for a deluge of tourists. But tourists did not arrive in droves as had been anticipated. Some who did visit decided to stay in Monticello and became citizens, who were politically and socially active.

The cotton plantations were supplemented with hunting preserves, and the large plantations were divided into smaller tracts and rented to tenants. These sharecroppers were barely able to eke out a living. Some had planted as much acreage in corn as in cotton, but corn seemed to draw bears, which wreaked havoc on several plantations close to town, so they were discouraged by the townspeople from planting corn. It got so bad that hunters were brought in from all over Jefferson County to track the bears down.

Conner and Harrison had gone heavily into watermelon production on Athea Plantation, as much for the seed as the melons themselves, and the last summer had shipped eight carloads of watermelons weighing an average of twenty-five pounds each on the *F R & N Railroad.* Last year they had filled orders for over two thousand pounds of seed and expected to surpass that amount with the twenty field hands they employed for two months in the summer after they had finished marketing the melons. Their LeConte pear crop was the best they had ever had, and the additional twenty acres Conner had purchased from the Bailey family had as good a potato crop as could be bragged about in the lobby of the St. Elmo.

All was right with Conner's world at last. He still had an eye for the ladies, especially those who traveled throughout the country with their theatrical companies. It was the talk of the town when Boyle

Coleman ran off with one of the actresses, and Ardeth had been so humiliated by it that she moved all the way to Atlanta to live with her sister. She had never got over her defeat by Juanita and Boyle's loss of his marshal's job and had even stopped going to church. The gossip was that she was glad that he'd run off, so she could leave Monticello.

Conner and Juanita seldom missed a production at the Opera House. Juanita could feel his energy heighten whenever they attended a performance. He no longer wore the white linen suits of his gambling days, but his suits had to be just so, or he'd raise a ruckus with Easter. He cut quite a figure in a spotless white shirt with high stiff collar, gray cravat with a large pearl stickpin, Chesterfield overcoat with a glossy velvet collar, whenever a northeaster blew in, and a black derby rakishly placed on his slightly graying hair. His black shoes were polished to a high sheen, and the nails on his slender hands were buffed smooth.

Juanita felt every head turn toward them when they entered the Opera House. She was proud of Conner. He had kept his physique in perfect condition, on occasion working right alongside the field hands. She'd added a few pounds since Young Nolan had arrived, but Rose had reassured her that they were becoming. Conner never mentioned it and seldom complimented her, but she had heard from some of her patrons what their husbands had told them Conner had said about her, that she was a woman before her time and undoubtedly the smartest business woman in all of Jefferson County. But she doubted that he had actually said it. She longed for a compliment - she hungered for one. She knew he needed her to fulfill his desires, but then she figured most men needed a woman from time to time, and she'd not deny that she needed him. When he'd be away for five or more days on a hunting trip on the Wacissa, she could hardly wait for his return. She laughed when she remembered this last trip. He'd been gone for over a week with a party from Tallahassee and some dignitaries from Washington. He'd not bothered to even bathe, so unlike him, and had angrily told Delia to go to bed a good hour before her bed time. He'd practically dragged Juanita up the stairs, and she went all girl on him.

"Grief! Conner, what's got into you? You act starved."

"And it's indeed starved I am..." Afterwards she had him remove his hunting boots to the balcony. "I don't believe you'd come to our bed smelling just like a pole cat. Heavens, I'll have to change the sheets before we can even sleep on them." He didn't bother to respond, just walked into the bathroom he'd had built between their suite and the guest room. She felt warm all over. I don't care if you talk or don't talk, Mr. O'Farrell. I hear enough talking all day long at the shop. It's a relief to surround myself with silence.

But silence was not Conner's companion when he was at the St. Elmo. Harrison referred to his visits there as "Conner's Court." There was no one who could tell a tale like Conner - no one who could entertain the townspeople as he did. Whenever a dignitary visited, Mayor Denham made sure Conner knew it and would invite him to have dinner with them. He was invited on all of the important hunting trips and was even asked to serve on the Jefferson County committee to discuss their participation at the Chicago World's Fair. Harrison had teased Juanita unmercifully about becoming Monticello's First Lady when Conner was elected Mayor, and she had displayed the appropriate amount of anger just to please him. Actually, she would have liked to see Conner get more actively involved in the local politics, for he was a natural leader and extremely intelligent, read people well and was dauntless. But the fact that they were not legally married did bother her, for she was sure that if he chose a more public life the truth would come out. That she did not want, not for herself nor for Delia or Nolan.

Juanita usually left the shop in the early afternoon. Rose and Seth would remain there, as they had taken the three rooms upstairs for their living quarters. When Seth got out of school he'd help make deliveries on his bicycle. He had turned into a very handsome young man, was active in the Jefferson High School, formerly the Jefferson Academy, that now had almost 120 students enrolled. He was an excellent baseball player and had also joined the Monticello Rifle Team. If Seth had any problems, they were minor, except for his over protection of Delia. It bothered both Rose and Juanita and thoroughly angered Conner.

Conner had not displayed his love for Delia as openly as he had before Maeve's death, but she knew he loved her, and she loved him beyond all reason. She was obviously jealous of his generous attention to Young Nolan and would make sure that all of Athea knew of her dislike.

"Can't we have any peace in this house?" Juanita questioned loudly as Nolan ran from a pursuing Delia while screaming his lungs out.

"Delia Rose, let him be! Now, do you hear? Here, Young Nolan, come to Mama, Honey. Come here, I said. Delia Rose, I said to stop chasing him. Good grief! You're ten years old and you act like a two-year-old."

"Delia pursed her lips, squinted her darkly fringed, pale blue eyes and stomped her foot loudly. "He's a big cry baby, that's what he is. I can't do a blasted thing around here for him spying on me - not a blasted thing!"

"Watch your tongue, young lady, or I'll wash out your mouth with soap. Do you hear? Now just what's he been spying on, I'd like to know. Heavens, he's just a little over three years old. What could he possibly see that's got you so upset?"

Nolan was kicking his muscled legs and wiggling so that Juanita had a hard time holding him.

"That's it, young man, I'll let Melvia take you to the back yard to play. Delia, where do you think you're going? Don't you walk out of here. I asked you a question."

Conner burst through the French doors that led to the upstairs balcony. "What in the Devil's name is going on here? Has he loosed his fiery tongue in this house?"

Juanita shrugged and shook her head. "It's Delia and Nolan fighting again. I'm at my wit's end, I declare I am."

Conner grabbed Delia's ear, turned her around and proceeded to lambast her. "So it's fighting you're after and with your wee little brother. Well, it's fighting you'll be getting!" He let that sink in, her face was now somber. "Put 'em up, Delia Rose. Put up your dukes. Don't want to fight your Da? I'm too big for you, am I? Well, it's the same for Young Nolan, Delia. It's the same. He looks up at you just like you're looking up at me - just the same."

"But he spies on me! I can't do a blasted thing in this old place but what he spies on me..." And with that she ran from the balcony and into her room slamming the door soundly.

Juanita put her book of E.A. Poe's works on the wrought iron table beside her. "I think we'd better start inquiring into one of the girls schools in Tallahassee, Conner. She's going to grow up like a wild heathen if she stays here. Seth defends everything she does, so she thinks she can have her way about everything. Now that he's in high school she's having to fight her own battles. Did you see that black eye she got last week? Did you?"

"Of course, I saw it, Cherie. How could I not? But I'd like to wait a while before sending her away to school. At least for a few more years. She's headstrong, and that's good. She'll have a need of it, I'm sure."

He opened the folding doors that led to his study off their bedroom. "Would you care to join me? How about a glass of sherry, my sweet?" Juanita relaxed and sighed. "You know, I think I would. I've been very tired lately."

Conner poured the sherry and his whisky into crystal glasses. He remained standing after she took the sherry from him, looking silently out over the land. Athea Manor was situated on the highest hill of the plantation and caught the easterly winds. The full pecan trees shaded the house on the west side, and the Reases had planted magnolias along the front, leaving the east free to catch whatever breeze there was. He finally spoke, "This is a beautiful setting, Cherie." He pulled the chair close to her and sat down. "I believe that I'm the happiest I've ever been."

She restrained her response, the tears welled up. Finally she spoke. "We've been blessed. Indeed we have." She would have liked to have said more, much more, like why don't you go to church with me, since there's no Catholic church closer than Tallahassee? Why don't you marry me, so that our children will be legitimate? Why? If you're so happy with me beside you, why don't you do what's right? If Maeve were here, she'd insist on it. Harrison has mentioned it to you numerous times, I know, 'cause he's told me, but you never even give him an excuse.

Conner began to smoke his cheroot, slowly inhaling. Juanita relaxed and watched him remembering the very first time that she'd seen him. Was it that long ago? Over fourteen years? It didn't seem possible. How could I have loved him for that long? How is it possible that I know so little about him? He's let so few people into his heart - only Maeve and Harrison. He shuts all the rest of us out. I'd like to think that I'm the happiest I've ever been, too, but I'm not. I'm still waiting to be allowed into that sanctuary.

She picked up her book. Oh, how she loved Poe. She usually saved him for when she especially wanted to be miserable - she gloried in the misery his works evoked. She had even told Conner that if the baby was a girl that she wanted to name her Annabelle Lee, but she got Young Nolan instead. She was not sorry.

The quiet was shattered when Young Nolan gave a blood-curdling yell. "What the devil!" Conner shouted and jumped up putting his head around the wrought iron post and calling into the yard. "Melvia, what's he yelling about now? Melvia?"

Juanita joined him. "I'll tend to it, Conner. You relax and I'll get us a cold supper. Would you like it served on the veranda?"

He walked toward the bar and while pouring another whisky said, "Yes, I'd like that, and tell Melvia that I want that young lad bathed and ready for bed and on my lap in a shake."

She couldn't believe it when he swatted her bottom as she left. "Conner O'Farrell, you stop that!" His laughter followed her as she went downstairs. "Maybe, just maybe the time is right. Maybe Rose is right. Perhaps he's mellowed and become responsible enough to truly want a settled life. But I'll not get my hopes up, at least not yet. I have an idea I'll be reading a lot of Poe in the future.

CHAPTER II THE PASSING TIME

The Year 1895

The year 1895 was the year of the Big Freeze that devastated the state's citrus industry and sent thousands of citizens packing up and returning to their former homes. It was written about and discussed in every parlor and on every front porch throughout the state. The cynics determined that the economic growth of the state would never regain its momentum, and the tourist trade, that had been as lucrative as the citrus industry, would never climb to the expected heights promised by the land dealers and tourist bureaus.

Layke and Berta's fortunes were not directly affected by the freeze, because South Spring had continued to deal mostly in cattle, but it was a very difficult time for their fellow ranchers. The Garvins of Bullseye had gone heavily into citrus. It would be a long five years before the newly planted trees would produce fruit, and Pierce and his sons were forced to sell off a large portion of their land, land that had been in the Garvin family since the British occupation. It was a sad day at Bullseye when they signed over 5,000 acres to the Atlantic Land Company.

Callie and Clay had moved into the big house on Tall Ten after Kate had died of a massive stroke the previous year, and as Jay had predicted, his children probably wouldn't see their grandparents on his side. Parker had failed terribly since Kate's death and seldom left the ranch.

James William Willett joined his sister Annie the January before the Big Freeze. He was a healthy nine pounder, and this time Clay had insisted that Callie move to town to be near the doctor. Clay's and Jay's book, *"Thom's Wilderness Adventure"* was in its sixth printing, and their new book, *"Arthur, Pride Of The Everglades"*, had just been published. As before, Jay and Clay traveled to New York City to meet with Mr. Dutton, who honored them with the 1894 National Children's Literary Award. Callie was so proud of them. The problems that first confronted her and Clay seemed to dissolve, and she was kept busy with the running of Tall Ten and seemed to be happy.

SuSu's and Jay's son, James Parker, III, called J.P., was a healthy and happy child and accompanied his mother to Tallahassee for a visit with his grandparents while Jay was in New York. The grade school in Carrabelle would have an opening for the fall term in October, and SuSu had been approached about teaching there and wanted to take a trip to Carrabelle before making a decision. She and Jay had discussed it at length and after much deliberation decided to make the move from Middleburg to Carrabelle. Her mother was delighted to have her close by and had assured her that she would have no trouble finding adequate help to care for J.P.

Carrabelle was a beautiful spot on the St. George Sound east of the county seat of Appalachicola in the bend of the state. The Williams family had spent many vacations there and at Alligator Pt. with the other senators' families, and it was SuSu's favorite spot in the entire world, she had told Jay. He was as anxious to get to that section of the state as SuSu, because he had also grown fond of it.

His time in Middleburg had been fruitful, his paintings hanging in some of the most prominent families' homes. The beautiful Chalker home on Palmetto St. alone boasted of six of his paintings, and the large galleries in Jacksonville had purchased some. His painting of the Great Blue Heron and magnolias hung in the county courthouse in Green Cove Springs, and his scene of the Anhingas on Black Creek was prominently displayed in the lobby of the Clarendon Hotel. He and SuSu had been warmly received by everyone in Clay County, and they would miss their association with them, but he was looking forward to painting the seascapes and seabirds of the Gulf in the panhandle of Florida.

Carrabelle was an old logging town mainly built around several large sawmills. The lumber and turpentine were brought down the Crooked and the New Rivers and shipped from the Carrabelle docks. SuSu's best friend in college, Mary Ellen Lampros, lived in the tiny fishing village of Eastpoint about ten miles west of Carrabelle and taught school there. And Berta's and Layke's old friend Jessup Sutherland, who had served in the senate with Layke for two terms, owned a home as well as several businesses in Appalachicola and Carrabelle, so SuSu and Jay would have ready friends.

Berta and Layke had always loved to visit Jessup even before the railroad was completed in '93. It wasn't the same since Marlene had died, but he was a gracious host and had a wonderful cook and cleaning lady. He had assured them that he'd assist the young Meades all he could, and they knew that he would. They would get to visit him more often, now that SuSu would be living so close to Tallahassee.

Harrison hadn't sat down on the kitchen chair for two minutes before Nolan had found his way to his lap. "Easter, how about pouring me another cup of coffee. Here, get down, Young Nolan. Now I don't want to spill this hot coffee on you." Easter stood beside the big black cook stove and stirred the various pots, smelling and tasting. She was younger than Harrison by at least ten years. Her husband had been killed in a logging accident soon after they had been married. She had been sorry that she had not been given a child and truly had expected to find someone to share her life. She was bright, had an even disposition and was a wonderful cook. A good thing, because Juanita had never enjoyed cooking. Actually, she had never done much of it and didn't plan to learn, she had informed Rose many times.

"Easter, are there any leftover biscuits?" Harrison asked. "I think I'll just eat a few, then go back to the fields. We need to get those melons seeded before sundown. Mr. Conner should be getting back from Wakulla Springs day after tomorrow, and I'd like to have the seeding completed by then."

She placed a plate of four large biscuits in front of him. "You want me to warm them? Won't take but a minute." He smiled up at her. She was a gentle soul, and he liked her, he truly did. She reminded him of his Ma Silvey. She put a mound of butter on his plate and the crock of cane syrup and jar of blackberry jam beside it. "How about a nice piece of ham, Harrison? I'll slice it real thin the way you like." He knew she was not his intellectual equal, but it didn't seem to matter, and the fact that she was past child bearing years didn't seem to matter either. They were comfortable together. He guessed he loved her - it was the very first time for him.

He had told Juanita that he planned to ask Easter to be his wife and wondered what she thought of it. She replied, "At least there is one honorable male at Athea. I can't say that for someone else I know, can I?" He couldn't find the words, the right words to answer.

"When do you think you'll ask her, Harrison? If you wed before planting time, I'm sure Conner will insist that you two take a little vacation, and I'll have to get someone from town to do the cooking."

"I wouldn't subject Conner to your cooking, Cherie," and they both laughed. But planting time came and went without a wedding. Whenever Juanita would bring it up, Harrison would say, "We're not in any hurry, probably by summer."

But the summer of '96 came and went as did the summer of '97 and '98. The world around them had changed rapidly. Henry B. Plant had completed his railroad system from Georgia to Tampa on the Gulf side of the state. The Kissimmee valley was bustling as new Floridians homesteaded the land, and tourists flocked by the thousands to both coasts to escape the frozen north. The effects of the Big Freeze of '95 were no longer visible. The abandoned groves had been replanted or plowed under. Only in the minds of those who witnessed it and were made penniless by it did the memory of the freeze remain.

It was May of 1899. Meade's school had just let out, and he and Callie were packing his trunk for his long awaited trip to Carrabelle to spend the summer with his Uncle Jay, Aunt SuSu and their children, J.P. and Elizabeth, who was just a year old. Jay had expressed many times to Callie that Meade had a definite artistic talent. Meade's teachers had told her the same. Jay suggested that he tutor Meade until school resumed in October. Excitement was high at Tall Ten. Lily Mae had been ensconced in Mattie's position, and she, Sap, Toad, Lillily and baby, Sister Fern, lived in Mattie's old quarters. Parker was practically bedridden, and Sap had given up his job on the railroad to tend to him. Clay spent a great deal of time traveling throughout the southeast on special assignments for two of the leading newspapers in Florida, the *Tallahassee Floridian* and the Tampa *Tribune*. He had decided to accompany Meade the next morning by train to Tallahassee, then take the train on down to Carrabelle, because he and Jay were working on another book, a sequel to *Thom's Wilderness Adventures*, and Jay wanted Meade to do some of the illustrations.

Tall Ten still participated in the spring cattle drives to Punta Rassa, but this year Jam and Slick would ride in the chuck wagon. Those were Callie's orders, and though they knew she was probably right, they also knew that after the first day out they would join the others and stand watch like they'd been doing for the past thirty-five years.

"I ain't taking no orders from that whippersnapper! Not me, are you, Slick?"

"Not on your life, friend. You know Parker'd never do this to us. Crippled, my eye. Hell, there ain't a cowman around who can handle the beeves like you and me - not a one!"

"My legs ain't good as they used to be, but they sure as hell can still sit a horse, and my arms can handle a whip near 'bout as good as before. Near 'bout!" Jam bragged.

Slick looked at him suspiciously. Jam's toothless grin transformed his wind-burned features into a painful smirk as he demonstrated his ability with the cowhide whip. He thought, that misery he had in his shoulder sure 'nuff acting up on Jam. He ain't gonna admit it, but maybe Callie is right 'bout the two of us. He ain't near as good as he used to be with that whip.

Callie was almost looking forward to the weeks that lay ahead when Clay, Meade and the cowmen would be gone. It would give her time to get her house in order, as Mama Kate used to say. Not that she had taken kindly to being a house woman, for she hadn't. But she wanted time to take Annie and Jimmy down to the pond, stretch out on an old quilt and daydream or think of absolutely nothing. Seemed like every time she turned around someone or something needed tending to. When Clay was home, he'd take some of the burden off her shoulders, and she was grateful, but lately what with the cowhunt and drive and Meade's trip she was in need of a rest.

Meade was so excited about his trip that he was driving them crazy with his questions and his "what if's". She had got so short with him at supper time that Clay had to intervene. "Meade, your mama is weary. Now if you have any questions why don't you wait 'til after supper, and you and I will tend to them." Meade had got up and gone to Callie, hugged her and told her he was sorry. She'd felt so guilty about her outburst that she'd left most of her supper on her plate and sought the solitude of her and Clay's room upstairs. About an hour later she heard the stair creak and knew it was probably Clay coming up to check on her. He always gave her enough time to work out her problems, then if she needed to she'd unburden her frustrations, and he'd listen, giving the appropriate responses. He understood the burden she carried without Parker's advice, since he had reverted into the past almost completely.

His condition was apparent to his old friend and fellow rancher, Jordan Northrup from the Big Lake spread, who had stopped by two days previously for a visit. He hadn't seen Parker since Kate's funeral and was saddened by his failing. One of the reasons he'd decided to visit Tall Ten was to talk to Parker about his top hand, Sweet Harrington. He'd been with Jordan for over ten years, but since he'd married Dotty she'd been pressuring him to move closer to Arcadia, where she was from. Jordan hadn't wanted to lose Sweet but knew that

Parker and Callie could use a good man now that Jam and Slick were getting up there in age and ability, so he decided to ask.

Callie had Sap carry Parker out to the front porch, so he and Jordan could visit. At least he recognized Jordan, she thought. "Daddy, Jordan was telling me that Sweet Harrington wants to move closer to Arcadia on account of Dotty. He's a good man, and we could sure use him. What do you think?"

"Your Mama'll sure be tickled to hear that, Honey. That Dotty can out sew anybody in Tater Hill."

Callie looked at Jordan, and he went along with Parker. "She's a fine seamstress all right. She makes most of Min's dresses and Ellen's and Molly's, too. She'll be a big help, I'm sure."

Callie spoke up, "Then it's all settled. Jordan will speak to him on the drive, and when Clay gets back from Carrabelle, he and I'll get the little house at Ole Piney fixed up for them."

"That's good, Callie," is all Parker said, his chin soon finding his chest as he gave in to sleep. Sap scooped him up effortlessly and took him to the bed in the parlor. It had become too difficult to get him up and down the stairs, so Clay had the cot moved from Jay's workroom to the big house. Parker slept most of the time, but when he stirred, there was usually someone in the kitchen or on the front porch who would hear him.

Callie had allowed Annie to put her playthings underneath the parlor table and had covered it with a sheet. She'd play by the hour there and let the entire household know when Daddy Parker awakened. "The only time that child is quiet is when she's underneath the parlor table, "Callie declared many a time. Meade had spent hours trying to teach her how to whisper but had finally given up on it, and her daddy had suggested voice lessons so she could move to Italy to become an opera star. But Annie took their teasing in stride, but not little brother Jimmy's. Jimmy could do nothing right except when Lillily wasn't around. Then Annie'd play with him.

She and Lillily had become almost as good friends as Callie and Pet Morgan had been. Lillily was tiny for her age, and although she was two years older, she and Annie were the same size. The only place Lillily couldn't venture was in Annie's hiding place underneath the parlor table, because that's where Annie would watch Daddy Parker breathe. She knew that when he stopped breathing that he'd be taken away and buried beside Mama Kate in the graveyard at Ole Piney Road. Annie was determined to see the angels take his last breath up to heaven like her mama had said they did with Mama Kate's. She'd been too little to see them before. So Annie looked and listened, sometimes for hours, for Parker's chest to stop rising and falling and his moaning sounds to cease, but so far the angels hadn't paid Daddy Parker a visit.

 Clay relaxed on the bed, trying to concentrate on his writing. He'd propped the pillows behind him but couldn't seem to get comfortable enough. He put the tablet down on the night stand and watched Callie brush her waist- long hair. She stood looking out the window. It was a dark night with an occasional hoot from an owl. The lamp light played on the red of her chestnut hair. *She's starting to look more like Kate since her face has filled out. I'm a lucky man. She always gets so quiet before I leave, but this time she's nervous, too. Maybe I should send Meade alone. She seems to need me here.*

 The new crop of spring frogs began chirping. Callie could hear thunder in the distance. Old Bay began to howl, and she heard Jam call to him, then let him inside the bunkhouse. *I hate to see him go, but I know I need the quiet. He's staring at me. I always know when he's looking at me. Oh, I hope Jimmy'll sleep the night through. I want this night for just me and Clay.*

 The wind picked up and the rains came, slowly at first, then slashing out hard against the weathered house. Callie pulled the curtains to and turned around. Clay tossed the covers back for her and blew out the lamp. They could hear Old Bay trying to compete with the thunder and the cowmen yelling at him, telling him to shut up. The lightning streaked and even through the curtains it lit up the room. When Annie yelled out, Callie sat straight up, throwing Clay's arm off as he said, "She'll go back to sleep, Honey, soon as the thunder dies down."

 "Not Annie," she sighed and got up. "I'll quiet her." He watched her leave and hoped the storm would hurry and end so Annie wouldn't be invited to share their bed, but the storm decided to pay a longer visit. Finally, he got up and stood outside Annie's door. He cracked the door and saw Callie sitting on the edge of Annie's bed, telling a sleepy Annie about the "thunder man" and what an important job he had. It was his job to inform folks that there was a storm on its way and that they'd better take shelter, and the cowmen should put on their slickers and get their catch dogs ready in case the beeves decided to stampede, and that she shouldn't be afraid of the thunder man's voice any more than

Jimmy should be afraid of Annie's loud voice. But Annie, always enjoying having the last word, said, "But Mama, Jimmy can see me and I can't see the thunder man. If I could see him maybe I'd like him."

"Can you see Mama Kate, Annie? Can you?"

"Well, no, not now, but when I was little I could, so I know what she looked like."

"I'll tell you what I'm going to do, Honey. I'll have Meade draw you a picture of the thunder man, then you'll know what he looks like."

"He doesn't know a bit more than I do. I already asked him."

"I give up, Annie. Just go on back to sleep, and don't you dare wake up Jimmy. I mean it, young lady. Go on now."

Reluctantly Annie pulled the covers up over her head, and Callie could hear her mumbling loudly, "Meade never even saw the thunder man. Never, never."

"Quiet, Annie. I mean it!"

Clay looked down at her, put his arms around her, pulled her to him and kissed the top of her head. "I love you, Callie Anders. I love you more than life itself." They could hear Annie's constant mumbling as they closed their door, and Clay laughingly said, "That child will either be a lawyer or politician. What beautiful children you've brought into our world, my sweet."

The storm stopped almost as suddenly as it began. "You warm my bed, you warm my heart, sweet Callie. You have made my life complete. It will be a very long two weeks..."

"It'll be long for me too, Clay," she sighed. "But Meade needs you, too, Honey."

The spring peeps drowned out their murmuring - soon there was none, just hesitant gasps...

****

"Layke, it's beautiful. I've never seen a more beautiful cameo - and even matching earrings."

"I had Clea Fontaine purchase them when she and Bernard were in Paris in May."

Berta was seated in front of the mahogany dressing table. Layke was standing behind her, watching her every move in the mirror.

"They're Limoges. I told Clea just what I wanted and that they had to have the blue of your eyes, my dear one."

"They're so dainty. I'm glad she got the earrings to match." She reached for his hand and squeezed it affectionately. "Does it seem like twenty-one years to you, sir?' she asked coquettishly.

"It's difficult for me to remember being without you, Berta, truly it is." He lifted her up and turned her around to face him. "Why don't you just slip out of this old dressing gown and..."

"Layke Williams! The entire family's downstairs waiting for us. Now what would they think?"

"Do you really care what they think, my love? Do you?"

She giggled and held on to him and sighed, "No suh, Mistuh Layke, suh - nosiree"

The dressing gown floated to the rug and Berta slipped underneath the deep rose coverlet.

"Why, Miss Berta, Ah do believe y'all is mighty hongry - mighty hongry!"

"Well, when a gentleman presents his lady friend wid sech a beautiful gift, it sho would be thoughtless of her to not thank him proper like, suh."

"Shhhh, my sweet, the time for talking is past - shhhh."

Lake and Berta entered the large parlor to the sound of applause and good wishes. They had decided to not invite outsiders but just their family for their twenty-first anniversary party. Their plans were to return to South Spring with Reuben, Leonora, and their children, Sammy and Oliver, and then spend some time in town with Jonah and Myra. Berta was very concerned about Trudy, who reportedly was in a bad way.

Wes was able to get home for the party from his instructor's position at The Citadel and looked handsome in his uniform. Berta thought when she looked at him how much he looked like Reuben's brother Ham, except his hair was wavy. He's grown so tall, almost as tall as Layke, and filled out. Oh, I wish he could find a nice young girl like Reuben and Jonah have. But, Wes is more than handsome. He's kind and caring, as are all my children...oops! I'll take that back, all except poor Raine. Why do I continue to think of her as poor Raine. She's stronger than most, but I sense that there is a troubled road waiting for her to travel. I've always felt that and pray I'm wrong, because there is a fragile little girl she's trying so hard to hide. But I'll have time to think about all this later...

"Berta, where are you my sweet? SuSu asked you if we're going back to Carrabelle with them?"

"I'm sorry, Honey, my mind was..."

"I know, it was far, far away. Well are we or not?"

"SuSu, I'm sorry but Young Reuben said that Trudy is in such a bad way. I do so want to spend some time with her. You understand?"

"Yes, I understand, of course I do. I wish we could join you, but Jay and Meade still have a lot of work ahead of them - the deadline, you know. Mr. Dutton said late September, and you know what bears they are when..."

"I understand, Honey, honest I do. I tell you what, we'll stay a few weeks in Old Town, then on our way back we'll take the train down for a visit."

"I'd like that, Mama." SuSu hugged her. Berta thought, it's so good to see SuSu so happy, and Jay... what a delightful young man! How can one family be so fortunate. I'm getting maudlin. Layke'll think I'm... Her thoughts were shattered by Raine.

"What on earth, Raine!" She was giggling uncontrollably, and Meade, who was a good head taller and not quite sixteen, was teasing the twenty-year-old Raine and enjoying her girlish reaction. Why can't she act her age? No matter what we do for that child, she has got to show herself. Well, I'll just have to speak to her father. She has gone too far.

Rosette announced dinner in the nick of time, and Berta, relieved, grabbed Layke's arm - she needed it. The chandelier was aglow. She had had it electrified years before but was still not used to its harsh light, preferring gaslight, so much softer, she thought. The menu had been chosen carefully, and Rosette and Salome had been preparing it for days. Berta had ordered oysters brought up from Appalachicola and kept iced. Salome's specialties were sauces, and the sauce for the oysters was her very own creation. It was a favorite of Layke and consisted of hot Louisiana pepper sauce, pureed tomatoes, green peppers and onions with just a touch of coarsely grated allspice and lemon rind. Following the oysters on the half shell, Brevard served shallow bowls of smoked mullet topped with thinly sliced, pickled cauliflower and red onions in sour cream accompanied by heavily buttered scones. Berta had decided against a soup or chowder because the summer heat could be very harsh in July, and the smoked mullet would be a nice replacement.

When Brevard brought out the steaming platter of leg of lamb with ginger and mint sauce, and Rosette the stewed hens with fluffy dumplings, the festivities began. Layke had ordered cases of Mumms champagne for dinner and afterwards a fine Spanish brandy for the men. Meade was taking it all in. He'd never seen anything like it - sure, he'd had chicken and dumplings, but he'd never had the cajun dishes Salome fixed. The rice had all sorts of red, yellow and green things in it. He was skeptical at first, but when Jay told him that they were just pimentos, capers and green onions, he decided to try it. He did and liked it. Raine, who was sitting across from him kept inquiring about his art in such an amusing way that he knew she was having sport with him, and he sensed that her mother didn't approve of her behavior, but he liked her, he truly did. She was fun. He felt he could say anything he felt like, well, almost anything. Her twin brother, Tucker, was enjoying her show. After all, he'd had a great deal of champagne and seemed to laugh even when things weren't funny. Meade understood why. Heck, he'd seen Jam, Slick and Burt act just like that when they'd had too much shine.

Brevard poured Meade a glass of champagne so he could join in the toast to Berta and Layke before the dessert was served in the parlor. I'll sure be glad to get out of here, he thought. The room was so formal that he'd been scared to death that he'd make a mistake. Now, he realized why his mama and Clay had insisted that he learn good table manners. He'd fought it like crazy but was now glad that they had persevered.

Berta had insisted on a formal dining room. After all, that was where Layke did a great deal of his policy making. She felt that if the room was warm and cozy that the men would not take things seriously. When she explained her choice of heavy, royal blue, velvet drapes and gold flocked wallpaper, dark mahogany dining table with an eight foot sideboard to match and a gold leaf encrusted mirror above it, Layke felt the room was much too dark - too formal. But when Berta added a room-sized, pale gold, blue and magenta carpet, the ecru lace panels at the French doors, and then covered the dining chairs in a silk brocade to match the rug, he could see her wisdom and exquisite taste.

She had indeed been correct in her choices, and lightened the room even more when she added the pale lace tablecloth topped by arrangements of flowers and fruit in crystal bowls. There was a regal warmth, although the room maintained a formal atmosphere. Whenever they entertained people Layke wanted to impress, the French doors were opened to the covered colonnade, and musicians would play sweetly throughout the festivities. It was an elegant room, and Layke was the envy of his fellow politicians.

Young Reuben was the first to toast Berta and Layke, and like his father before him would have, he did an eloquent job. Jonah was more hesitant, but the champagne had loosened his tongue, and Myra clapped longer and louder than the others to show her support. Berta was enjoying her children. She and Layke had done a commendable job, she decided. When SuSu stood, she pulled Jay up so he could join her. They raised their glasses toward Berta and Layke and simply said, "We wish you twenty-one more wonderful years." Layke was so touched he didn't bother to wipe the tears that seeped out. Wes stood tall and erect and was more formal with his toast than the others, but they all knew how much Layke meant to him. They were closer than ever since he had decided to follow in Layke's footsteps by attending The Citadel.

Raine grabbed Tucker and grinned, "I'm older, I know, and naturally wiser," - they all laughed - "but I do think it appropriate that Tucker and I propose our toast in unison. All right, Tucker? Now just as we practiced. Ready?" He looked sheepishly at her. She knew he'd forgotten his lines. "Oh, well, I'll toast you all by myself. I don't know how he thinks he can follow you in the senate, Dad, if he can't even remember a simple toast."

Layke and Berta turned toward each other, then back to Raine.

"Oh, I thought you knew that Tucker longs for the stuffy halls of the senate and plans to study law... or is it political science?"

Tucker's face reddened. "Raine, you promised you'd not tell - you promised!"

Berta was about to chastise her when Layke stood, walked around the parlor table and put his arm around Tucker's shoulder. "I'm sorry Raine spoiled your surprise, son, but you couldn't have given me a better anniversary gift. We'll have to get busy and get those letters off to William and Mary."

Raine shouted, amused, "His grades will never be good enough to get him in there, Dad. You'd better settle for Stetson."

Berta had had enough. "That's quite enough, Raine. That's for Tucker and his dad to decide, and speaking of grades, young lady, we just received yours from Mrs. Baldwin. It's a good thing that you don't wish to further your education..."

"Now, Honey," Layke interrupted, "lets not get into that tonight."

But Raine would not give in to her, not for a minute. As she walked triumphantly away she said so all could hear, "She always takes up for baby Tucker - poor baby." Meade decided that he didn't much like Raine Williams after all and that he'd better stay close by Jay and SuSu.

Berta had filled the large urn with cut flowers and ferns from her sizable flower garden and placed it in front of the fireplace. The brass and crystal wall sconces were lit, their light and shadows played on the pale gray damask-covered walls. It was a lovely, large room with French doors leading onto the covered colonnade. When the musicians began to play, Layke very formally bowed to Berta, resplendent in her deep violet gown and flushed with happiness. She reached for his outstretched hands, and they were quickly twirling around and around to the lilt of the violins. Layke called out, "Come on, all of you, this is a party - join in."

Meade saw her coming toward him, and before he could escape to the colonnade, Raine was beside him. "Gotcha!" is all she said, and he felt himself pulled out onto the dance floor. He'd never in his entire life waltzed. He'd danced at the Gathering and at the Social, the two important get-togethers in Arcadia, but that was square dancing and this was round.

"Don't look at your feet, silly. Here - one, two, three and four - one, two, three and four - that's right. You dance better than Tucker already."

All he could think to say was a breathless, "Thank you."

"You're welcome, Mr. Garvin. You're most welcome."

Why can't she leave him alone, Berta thought. She just seems determined to spoil everything. Layke looked down at her and shook his head. "This is our night, Honey. Let her be. Meade can take care of himself." She sighed and thought, I certainly hope so. What can she see in him anyway? He's at least four or five years younger than she. But she is so child-like sometimes. But Layke's right. I've got to let it go, and so she did.

Brevard drove Young Reuben, Leonora and their boys to the hotel, and SuSu and Jay followed in the buggy that Layke had rented for their use during their visit. Meade stayed in the room with Wes, and Jonah and Myra, who had no children, stayed in the guest room. Meade was relieved to be in the room with Wes. He'd not put it past

Raine to pay him a visit during the night. He'd heard of girls like that - forward - but had never in his entire life known one like Raine. Whew! She sure was determined.

Just before the party ended she had announced to all who would listen that she wasn't about to stay at stuffy Mary Baldwin College any longer and that she was going to New York City and join Susan B. Anthony's women's suffrage movement.

Berta couldn't help but laugh out loud. "You know, Raine, that might not be a bad idea."

Raine glared at her with open hatred. A cold shiver ran up SuSu's spine. "What on earth's wrong with her?" she whispered to Jay.

"I think Layke had better sit on that one," he responded.

"I'm afraid he's too late, Honey. He should've sat on her a long time ago, I'm thinking. Well, I've had just about enough of her, I have."

SuSu walked over to Raine, took her firmly by the arm and said, "Raine, I think you and I had better have a little talk."

Raine jerked her arm away. "What on earth about, SuSu?"

They were now outside the parlor doors. "You could have been pleasant this evening. I know that it's not your nature, Raine, but this is a special occasion, and it wouldn't have hurt you one little bit."

Raine glared at her. "You've always been such a namby-pamby, SuSu. Can't imagine what such an exciting and handsome man like Jay sees in you, anyway. You, SuSu, are very predictable. He's probably already tired of you." She tossed her long curls and whirled away from SuSu, who tried to hold her mouth firmly closed when she saw Berta approach them, but giving in to her feelings said, "I'd gladly strangle that one. I can't believe that we're even kin!"

"What's wrong?" is all Berta said.

"Well, Mama, I needed to give that young lady a piece of my mind, but I doubt it'll do one bit of good."

"Oh, Honey, don't! Don't let Raine get to you, too. It's enough that I have to put up with her willfulness. In a way she's pathetic. No, I mean it. She has this silly jealousy toward me. She thinks that she's plain and resents it when anyone makes a fuss over me, especially Layke, her own father. I just pray she outgrows it. I'm worried about her, SuSu. When she was younger we thought she was just mischievous, but ever since we sent her away to school, she's done her best to irritate me, talking really ugly at times. Layke's talked to her, but it hasn't helped. It's as if she hates me..."

"Oh, Mama, don't, now don't you cry. Please. Let's not let her win this one. I think it'd give her great pleasure to see you like this. I'm sorry to say it, but I really think it would."

Berta looked at SuSu, "What am I going to do? I hate feeling this way about her, truly, SuSu."

"What are you two doing out here in the dark?" Layke called. Berta sniffled, brushed her wet cheeks and light-heartedly responded, "Can't SuSu and I have a girl talk, sir? We'll be right there, Honey."

They entered the room smiling, but when Berta saw Raine duck from behind the velvet drapes, she realized that she had been hiding and listening to her and SuSu. Raine, with a triumphant smirk on her face, reached for another glass of champagne, raised it toward Berta, drank the entire glass, gathered her full, emerald green, taffeta skirt, hiked it up high and ran upstairs laughing all the way.

Oh, dear Lord, have we created a devil? Have we? Berta thought helplessly.

Raine kicked the dark stained door shut soundly behind her and whirled around toward the vanity. Raine Trudy Williams sat down hard on the birdseye maple vanity chair. Her full taffeta shirt billowed over its arms. She glared in the mirror and said aloud, "You're plain, Raine Williams. Plain, plain, plain. Everyone knows it! You'll never be beautiful like your golden-haired mother. Never!"

Getting up quickly and ignoring the chair falling behind her, she threw herself onto the quilt-covered bed. The abandoned tears soaked the dark red squares on the old quilt, that her godmother Trudy had made before the War and given to her when she was born. Sobbing sporadically, she flipped over onto her back. Raine never did anything smoothly or evenly - every movement was impulsive, abandoned.

Why did Tucker have to have the gold hair and blue eyes? Why? He's such a namby-pamby, doesn't even know how to use his good looks, she sighed.

"No one will ever look at me the way Father looks at her - never!" She removed her gown, fighting every stubborn covered button on the bodice. When she saw herself in the mirror, the tears flowed again. "Hell, I look like a blooming boy! No one will ever love me - no one!"

Not able to dwell on her disappointment for long, she fell asleep and slept soundly 'til first light. She hurriedly dressed so she could get downstairs early with the hopes of catching Meade alone. Boy, that would really burn her mother up. She licked her lips in anticipation...

CHAPTER III   CARRABELLE

"Now, why on earth does he feel he has to jump whenever any of his friends say so, Harrison? Actually, they're not friends, just acquaintances. You can't call Mr. Kelly a friend." Juanita was more than perturbed; she was downright angry. Conner had left for Columbus, Georgia, by train a week earlier to visit Mr. John F. Kelly, who was the president of the Merchants and Planters Steamboat Company, to assist him in selecting a race horse. Conner's uncanny ability to select winning horses and prize dogs was becoming well known, and he was often sought, paid handsomely and treated like royalty for his services. He reveled in the recognition, and Juanita resented it. It meant more time away from Athea Manor, the plantation and her and the children. She honestly felt that he had begun to believe his own aura and that he was gifted, like people said.

It was the last of July, and the summer heat had taken its toll on her nerves, that and having sixteen-year-old Delia Rose home from school for the summer. Conner had insisted that she attend St. Joseph's Academy in St. Augustine rather than Mrs. Baldwin's school in Virginia. Juanita had not approved, but had relinquished her desires. She and Rose had been so busy at Cherie's that making one more decision or having to participate in another confrontation with Conner was just too much for her to tackle. She was sure that it was a good school, and goodness knows, Delia could use the discipline from the good sisters, as Conner said. But Juanita was positive that it would take more than school to straighten out Delia Rose.

Delia had in the last few years become a little more sensitive and understanding of Juanita's responsibilities and standing in the community, but she was still headstrong. She had become a real beauty, lit up a room whenever she entered, and had her da's charisma as well. But, poor thing was almost as tall as Conner, towered over most of the young men in Monticello, and even when wearing the tiny Louie heels she was still almost six feet tall. Juanita insisted that she wear her hair off her face, slicked back with a large, low chignon to eliminate any extra height. Delia could not have cared less and often asked what possible difference did it make anyway, because she was not interested in any - and she meant any - boy in all of Jefferson County. And who said that the man had to be taller than the woman. It made absolutely no difference, so why all the fuss.

"Do not slump, Delia Rose. Be proud of your stature," Conner was constantly reminding her, and because her da said it, she stood as straight as she possibly could and, as her mother said, straighter than an army soldier. But when she accompanied Juanita and Conner to the Opera House or to some important function, they indeed turned heads. She was never as proud as when she was with her da.

Nine-year-old Nolan was also tall like the O'Farrells. Since Delia had been away at school, they had actually become closer. Unfortunately, he had his da's devil streak and was such a prankster that when Delia was home, there was constant pandemonium. The colored folks loved him and the excitement he caused, even Harrison, who should have known better than to allow Juanita to know of his amusement.

Delia never knew what kind of critter, dead or alive, she'd encounter hidden in her bed covers or her slippers or her dresser drawers. Juanita and Conner both threatened to send him away to school, but Nolan knew they were just threats. He, too, was of the cloth of the O'Farrells and could read them, his teachers, and the people at Athea, and read them well. He knew just how to play them. Of course Juanita and Conner were on to him, but it just made him that much more delightful.

"He'll be outgrowing these shenanigans in a short time, Cherie. Don't you fret," Conner said, and she, "And just what do you expect from your son, Mister O'Farrell? Should he be without the Devil in him, sir, and a perfect angel like I'm sure his da was at that age? Now, should he?" And they'd both chuckle. But when she'd say, "We're too old to be putting up with the likes of Young Nolan, Conner, honest we are," she didn't add that after all, she was approaching forty years, thirty-eight to be exact, for Juanita tried not to think of age, hers or Conner's. But Conner was staring at sixty years. No one would have believed it, not even Juanita, had she not known. The only time his age showed was when his face was in repose, usually when he was concentrating on an article in the newspaper, and she'd watch him and think, my gracious, Conner is almost sixty years old. But the minute he'd speak his entire face changed, and his love of life would emanate - there was a lot of fire in Conner. He was blessed with a beautiful curiosity about everything around him, and Young Nolan had inherited that gift. It was indeed a good gift for his son, Juanita often thought. It'll keep him as interesting as his da.

Good health was Conner's companion, he never complained, but neither had Mr. Crawford, who owned the ice cream parlor down the street from Cherie's. He was in perfect health, his wife had said, but he dropped dead while mixing a chocolate soda for Eileen Dockham right there in the store, and he was Conner's same age. After that Juanita questioned herself about her true feelings for Conner. She knew that she loved him, and she could not conceive of a happy life without him. But Mr. Crawford was sixty and Conner would be soon, and there was the possibility that the Lord would decide to take him just like he did Mr. Crawford. "I'd simply not be able to stand it. I know I couldn't. I guess that's how Conner felt when Maeve was taken. Would it take me that long to get over him, I wonder? No...I'll not think of it. I'll not." And she didn't.

But she was certainly put out with him this time. Mr. Kelly not only wanted him to help select a horse, he had also asked him to oversee the refurbishing of his private cabin in his new sternwheeler, the *W.C. Bradley*, the 163-foot boat that he was so proud of. He had commissioned Conner to decorate the state rooms, as well, and to design the brochures and the menu folder, and even to plan the menus. "Why Conner?" she had asked Harrison. Conner had confided to her that he had grown up eating mostly mutton, boiled potatoes and cabbage. How could he have developed into such a sought after connoisseur, she asked. Heavens, he didn't even like to eat, wasn't a hearty eater at all and never had been. Even the St. Elmo Hotel asked his advice on its menus, and darned if he hadn't planned and designed its newspaper ads as well as its brochures.

Nestor Whitfield, the manager, hadn't paid him for his services, but Conner dined there several times a week as his guest, and he and Juanita often stayed for an overnight after a performance at the Opera House instead of riding all the way back to Athea Plantation, and always as the guests of Mr. Whitfield. She guessed it was worth his time and efforts, but it did rankle her a little.

"Harrison, normally I'd not be upset with him about an old trip, but Delia isn't with us for very long, and you know how she dotes on her da." Harrison knew that wasn't the only reason that Juanita was upset. She was overworked, the heat had become unbearable and she and Conner needed to get away, just the two of them. He had even suggested it to Conner, who had thought on it and said that he'd "entertain the idea". Perhaps he had, but he had not acted on it. At least Juanita hadn't mentioned it.

Harrison, being Harrison, took it upon himself to intervene and propose the idea to Juanita of perhaps joining Conner on the *W.C.*

Bradley after Conner's stay in Columbus with Mr. Kelly. She could take the train to Columbus, join Conner on the steamboat and have a relaxing trip down the Chattahoochee and Appalachicola Rivers, depart at a convenient river landing and return by train to Athea. When he mentioned that it would be much cooler on the river, she seemed interested, but when she questioned him whether Conner had been the one to suggest it, he could not lie to her. That did it!

She was a proud woman and would not stick her chin out, not even for Mr. high-and-mighty O'Farrell. If he'd wanted her to join him, then he could do his own proposing, he could. Anyway, he wouldn't be gone but for a few weeks, and she could stand being in hot old Monticello without him for that long. Maybe she'd just take the train to Savannah - maybe. He wasn't the only one who could just take off at will without even a mite of concern for Athea or the children. She could just hop on an old train too - but she didn't.

****

July 28, 1899 Carrabelle, Florida

It felt good, SuSu thought, to just relax and watch Jay sketch the sandpipers and gulls along the shore on the St. George Sound. J.P. and Elizabeth were playing at the edge, squealing at every tiny ripple, especially Elizabeth. She looked like the Meades, as did J.P., but Berta had told SuSu that she did resemble her sister Lamorah when she was that age. There was not a cloud in the sky, and the sound was almost like glass. J.P. was busily counting the tiny fishing boats and tugboats that came out of the Dog Island loading berths. The Meades often took the ferry to Dog Island across the sound from Carrabelle, because Jay liked the isolation of the beaches and J.P. liked the activity on the water. SuSu and Elizabeth just liked being there enjoying the warm breezes of summer and relaxing.

SuSu watched the tiny, toy-like boats bob along. How can anyone be as happy as I, she questioned. Why has fate been so kind to me, when poor Mary Ellen is so unhappy? And just when I thought that she'd found the right man for her, he decides to return to Maine. She'll never see him again, and I believe even she knows it, I don't care what he told her. Guess we weren't sophisticated enough for him. Not that being the editor of the *Appalachicola Times* should make him any better than anyone else.

SuSu had laughed at Jay that morning before they took the ferry to the island after he commented on Cedric Rushmore's leaving Appalachicola. He said, "Oh, SuSu, he's just gone Yankee on Mary Ellen." Now, she knew that Jay Meade didn't have a prejudiced bone in his body, and he was dead serious when he said it. So when she showed her surprise at his statement, he commented, "You'd have to stay in New York City for a while and deal with the folks up there to understand Cedric and his like," and when she asked for further explanation he replied, "Talk about narrow-minded people, Honey. Well, they treat Clay and me like we're the defeated - the War you know. Now here they are publishing our books and awarding us recognition and praise as they make a great deal of money from our efforts. Well, as Mattie would say, `Miss Kate, dey jus breathin' dat high air, so don' ya worry 'bout 'em,' and she'd be right. In other words, they enjoy playing the superior, the victorious role, and Cedric fits right into that mold."

"Why, James Parker Meade, I didn't know that I'd married myself a philosopher," and she began to tickle him unmercifully, something he simply could not handle. Next they were playing on the small, parlor floor and J.P. joined them. "SuSu McRae, you'd better stop that," Jay managed through giggles. "J.P., tickle your mama - get her J.P." Soon they were exhausted, gasping for breath.

"Let's go to Dog Island to swim, Mama. Can we, huh? Please!"

"Anything to get away from your mama's tickling, son. But I have to go to the post office first. Clay asked me to write, since Meade hasn't done much of it."

"When's Meade coming back from Wakulla Springs, Mama? I don't think I'm too young to go on overnights - I don't. Why'd Mr. Key say I was."

"Now, son, you know the rules. He's in charge of the summer program at the church, and it's his job to make the rules. Besides, Meade hasn't had many outings since he's been here, and I think it's wonderful of the Methodist Youth Group to sponsor the outing and even more that they allow boys from every denomination to participate. Jerry and Angelo Fortuna even went, and they're Catholic. For such a small town they do a wonderful job of keeping the youngsters busy when they're not in school or working at the fish houses or sawmills, don't you think so, Jay?"

He nodded his head in agreement as he prepared the letter for Callie and Clay. SuSu continued, "Have you ever seen Meade so excited? He's a delightful young man, and I'm so glad we've had the opportunity to get to know him. Please tell Callie that, Hon. I'd like her to know."

"I've already sealed it."

"I'll try to write later in the week. He's been a big help to you, too, wouldn't you say so?"

"I'd say anything you want to hear, lady mine. Just don't tickle me."

"You're a big old sissy, Daddy. I'm not afraid of Mama's tickling. Here, Mama, tickle me. I won't laugh one little bit. Please tickle me, Mama - please..."

"I'd rather kiss you, James Parker the third!"

"Don't you like to kiss Daddy?"

"Oh, I love to kiss your daddy, and I'm going to catch him and kiss him all over the place..."

"She sure does, J.P. See...watch your mama kiss your daddy." Jay put his slender arm around her waist and hugged her to him.

"Whoops! We've awakened Elizabeth with all our carrying on. Elizabeth, I'm coming, Honey," SuSu called into the children's bedroom, one of the four rooms in the tiny house. "Jay, I'll get her changed and fed, and we'll meet you at the post office. There'll be plenty of people to visit as always, and oh, Jay, please buy the paper. I'm anxious to see how the new editor is doing."

"Will do, lady mine."

SuSu watched him walk past the window. "Would you just look at your daddy, Elizabeth? I've caught myself the handsomest man in all of Franklin County, I have," and she hummed happily as she changed the wiggling Elizabeth. "We're going to have a beautiful day, young lady. Not even an afternoon storm's brewing. Imagine! J.P., hurry up so we can join your daddy, hear!"

****

South Spring in the summer was as hot as the Devil's den, Layke often said. "If we didn't have the afternoon storms to cool us off, I don't know how we'd stand it."

"You're spoiled, Honey," Berta replied. "If we had built the ceilings higher, it'd not be so hot, and we could put in the paddle fans like they have in the hotels. As low as these ceilings are, why the fan's would cut your handsome head right off."

"That's a disconcerting thought, Miss Berta. Cut my head off, huh? In that case I'll quit complaining and go to the river to see if I can catch a breeze. Wanta join me?"

"You know, I would. Ever since I sat with Trudy yesterday I've been low, I really have. Honey, I'm afraid that it's just a matter of time now. She's so weak, and if Dollie didn't turn her often, those old sores would really give her a fit. It's so hard for me to see her like that, it really is."

"She's been our good friend for so long! We're just fortunate to have known her. Now, I mean that. Not just because she helped you during your birthing time but because she's the core, the hub of Old Town, and I don't know anyone who is going to care as much as she, do you?"

Berta closed her eyes tightly and responded, "I love Jonah and Myra, and I think that they're wonderful, caring people, but you're right, they're not a Trudy Stucky. They just aren't!"

"They'll do a fine job with the hotel. We both know that, but they have each other and us, their family, whereas Trudy had everyone in the area for her family. Heck, she helped most of them enter this old world. A large part of our lives will be gone when she departs. But, Berta, she's left us with our memories. How many times have I told the story of when Bucko and I and Tag rode up to the Stucky front porch that first time? How many times?"

They were sitting on the South Spring landing on the Suwannee. Berta had spread an old quilt, and Layke with his pants rolled up and Berta with her skirt hiked up over her knees were dangling their feet in the dark amber water. There had been so much rain that the river was high, but since Young Reuben had moved the chicken coops and garden to behind the knoll on the other side of Big Dan's and Aunt Willa's old house, they weren't as concerned about the high water. The Suwannee was always a threat but Young Reuben had a good head on his shoulders, as Trudy would say, and was a take-charge person.

"Do you have a set time when you want to return to Tallahassee, Hon?" Layke asked while stroking her back. Berta replied lazily, "I told SuSu that we'd go down to Carrabelle for a visit with them, but I'd like to visit Marlene and Simon in Jacksonville before, and, oh, go on over to see Jessup in Appalachicola. He's been a dear helping the children out the way he has. Why, they'd have had to live way over in Appalachicola if he hadn't found that little house in Carrabelle for them."

"Yes, and SuSu would've had to take Captain Wing's mail boat every day from Appalachicola to the school in Carrabelle, and with Elizabeth on the way I don't know how she'd have done it. It was good of Jessup, moving the Parlins to the bigger house in Lanark so the kids could have the smaller one. Well, I'll be glad when the new high school gets finished next year. SuSu's very excited about being asked to teach there. Lets plan on staying with Jessup for a while. You know SuSu and Jay really don't have the room."

Layke listened to Berta ramble. "Are you avoiding answering my question about when you want to leave? Because if you want to stay with Trudy longer that will suit me fine."

"Oh, Layke, I'm torn, really I am."

"I know you are. And I understand, but a decision does have to be made. Why don't we do this, go on back to Tallahassee, visit SuSu for a week, that will be a long enough visit, and come back here for the rest of the summer."

"Would you be willing to be away for that long? I can't believe you'd be able to ..."

"I love this place, Honey, and am more relaxed here than anywhere I've ever been. I thought you knew that."

"Well, yes, I know that, but it is, as you always say, hotter than the Devil's den ..."

"I haven't told you, but now seems to be the right time. I'm thinking seriously of not running for another term."

"Layke Williams! I'm not believing what I'm hearing!"

"You believe it, lady mine," and he nuzzled her on the back of her neck. "I would like to travel, Berta. I'd like to take you to Europe for an extended vacation, and I'd like to write... now don't you laugh. I'm serious. I've always wanted to write about my experiences in the War and about the bravery of the men around me. The older I get the more I realize a book of that type needs to be written."

"I'm flabbergasted. How did you manage to keep all this away from me, Layke Williams? And here I was just telling SuSu that we can almost read each others minds and..."

"Berta, your tiny slaps are not effective, you know," and grabbing her hands, he pulled her back onto the quilt laughing.

"I'm so excited about this, Layke. I think it's a wonderful idea, the writing, I mean. I'm not too sure about the extended vacation to Europe. You know how I'd miss the children. I'm not sure I could be away for long. How long did you have in mind?"

"We'd stay for as long as you want. But we'd have to plan it carefully, because there are some places I must see."

"Probably the girly shows in Paris, huh? Is that it? Because if it is, then I'll just find something just as daring to watch myself..."

"Oh, this is going to be a contest, is it?"

"Oh, Layke, seriously do you really not want to run again? I can't imagine..."

"Yes, I feel my effectiveness is wearing thin, Honey. I'm not as ferocious as I was. I honestly believe I've lost some of my drive and need to change direction."

"Lets do it!" She stood up pulling him with her. Getting on her tiptoes, she kissed him. "Lets do it, Layke. We're not old stodgy people like some we know. We have a lot of life in us yet, and with the twins away in school and the others settled there is simply no reason that we not do some of the things that give us pleasure."

"I love you. I knew you'd be as fascinated by the idea as I am. I can always count on my Berta." He kissed the top of her loosened hair and as they stood on the landing a soft breeze kicked up and began blowing the gray Spanish moss, that was thick on the river oak overhead. Around the bend came a small sternwheeler, and they waved to the passengers.

Captain Bennett tooted the horn of the *Cedar Key Queen* and turned to the passengers and said, "And that, ladies and gentlemen, is the South Spring landing, where Senator Layke Williams and his wife Berta live. It's one of the grandest ranches on the Suwannee and..."

****

"Read it again, Mama," Annie said to Callie. They were sitting on the front porch trying to catch an afternoon breeze and reading the letter from Meade, that had been read dozens of times already. Callie could hear Parker, who was on the cot in the parlor just inside the porch door, and he was breathing heavily. She was especially concerned about him and had told Clay that she felt they should have Doctor Benson come out from town to check him. Lloyd Benson was Doctor Spooner's new assistant, and they both liked him. He had practiced up in Jeffersonville, Indiana, before coming to Florida and was in his mid thirties. Callie and Clay had invited him, his wife Gertrude and children, Julia and Harold, out for Sunday dinner, they'd had a wonderful time. Even Annie and Julia had got along. Gertrude had already become involved in the church, and Lloyd had volunteered to help coach the baseball team. It was good to have new people move into town.

Meade's letter was just two short pages, but they could tell that he was having a wonderful summer, and he didn't mention being homesick. Jay had kept him busy helping with the illustrations for the new book, and when not doing that he spent his time on the Sound or Appalachicola Bay or on the Gulf. He'd met several boys near his age that he palled around with, and SuSu had written that she seldom saw him when he and Jay weren't working. He had also said that they might not recognize him when he got home because he was very sun-tanned and his hair was bleached from being in the sun so much. But all the girls seemed to like it.

When Callie read that she got such a catch in her throat. He's almost a man grown, she thought. Now why shouldn't the girls think he's good looking, because like his father before him, he is. He isn't as outgoing as Thom was, but he laughs easily and, after having found his tongue, he is now quick to use it. Clay had been such a good influence on him, and having Annie and Jimmy practically worshiping him gave him needed self assurance.

"Mama, please read it again, please."

"Annie, I told you that I'd read it once, and once it is."

"But I don't have anything to do. Lillily won't play with me any more. Whoops!" and her hand quickly found her mouth.

"What did you say? Now, when did all this happen? Cora Anders Willett, don't you dare jump off this porch, young lady! I asked you what happened between you and Lillily?"

"She's just so bossy that I hit her one. But I didn't mean to hit her that hard."

"You come here this instance. I wondered why you were so quiet and still. Now the truth will out!"

"Mama, don't spank me," she wailed. "I think I hear Daddy Parker, Mama. I think the angels are here, and they're taking his breath up to Mama Kate! Honest. I think I see them, Mama. Don't spank me!"

"So you think I'll fall for that trick, do you? Do you?" Callie was holding on to her arm tightly and shaking her finger in her scrooched-up face.

"No ma'am, I really think I hear them, and they're all around his bed, and I been waiting and watching for them almost every day and..."

"Annie, if you're fooling me, I'll really give you what for! Now, let's just go inside and see if what you're telling me has any credence, young lady. Eight years old and acting like a...come on, don't you pull away from me."

When Callie closed the screen door behind them and turned around to look at Parker she gasped, "Oh, Daddy! Daddy! Oh, not now. Not now."

"Mama, don't cry, please don't cry, you're making too much noise. I'm trying to see the angels, and you've up and scared them away. Please don't cry, Mama." Annie sat beside Parker, and staring around the parlor she said softly, "Come out, come out wherever you are," just like she and Lillily did when they played hide and seek. "Come out, come out wherever you are. See, Mama, you scared them away, and they've already come and gone with Daddy Parker's breath. Doggone it, Mama!"

"I know I'm right, Clay. There is no need for Meade to come home. We'll send a telegram to Jay and suggest that just he come and that SuSu stay with Meade and the children. Honestly, that's how I feel about it. This is the very first time Meade has had a carefree time, and I don't want it spoiled. I'll sit right down and write him to explain how I feel about it."

Clay could see that she was adamant and that there was no need in talking about it any more. And she was absolutely right. It wasn't necessary for Meade to come home. He'd been a wonderful grandson, and Parker would have wanted him to continue having a good time in Carrabelle. Yes, Callie was right.

****

"Here, Honey, let me help you with that," SuSu said to Jay. "Are you sure that you don't want..."

"We've gone all over that, Honey. Of course, I'd like you to be with me but Callie is absolutely correct. I think it's more important that you stay with the children and Meade. Now, that's how I feel, and that's how Callie feels, so it's settled. There's no reason for Meade to have to come home from his overnights at Wakulla Springs. No reason."

"Bernie said that they should be back by the... let's see, today's the 28th, and he did say they'd be back in three more days, so that would make it the first, August first. Can you believe that it's almost

August?" She kissed him and continued making small talk while helping him pack his valise. "I'm so sorry that Mama and Layke won't be able to attend the funeral, but when I re-read her letter and realized that they were going to be in Jacksonville visiting Mama's cousins, then stopping off in Lake City for a visit..."

"SuSu, it doesn't matter. I know that they'd get the next train to Arcadia if we could get in touch with them. I know your folks pretty well, young lady."

"I know you do." She hesitated and said, "I'll miss you, and, Honey, if you change your mind after you get there and need me or..."

"I'll not change my mind. I loved Daddy Parker and know full well that he's where he wants to be - beside his Katie. Now, SuSu, I rightly know that."

****

"What're you laughing about, Harrison?" Easter questioned while enjoying his relaxed attitude.

"That Cherie has got herself in some kind of snit, she has. I've never seen her so put out with Conner. When Martin brought that telegram to the shop this morning, I thought she was going to have a fit right in front of that prissy Mrs. Landover, and that all two hundred pounds of that woman were gonna come tumbling out of the fancy gown she was trying on. Rose had to come into the back room, she was so tickled."

"Well, Ah for one don't blame her. Mr. Conner doesn't hafta stay fer another week. Now, why can't he come on home and be wid his fambly? That Mr. Kelly seems ta be upping Mr. Conner wid his wantin' more and more."

"Easter, that's not quite how it is, Honey. Conner doesn't get upped by anyone, and that includes Kelly. Well, you don't know him like I do and like Cherie does. Conner doesn't get upped by a living soul, nor, I've an idea, by any of those in Purgatory."

"Where's that, in Georgia?"

"You mean Purgatory?"

"Ah never heard of it. Mus' be in Georgia. Heard of Perciville, though. What'd Ah say now?" Then with arms akimbo, "What're you laughing about, Harrison?"

"Oh, Easter, you're the light of my life, honest you are." He rose from the straight backed chair, took hold of her shoulders and said, with great seriousness, *Love is lost in immensities; it comes in simple, gentle ways.*

"If you're funnin' me, you in fer a heap o trouble, Harrison."

"Do you realize that it's almost August, Rose, and Mr. high-and-mighty is still dressing the cabins in Columbus and that fancy state room on that blooming steamship, and here we sit in this tiny shop in Monticello just about to burn up in this blasted heat? Do you also realize that I'm just about to..."

"Juanita, the entire town realizes that you're upset with Conner. Why, I thought that Selma Smart was going to, as Millie would say, bust a gut this afternoon when you got started on how you didn't need any man alive and... what else did you say?"

"Oh, who cares, anyway? Certainly not one Conner O'Farrell. You know, I truly wonder if he cares about anyone other than himself - I truly do. But I'd have to add Harrison to that."

"Then you never see how he looks at you. No, I mean it. Now, I'll have to admit that I didn't used to be absolutely sure that he really loved you, but not anymore."

"Really? Really, Rose?"

"Yes, really Juanita. Mostly in the last few years he's..."

"How many? I mean, how many years, would you say?"

"For crying out loud, Juanita! I'm not exactly sure just how many."

"Go on. What else."

"Well, he looks at you sorta soft like... like, oh, Juanita, you know I'm not good at using words, you rightly know that."

"That's all right, Rose. That's all right, and thanks for telling me. I was beginning to feel, well, you know - unloved." Juanita sighed, took the bundle of fabric into the back room and began singing a song they'd heard in the Gilbert and Sullivan operetta they and Conner had seen a few weeks before.

She'll be alright, Rose thought. He really does look at her differently now, and I can see that he's winding down and will probably marry her ... well, maybe not that, but he does appreciate her more than he used...well, I'm really not sure what he...oh, well, that's Conner for you. She'll be all right.

****

"Mr. Key, do you want Jerry and me to gather more wood for the fire?"

"Meade, that would be kind of you. Very kind, indeed. Now, I wish the other lads would be as thoughtful as you are. That I'd wish."

"What're you laughing about, Garvin? Hell, he's got enough wood to build the bloomin' ark!"

"Hell, I know it, Fortuna! You think I'm some kind of pantywaist? Not Meade Garvin! You oughta see what all we pull down in Arcadia!"

Jerry thought, boy, that Arcadia must be some kinda wild town! Man! That Meade Garvin's some kinda wild!

"Now, when he gets to snoring, like he did last night, then we'll mosey on over to Sparkle Creek and see what those pretty little lassies from up at Woodville look like," Meade said confidently.

"He's not gonna like that, Garvin. Not gonna like it at all."

"Fortuna, he ain't gonna know a blasted thing about it, now is he?"

"Well, I don't know. He might wake up in the middle of the night and do a lantern check, and we won't be there, and neither will anyone else...."

"Whaddaya mean, anyone else? You didn't go and tell 'em did ya? I'll swear, Jerry, you got the brains of a rhinoceros! Well, now that the whole blooming group knows, we might as well go to bed like all the rest of 'em. And Jerry, thanks a lot, ya hear? I was looking forward to a piece from one of those Woodville girls. We're going back to Carrabelle tomorrow, and now there ain't a chance. Thanks a lot, Jerry!"

Whew! Meade thought. I got myself out of that one. I'm gonna hafta be more careful in the future. One of those wiseacres might put me to the test, and I'd hafta do some of the things I've been bragging about. I'd sure better be careful. I wish Clay were here. He'd tell me what to do. Clay knows all about this growing up-business. Meade was soon asleep and didn't hear the wind start up, and if he had, he'd have thought that it was just another summer storm. He'd have been wrong.

****

It was on the morning of August first. The *W.C. Bradley* hadn't left the Columbus harbor when word came about the devastating hurricane that had hit Carrabelle at four that morning. The winds were already about 150 miles an hour, and the eye of the storm hadn't even hit. It looked like it would be there for the entire day. They predicted that it would level Carrabelle, and they were told to make haste to Appalachicola with supplies for the people that were sure to have need of them. There would probably be a lot of casualties. Captain Lacey had alerted the crew, and since Conner was already on board with plans to depart at the Blountstown landing to take the train back to Athea, he stayed on board and was already engaged in a friendly poker game in Kelly's newly refurbished stateroom.

"There's no more word on the terrible hurricane," Captain Lacey told his first mate, Rooney Muldoon, recently come over from the city of Cork, Ireland. "When Johnny brought the news of the twelve-foot tidal wave hitting that wee fishing village, I told Ruthie that there wouldn't be a living soul left there, not a living soul. The poor girl cried, and she not knowing anyone in the place. Tender hearted, she is. Tender hearted."

"And would it be fittin', Captain, that me and Johnny should be gettin' some extra supplies from the store shed?" asked Muldoon.

"I'm wishin' that I'd be knowing, I'm wishing that. But we'll be casting off directly, and I'll not be able to get Mr. Brooker to give the go ahead, seeing as how he's in Eufaula, and only the dear Lord will know what we'll be finding in Carrabelle." Muldoon crossed himself and mumbled something in Latin. Johnny figured that it was from his foreign Bible, but every person for himself, he thought. He was that kind of man, and Muldoon respected him more than most, even though he had little formal education. But smart he was about the river and anything pertaining to it, so they got along just fine.

"Mr. O'Farrell, sir, Mr. Kelly cautioned me of your winning ways at cards and the likes, but I, sir, am from Kansas City, and we Missourians hafta be shown, not told. So, sir, would you allow me to sit in?"

"And you must be Maurice Downs. Kelly spoke of you, and of course you may sit in. Now, this is just a friendly game, you know, we don't want the authorities to descend on Kelly's *Bradley*, do we?"

Conner whispered to Kelly's man that he'd like an extra bottle of brandy for the gentleman from Missouri and a plate of biscuits and whatever meat and cheese he could find, that he'd been a little light headed all morning long and that it was obviously from need of food. "And, Homer, could you add some sliced peaches and a sprig of mint to that? I'd like to cleanse my palate before starting on the serious drinking." He gave a deep laugh and shuffled the cards. There were two other players, all friends of Kelly's, and Conner was told that they were his equals.

He was excited because he'd not had a good, serious game in a very long time. He could feel his pulse race, and he remembered his days on the Mississippi and the St. Johns. Those had been grand days, and he was glad that he had lived them. But he liked his life now just as much, maybe more. It was not as exhilarating, but it was definitely satisfying. Maybe it is as Cherie says, that we're getting old. He blew the smoke from his Havana and dealt the cards.

"Gentlemen, a game of stud?"

****

"I'm glad that we decided to visit Marlene and Simon, Honey. They're delightful company, and I'm always amazed at the progress Jacksonville is making. Here, Berta, let me help you with that." Layke took the trap from her and handed it to Brevard and asked how things were at home. Brevard handed Layke the telegram, and Layke immediately thought of Trudy. I'll not mention it to Berta 'til morning, she seemed so tired in Lake City. Brevard assured him that things were just fine and that they had all missed having Mr. Tucker and Miss Raine home, because things were much too quiet, but now that they were home things were back to normal.

Berta asked him sleepily to repeat what he'd said about Raine and Tucker, and Layke answered for him, "Honey, you're half asleep. Brevard just said that they had missed Raine and Tucker, but since they returned things are not as quiet."

"Well, I declare," is all she managed and fell fast asleep on Layke's shoulder. He read the telegram and thought, so it was Parker and not Trudy. Well, I still will let her sleep. There is no way that we can get back to Arcadia in time for the funeral. Berta slept all the way home. They undressed hurriedly, and Layke told Brevard to tell Rosette to not awaken them early, that they wanted to get some extra rest because they were dead tired.

When the door bell rang at nine o'clock that August morning, Layke and Berta had not yet awakened. "I'se comin', I'se comin', Rosette called. "Cain't let a body even git de biscuits roll out. I'se comin'."

Berta stirred and rolled over. When she opened her eyes, she was astonished that she was in their room in Tallahassee. She listened and said to herself, "Is that the doorbell? Can't be, it's too early. Can't be." and turned back over on her side.

The rap on their door was not a hesitant one, and Berta answered immediately. She was pulling on her dressing gown when Layke stirred and asked what in tarnation was going on. Rosette handed her the telegram and waited like Berta told her to. Layke was sure that it was from SuSu telling them the time of Parker's funeral and wasn't too concerned, but when he saw Berta's face he hopped up.

"Close the door, Berta. Rosette, tell the man to wait. We might have a reply. Sit down, Berta. What is it, Honey? You're white as a sheet!" He took it from her and exclaimed, "My God! When did this happen? It's from Jessup. It struck at four this morning and it looks bad. My God!"

"Rosette, get Brevard and tell him to get the buggy ready. Miss Berta and I are taking the train to the Blountstown landing. We'll have to go in by boat. If it's as bad as Jessup fears, even the train tracks into Carrabelle will be torn up, and we'll have to .." he gasped, "we'll probably have to take the Appalachicola River. It'll be our best bet. Hurry, woman! Now!" he yelled to Rosette.

"Now, Berta, listen to me. You know they always make these things out to be worse than they really are, dear. Berta, I said listen to me. All Jessup said was when it hit and that it looked real bad, that's all he said. You have to get dressed and packed. We're going to SuSu, dear. Everything will be all right. Berta, do you hear me? No, I guess you don't."

"Rosette," Layke called through the cracked door, "call Salome and get her up here this minute. Her missus needs her. And, Rosette, get the smelling salts."

"It's gotta be bad, Brevard, or the mistuh wouldn't be so upset and yellin', and you bes' git dat horse hitched up 'cause he's sure 'nuff on a rampage and... Lordie, he's a talkin' 'bout a train wreck and dem havin' ta take a boat and Ah don' knows what all. Dere goes dat bell. Mus' be Miss Raine actin' lak de queen again dis mornin' and me wid all dis work to do...I'se comin', Miss Raine."

"What'd you say, Rosette? Who died? For heaven's sake you could have found out who it was. Probably just Trudy."

"No'um, Ah don' tink so. More dan dat. Someting 'bout havin' ta take a boat 'cause de train busted up, and..."

"Oh, for heaven's sake, I'll get my own tea. Go on, get out. I come home and the first thing that happens is someone dies, and that means I'll be expected to go to a blasted old funeral and..."

****

"It is indeed lucky I am this morning, gentleman," Conner quipped. It had been a good game, and as Kelly had said, the men were on a par with Conner. They had kept the stakes low, the conversation brisk and the coffee with brandy drunk. Conner leaned back in the oaken captain's chair. He had insisted on a maroon leather seat with brass nail-head trim. He had told Kelly, "You can afford the best, so why not enjoy the luxury." It was a comfortable stateroom that was definitely masculine in feel, but Kelly had ordered another room adjacent to his for his wife, and Conner had been allowed to use his innate sense for color.

Not being sure of Margaret Kelly's taste (the room was to be a surprise for her) he had asked what her coloring and age were. Told that she was a true brunette with light brown eyes in her late thirties, he knew immediately which color combinations he wanted. He selected rich shades of magenta and royal purple, softened with jade and smokey blues, in a feather design brocade for the Queen Anne chairs. He wanted the fluid lines of the Queen Anne style but the richness of color to complement her coloring. A matching floral cloth covered the round table, topped by heavy ecru lace. It was indeed an elegant room and, she was delighted with it. As a matter of fact, she had insisted in having a dinner party in his honor to show her appreciation.

Conner was glad to leave Columbus. Maggie Kelly was a charming woman, but he was concerned that her appetites weren't being satisfied by Kelly. There was a great disparity in their ages, but then he was over twenty years older than Cherie. Perhaps I am too sure of my Cherie. Perhaps I should not take her for granted, for he could see that Kelly had no suspicions concerning his Maggie. Think I'll leave on the first and not stay those extra few days, for if I have need of my Cherie, then perhaps she has needs too. Yes, I'll leave early.

"Homer, do we have much time before we arrive in Blountstown? Say, time for a few more hands?" Homer assured him that there was plenty of time. "Gentlemen, it is on you are, then. Now, Mr. Hogrefe, what was it you were saying about the big lake, Lake Okeechobee? Is the land there as fertile as reported by the land sharks?"

Charles Hogrefe had been extolling his latest acquisition in an area called East Beach on the southeastern shores of the big lake and was enroute to see first hand what he had actually purchased. Conner and the others were having sport with him, because anyone who would purchase land from one of the land agents, sight unseen, could not be very bright. He seemed to be a shrewd poker player, that is until the last hand, and it amazed Conner that he would have done such a stupid thing.

"Mr. O'Farrell, it is indeed true. My cousin, Duncan Padgett, has visited East Beach in person and has allowed that the beach is more beautiful then the beaches in Daytona, although not as wide. At present there are only a few fishermen living there, no town to speak of, but it is only a matter of time until it's discovered. And Duncan is a wise man. Heavens, he owns a large acreage in Palm Beach itself right on the Atlantic and bought it for next to nothing. Yes, Cousin Duncan is a wise man." With that additional information, Conner and the others barraged him with more questions. The game progressed, and again Conner's luck held. Hogrefe was getting in over his head, as the stakes had been raised considerably along with the consumption of brandy. When he became totally without funds, Conner suggested that he put up his East Beach land holdings rather than an IOU note, and not thinking too clearly, he did.

"Now what in the devil will I ever do with this?" Conner asked the Missourian looking down at the land deed he'd just won.

"It is worthless, I'm sure, but one never knows about this state. My uncle inherited some land near Ocala, and darned if they didn't discover a beautiful spring on it, and now he can't spend his money fast enough. He's even got girls dressed in mermaid costumes sitting around on rocks and people come from all over the blooming world to take their pictures and drink the medicinal waters and ride around in little glass bottomed boats. Never saw the likes of it. Yes, this is a different kind of state. Maybe that piece of paper will do the same for you, Mr. O'Farrell." And they both laughed.

He and Maurice Downs stood on the deck watching the river traffic. Conner was smoking his Havana and finishing his brandy. He turned to Maurice and started to say something, his glass fell in the river and he clutched his chest with his other hand. Maurice caught him as he went down.

****

"You don't need to drive me into town, Harrison. Your help is needed more on the plantation. Now, I don't care what Mr. high-and-mighty told you to do, it's my shop, and I am not in any danger driving these few miles."

"I need to get some supplies anyway, Cherie. And besides, I want to find out what time the train arrives from Tallahassee. I know Conner will expect someone to meet him at the depot."

"Expect, expect. He sure expects a lot from all of us, and what do we get in return, I ask you? What?"

Juanita was still so put out with Conner that she was taking it out on everyone at Athea and the shop. Rose had actually told her yesterday to stop her complaining or to go on back to Athea, that she and Sophia could finish up Dorothy Wilkinson's trousseau without her expert advice. Harrison had never heard Rose so much as raise her voice to Juanita. He had got so tickled at Juanita's expression that he had to get out the back room in a hurry.

Juanita was late getting into the shop, and Rose and Sophia had already fitted several customers. Juanita took off her hat, placed the hatpins in it and put it on the high dresser in the back room. When she came out to the waiting room, she asked Rose if they had bought the paper, and she said that they had been too busy. So, she sent Harrison over to the ice cream parlor to get it and also asked him to check with Mrs. Crawford to see if the latest Saturday Evening Post had come in, complaining about how long it took anything important to arrive in Monticello, and she didn't know why she'd moved to such a backward town and...

Rose and Sophia just rolled their eyes at each other and realized that it would be another of Juanita's complaining days, and they could hardly wait for Conner to return so she'd be her old self. Rose had said to Sophia that she was getting sick and tired of having to listen to Juanita complain. But Sophia knew that it was the heat as much as anything. She'd never seen such a hot July, and it looked like August was going to be just as bad.

Harrison was reading the front page and muttered about not seeing anything about a hurricane down in Carrabelle, that he didn't know what Mrs. Crawford was referring to. About then Seth rode up on his bicycle with a telegram for them, that Mr. Harbin from over at the telegraph office had told him to give to Miss Cherie and in a hurry because it was urgent.

"You'd better take this, Harrison. It's bad - I mean real bad news about Conner."

Harrison thought that he was referring to Conner's staying for another few days but became ashen when he read it.

"Don't say anything about this until I talk to Rose, Seth. Now, I mean it, and ride fast as you can to the depot to see when the next train leaves for Tallahassee and Blountstown. Now, I said!"

There is absolutely no reason to go to Athea for any clothing. I just want to get to him, Harrison. Now! Right now!"

"Cherie, the next train isn't due for two more hours, not until two this afternoon, and that'll give us time to go for Delia and Young Nolan and..."

"No, I said. Maybe Delia Rose but not Nolan, now I mean it. I don't think I could stand for Nolan to see him like that. I don't think I could stand.."

"Rose, talk some sense into her, would you please. I give up!"

"Juanita, no, don't fight me, for I'll not stand for it. Now, you listen to me. Harrison and I are going with you to Athea, and we'll pack your things and also Delia's, and then we'll ride back to town and you'll board the train for Blountstown. Are you listening, Juanita? Are you?"

"Who in tarnation can help but listen when you're yelling. Of course I'm listening. But, Rose, they just said that he had a stroke or heart attack... They didn't say that he was dead, did they? I'm sure I read that he wasn't dead..."

"That's right, dear, they said that he had a heart attack... but we need to get to him in a hurry, Juanita. He needs you and Delia beside him, dear."

"Harrison," Rose added, "I'll send Seth out to tell Easter to tell Delia about her daddy and to start getting ready. He can ride out a lot faster than we can."

"Good thinking." Hold on Conner, he thought, flicking Thunder's rump. You don't want to go out this way. This just isn't dramatic enough for you, Conner O'Farrell. Hold on, my friend. Hurry Thunder, your master needs us. He wiped his eyes and didn't care who saw him.

****

"And who else should you bless besides your mama and ..."

"God bless Daddy and Aunt Callie and Meade and.."

"Hurry up J.P. We'll be here all night," SuSu said with a smile. She had put Elizabeth to bed early, and she and J.P. had sat on the front porch of the frame house until the bugs chased them in. What a beautiful night it was! The afternoon rain had cooled it off, and it was a typical southern summer evening. SuSu thought, I'll just lie next to the window and watch this night. I miss Jay so that I can't even concentrate on my reading.

"Now, J.P., I said go to sleep now. Mama will be in the next room, and before you know it, it'll be daylight. Go on, Honey, don't make mama fuss at you. We'll do something special tomorrow." As soon as she said it, she knew it was the wrong thing to say, and sure enough he began. "What, Mama? What are we gonna do?"

"We'll go to the post office and watch them hoist the flag and post the news of the outside world on the board, and then we'll go over to the ice plant, and I'm sure Mr. Pickett will give you some ice shavings, and then..." He'd finally dropped off while she was thinking of all the things that they could do together. I'll just turn in, too, son, because I am as nervous as you seem to be without your daddy here. And she did, and when the wind whipped up about midnight, she was sound asleep. She didn't awaken until J.P. shook her and asked why the wind was blowing so hard. When she looked out the window, she couldn't believe that she'd been able to sleep through it. "I don't know, son, but I think I'd better find out." About then they heard the alarm sound from the Methodist church, and Susu looked at the clock. Six o'clock, not quite daylight. She knew that they were in for trouble.

"What's that, Mama? What's that noise?"

"It's the alarm from the church, son. They want us to get dressed and go over there so we can all be together during the storm."

"But why can't we stay here in our own house?"

"J.P., listen to me. Do you see that wind blowing? Yes, I can see that you do. Now, if it gets any harder our little wooden house won't be able to stand the high winds, whereas the church is stronger and... J.P., I am getting dressed, and I want you to do the same. Then I'm going to dress Elizabeth and take some extra clothes and blankets..."

"But it's not cold Mama..."

"J.P.," she yelled, and he began to cry. "Now, see what you've done? You've made me yell at you, and you know how I hate to yell at you - oh, Honey, don't cry. I'm sorry, but we need to hurry."

"I want my Daddy."

"So do I, but he's not here, so hurry and get dressed like I said!"

By the time they got to the church they were soaked and out of breath. The wind was blowing a gale, the palms almost bent double. The church was already filled with people, but no one seemed to have much news. Mr. Coombs from the Franklin County Lumber Company had said that it was going to be a bad one and that the Reynolds sawmill was already damaged. The men had brought in containers of drinking water and tins of food, but SuSu had forgotten theirs, even after she and Jay had gone over and over just what they were supposed to do in case of a hurricane. She was so upset with herself that when Laurel Ogletree asked her if she had remembered the candles and blankets, she started to sniffle and couldn't seem to control herself. All she could think was that she'd have to tell Jay what a goose she was.

Laurel patted her on the back and made clucking sounds, and that made SuSu even more angry at herself, so when she saw some of her pupils stare at her, she sniffled her last sniffle, gulped and got up to ask Laurel what she could do to help.

The hurricane raged on and on without any let-up until the lull about ten o'clock; then the winds switched to the southwest, and they were told later that the winds reached 150 miles an hour. I'll never take another wind lightly as long as I live, SuSu thought. They stayed cramped in the small church until eight o'clock that evening. They finally opened the church doors, and nobody could believe the destruction.

Billy Webber said that the twelve-foot tidal wave took boats a quarter of a mile inland and threw them high up in the trees, and they looked like they were decorating a bunch of blooming Christmas trees. The ships that had been berthed in the upper anchorage just inside the eastern point of St. George Island were totally destroyed. It had been lucky that there were no ships tied up at the Dog Island loading berth, or there would have been more damage.

SuSu kept asking Marsha Daniels how they were going to get word to their folks, that she had to get word to Jay and her folks in Tallahassee. Marsha looked at her like she was some kind of nut. "Well, Marsha, I've never been through a hurricane, so I don't know about these things." SuSu could tell what she was thinking, "And that woman teaches my children!" Well, let her think what she wants. I have to let Jay know that I'm all right.

"Mrs. Meade," she said in a superior tone, "there won't be a telegraph pole left standing between here and Tallahassee or anywheres else."

Boy, that really got to SuSu. "Well, Marsha, just maybe the hurricane didn't destroy everything over in Appalachicola, because it came from the other direction, and I'm going to find out if just maybe there's a boat going in that direction. And if there is, I'm going to get word to my husband and parents, Marsha." After having had her say, she felt better, and she and the children made their way home. But there was no home left. She thought of all her pretties and Jay's work and art supplies worth so much money, and caught herself before giving into her feelings as she looked at the match stick shambles that had held their things.

SuSu felt an arm surround her shoulder and heard Laurel do her clucking sounds again, but they were welcome. "You've got your lives, Mrs. Meade," is all she said, and SuSu responded, "Yes, Laurel, we have our lives and each other. A body shouldn't want for more." They walked back to Laurel's house, and that's where she and the children were when Jessup's man found them. She had not even thought of Meade. "Oh, dear Lord! What if something happened to Meade!" Laurel assured her that Mr. Key wouldn't have come back during a hurricane, that he was a native of Carrabelle and understood such things. He and the boys were probably nice and dry at one of the hotels in Wakulla. And as it turned out, that's just where they had been.

****

"Mrs. O'Farrell, I'm so glad you got here when you did." Maurice Downs whispered while holding the door open to the stateroom. Harrison was beside her, at her request, but she had asked Mr. Downs to please stay with Delia Rose. She wanted to see Conner by herself, except for Harrison of course. Maurice took Delia to Mrs. Kelly's cabin and had Homer get her some refreshments from the galley.

"My God, he's dead, Harrison!" is all she could think to say.

Harrison reached for his wrist and assured her that he was not, but when he looked at Conner he said to himself, I'm thinking that this is it, though. He made up his mind at that moment. He turned toward her and said, "Cherie, I want you to go the room where Mr. Downs took Delia. Now, don't argue. Just do it!"

She actually seemed anxious to leave, and followed his suggestion. Now, he thought, if I can convince the captain, then we've done it, Conner, old friend. He asked for the captain and was told that Captain Lacey wanted to speak to him also. He had been unable to find a doctor at the landing and was so concerned by his failure that he wanted to express his feelings to Juanita and Harrison.

The captain came out onto the deck to talk to Harrison. When Harrison told him of Conner's request, Captain Lacey got tears in his eyes and told Harrison to wait for him in the stateroom until he got his Bible. He left muttering all the way down the deck about what a fine man Mr. O'Farrell was, and that he thought that was the loveliest gesture he'd ever heard a dying man make. He cleared his throat all the way to his cabin.

When Harrison told Juanita what Conner had requested, she clasped her hand over her open mouth and began crying. He told her that he'd expect her in the stateroom with a smile on her pretty face just like all brides wore. Delia couldn't understand why her da would wish to repeat their wedding vows on his death bed, and Harrison explained to her that it was not an unusual request, that it was done all the time. He was sure she'd not know the difference.

When Harrison got back to the stateroom and looked at Conner, he knew that he was dead. "Not now, you don't, Conner O'Farrell! Not now!"

Captain Lacey, Juanita and Delia entered the room and spoke not a word, just stared at Conner. Harrison whispered something to the captain and he nodded that he understood. Juanita was radiant - expectant - but when she looked at Conner closely, she pulled on Harrison's sleeve and whispered, "Are you sure Conner requested this, Harrison? He doesn't even look alive." She was getting scared, because Juanita didn't like the idea of being around dead people.

"Cherie, he's alive, though barely, but he can squeeze my hand and whisper. Now let's proceed with his last wish."

Captain Lacey gave the appropriate hurumph to clear his throat and read from the Good Book. When he got to the part, *do you take this woman to be your lawfully wedded wife,* Harrison put his head down to Conner's lips and his hand in Conner's, pretending that Conner was whispering and squeezing his hand and smiled up at the captain to assure him that Conner indeed did. And when he asked Juanita if she took Conner, she said "I do" even before he had finished. "I now pronounce you man and wife, and, Mrs. O'Farrell, I want you to know that when I get back to Georgia, I'm going to insist that Ruthie and I renew our wedding vows just like Mr. O'Farrell and you did. That was the loveliest ceremony I've ever conducted."

But Juanita wasn't hearing a word he said. She just wanted to get out of there and onto the deck to feel the wind blow through her hair and to be alone with her emotions.

As soon as they left, Harrison took Conner's hand in his. "Now, that's more like it, Conner, my friend. You should have done that a long time ago." He bent down, kissed his forehead and his closed eyes and said, *"Grief can take care of itself; but to get the full value of joy, you must have somebody to share it with."* Samuel Clemens, my good friend, or as he's calling himself, Mark Twain.

"Who is that Delia is talking to, Harrison?" Juanita and Harrison were on the deck as the ship was approaching Appalachicola Harbour. She thought, at least he's tall enough for her. Harrison knew who he was but was hesitant to tell Juanita.

"It's Tucker Williams, Senator and Berta Williams' son, Cherie. Do you want me to go for her?"

Juanita looked surprised that they would be on board, but when he told her about the devastating hurricane in Carrabelle and that they were going to see if they could find out about their daughter and grandchildren and the Garvin boy, Juanita said that she understood and, no, not to go for her, that Delia should enjoy herself. When he looked down at her, she had a funny expression on her face.

What goes around comes around, huh, my husband? The way your Delia's looking at the Williams boy, I think that we just might be seeing more of the senator and his lady.

Harrison wondered what the devilish smile could mean, but knowing Cherie, he was sure he'd find out soon. The drama continues, friend Conner. Harrison stood in the shadows. What can she be thinking with that faraway look on her face? She looks content, Conner. We gave her her dream and I enjoyed it almost as much as when you secured that horse Guinevere for us. Almost...

He watched Berta and Layke greet their friend. I guess their news is good news from the way they're hugging each other. He watched Tucker bound up the gang plank and tell Delia something, then he turned to watch Juanita, and she smiled up at him. *She's got something up her sleeve, for sure.* He returned to the stateroom where they had laid out Conner until they got back to the station in Blountstown and patted his hand. "Conner, can you see this? I'm going to pretend that you can, for I don't want you to miss out on Cherie's and your children's adventures. They'll keep a smile on your face, my dear friend, until I join you." Harrison continued to keep the vigil, because Juanita simply could not, she explained to everyone, that as his wife she knew it was her place, but...

"Oh, Mama, did you hear the good news? Tucker's sister and everybody else are safe. They weren't killed in the terrible hurricane after all. Isn't that grand news?" Delia asked animatedly.

"Yes, my sweet, that is grand news. Now when may I be introduced to your new friend?"

"He's so nice, Mama, and look at how tall he is? I do so hope he can come to Monticello for my debut!"

Juanita almost said, "What debut?" because Delia had been fighting it for over a year, but she caught herself in time.

She'll miss her da something terrible, I know, but the young heal so rapidly. But, my own sweet husband, I'll not be healing quickly. I'll be reading a lot of Poe. And, Conner, she gulped, then continued her thought, *I'll see you on the far side of forever, my dear one...the far side*

VOLUME V PAHOKEE

to be published in 1992

The continued romance of Old Florida
in the compelling series
THE FLORIDIANS

About the author:

Ann O'Connell Rust is a native Floridian, a "cracker". Her parents were pioneers in the Everglades in the early part of the century. Her father, Frank O'Connell, moved to Canal Point on Lake Okeechobee to work on Conner's Highway—the first hard road into the Glades. Conner was a friend of the West Palm Beach O'Connells, and young Frank wanted to be a part of Conner's thrust into the mysterious Glades. There he met Onida Knight, one of the beautiful Knight girls, whose father had homesteaded their land the previous year, and opened his own Knight's Grocery and Dry Goods Store in Canal Point. Luther Knight ultimately became a farmer/rancher and her father, a farmer, deputy sheriff and chief of police in Pahokee.

After schooling in Palm Beach County schools, Ann embarked on a very successful career in modeling—in Miami and New York City, where she met and married Allen, an FBI agent, and followed him to Puerto Rico, New Mexico, Washington, D.C., Mexico City and finally back to her love — Florida. She has had an on-going love affair with romantic old Florida all of her adult life .

She is the owner of a modeling and talent agency in Orange Park and since her retirement has devoted all her energies to writing and sharing her love of this magnificent state. She and Allen spend their time between their home on the St. John's River and their ranch in Wyoming.

Are you unable to find *"The Floridians"*
in your book stores?

Volume I Punta Rassa: Fiction, 1988, 275 pp., Softcover
Volume II Palatka: Fiction, 1989, 231 pp., Softcover
Volume III Kissimmee: Fiction, 1990, 208 pp, Soft cover
        and hardcover
Volume IV Monticello: Fiction, 1991, 232 pp, Soft cover
        and hardcover

Mail to: AMARO BOOKS
             5673 Pine Avenue
             Orange Park, Florida 32073

Please send check or money order (No cash or C.O.D.s)

I enclose $ _____ for books indicated.

Book Title: _____

Number of books: _____

Name: _____

Address: _____

City: _____

State: _____

Zip: _____

Please enclose $12.95 per book plus $1.50 for postage and handling of first book and .50 for each additional book. For hardcover please enclose $17.50 per book plus $2.00 postage of first book and $1.00 for each additional book. Florida residents add 7% sales tax. Please allow 2-4 weeks for delivery.